Five Days
Left

Five Days Left

Julie Lawson Timmer

CENTURY

Published by Century 2014

2 4 6 8 10 9 7 5 3 1

First published in Great Britain in 2014 by
Century
Random House, 20 Vauxhall Bridge Road,
London SW1V 2SA

www.randomhouse.co.uk

Addresses for companies within The Random House Group Limited can be
found at: www.randomhouse.co.uk/offices.htm

The Random House Group Limited Reg. No. 954009

A CIP catalogue record for this book
is available from the British Library

ISBN 9781780892139 (Hardback)
ISBN 9781780892146 (Trade paperback)

The Random House Group Limited supports the Forest Stewardship
Council® (FSC®), the leading international forest-certification organisation.
Our books carrying the FSC label are printed on FSC®-certified paper. FSC
is the only forest-certification scheme supported by the leading environmental
organisations, including Greenpeace. Our paper procurement policy
can be found at www.randomhouse.co.uk/environment

Typeset in Sabon LT by Palimpsest Book Production Ltd, Falkirk, Stirlingshire

Printed and bound in Great Britain by CPI Group (UK) Ltd, Croydon,
CR0 4YY

For Ellen

PART I

Tuesday, April 5

Five Days Left

1

Mara

Mara had chosen the method long ago: pills, vodka and carbon monoxide. A 'garage cocktail,' she called it. The name sounded almost elegant, and sometimes, when she said it out loud, she could make herself believe it wasn't horrifying.

It would still be horrific for Tom, though, and she hated herself for that. She would rather do it without leaving a body for him. But as much as she'd love to spare him from being the one to discover her, she knew not letting him find her would be worse. And at least this was the tidiest option. He could have someone come and take her car away. Fill her side of the garage with something else, to block the image. Bikes, maybe. Gardening supplies.

A second car for himself. Maybe she should arrange to have one delivered after. Would that be too weird, though? A gift from your dead wife. She should have given him one years ago. For their anniversary, or to celebrate bringing baby Lakshmi home. Or just because. She should have done so many things.

Mara frowned. How could it be that she had spent almost

four years ticking off all those items on her long list of things to do before she died, yet here she was, five days from it and still thinking of things she should have done?

Ah, but that was the trick of it. Tell yourself you'll wait until you've accomplished every last thing and you'd keep putting it off. Because there would always be one last thing. Which might be fine for someone who had the luxury of delaying a few more weeks, or months, or years even, until they were finally out of excuses and ready to go through with it.

Mara didn't have that luxury. In less than four years, Huntington's disease, the mother of all brain cell destroyers, had already done more damage than she and Tom could have ever prepared for. She had the severance papers from the law firm to prove it. The once graceful, athletic body that was now slow to react, reluctant to cooperate.

If she allowed herself to experience that one more moment with her husband and daughter, to travel to that one last must-see destination, she might wake the next morning to find it was too late, and Huntington's was in control. And she would be trapped in the terrifying in-between of not being able to end her life on her own, and not truly living, either.

Time was against her. She couldn't risk waiting any longer. She could make it to Sunday, as she had planned. But she couldn't wait past then.

Mara took a long swallow of water from the glass on her bedside table and stood. Inhaling deeply, she reached to the ceiling with both hands and focused on the bathroom door across the room. It was tempting to cast her eyes up toward her hands, the way the move was supposed to be executed, but she had gotten cocky before and the hardwoods always won. She counted to five, exhaled and tilted forward slightly, pressing her hands toward the floor for another count of five. A Sun Salutation modified beyond recognition, but enough to clear the fog from her brain.

The hiss of the shower stopped and Tom emerged from the bathroom, toweling his dark hair. 'Good morning,' she said, eyeing his bare torso. 'You're wearing my favorite outfit, I see.'

He laughed and kissed her. 'You were out cold when I got up. I was planning on asking your parents to come over and get Laks on the bus.' He tilted his head toward the bed. 'I can still call them, if you want to catch a few more hours.'

Laks. Mara's throat closed. She reached the dresser and put a hand on it to steady herself. Turning away from her husband, she pretended to fuss over some spare change and loose earrings on the dresser. She swallowed hard and coaxed her throat into releasing some words.

'Thanks, no,' she said. 'I'm up. I'll put her on the bus. I need to get moving myself. I've got errands to run.'

'You don't have to run errands. Why don't you write out a list and I'll get anything you need on my way home.'

He walked to the closet, pulled on dress pants, reached for a button-down. She made a furtive wish for him to choose blue but his hand found green. She would try to remember to position a few of his blue shirts in front so he would reach for one before the end of the week and his cobalt eyes would flash one more time.

'I'm capable of running a few errands, darling,' she said.

'Of course you are. Just don't push it.' He tried to sound stern, but his expression showed he knew she would take orders from no one.

He put on his belt – third hole – and she shook her head. He hadn't gained a pound in twenty years. If anything, he was in better shape, logging more miles in his forties than he had in his twenties, a marathon a year for the past ten. She supposed she could take some credit for it, since these days he ran partly to manage stress.

She walked to the door, lightly touching his shoulder as she passed him. 'Coffee?'

'Can't. Patients in twenty.'

A few minutes later, she felt him wrap his arms around her from behind as she stood at the kitchen counter, inserting a premeasured coffee pack into the coffeemaker. Loose grounds tended to end up on the counter or floor rather than in the filter these days.

Tom kissed the back of her neck. 'Don't do too much today. In fact, don't do anything at all. Stay home, take it easy.' He turned her around to face him and smiled in defeat. 'Don't do too much.'

Mara watched him disappear into the garage. She willed her breathing to slow and her eyes to stop burning. Turning to the coffeemaker, she made herself focus on the *plip, plip* of the coffee as it dripped into the pot, the scent of hazelnut, the steam rising from the machine. She set a cup on the counter, filled it halfway and gazed at it longingly. As tempted as she was to take a sip, she had learned to let it cool. Her hands couldn't be trusted to stay steady, and it was better to have only a stain to clean than a burn to soothe. Calmer, she made her way down the hall to her daughter's room and peeked in the doorway. A small head lifted drowsily from the pillow and a wide grin, gaping in the middle where four teeth had recently gone missing, greeted her. 'Mama.'

Mara sat on the bed, spreading her arms wide, and the girl climbed into her lap, pressing her body close and gripping tightly around her mother's neck.

'Mmmm, you smell so good.' Mara buried her face in her daughter's hair, freshly clean from last night's bath. 'Ready to take on another day of kindergarten?'

'I want to stay with you today.' The little arms clutched tighter. 'Not letting go. Not ever.'

'Not even if I . . . tickle . . . right . . . here?'

The small body collapsed in a fit of giggles and the arms loosened their grip, allowing Mara to wriggle away. She stood, took a few steps toward the door and, calling forth her best 'Mommy means business' look, pointed to the school clothes laid out on the glider chair in the corner of the room.

'All right, sleepyhead. Get dressed and brush your hair, then meet me in the kitchen. Bus comes in thirty minutes. Daddy let you sleep late.'

'Oh . . . kay.' The child stood, stepped out of her pajamas and walked to the chair.

Mara propped herself against the door frame, pretending to supervise so she could steal a few precious seconds watching the waif whose skinny, olive-colored frame still took her breath away.

As she dressed, Laks sang one of her rambling songs, a play-by-play of what she was doing, set to her own meandering tune. 'Sprite music,' Mara and Tom called it.

'Then, I put my jeans on,
with the flowers on the pockets,
and a pink shirt,
that is so pretty.'

She stepped away from the chair and did a pirouette, arms raised above her head, hands in 'fancy position,' as she had seen the big girls do at ballet school. Striking a final pose, she looked at her mother and smiled triumphantly. Mara forced her trembling lips into a smile and, not trusting her voice, held up a hand, fingers spread wide, indicating the number of minutes the girl had to make her way to the kitchen.

2

Mara

Lying in bed on the night of her diagnosis almost four years ago, Mara had stared into the darkness while Tom, heart-broken beside her, slept fitfully. Long before the first gray streaks of dawn pushed away the inky black night, Mara made herself a promise: she would choose a date and not waver from it. No second-guessing, no excuses.

She would live like hell until that date arrived, as much in control of her remaining days as she could be. Give Huntington's a run for its money before she finally flipped it the bird, swallowed her cocktail and exited the world the same way she had lived in it – on her own terms. She wouldn't give the sonofabitch disease the satisfaction of taking that from her.

Choosing a date was easy: April 10, her birthday. She knew Tom and her parents would mourn her on that date no matter what, and it didn't seem fair to give them a second day to feel so sad. But which April 10, which birthday? Not the first one after her diagnosis, she decided – surely she had at least one good, full year left before the disease moved into the next stage. The second seemed too soon as well. But the fifth could be too late.

By the time the Texas sun had cast its earliest rays through the spaces in the blinds, turning their bedroom ceiling from light gray to white, Mara had concluded the safest plan was to choose a symptom that signaled the beginning of the end, a warning that the disease had moved out of its early stages and into the more advanced. Once that symptom occurred, she would give herself until the next April 10, and then she would lower the curtain.

As she waited in the kitchen for Laks, a sudden wave of nausea hit her and she gripped the side of the counter, hoping the feeling would pass before her daughter appeared. She squeezed her eyes tight but there was no escaping yesterday, and her queasiness only worsened as the previous morning replayed itself on the inside of her eyelids.

She had been standing in the cereal aisle at the grocery store. A small boy stood several feet away, a chubby hand resting on his mother's hip as she bent to retrieve something from a low shelf. The boy smiled shyly at Mara and she smiled back.

He raised a hand and she was waving in return when, without warning, she felt the overpowering need to go to the bathroom. She tried to recall where the store's restroom was and wondered why her body was acting so impatient. Before she could come up with either answer, it was too late. Slowly, she tilted her head to inspect her light gray yoga pants, now showing a large wet patch at the crotch. A thin, dark line trailed down the inside of her right leg. 'Oh my God,' she whispered. 'Oh no.'

She put a hand in front of the biggest part of the stain,

trying to hide it. But the boy had already seen, and his mouth formed a surprised 'O.' Mara tried to smile at him again, to reassure him there was nothing to be upset about – and nothing to tell his mother. Her mouth wouldn't co-operate, though, so she raised a finger to her lips. But the boy's mother straightened then, and he tugged on her wrist with one hand and pointed at Mara with the other. 'Mommy! That lady didn't get to the potty on time!'

Mara's face caught fire. She reached for the jacket she always carried in her shopping cart to ward off the store's high-powered air-conditioning, but it wasn't there. She had forgotten it in her car. Frantically, she searched for something she could cover herself with.

The boy's mother, her face impassive in the studied manner of someone trying not to react, grabbed a package of paper towels from her cart and ripped them open as she walked toward Mara, her son in tow. 'Don't stare,' the woman whispered.

But the child's eyes remained fixed on Mara's wet pants. As they got closer, he pinched his nose with a tiny thumb and finger. 'Ewww.'

This brought a reprimanding hiss from his mother. 'Brian!' Reaching Mara, the woman held out a ream of paper towels. 'Maybe if you pat it?' Despite her neutral expression, her face was bright red and her nose twitched almost imperceptibly. 'I could get a blanket from my car but,' the woman said, nodding toward her son, 'by the time I get him all the way there and back . . .'

'Thank you,' Mara whispered, reaching for the paper towels. 'This has never happened before.' She blotted at her pants while Brian pulled on his mother's wrist. After a minute, Mara lifted wet, shame-filled eyes to the woman's

11

soft, sympathetic ones. 'You don't have to stay. I don't want to upset your son.'

'He's fine,' the woman said, tearing off more paper towels and handing them over. Mara searched for somewhere to put the used sheets, finally shoving them into her purse. This earned a gasp from the boy, who renewed his efforts to pull his mother down the aisle. The woman tugged the wriggling child to her side and put a flat hand on his head, anchoring him in place. Bending so her lips were beside his ear, she whispered, 'This nice lady needs our help, and we're going to give it.'

'But—'

'Shh! Not one more word.'

Mara stopped working on her pants and raised her head, parting her mouth to speak. She'd had too much coffee, she wanted to tell them. Not to mention all the water she had to drink to get the pills down. And the protein shake Tom insisted she drink every morning to keep weight on. Also, she'd been distracted by the long list of errands she had to run. She hadn't taken time to go to the restroom in the past few hours.

She closed her mouth. She wouldn't burden someone else with her story. Lowering her head, she dabbed more frantically but it was no use. The pants were too light, the stain too dark. And now she had white flecks all over from the paper towels. 'I don't think it's working,' she said to the woman, and a jagged shard of humiliation shot through her as she heard her frustration come out in a high-pitched whine. She stared at the wet paper towels in her fist. She would need a long, soapy shower to remove the stench.

Mara glanced at the boy again, disgust evident in the curl of his lip, and thanked God she was here alone with only strangers as witnesses. What if Laks had been with her? Or Tom? The thought drained the blood from her head and she put a hand on her cart to steady herself. 'I'm so sorry about this,' she said, looking from mother to son.

'What's wrong with her?' Brian whispered, and his mother and Mara locked eyes briefly, a wordless agreement they would both ignore the boy's question.

'He's darling,' Mara said, not wanting the woman to be upset with her son for his reaction. Who could blame him? 'I hate to do this, but I'm going to leave my cart right here and make a run for my car.'

'I can reshelve your things,' the woman said. Gesturing to Mara's pants, she said, 'It's a little better, actually.'

But her smile was plastic, and Mara felt like a child being told her self-cut hair looked 'fine.'

'Thank you for your kindness,' Mara said quietly. 'Please know how sorry I am.'

'Not at all. You take care now.'

As Mara retreated down the aisle, she could hear the woman's too-cheerful voice reading the rest of her grocery list aloud, drowning out the noise of the child beside her who was, Mara was certain, asking his mother what was wrong with the crazy lady with the purse full of pee-filled paper towels.

She forced herself to hold her head high as she walked past the cashiers and out the front door. By the time she reached the parking lot, her lips were trembling and she could feel the familiar pressure in the top of her throat, signaling impending tears. She toppled into her car, pulling the door closed almost before her feet were out of the way, and fell against the seat, hands covering her face.

'Oh my God, oh my God. Oh my God!'

Sobs tore from deep inside her and she gasped for air around them. When she was too exhausted to hold herself upright, she dropped her body forward, letting her head fall to the steering wheel. She stayed like that, bent forward and weeping, for an hour, rewinding the episode in torturously slow motion over and over in her mind, each time wishing for a different ending.

Finally, her body was too spent to produce any more tears or noise, and she became vaguely aware of cars pulling up nearby, the sound of radios, slamming doors, children calling to parents. She let herself rest against the steering wheel a little longer before she straightened, wiped her cheeks and nose with a sleeve and met her own gaze in the rearview mirror.

'That's it, then,' she said grimly to the puffy, red-rimmed eyes staring back at her. 'My birthday is on Sunday. I've got until then.'

Five days left, as of this morning. So little time. But she had started preparing almost four years ago, that early dawn as she lay beside her husband, settled on her deadline and promised herself she wouldn't make any excuses for letting it go by.

Since then, she had savored each moment as though it were her last. Big ones: Laks's birthdays, Thanksgiving, Christmas, their anniversary. And small ones: cooking with her mother, watching her father read bedtime stories to Laks, sitting on the bench out front, blowing bubbles while Tom and Laks raced to see who could pop them first. The small ones, she had decided, were the ones she would miss most.

'Mama?' Laks, backpack slung over one shoulder, the same as the big kids on the bus, trotted into the kitchen, reaching for the ballerina lunch bag on the counter. 'You didn't forget to pack me a cookie again, did you?' She eyed her mother suspiciously and unzipped the bag to peek inside. Satisfied, she zipped it up and thrust a hand out. 'Ready?'

A clump of hair stuck out over the girl's right ear, the result of a glue incident a week earlier. Laks's best friend, Susan, accidentally smeared some in her friend's hair and, in an effort to rectify her mistake, cut out the mess with safety scissors. In the days since, Mara had made a few attempts to get the child to wear her hair in a ponytail to hide the tufts, but each effort had ended in arguments and tears and Mara giving in. A lump the size of a fist blocked Mara's throat at the sight of her daughter, bristly-haired and gap-toothed and beautiful.

How could she ever be ready?

But this is why she had made her promise. So she would go through with it, ready or not.

'I'm not putting it in a ponytail, Mama,' Laks said, her chin jutting out a fraction in determination, a carbon copy of her mother even without the shared DNA, Tom often remarked. 'They're too pully on my hair. I told you.' She put a hand on her forehead and pulled the skin toward the back of her head, demonstrating.

Mara cleared her throat and stood. 'I know,' she said. 'I wasn't thinking about your hair. I was only being slow to answer.'

'Oh.' Laks nodded, appeased. 'Then, are you ready?'

Mara kissed the top of Laks's head and ran a gentle palm over the bristles before taking the small hand. 'Yes, sweetie, I'm ready.'

15

3

Scott

Scott pulled into the driveway and parked close to the sidewalk to leave room for Curtis, who was shooting hoops at the net attached over the garage door. Granny shots, the saving grace of an eight-year-old, he thought. Hearing the car, Curtis turned and waved.

'Nice arc on those shots, Little Man.'

'Ugh. I'm *so* tired of doing grannies but it's all I can do on this net.' The boy held the ball in front of him, eyeing it like it was a traitor, then nodded. Scott dropped his keys and briefcase onto the driveway and in one graceful movement he caught a sloppy bounce pass, set up a quick shot and sank it. Swoosh. Curtis grabbed the rebound and tried a similar shot. Short on grace and shorter on height, the ball arced a good two feet below the rim. He arched an eyebrow. 'See?'

Scott took the rebound. 'I know, I know. I should've bought one of those adjustable stand-alone hoops when we retired your friend over there.' He nodded toward a worn plastic basketball hoop leaning against the garage. Sinking another shot, he stood, arms open wide, and the boy ran to him, throwing his arms around Scott's waist. Scott stroked the head that rested against his stomach, his hand pale white in comparison to the brown skin showing through Curtis's wiry black hair. Leaning down, he pressed his nose and mouth against the top of the small head and breathed in the smell of little boy sweat and Michigan spring.

'I'm going to miss you,' he said. The child nodded and hugged tighter. They stood for a few moments, arms around each other, until Curtis broke free, dragged a dirty hand across his wet eyes and ran after the ball.

'Where's Laurie?' Scott called after the running boy.

'Kitchen. Makin' lasagna.'

This earned an approving smile. 'What'd you do to deserve that?'

'Miss Keller put a check mark in my planner 'cause I had a real good day.' He gave a 'How do you like that?' look and reached out for a fist bump.

'Nice. That's two for two this week. Three more and you stay up late on Friday.'

'Popcorn *and* a movie. Till *ten*.' The boy's mouth twisted in exaggerated dismay. 'But Laurie wants to watch, too, since it's our last one, so it's gotta be a movie a *girl* wants to see. No splosions or anything.'

'Still, ten o'clock bedtime rocks, right?'

Curtis brightened. '*And* popcorn.'

'So, nail the next three days. I'd better go check in. More hoops after dinner?'

'Maybe. But I have to read tonight. Laurie said. *And* practice math.'

Scott smiled at the pretend anger. The boy thrived on the expectations and rules at the Coffmans' house, but he was old enough to know he wasn't supposed to admit it.

Scott played along. 'School's important, Little Man. Come in soon for dinner.'

He bent to pick up his things and started for the front door. Behind him he heard a loud 'Dang *it*!' as the ball, he guessed, came short of the net once again.

Pushing the door closed behind him, Scott set his keys on the front entryway table and inhaled deeply: garlic, tomato, basil, cheese.

'Laur?' he called. 'Smells fantastic in here.'

He dropped his briefcase at his feet and bent to examine a floor nail that had worked its way loose and now threatened to catch on the next sock that ran across it. Pushing the nail down with his heel, he checked the rest of the entryway for others. It was ten years since he had resanded these floors. He put a hand reflexively on the small of his back.

His wife's vision of a dream house hadn't exactly matched their fixer-upper budget. Restoring the hundred-year-old 'needs love' colonial had involved a three-page to-do list and every weekend and evening for over a year. It was the price of entry, they told themselves, to the kind of house she had always wanted and he was determined to give her: a big, rambling place with wood floors, built-in shelves and two fireplaces. Full of character and, one day, children.

He ran a flat hand over the entryway wall. Removing all the layers of wallpaper took them two months alone. Then there was all the painting – the same neutral Warm Ecru throughout the house with a bold-colored accent wall in every room, carefully chosen after they compared several patches of different shades of multiple colors. They joked about putting the paint department guy at the hardware store on their Christmas card list.

He reached the doorway to the kitchen and leaned against the frame. His wife was bent over the oven, her large-bellied profile still a surprise to him. She hadn't changed out of her work clothes, though she had captured her wavy blond mane in a ponytail.

'Smells fantastic,' he said again.

'Oh, hi there, you. I didn't hear you.' She set the lasagna on the stovetop.

He crossed the room to kiss her. 'He had a good day, I hear.' Tipping his head over the lasagna, he inhaled again. 'Mmmm. Glad he did. I've been craving your lasagna myself lately.'

She made a face and put a hand on her stomach. 'That makes two of you. I can barely stand the smell of it.' In response to his look of concern, she waved a hand. 'It's nothing. We had fattoush salad at lunch from that new place near the office and it was a little too oily. Anyway, don't get too excited about the good day. I talked to Miss Keller when I picked him up. She's going easy on him this week because of the transition. He only met half his behavior goals, but she decided to give him full credit. I think she's worried if she doesn't help him build some positive momentum, he'll fall apart completely by Friday.'

'Maybe Miss Keller knows a way to keep me from falling apart,' Scott said. Sighing, he moved aside the curtain on the small window above the sink and spied on the boy in the driveway until a hand on his back reminded him whom he was supposed to be paying attention to. He let the curtain drop and turned to his wife.

'I'm surprised you're going along with the leniency,' he said. 'Lasagna, when he didn't really meet all his goals?' All year, Laurie had been the one to lead the discipline charge. He put a hand on her round stomach. 'Impending motherhood's making you soft, huh?'

She lifted a shoulder. 'I was going to make it anyway, no matter what I heard from Miss Keller. I wanted to be sure he had it one more time before he leaves. I'll do spaghetti tomorrow, and let him help bake cookies for dessert. Homemade pizza on Thursday. I thought about baking a cake on Friday, and you could grill burgers on Saturday. All his favorites, you know? Although I'm tempted to have him eat nothing but vegetables and fruit until he leaves, just to get some nutrients in him before he goes back.'

Scott winced.

'Sorry,' she said.

'No, it's okay. There's no use pretending. He's not moving into the Ritz when he leaves here, and that's the reality. And it's okay – at least, that's what I've told myself a hundred times a day for the past few weeks.' He closed his eyes as if reciting a mantra. 'It's going to be okay. Even if he eats cold ravioli from a can and only showers once a week and goes back to all his old stunts. All of that is better than being separated from his mother. Even if she lets him get away without doing homework, sends him to school without eating breakfast, the best thing for him is to be with his mom.'

'All of that is entirely true,' Laurie said, and he could sense the small tinge of frustration in her voice. 'And it almost sounds like you believe it, this time.' She didn't add 'finally,' but he knew she was thinking it.

'Almost,' he said. She started to speak, and to avoid hearing what he knew was coming, he jumped in ahead of her. 'Thanks for picking him up, by the way. Sorry about the eleventh-hour change of plan. So, can I help with anything in here? Set the table?'

It worked. She handed him three glasses and a basket of rolls, armed herself with cutlery and paper napkins and led him into the dining room. 'You're welcome, but I thought the whole point of having Pete cover practice this week was to give you more time at home, not more time for last-minute meetings with parents. Why didn't you ask the woman to wait till next week?'

She spoke in the too-light tone he recognized as reproach wrapped in politeness, her question more of a challenge. She had posed similar ones many times: Why did he get up early Saturday mornings to make the thirty-minute drive to inner-city Detroit, when he could be sleeping late? Half the kids who attended the Saturday tutoring program he ran were only there for the free pizza lunch anyway, didn't he see that? Why did he spend his summer evenings at the run-down outdoor court in front of the school, playing pickup with kids most teachers were thrilled to have a two-month break from, or be freed of entirely, now that they had gone on to high school?

Scott held his palms toward her, begging forgiveness. 'You know how my parent-teacher conference nights go at that school. I read *Sports Illustrated* for an hour with maybe one or two people bothering to stop by. If someone's going to finally get involved in their kid's education, I've got to be there to meet with them. If I put her off till next week, there's no guarantee she'd show.'

'You can't single-handedly save every student at Franklin Middle School.'

'I know. I won't get to all of them. Three years isn't enough time.' He flashed a lopsided grin and hoped it was irresistible.

She let out a breath as she returned to the kitchen. 'That

was not the point I was making, and you know it.' Following, he reached in the fridge for a beer and opened it, then filled a glass of water from the tap. He handed her the glass and raised his bottle. She clinked her glass against it, took a sip and made a face, a hand on her stomach.

'You sure you're okay?' he asked.

She sighed. 'You know how it's been. I eat one wrong thing and it throws me off the rest of the day.'

He raised his beer again. 'Here's hoping the last trimester will be better.' The last trimester was two weeks away. She was due July 15.

'Hopefully.' She set the glass on the counter and kept her gaze fixed on it. 'I never feel like it's the right time to say this, and it's not now. But I really think having our life back is going to make things better.' She caught his expression and quickly added, 'Or, not "better" necessarily. Just, you know, easier. Being able to come straight home from work and sit? Relax? Instead of having to be taxi driver, afternoon snack server, homework supervisor, all of that?'

Scott looked out the window again at the boy in the driveway and didn't answer. He didn't have a list of things he'd rather do than spend time with Curtis.

'Would you rather sit by yourself and read or come and shoot hoops?' Curtis had asked once. 'Laurie says I have to ask you what you'd rather do, instead of just expecting you to come out and play every time.' Scott dropped his book to the floor. 'I'd always rather be with you. But would you rather shoot hoops alone and be unopposed, so you can tell yourself later you were the best out there? Or have me come out and wipe the court with you?'

Would you rather. It had become their language. A second-grade boy's version of 'I love you, too.' Would you rather eat glass or walk on it? Would you rather swallow a handful of live spiders or stand for an hour in a roomful of bats?

Scott heard Laurie clear her throat behind him. Would you rather keep watching the boy and have your wife ticked off for the rest of the night, or pay attention to her? He turned from the window.

'I'm going to miss him, too,' she said. She reached in the drawer for a knife and started slicing the lasagna. 'But I'm focusing on the bright side now, and that's what you need to do. I've already planned out next week: Monday, I'm coming home from the office, sitting on the couch with that stack of baby books I haven't had a chance to read, and not moving till dinnertime.' She pointed her knife at him. 'I'm counting on my husband to take me out to dinner that night. Maybe even a movie after. When's the last time we had a date night?'

She paused, waiting for him to notice his cue. He gave his impression of an eager nod and, satisfied, she went on. 'Tuesday, I'm finally getting that pregnancy massage the girls at the office gave me the certificate for. I cannot wait.' She put a hand on her lower back and rubbed. 'Wednesday . . . well, I've only gotten to Tuesday in my plans. The rest of the week will probably involve a lot of sitting with my feet up, reading, in absolute silence.'

'Nice.'

'Think of everything you'll be able to do in your newfound spare time,' she said. 'Reading baby books with me for starters. We're six months along and about six months behind in learning what's going on in there.' She indicated her belly and he put a hand on it. She covered his with hers, leaned against the stove and smiled.

'Sometimes, I still can't believe it, you know? After all this time. A baby. In this house. In July.' Her smile widened. 'Can you believe it?'

'I'm a grinning idiot every time someone asks me about it,' Scott said. 'So Pete tells me.' Pete Conner was a fellow English teacher at Franklin, assistant basketball coach to Scott and his closest friend.

She snapped her fingers. 'Oh, I almost forgot. Bundles of Joy called. That crib we looked at? The one with the claw feet, that was already sold? Turns out they have another one coming in on consignment, end of the week or Monday. It's gray, but a few coats of paint will change that. They're going to put our name on it.'

'Great news on the crib. Not so much on the painting.'

'Come on, it'll be fun. And only one room this time, right?'

He squinted, letting her know he was on to her. It might only be one room, but he had seen her to-do list for the nursery and it was as long as the one she had made for their attack on the entire first floor. She laughed and punched his shoulder. 'Stop,' she said. 'You're going to love decorating as much as I am.'

'Yeah, I know,' he said. 'I'll go get the kid.'

The front door flew open before he reached it and Curtis fired himself through at a run. At the last second, Scott opened his arms to catch him, Curtis laughing at the impact. Reluctantly, Scott pulled himself away and put a hand on the boy's shoulder, steering him toward the kitchen. 'Wash your hands, LeBron. It's dinnertime.'

4

Mara

After the bus left, Mara stood at the kitchen counter and ran a hand over the cool granite. This was her favorite room in the house. She had always found it so seductive, with its sleek, gunmetal granite counters run through with a thin line of limestone green, its tall, rich-warm cherry cabinets, its sexy slate floor, lighter gray than the granite but with a delicate vein of the same limestone green.

These days, the room posed a few challenges for her, but she still loved it. The oven door felt heavier every day and it took a practiced combination of arm, leg and hip movements for her to open and close it. The countertop had to be given a wide berth; she had plenty of hip-level bruises to remind her how painful the granite could be on impact. And the beautiful slate floor would not be trifled with; when she lost her grip on a glass or plate, she knew not to waste time hoping it survived and, instead, walked immediately to the pantry for the broom and dustpan.

Tom was always urging her to spend more time on the soft couches and carpeted floors of the living room and family room, rather than the hard wooden chairs or bar stools in the kitchen. But Mara loved the way the sun streamed through the sliding glass doors that led from the kitchen to the backyard. The suncatcher hanging in the doorway harnessed the light and shot it in concentrated rays into the kitchen, a million laser beams of color that always infused her with energy, even on days that followed sleepless nights or unsettling appointments with Dr Thiry at the Huntington's disease clinic in downtown Dallas.

Mara, Tom and Laks ate their lunches at the kitchen counter and their dinners in the dining room, leaving the kitchen table to serve as Mara's workstation. Her laptop lived there, along with several legal pads, a cup filled with pens, and at least ten packages of sticky notes. A stack of legal files used to reside there, too. Now Mara used that space for the magazines and novels she turned to when she was still wakeful in the middle of the night and had run out of things to look at online.

Until recently, she had gone straight to the table after her early-morning date with the elliptical machine and dumbbells they kept in the guest room, squeezing in an hour or more of work before the rest of the house woke up. She would return there later, after Laks was in bed, until Tom finally goaded her into calling it quits for the night and joining him on the couch in the family room, or in winter, in front of the fire in the living room.

Mara headed to the table now, and sitting, she peeled a large-sized sticky note from the top of a package, chose a pen and considered everything she needed to accomplish in the next five days. She had to plan every detail of Sunday morning. Arrange for Laks to be out of the house on Saturday night. She had goodbyes to say.

Task number one – finalizing all the details – was largely

complete. There was a full bottle of vodka in the liquor cabinet. She had been stockpiling sleeping pills for a few months and thought she had enough, but she would count them out later, to be sure. If she felt she needed more, a quick call to Dr Thiry's office would solve that problem. Three simple words, 'I'm not sleeping,' and thirty more little white pills would be hers.

Task number two – arranging for Laks to be out of the house – was a minute's easy work. Mara picked up the phone and dialed her parents.

'Morning, daughter.' Pori loved his caller ID.

'Hi, Dad. Mom around?'

'She is, but so am I.'

'Great. Want to talk about plans for Saturday night?'

'I'll get your mother.'

Mara laughed as something rustled on the other end of the phone. 'Marabeti,' Neerja said. 'How are you feeling? How did you sleep?'

'Never better,' Mara lied. 'Mom, could I ask a favor? Could Laks sleep at your place this Saturday?'

'Of course. Your father and I would love to have her. Is everything . . . ?'

'It's all great. Tom and I want to . . . We have . . . There's something we need . . .'

Her mother laughed. 'You don't have to be shy around your mother. Lakshmi is welcome here, and you and Tom can enjoy your . . . something.' She chuckled softly.

'Mother. Please.'

'I'm only teasing, Beti. We should all be so lucky. What are you up to today? Resting, I hope?' When Mara didn't answer, Neerja added, 'Well, don't do too much.'

'Thanks for Saturday. Laks'll be thrilled.'

'Rest, Mara.'

'Yes, Mom.'

Task number three – saying goodbye without raising suspicion – would take more time. Mara drew three columns on the sticky note.

People she would talk to in person: Tom, Laks, her parents. 'Those Ladies' – Laks's name for Steph and Gina, Mara's two best friends, who appeared so often as a unit that everyone understood why Laks would lump them together with one name. In truth, when Laks had first come up with it, she called them 'Dose Yadies.' Now that she could pronounce the words properly, she didn't like to be reminded of a time when she couldn't.

Perfect timing: Those Ladies were taking Mara to lunch on Saturday to celebrate her birthday. Another benefit of having chosen April 10 for her deadline. She would ask Tom to take her to their favorite place for dinner on Saturday night, she decided, and she made a note of it beside his name, so she wouldn't forget.

People she would call: her closest McGill friends in Montreal, her best law school friends after Steph. Tom's mother and sister in New York, who would be expecting Mara's semiannual update call about now anyway, so wouldn't think twice. It had always been enough for them to hear in her twice-yearly phone calls, and her annual holiday card, how their son/brother was, how much the granddaughter/niece they'd only ever seen in pictures had grown since the last update. So different from the constantly hovering Pori and Neerja, who knew before Mara did when Laks lost a tooth or outgrew her shoes. 'This is the risk you run,' Tom had said with resignation, not bitterness, 'when you confront family members about alcoholism and they choose shooting the messenger over hearing the message.'

People she would e-mail: a handful of people at the firm where she and Steph had worked since their graduation from SMU Law School, a few mom friends from Laks's school. And, of course, Mara's dear friends from the Not Your Father's Family forum, an 'online community of adoptive, step, foster, gay and other nontraditional families.' She had found the forum a week after she and Tom arrived home from India with new baby Lakshmi, plucked out of the same Hyderabad orphanage from which Neerja and Pori had rescued Mara thirty-seven years earlier.

For the past five years, Mara had chatted a few minutes almost daily with her fellow forum members, about nontraditional parenting arrangements and so much more. Work, cooking, exercise, finances, marriage, sex – no topic was off-limits. Plenty of people had come and gone from the forum once their specific question was answered, but a core group of regulars remained, Mara among them. The reason each of them had joined the forum had long been supplanted by the reason they remained: friendship.

With a few members, she had ventured beyond group discussions and into the private world of personal messaging. It wasn't uncommon for a discussion to begin on the broader forum, only to have one poster ask another to 'PM' to continue to talk about it. The PM accounts were set up through the forum – a double click on a member's username allowed you to send a private message to that member – so PMs didn't reveal the members' identities any more than the main message board itself.

SoNotWicked, the founder of the forum, requested that members remain anonymous to protect the foster parents among them, most of whom were under confidentiality agreements with their states in connection with the children they were taking care of. But all the members agreed the anonymity factor was one of the main benefits of the forum; not sharing names made it easier to share details they would never reveal to people they actually knew. Mara had mused to Tom many times over the years how odd it was that she was so private 'in real life,' yet so comfortable sharing profoundly personal details with people she knew only as PhoenixMom, MotorCity, flightpath, SoNotWicked, 2boys.

Mara wrote MotorCity's name on her sticky note and drew a circle around it. For a year, he and his wife had been guardians of a boy who was scheduled to return home next Monday, to live with a mother who had paid the boy less attention in his entire eight years than MotorCity had in the past twelve months. It was easy to see MotorCity loved his 'little man' like his own, and while he had professed many times that it was best for his temporary charge to be reunited with his mother, everyone could tell it was killing him that Sunday would be his last day with the boy.

MotorCity would need a friend on Monday.

Mara would be dead on Sunday.

Her chest tightened with guilt and she turned from her sticky note to her open laptop, clicked open the forum and her voice-recognition software and dictated a quick post.

Tuesday, April 5 @ 8:32 a.m.
@MotorCity – I've been thinking about you all morning. Five days left with your LMan (not that you need a reminder). Sending positive thoughts your way, friend. I'll check in later to see how the day's going at your end.

She clicked the 'post field' button at the bottom of the screen and waited to see her message pop up as a new comment. When it did, she read what she had posted and frowned. A line or two about 'positive thoughts' was so inadequate.

She scrolled to the top of the page to see what SoNotWicked had posted for the day's topic of discussion. It was about MotorCity's situation: How have other forum members managed to keep it together when returning their foster children to their families? What advice could any of them give to MotorCity to make his coming days less sad?

The forum would light up today, Mara knew, and the thought made her chest relax. The members were for the most part a busy group, with little spare time, but the 'regulars' made it a priority to spend the minute or two it took to check the day's topic and fire off a post before returning to their children or work. Even at Mara's busiest, she had made time to offer a line or two of encouragement whenever a fellow member needed it.

Mara had never told her online friends about her illness, and months ago, a daily, raging debate had begun in her mind over whether she was sparing them or depriving them. It seemed disloyal to have kept it from them for so long. And now, the thought of simply disappearing without explanation, especially when MotorCity needed every friend he had, felt unforgivable. Mara leaned forward toward the laptop's tiny microphone and spoke.

Tuesday, April 5 @ 8:34 a.m.
While we're on the topic of five-day countdowns, there's something I should have told all of you a while ago:

She read what she had dictated so far and considered how to continue. It would help MotorCity, she thought, to know she had more than bland compassion for what he was going through, a thousand miles away. She, too, was preparing to say goodbye to her child.

She understood the suffocation he must feel when he thought about letting his little man go. The vise grip of panic that must squeeze his chest each time he pictured his life without the boy. How he must choke away tears every time he tucked him in at night, knowing tonight's goodnight kiss was one of the last. She felt those same things, she could tell him now. He would appreciate knowing a friend was going through the agony with him, wouldn't he?

Or would he be horrified, knowing she had a choice in the matter and was choosing only another five days with her daughter instead of another . . . however long she might have? Would they all be horrified? Was it better to slip quietly from MotorCity's life, from all their lives, and not burden them with the reason why?

There was a time, a few months before, when Mara's fine motor control had begun to mutiny. More disturbing than the issue of coffee grounds all over the counter and floor, her posts to the forum suddenly read as though written by a barely literate second grader. When 2boys finally asked about it in his characteristically abrasive way ('wtf, laksmom – you been knocking a few back already this morning?'), Mara lied and told them she had broken her arm and was using only one hand to type. She spent the following hour downloading voice-recognition software onto her laptop and phone.

If she confessed everything to them now, would they

blame themselves for not having noticed the too-quick restoration of her typing ability, the too-quick recovery of her allegedly broken bone? Would telling them now benefit them, or only her? She would die without the guilt of having disappeared from the forum without explanation or goodbye, but they would live on with the knowledge that their friend had been suffering all this time and they hadn't done anything to help. They would never forgive themselves for not being there for her, and the fact that she hadn't given them the chance wouldn't make them feel better.

At first, it wasn't a conscious decision, keeping her illness from them. She was in denial in the beginning, as loath to admit to herself that something was wrong as she was to admit it to them. But then, after her diagnosis, everyone around her became so overly concerned, so insufferably attentive that she started to regret anyone knew. As much as it was a relief to have a diagnosis in hand, it was infuriating to watch herself deteriorate in the eyes of the people around her. Use the word 'disease' and suddenly everyone will instantly treat you like you're ill, Mara learned, even on days you feel fine.

The forum had become the last vestige of normalcy in her life. The one place where people weren't constantly urging her to slow down, take it easy, conserve her energy. There, she wasn't treated like Mara the patient, Mara the sick, Mara the pitiful soul who wouldn't even outlive her own parents. On the forum, she was simply LaksMom: adoptive mother, full-time lawyer, wife to her college sweetheart, helpful friend. For that reason, the forum had been her lifeline, many days. The rope, however frayed it sometimes felt, that tethered her to sanity.

Mara read again the beginning of the post she'd dictated. If ever she needed an aid to maintaining sanity, it was this week. This was not the time to let them in on her secret. She positioned her cursor at the bottom of the screen and clicked 'delete field.'

5

Mara

Mara lay beside Tom in bed, running her hand over his shoulder and chest as he slept the contented slumber of a man who had just been made love to. To her, it had been a desperate, clinging kind of lovemaking. Part apology for what she was about to put him through, part gratitude for everything he had done for her and would do for their daughter. Part goodbye. To him, it had been hot.

Now, a half hour after, he didn't stir as she moved her hand over him. She ran her index finger gently down the long bridge of his nose, over the stubble along his square jawline. He wasn't the least bit vain but he was troubled lately by the salt and pepper of his sideburns and the way his beard grew in half gray, not that he ever let it grow for more than a long weekend. Mara loved it, though. It was as if the gray hairs were little spotlights, drawing attention to the contrasting blue of his eyes.

Neerja once told Mara that 'they' say the combination of dark hair and blue eyes, rarely occurring, tends to result in exceptional beauty. Certainly Mara's study subject of one, sleeping beside her, proved that theory. He was constantly being hit on, by both men and women. How many invitations, propositions, had he turned down in the past twenty-two years? she wondered.

How long would it take him, after she was gone, to accept?

She drew her hand away.

Disentangling her limbs from his, she crept out of their room and into Laks's, a short detour before she made her way to the kitchen table and her waiting laptop. It was an instinctive nightly habit – a few seconds to pull up the covers, thin out the herd of stuffed animals the girl had wedged in beside her, kiss her forehead and whisper 'I love you,' before she settled at the table to work or read or surf the Internet.

Only tonight, Mara was frozen by the sight of the slender little shoulder above the covers, and she stood watching it rise and fall, rise and fall, until her legs felt weak. She sat on the edge of the bed then, and when she realized her weight on the mattress hadn't made the girl stir, she stretched carefully on the bed, inching herself closer to the sleeping body.

She put an arm around Laks and slowly pulled her closer until they were spoons, the child's tiny bottom pressed against Mara's stomach. She buried her nose in her daughter's thick hair, inhaling deeply. Laks had talked her way out of a bath earlier that evening, and her hair smelled faintly of the prior night's shampoo and . . . honey? From lunch, Mara supposed: five days a week of butter and honey on whole wheat, no crust. Six baby carrots. A bottle of water. And the blasted cookie, of course. God help the person who forgot to include the cookie.

Mara moved her nose to the girl's neck and felt something sticky. Grinning, she pictured Laks in the lunchroom, waving her sandwich in the air as she chatted away to her friend Susan and others, suddenly feeling an itch on her neck and reaching with the same hand to scratch it. The fact that she had smeared honey on herself wouldn't have fazed her. She would have shrugged – regretfully maybe, or maybe not – and just gone on talking. 'Miss Messykins,' Tom called her.

Mara pulled Laks closer still, an outstretched hand spanning the small rib cage. She could feel the girl's heart beating into her palm. Slowly, she moved her body down on the bed and pressed her nose and mouth against the little pajama shirt, the waffle fabric rough against her lips. She inhaled again: morning body.

'This kid doesn't have morning *breath* when she wakes up,' Tom once said, 'she has morning *body*.'

Not that they had any other child to compare her to, but it had surprised them how sour-smelling she was at the end of a night's sleep. It was some combination of little-girl sweat and dried drool. And on no-bath nights such as this one, her scent was 'enhanced' by the fragrance of whatever food she had managed to get on herself during the day.

'It's a little gross,' Tom had said.

It's the best smell in the world, Mara thought now.

She closed her eyes and breathed in again, pressing every inch of herself as tightly to Laks as she could, trying to implant in her memory the precise feeling of her daughter's warmth, her knobby vertebrae, her bony bottom. The way she smelled. The way her breath sounded as she slept, the quiet little catch at the start of her inhale. The way she looked, so still, so small, so peaceful.

37

A sob thrust its way out of Mara's chest. A panicked, terrified sob that made her tighten her hold instinctively. Laks stirred and tried to roll over, but her mother's body blocked her on one side while twenty stuffed animals trapped her on the other.

'What? Mama?' She wriggled out from Mara's grip and turned to face her, awake now, confused.

'It's okay, sweetie,' Mara said, standing. 'I came in to pull up your covers and you looked cold, so I thought I'd hug you a bit first, warm you up. But I was just leaving. Go to sleep.'

She leaned down to kiss the girl's cheek and felt both relief and sadness as Laks blinked once, then drifted off.

Mara made it into the hallway before her knees gave out. She shot a hand out against the wall to brace herself. Straining, she could hear Laks's quiet breathing through the doorway, and in the darkness she closed her eyes and saw the narrow shoulder rising and falling. She smelled morning body and stale honey.

A low moan left her throat before she could stop it and she clapped a hand over her mouth. Aching to feel the small body against her again, she stepped toward the doorway. She heard the catch at the end of the girl's breath and clamped harder against her mouth as another moan sounded, this one louder than the first. Laks stirred and Mara stepped back, away from the doorway.

It was too soon.

She couldn't do it. Sunday was far too soon.

What if she had another twelve months? Another full year of packing lunches, giving baths. Of hugs and tears and giggles and tuck-ins. Of waffle pajamas and morning body.

Maybe it was an isolated incident, what had happened in the grocery store. Maybe she should talk to Dr Thiry or one of his staff about it before she so hastily concluded this was the beginning of the end. Huntington's was different with everyone, they would tell her – they told her this at almost every appointment. One incidence of incontinence might signal the beginning of major decline for one patient, but it might be a random, insignificant, one-time thing in another.

In the kitchen, she reached for the phone, pressed the speed-dial button for Dr Thiry's clinic and left a message asking them to fit her in tomorrow for a brief consult, even if only by phone. Nothing urgent, she added, just a quick question or two about a minor incident. It was probably a molehill, and their answers would surely keep her from making it into a mountain.

She felt her pulse slow as she stared at the receiver in her hand. Maybe she had until next year's birthday.

6

Scott

Scott leaned back in his chair and patted his stomach. 'You are one great cook, Laur. That was terrific.'

'Thank you.' She pushed her largely untouched plate toward him.

He took a few bites before holding up a hand. 'That's it for me.'

Turning to Curtis, Laurie said, 'I thought I'd make spaghetti tomorrow. Maybe you'd like to help bake the cookies for dessert?'

Curtis, his mouth full, smiled and stuck one thumb up.

'Not because of the glowing report I know Miss Keller will write in your planner tomorrow afternoon, but just because.' She put a hand on his and Scott grinned as he saw the boy look suspiciously at the fingers that held his; he knew what was coming. 'It shouldn't always be such a big deal that you behaved properly in class,' she said, her voice stern but gentle. 'You know that. It should be something you do all the time, because it's the right thing.'

Curtis nodded, still chewing.

'One day, you'll have to be able to act the way you're

supposed to even when there's no sticker chart to fill in, no special dinner, no movie night, no me or Scott looking over your shoulder. Because doing the right thing doesn't come from a sticker chart, right?'

The boy shook his head.

'It comes from . . . ?'

He pointed to his forehead.

'Right. And where else?'

He pointed to his heart.

'That's my guy.' She patted his hand. 'You got this. You can do this. You don't need me, or Scott, or the chart, or even Miss Keller. You've got everything you need, right here' – she pointed to his forehead – 'and here.' She pointed to his heart. 'Right?'

'Right,' he said, now finished with his bite. 'Like today, when I did everything good. Everything I was supposed to. Just like it says in my planner.' He glanced at each of them briefly before snapping his chin down to study his plate.

Scott looked sideways at his wife, wordlessly betting her she wouldn't be able to let the lie go. 'And that's why you got such a great note from Miss Keller,' she said to the boy before turning to grin victoriously at her husband.

He leaned over to kiss her. 'Getting soft,' he whispered as he pulled away. 'By the time the baby's born, you'll be as lax as me.' A hand landed emphatically on his knee and he covered it with his own. 'Tell you what,' he said, 'why don't you let Little Man and me take care of the dishes while you get ready for book club.'

When she left to change, Scott and Curtis stood to clear the table. 'Would you rather have me help, even though I might drop all these dishes on the floor and break them,' Curtis asked, the dinner plates balanced in his hands, 'or do it yourself, so you can be sure nothing gets wrecked? While I sit at the table, real careful, not busting anything and maybe just telling you some of my new jokes.'

'Would you rather sweep out the garage, including all the corners where the biggest, hairiest spiders live, or go down to the basement to see if we caught anything really big and ferocious in the mousetraps?'

'Ewwww.' The boy gave an exaggerated shiver and got to work.

Fifteen minutes later, Scott was putting detergent in the dishwasher when he heard his wife come down the stairs. He looked up and let out a low whistle. Her long waves of hair, released from the confines of the ponytail, spread out past her shoulders, and the color of the dress she had changed into – cinnamon, he thought he'd heard her say – set off every feature. Her eyes shone, her face glowed, her hair looked especially rich. All that, just by wearing the right dress.

And by being pregnant, he thought. It truly had softened her, not just in the way she was with Curtis, but physically as well. It had relaxed the tightness around her temples and mouth, where her disappointment, her frustration, her resentment used to sit. Those things flashed in her expression from time to time, and in the tone of her voice, but she no longer carried them constantly.

He was happy to see she had traded the small, conservative earrings she had worn to work for the thick teardrop-shaped ones they had bought together at an art fair years ago. The earrings were long and dramatic and he thought they made her look cool and artsy and sexy. Knowing he felt that way, she used to wear them on every date night, leaving them on at the end of the night while they made love. Lately, if she wore them at all, there was as much chance the night would end with nothing more than a peck on the cheek before they each rolled toward opposite walls. But his heart sped a little anyway.

'Wow.' He crossed the room to her and moved a strand of hair out of her face. 'Do they allow men in your book club? I mean, to sit and observe?'

Laughing, she craned her body around him to talk to Curtis, who stood at the kitchen counter drying the lasagna pan. 'Five pages tonight, right?'

Curtis looked at her over his shoulder and nodded unenthusiastically.

She held up a hand and counted some other items on her fingers. 'Also math. And a shower.'

He opened his mouth wide in exaggerated protest.

'I know,' she said. 'It's a great injustice.'

She stepped past Scott to give the boy a hug and kiss, grazed her lips quickly past her husband's cheek and headed for the front door. 'See my two best men later,' she called. 'One of you had better be asleep when I get home.'

'If we both are, feel free to wake one of us,' Scott called.

He heard the tinkle of her laugh before the front door closed.

Scott and Curtis were settled into their nightly positions in the family room: Curtis disappearing into the overstuffed cushions of the couch, counting down the pages until he was freed from his reading practice, Scott at the built-in desk beside the window, poised with a red pen to attack a pile of seventh-grade English papers. On the other side of the window were the floor-to-ceiling bookcases Laurie had dreamed of, now covered in two coats of Warm Ecru and filled to capacity with books and framed photographs.

A large stone fireplace sat on the back wall of the room. Scott had started a fire after dinner and it crackled lazily now, almost ready for another log. They had chosen the wall opposite the fireplace for the accent color – Deep Moss Green – and it took on a textured appearance when the light from the fire danced across it, making it look as though it were covered in velvet.

A large, dark wood frame in the center of the green wall held his favorite photograph – him and Laurie, soaking wet on the bow of the *Maid of the Mist* at the bottom of Niagara Falls. Honeymooners, their faces pressed closely together as Scott held the camera in front to snap the picture. They were drenched and freezing and a little motion sick, both of them, yet smiling like they had won something.

At least half of the pictures around the room were the same: the two of them laughing, cheek pressed to cheek while one of them held the camera out in front. Or standing, arms around each other, as someone else captured the moment for them, bodies as close together as they could get them. Framed reminders of how happy they had been.

There were more recent shots, too. Laurie and Scott standing in the doorway of their bathroom last October, their mouths wide in excitement and disbelief as she held up a white pregnancy stick and he, arm extended, snapped the photo.

Scott and Curtis in the driveway, Curtis holding a basketball against his chest with one hand, the pointer finger of his other raised to announce his self-declared number-one status in their two-man driveway league. Scott was crouched beside him, his hair dark with sweat, eyes cast skeptically at the boy's proclamation of victory, left hand poised near the ball, ready to steal it and resume the game once the picture was snapped.

Scott, Pete and Curtis on the porch steps last November, each holding a football ticket high in the air and dressed in the maize and blue colors of the University of Michigan, Scott and Laurie's alma mater, on whose campus they had met as sophomores almost fifteen years ago. In the lower right corner of the photo stood Curtis's older brother, Bray, a former student and basketball player of Scott's.

Bray was now a sophomore on a basketball scholarship at Michigan. His life was so full of promise that when the boys' mother, LaDania, had been sent to jail for a twelve-month sentence last April, Scott jumped at the chance to look after Curtis for the year so Bray wouldn't risk his future by taking time off. In the photo, Bray is standing on the grass beside the porch, holding up his own ticket. Even from his handicapped position on the ground, his hand reached a full three feet above his younger brother's head.

Laurie and Curtis in front of the stove on the boy's first day with them last spring, a sheet of cookies between them, Curtis holding one high in the air, a prize. The first cookie he'd ever had that didn't come out of a package, he told them. They wondered if he'd be reluctant to eat it – for about two seconds. The instant the boy heard the camera click, he popped the cookie into his mouth. They weren't sure he even chewed it before swallowing.

He wasn't so cavalier about his birthday cake a couple months ago. He hollered when Laurie held the knife over it and begged her not to cut. He wanted to keep it forever, he told them. It was nothing special, Laurie said – a plain old sheet cake turned into a battlefield with the help of green and brown food coloring and a new package of

45

plastic army men. She could make him another anytime. And she'd record this one for him, she added, lifting her camera and firing off half a dozen shots.

But Curtis held both hands over the cake, protecting it from the knife as Scott, Pete and Laurie exchanged confused glances. Finally, Bray whispered over his brother's head that it was the first time Curtis had ever had a birthday cake. Later, he would explain that while LaDania had almost always managed to produce a present or two on each boy's birthday (still in the store bag and usually with the price tag still on), organizing finer details like having a cake and candles ready, or wrapping the gifts with paper and bows, was more than she was willing or able to do. By then, Scott and Laurie had done so many firsts with the child, they weren't surprised to hear it – first set of clothes that weren't hand-me-downs or from a resale shop, first haircut at a barber instead of at the kitchen table, first time having someone pack him a lunch instead of eating the glop in the school cafeteria.

Laurie ran a soothing palm over the child's head as she assured him again she would make him more cakes, just like this one. A cake every month, if he wanted. So he should feel free to let everyone gobble this one up today, and not worry it would be the last.

'That's right, buddy,' Pete told Curtis. 'You've seen how much Laurie loves to bake. She can make another one of these anytime.'

'But once this one's gone,' Curtis said, pointing to the edible war scene in front of him, 'my birthday will be over.'

'Yeah, but you'll have another one next year,' Scott said, sitting beside the boy and putting a hand on his shoulder. 'This isn't your only birthday, Little Man. Right?'

Curtis's response was so quiet Scott couldn't hear. 'What'd you say?' he asked, leaning closer.

The boy lifted his head, put a small hand on the back of Scott's head to pull him closer and whispered in his ear. 'I said, it's my only birthday with a father.'

Scott heard a distant click as Laurie snapped another photo: Curtis and Scott, their foreheads pressed together, each with a hand around the other's neck, gripping as though neither wanted to ever let go.

Scott kept that picture on his nightstand.

7

Mara

Mara and Tom had told Dr Thiry that looking back on it, there were probably signs as early as law school. Memory, mostly; she had walked to the store for wine once and returned home with nothing. She reached the corner and forgot what she had gone out for, so she turned around and went home to find a surprised husband sitting at the table, two empty wineglasses in front of him. It was the stress of finals, they decided, laughing about her 'law school-induced dementia.'

Another time, Tom arrived at the law school library to take her out for their anniversary, something they had talked about all week. She stared at him like he had invented the entire thing. He managed to coax her into letting him at least buy her a cup of coffee but she drained it in a few minutes and sent him home, mildly annoyed he had interrupted her studies. Later that night, walking home from the library, she suddenly remembered. She ran home and crawled into bed beside him, covering him in kisses and apologies and tears as he grinned salaciously and told her not to worry about it, he'd already thought of a way for her to make it up to him.

When they thought about it harder, they recalled more incidents, a few each year since their grad school days, followed by a marked increase after she became partner. It was only little things at first: a forgotten item or two at the grocery store, a missed trip to the dry cleaner. Even when the overlooked things became not quite so little, they still joked about it. It was a funny thing, 'endearing,' Tom said, not something either of them saw as cause for concern.

She missed a hair appointment, and the salon called. She forgot to leave a check for the housecleaning service and had a not-so-friendly call from the manager. She was a no-show for a dentist appointment and received a bill in the mail, with 'Second Missed Appointment – Charge' stamped across it. As she rebooked the hairdresser and the dentist and wrote the check and a note of apology to the cleaner, she laughed and told Tom she hadn't even noticed her hair needed retouching, her teeth needed cleaning and the bathrooms needed scrubbing. If she was okay with the state of things, why were the hairdresser, dentist and cleaner all up in arms?

And then one September, only a few months after they brought the baby home, it stopped being funny. Her cell rang at nine fifteen one morning and Gina, who worked as Mara's secretary back then, was frantic on the other end. 'Where are you? They're here!'

'Who's there?' Mara asked. She was sitting in the family room with her mother, Neerja, sipping coffee and watching baby Laks gurgle on the floor in front of them. Mara and Tom had planned to hire a nanny to stay with the baby while they continued their twelve-hour workdays. But Pori and Neerja wouldn't hear of a stranger raising their only grandchild, and Mara's pleas that they not waste their retirement on diaper-changing duty went unheeded. They cheerfully arrived early each morning, shooing Tom and Mara out the door with instructions to work as late as they wanted, the baby's Nana and Nani had things under control. That day, Pori had run out to do errands and, on a lark, Mara decided to spend a leisurely hour with her mother and daughter before heading to the office.

Mara bent to touch the baby's stomach and flinched as Gina's voice blared in her ear. 'The mediator! The Torkko executives! Mr Hoskins! Everyone!'

When Mara didn't respond, Gina said, 'The Torkko mediation? Nine thirty this morning?'

'Oh, shit!' Mara stood and the baby, startled by the shout, began to cry. Neerja scooped her up and carried her out of the room as Mara checked her watch. She was thirty minutes from the office, without traffic. 'I can be there by nine forty-five, ten at the latest. Stall them.'

Later, when the elevator doors closed and the clients were gone, Mara grabbed Gina in a tight hug and kissed her on the cheek. 'You are a godsend! What would I do without you? Come on, I'm taking you to lunch. No deli takeout for you today!'

Gina smiled proudly but waved her hands in protest. 'Doing my job, is all. And do we have time to go out? It's already after noon, and the Winchester Foods brief still needs a lot of work, doesn't it?'

Mara stared at her blankly.

'The Winchester Foods appeal,' Gina repeated. 'Our response brief? Due today . . . ?'

Mara's hand flew to her mouth. 'Oh my God! I totally forgot!' She looked wildly at Gina as the memory of hours spent on the Winchester Foods appeal brief the prior day came back to her, along with the work left to do before the hours-away filing deadline.

'Are you okay?' Gina whispered to her boss, taking her arm. She led her past the reception desk and around the corner to her office, where Mara flopped into her chair.

'What on earth, Gina? I'd have spent a long lunch whooping it up over the Torkko relationship being mended while I committed malpractice in the Winchester Foods appeal. What is the matter with me? We worked on that thing all day yesterday. It's the only thing we talked about the entire day.'

Mara moved her hand from her mouth to her eyes and pressed her thumb hard against one temple, her fingers against the other. It was one thing to forget a dentist appointment or to pay the housekeeper; those things were easily remedied with an apology and extra money. Forgetting work deadlines could get the firm sued, and Mara fired. She couldn't muse with idle curiosity about her memory problems any longer. She needed to take action.

But first, she needed to get the Winchester Foods appeal brief finalized and filed with the court. For the next three and a half hours, they tore through the revisions to the brief, handing it to the courier with no time to spare before their filing deadline. When the runner left, Mara closed her office door and sat at her desk, motioning for Gina to take one of the guest chairs.

'We can't let this happen again,' Mara said. 'I can't count on clients being so understanding about forgotten mediations. And a missed court deadline is malpractice.'

Gina started to interject but Mara raised a hand to stop her. 'Last week, when you had your doctor's appointment over lunch? I was supposed to speak at the noon litigation meeting. I almost forgot to go at all, until Steph came to get me on her way there. And it wasn't until they introduced me that I remembered it was my day to give my annual civil procedure rules update.'

Gina's mouth opened wide. 'I assumed . . .' she started, but stopped herself.

'You assumed I knew about it?'

Gina nodded.

'Because . . . we talked about it?'

Gina winced.

'Jesus!' Mara slapped her hand on her desk. 'We talked about it?'

'You're the hardest worker at the firm. Everyone says so,' said Gina. 'I've wondered myself how you keep track of it all. Maybe after a while, you just can't.'

'Well, "can't" isn't an option. We need to come up with a solution.'

'What about slowing down a little?' Gina asked. 'All the other female partners have done it, at least for a little while, after they had their babies. Even Steph—'

'Gina.' Mara shot the other woman a warning glare. The subject of how hard she worked was off-limits – to Gina, to Tom, to Mara's parents, to her best friend, Steph, a fellow partner at the firm. Not that they hadn't all tried, some of them more than once, to get her to ease up. But this was who she was: Mara the workhorse; Mara the woman who was married and had a new baby but still billed the hours of a single woman.

It's how she'd always been, doing all the extra-credit projects in elementary school, reading all of the 'suggested' books on the summer list in high school while her friends were sleeping late, squinting at her texts under the dim bulb of her desk lamp long after her college roommate had started snoring in bed a few feet away. Even in law school, a place rampant with workaholics, she was known for her marathon sessions in the law library, her refusal to join her classmates for Friday evening happy hour if she hadn't fulfilled the requisite studying for the week (a standard she set for herself).

And it's how she always would be, she told them. So they could keep their warnings and cajoling and pleas to themselves. Nothing made her feel as alive as a long, hard day of productive work at the law firm. And nothing – not friends or parents or happy hour or a husband or even a new baby – could make her give that up.

'Okay,' Gina said, reaching for a notepad and pen on Mara's desk. 'Let's take some time right now and go through your calendar to make sure I have all the deadlines down. Then I can remind you when things are coming up.'

'Thanks. That will help. But it's more than just deadlines. It's everything. It's as though my entire short-term memory is on strike. We need a system of some kind, something foolproof.'

Gina leaned forward, put both hands on top of Mara's and smiled. 'We'll sort it out.' For the rest of the afternoon and into the evening, they went through every open file in Mara's office. Gina was armed with a desk calendar, a notepad, a stack of sticky notes and colored pens. By the time they stood to stretch, a little after seven, Gina had ten pages of notes and a calendar full of colored markings, and she had put sticky notes on over half of Mara's files, with different colors signaling different levels of urgency.

'I'll go input all the deadlines into the calendar on the e-mail system,' Gina said, gathering her things, 'and I'll send you meeting notices for each one. And I'll set that calendar alarm to give you several reminders for each deadline.' As she reached Mara's door, she looked back thoughtfully. 'Let me get that finished, and then I'll think about what else I can do to make sure we stay on top of everything.'

'Thank you, Gina. This is all so far above and beyond.'

'You know, you're the only lawyer I know who's been keeping track of your own deadlines. It's about time you let me help with all of this.'

It made Mara feel better to hear it. She wasn't the only one who was under too much stress from work, and from the frenetic pace involved in balancing work and family, to be able to keep track of everything.

'Yes, well, you've hardly been underworked,' she said to Gina. She waved a hand around her office, indicating the hundreds of neatly labeled files that Gina spent hours each week keeping updated. In her five years working for Mara, Gina had put in countless hours of overtime without complaint; she was the only secretary Mara had ever had who was able to keep up with the workload, the constant deadlines and the requirements of a perfectionist boss who wanted every brief reread one more time for errors, every stack of exhibits checked one more time for completeness.

'You're my guardian angel, Gina.'

'The feeling's mutual. You seem to be forgetting that.' Mara didn't respond, and Gina said, 'Don't pretend. You know exactly what I'm talking about.'

Mara rolled her eyes. So she had flown to Oklahoma for Gina's dad's funeral, and ended up staying over a week to help Gina's mother sort out her financial affairs. When

Gina's mom died two years later, Mara traveled to Oklahoma a second time, staying another week when she realized how much Gina had to contend with in packing up and selling her parents' house. It was weeks before Mara's first oral argument in the Fifth Circuit Court of Appeals in New Orleans, and she should have been back home preparing.

But she had refused to leave Gina to face it all alone, and had the firm overnight three boxes of briefs and exhibits, which she reviewed late at night, after she and Gina had finished the day's packing, or meeting with the family's lawyer, or whatever else needed to be done. Back home in Dallas, Mara had insisted Gina spend Thanksgiving with Mara's family so she wouldn't have to face the holidays alone.

Mara waved a dismissive hand at Gina. 'Please. Anybody would've done those things.'

'You mean nobody. Nobody does those things. Nobody offered, and nobody did. Except you.'

Mara shook her head and Gina walked resolutely over and put a hand on Mara's. 'Did you hear me? Nobody. Except you. You have been my family. The least I can do is be your memory.' She squeezed Mara's hand, turned around and walked out. 'I'll be at my computer,' she called over her shoulder. 'You're about to get seventy-five meeting notices over e-mail.'

'If I start forgetting to check all the sticky notes we've got everywhere,' Mara said, following Gina to the door, 'then I'll really be screwed.'

'Then I'll start calling you, to remind you to read them.'

'Oh my God, Gina. If it comes to that, please push me off a cliff.'

8

Mara

By the following September, Laks was a year old and Mara was finished with the jokes about her forgetfulness. She no longer made self-deprecating comments about it, and she wouldn't tolerate Those Ladies, Tom or her parents making light of it, either. In fact, she could barely tolerate any of them at all, for any reason. She had turned irritable, moody. No one was immune to her sudden rages, especially not Tom.

One evening in late November they were standing in the kitchen. Mara was stirring soup on the stove and Tom slicing a loaf of French bread. 'We're about three weeks behind on laundry,' he said. 'I thought after dinner—' He stopped when the wooden spoon she had been holding flew past his head and clattered against the kitchen table, soup splattering across the floor and walls.

Tom looked in astonishment at the spoon and then turned back to Mara, his mouth open to speak. She didn't give him a chance. 'I can't believe you! I'm standing here making you homemade soup after twelve hours at the office and all you have to say is I'm behind on laundry?!'

Tom raised his hands in the air, questioning. 'What are you so upset about? I didn't say *you* were behind on laundry. I said *we* were. And I was about to say I'd get a load started after dinner—'

'Bullshit!' Mara spat. 'You were accusing me. You know I feel terrible when I get behind on things around the house, and you're just trying to make me feel bad.'

Tom put his knife down and walked toward her, his arms open. 'Mara, when have I ever—'

She backed away from him and as she did, she untied the apron she was wearing over her suit and threw it to the floor. 'Make your own damn dinner!'

She stormed out of the kitchen and into their bedroom, slamming their door behind her, and paced in front of the bed, her fists clenching and unclenching. Finally, her pacing slowed and she walked into the bathroom and looked at herself in the mirror, embarrassed by the red, blotchy, angry face staring back at her. She'd acted like a child. Wetting a washcloth with cold water, she pressed it against her face for several minutes before leaning close to the mirror and peering intently at herself as though she might be able to find, on close inspection, the thing that was making her act so crazy. 'What. On. Earth.'

Back in the kitchen, she found Tom standing at the counter, the bread sliced, a drink in front of him. He raised his eyes to meet hers, a look of such pain on his face that tears immediately sprang to her eyes. She rushed to him and put her arms around his waist, kissing him. 'I am so sorry. I have no idea what just happened.' She hugged him and took a step closer, pressing her entire body against his until she finally felt him relax. 'I don't know what got into me. You didn't deserve that. Please forgive me.'

He sighed and kissed the top of her head. 'I forgive you,' he said.

But after that, she stopped apologizing. She would yell at him for charring the vegetables on the grill one night, only to push them aside the next night, complaining they were undercooked. For weeks at a time, when he reached for her in bed, she feigned exhaustion or flat out expressed her disinterest. And then accused him later of not wanting her anymore because they hadn't had sex in so long.

She became irrational, paranoid. Depressed and anxious. Over Christmas, Tom begged her to see her doctor, but she refused. She couldn't remember what reasons she gave. But then, that was part of the disease – it didn't just go after your ability to think and move, but attacked your emotions as well. A three-pronged assault, each prong as deadly as the other two. Like the devil's pitchfork.

A few weeks after Valentine's Day, they had tucked Laks in and were sitting together on the couch, something they hadn't done in months. Tom seemed quiet, and Mara asked what was on his mind. He regarded her cautiously. 'I'm worried about you,' he said, reaching for her hand. 'I think you need to see a doctor.'

Mara pulled her hand away and stood.

'Don't be angry,' he said, reaching for her again. She stepped backward, out of his reach, and crossed her arms over her chest.

'I only want you to be happy,' he said, 'like you used to be. You don't seem to enjoy things anymore – work, us, anything. Tonight has been lovely, but it's not the norm. Not anymore.'

'I am so tired of this conversation,' she said. 'I keep telling you, I don't need to see anyone. Normal life things, like a bit of forgetfulness, occasional irritability, are not diagnosable. You don't run to the doctor for that sort of thing.'

'That's the thing, though,' he said. 'I'm not sure these are "normal life things." I think it's become more than that.' He looked at her plaintively, one hand still extended toward her. He was still trying to discuss this nicely, calmly. It infuriated her.

She curled her lips into a sneer until he lowered his hand to his lap. 'I'm not sure you even know what "normal life" is,' she said. 'For our entire marriage, I've done everything around here, in addition to dealing with an extremely demanding, incredibly stressful job. I've tried cases all day long, and then I've come home to raise your daughter, make your dinner and fold your laundry. While you've put in your cushy dermatologist hours and then gone for long runs.'

He snapped his head back, shocked by her accusation. She let out a sharp cackle, enjoying the blow she'd landed and not caring that it was completely unjustified. He was more helpful around the house, and with Laks, than any husband she knew. Having grown up with a father who was generally too drunk to help with the household or parenting, Tom had made a point of being an engaged and helpful father and husband. The suggestion that he had failed at either – or worse, hadn't even tried – was the most damning thing anyone could say to him. For a split second, Mara considered backing down.

But she pressed on. 'You want me to be happy?' she asked. 'You want me to enjoy my life more? Try helping out more around here. I don't need a diagnosis, Dr Nichols. I need you to act like an adult. Try that for a while, why don't you, and then let's see if you still think I need a doctor.'

'Mara,' he finally said. 'That's completely unfair.'

She regarded him coolly for a second. He was leaning toward her, his expression open, trusting. He expected her to admit her meanness and apologize, as she had done before. Instead, she sneered again and said, 'You think you're such a great dad. A great husband. Well, you're not. You're just like your father.'

Tom stood with such speed that Mara flinched and jumped backward. 'That's enough, Mara! You don't get to say things like that to me! You don't get to make up terrible, hurtful bullshit like that and throw it out at me because you're in another bad mood. This has gone way beyond simple work stress, and I've put up with it as long as I'm going to. I don't know if you need antidepressants or iron supplements or just a very long nap. But this needs to stop. I'm not asking you, I'm telling you. See a doctor. Or I'm leaving.' Mara watched him, her mouth slack with shock, as he stormed into their bedroom, slamming the door behind him.

The next day, Mara let Tom make an appointment with Alan Misner, a neurologist Tom knew from medical school who offered to see Mara after office hours that evening as a favor to his former classmate. She didn't agree to listen with an open mind, however, although she didn't point this distinction out to Tom. She almost felt guilty about it; he was so happy about her concession to see someone.

As they drove in silence to Dr Misner's office, she let Tom believe she was preparing herself for a discussion about what medical condition she might have. But really, she was readying herself to give Tom an I-told-you-so look after his colleague informed him Mara had been right all along – other than the expected changes that came with middle age, she was in perfect health. And later, at home, she'd tell Tom she'd followed his order, and now it was his turn to follow hers and never raise the issue that 'something isn't right' again. She predicted her ultimatum delivery might come with some slammed doors of her own, so she arranged for Laks to stay overnight with her parents.

In the doctor's office, she and Tom sat in space-age black leather chairs in front of Dr Misner's desk. Mara would never forget the desk – one of those ultramodern black affairs that looked more like a spaceship than a piece of furniture, with gleaming chrome legs that matched the ones on the chairs. It was more whimsical than serious, she thought, and she wondered how people who actually had medical issues responded when the doctor delivered bad news to them from behind it. He might have the sympathetic eyes, warm hands and soft voice of a physician skilled in delivering sobering news, but all of those effects would be completely undercut, she guessed, by the unconventionality of the desk.

While Mara occupied herself with thoughts about office fixtures, she could hear the former classmates catching each other up on the missing decades between medical school and that evening. She smiled while the two men compared notes about practices and office staff and children, confident that she and Tom would be on their way back home shortly, this futile appointment behind them.

After the reunion chatter was complete, Dr Misner turned to Mara, smiling kindly, and asked how he could help. She smiled back blandly and said nothing.

'Well,' he said, unfazed, 'why don't we start with an easier question? Let's talk about your medical history.'

As much as Mara was determined not to take the entire affair seriously, she decided it would be good cover to at least appear cooperative. And her medical history wasn't complicated; it began and ended with her, since the orphanage had given her parents no information about her birth parents' medical condition or history. She told him as much as she knew.

'Okay, then, now we're rolling,' Dr Misner said, clearly pleased with himself for having established some rapport with his recalcitrant patient. 'Let's start again with discussing why you're here,' he said, and before Mara could fix him with the same blank stare she'd begun with, Tom jumped in.

'Would you rather I cover it?' Tom asked, reaching over and taking her hand. Mara nodded, and with his hand still around hers, Tom spoke quietly, almost apologetically, as he described to the other man the changes he'd seen in his wife. While he spoke, Mara stared at their joined hands and told herself the stories she was hearing weren't about her. She had been forgetful, somewhat impatient, a little irritable. But the woman he was describing sounded psychotic – objects hurled at the walls (or Tom) on what sounded like a weekly basis, doors slammed over minor misunderstandings, expletives shrieked not only at him, but at Gina, too, and Steph, and even Pori and Neerja.

After a while, she tuned out the physician she was married to and watched the one behind the desk. He was making notes on a yellow pad as he listened. Mara tried to peer surreptitiously over his desk to see what he was writing, but she wasn't able to make out any of the words. Now and then, she saw him underlining certain words, sometimes adding big, loopy circles around them. He asked a number of follow-up questions, and as Tom answered, Dr Misner added more lines under words, more circles around others.

Mara shifted uncomfortably in her chair, pulling her hand away from Tom's. It was clear Dr Misner felt he was on to something, and she grew increasingly anxious, and increasingly unsure of her defense strategy.

When Tom was finished with his recital, Dr Misner looked up from his notes, glanced at each of them in turn and asked, 'And how long have the involuntary arm movements been going on?'

Mara asked, 'What involuntary arm movements?' while at the same time Tom said, 'Over a year.'

They turned to each other with gaping mouths, each stunned by the other's answer. Though she didn't want to do it, Mara forced herself to look at her hands. To her horror, they were moving back and forth over her legs, out to the arms of her chair, back to the middle again, as though her lap were a piano and she were playing a complicated piece. Quickly, she shoved her hands under her thighs, pressing her legs down hard. Tom murmured something soothing and patted her leg.

Dr Misner circled a word on his yellow pad. He circled it again and added an underline. Then he nodded thought-fully, studying his notes for a moment before raising pained eyes to Mara. She cleared her throat and shifted again in her chair as he reached into one of the drawers in his space-ship desk and took out a business card. Rising slowly, almost reluctantly, he walked around the desk to Mara and Tom's side. He leaned against the desk with a tired sigh, folded his hands in his lap and trained his soft eyes on Mara.

The expression on his face made her lips start to tremble, so she cast her eyes to the floor. His shoes, expensive black loafers, were tapping a rapid beat against the carpet. She stole a quick look at his face again and realized: he was nervous. Her lips trembled more.

She wanted to get up and walk out before he could tell her what he was anxious about. But Tom would only say she hadn't met her obligation, and would drag her back again another day. She took her hands out from under her legs and gripped the arms of her chair, forcing herself to stay put.

'Mara,' Dr Misner said gently. 'Tom. I can't express how sorry I am to deliver this news. And before I go on, let me say we can't know for sure without a blood test. But based on everything you've told me, about the forgetfulness, the mood swings, the irritability, the depression and anxiety, and based on Mara's physical symptoms, I'm afraid I'm unable to rule out Huntington's disease at this time. I'd like you to see a specialist. There's a Huntington's clinic at Baylor Hospital, downtown. Evan Thiry is the man who runs it.' He handed the business card to Tom, then folded his hands again.

'Dr Thiry can take you through some cognitive and physical tests to determine whether Huntington's is a real possibility. If he agrees with my theory that this may be what's going on with Mara, he can confirm it or rule it out with certainty by doing a blood test, which you may or may not decide to undergo. But whatever you decide, Dr Thiry's clinic can provide a number of services, both medical and emotional, that I think the two of you may benefit from. And later, when she's old enough, your daughter. They have wonderful pediatric social workers on staff who can help children deal with—'

He paused for a second before speaking again. 'I'm so

sorry. I'm getting ahead of myself. I'm looking at Tom here, and I know he understands Huntington's. But I shouldn't have assumed you know about it, Mara. Have you heard of Huntington's?'

She thought she had. She remembered hearing Tom talk about it once – after he'd read about it for a class in medical school, maybe? Or had one of his partners treated a Huntington's patient? She couldn't recall, and she wasn't sure she'd ever heard all the details about the disease, but she could guess now, based on how Dr Misner was acting, that it was something truly horrible.

She turned to Tom, to ask him to remind her what it was he'd told her about it. She hoped he'd roll his eyes and tell her the other man was way off base, that whatever it was that was going on with her, it didn't warrant Dr Misner coming around to the front of his ridiculous desk, leaning toward her the way he was leaning, looking at her the way he was looking, talking about specialists and blood tests and social workers who could help her daughter cope. But Tom's eyes, shining with tears, told her something else.

Mara turned back to Dr Misner and shrugged, and he put a large hand on one of hers. His eyes never leaving her face, he described the disease in a low, gentle voice. Tom pulled his chair closer to Mara's and put an arm around her, and out of the corner of her eye she could see him studying her expression as Dr Misner went on. She tried to focus on the doctor's words as her mind raced, first to make sense of what he was telling her, and second, to prepare an argument as to why he was as wrong as her husband in suggesting there was anything wrong with her beyond mere work stress and advancing age.

She only managed to pick up on every fifth word or so. The rest of Dr Misner's sentences were muffled, as though he were speaking over a car radio that was going in and out of frequency.

Degenerative neurological disease.

Progressive brain cell death.

Caused by a genetic disorder. Every child of an affected parent has a fifty percent chance of inheriting.

This is why he'd asked so many questions about her birth parents, Mara thought. If only the orphanage had provided records to Pori and Neerja, she could whip those out and show Tom and his classmate how cracked they were.

Unless the records didn't show that. She pressed her eyes closed quickly against the thought. But she allowed herself, before she opened them again, one more notion along the same lines: thank God Laks was adopted, and didn't share Mara's genes. Laks's birth parents, Tom and Mara knew from the thick file they'd received, had no malfunctions in their DNA.

Characterized by decreased mental function.

Gradual loss of physical control.

Mara sat a little straighter and almost laughed with relief. Dr Misner was as overly dramatic as her husband; neither of those things applied to her. She was functioning perfectly fine, mentally. And she certainly had no problems with physical control. She dropped things from time to time, but didn't everyone?

Although, if she thought about it, she would have to admit she'd been doing it more often lately. She had fallen out of Downward Dog pose in yoga class twice last Saturday. Steph, on the next mat, had teased under her breath, 'It's not Drop Dead Dog.' But clumsiness didn't amount to 'loss of physical control,' Mara told herself.

Involuntary movements of the face, body and limbs, commonly known as 'chorea.'

Mara regarded her hands. To her dismay, they weren't gripping the chair arms as she'd intended, but were instead moving up and down the arms, back to front, front to back, in a rapid motion she had been completely unaware of. She shoved them back under her legs and pressed her thighs against them again, harder this time.

Other symptoms include depression and anxiety. Mood swings and personality changes.

She felt her cheeks warm.

Forgetfulness.

She swallowed hard and swung her eyes from Dr Misner to Tom. He was biting his lower lip and his face was ashen.

Gradual decrease in ability to perform daily activities such as work, driving.

Eventual inability to walk, speak, swallow, perform self-care.

Completely dependent on others in late stages.

Wheelchair. Nursing home. Feeding tube.

Limited awareness of surroundings. Inability to speak. May not recognize family members.

Life expectancy ten to fifteen years after onset of symptoms.

No effective treatment to slow progression of brain cell death.

Fatal.

No cure.

When Dr Misner was finished, he put a hand on her

shoulder. 'It's a lot to take in,' he said gently. 'I'll give you a minute to absorb it, and then we can—'

Mara couldn't force her lips to stop trembling. There was no way she'd be able to deliver a convincing argument against both of these men in her present state. She revised her strategy: if she could make it out of the office without crying, without letting them think they'd gotten to her, she'd consider that a victory. She stood abruptly, shrugging the doctor's hand off her shoulder. 'No need,' she said.

Dr Misner moved toward her and she turned quickly, making it to the door before he could get past her chair. She couldn't take another second of his soft voice and understanding eyes and his prediction that what was wrong with her was so much worse than mere job stress. Tom stood quickly, too, and followed her into the hallway, a hand on the small of her back as he led her to the elevators. Dr Misner caught up with them and walked beside Tom. Mara saw them exchange knowing glances and nods and saw their lips move, but the blood in her head was swirling too loudly for her to make out their conversation.

In the car, she closed her eyes and lay back in the seat, pretending to be too exhausted to speak as she thought through the long, dreadful list Dr Misner had recited and told herself none of those things would ever happen to her. Tom drove in silence, a hand on her leg. When they pulled into the garage, he hurried to get her door for her but she pushed it open herself and brushed past him. She busied herself in the kitchen, filling and then slowly drinking a tall glass of water while she waited for her nerves to settle.

Tom stood nearby, waiting. The look on his face – all

compassion and sympathy without a trace of the 'I told you so' she'd been expecting – made her feel enraged.

'Of course, Misner could be wrong,' he said, reaching to put a hand on her back. She stepped out of his reach. 'I hope to God he's wrong.' He moved closer and tried to wrap his arms around her but she edged sideways, out of his range again, and he let his arms fall to his sides.

'I could call Dr Thiry's clinic if you want,' he said. 'Arrange for the blood test. You tend to want certainty about things. The tests would give you that.' He touched her shoulder briefly, drawing his hand back before she could move away.

'You don't have to get tested, of course,' he said. 'It's up to you. This might be the one time you'd prefer not to have certainty, and that would be totally understandable. You heard what Misner told us: since there's no cure, a lot of people who're at risk decide they'd rather live with a fifty-fifty chance they don't have it than a one hundred percent certainty they do.'

Mara considered her husband. She hadn't heard Misner say that. She wondered what else she'd missed. It didn't matter, she told herself. Tom and his med school pal were both way off base.

'And I'd understand if that were your decision, too,' Tom said. 'But like he also said, you can still get treatment for some of the symptoms, whether or not you want to have the confirmatory test. Depression, anxiety – those can be treated with medication. I know I've said this before, and you haven't wanted to hear it. But if you took something for those things, you'd be happier. Less bothered by . . .' He paused. 'Everything.' He was so dramatic, she thought. She wasn't bothered by everything. Not all the time, anyway.

'And if you do want to get tested, and if it turns out positive, there's still hope. They're doing research all the time to find a cure, to figure out how to slow it down.'

Mara wondered if Misner had told them that, too, or if Tom happened to know it on his own. He waited for her to respond, and the hopeful look on his face annoyed her. She fought to control her anger – no sense in proving Tom's case for him.

'Thank you,' she said stiffly. 'But with all due respect, I think your wonderful Dr Misner is as far off about this as you are. It was a moving speech he gave, and he played the part extraordinarily. But there's nothing wrong with me.'

Tom's eyes widened.

'Fine,' she said, 'I forget things. But I am a working mother with a high-stress job. I'm almost forty.' He started to speak but she held up a hand. 'And maybe I'm irritable sometimes – more than I used to be. But we've had some hard times lately. We've grown apart. We're not the team we used to be. And that's making us both act differently.

'And yes, I'm a little klutzy all of a sudden, a tad fidgety now and then. While you, I will point out, are easily annoyed. Impatient. And obsessed, so it would seem, with finding some kind of medical issue on my part that you can blame all our troubles on.'

He made a noise in protest but she shook her head and raised a finger to stop him from interrupting. 'I admit I haven't been easy lately,' she said, 'and I'm sorry for that. But neither have you. And at least I'm not dragging you around to old classmates of mine, having them describe some horrible, degenerative, fatal disease and telling you, "I think you might have this." If I were, I expect our troubles would get a lot worse.' She arched a brow, driving home the point: after this stunt, he only had himself to blame if things became even more tense between them.

He reached for her again. 'Mara.'

She stepped quickly around him and walked to the doorway. 'I'm going to bed,' she said as she left the room. 'I'll put your pillow and a blanket on the couch.'

9

Scott

Unable to focus on spelling and grammar, Scott shoved the English papers aside and opened his laptop. As he waited for it to boot up, he craned his neck to listen to Curtis read. He loved how the boy sounded out each word in a whisper, running his finger slowly underneath the sentence.

'You . . . can . . . take . . . the . . . plate.'

He listened for another few seconds, then opened his favorites list and clicked open the Not Your Father's Family forum, the online support system he had relied on since the night he and Laurie agreed to keep Curtis for the year. Panicked at the thought of becoming an instant father, however temporarily, he had surfed the Internet for hours before stumbling on the hodgepodge of regular posters: 2boys, a widower raising his own son and a stepson; flight-path, an older poster who had been a single mom to two daughters after divorcing their alcoholic tyrant of a father; LaksMom, an adoptive mother; SoNotWicked, a stepmom and the creator of the forum.

Over the past year, Scott had talked to them almost daily about everything from parenting-related topics like discipline, bedtimes and homework supervision, to more general lifestyle-centered issues like balancing work and family, career changes and favorite recipes. And eventually to far more personal subjects, like disagreements with friends, marital problems and even sex. His online confidants didn't know his real name or what he looked like, but they knew as much about the joys and stresses of his relationship with Laurie as Pete did, and as much about his love for his little man.

He scrolled to the top of the page to read the day's topic.

Tuesday, April 5 @ 7:55 a.m.
SoNotWicked wrote:

MORNING, everyone!! I had initially planned to spend today talking about summer camp – there's been chatter on here lately about how the last day of school isn't far away. It's THAT time of year AGAIN – time to think about what we're gonna do with the munchkins for TWO months. But I'm gonna save that one for ANOTHER time.

I don't know about all of you, but ever since MOTORCITY reminded us about LMan's upcoming departure, I've been thinking about this: HOW do you foster parents and guardian types let yourself pour all this love and attention into a kid you might NEVER see again, once he goes home? Do you protect yourself a bit by holding SOMETHING back, stop short of investing yourself 100%?

I personally can't IMAGINE putting in the kind of time and energy it takes to look after a kid without having some assurance that in return, I'll get lifelong love and loyalty. Someone to visit me when I'm old and decrepit and muttering my days away at SHADY PINES! And here you guys are, doing all this for kids who may never contact you after this. How on EARTH?

Scott ran a hand across his chin and wished SoNotWicked had gone with the summer camp topic. Scanning the day's responses, he lingered as always on the posts by his closest forum friends. The first was from LaksMom, sending a 'thinking of you' message as she had done every morning for the past several weeks.

At first, he had pictured LaksMom sitting in the lotus position on a big shiny purple cushion, her laptop balanced on her knees, long black hair hanging in a braid down the length of her back, a beatific smile on her face as she chatted away to her online friends. It was a stereotyped vision, to be sure, and likely racist. And completely inaccurate, he thought, now that he knew her better. Now he imagined her in an expensive suit, briefcase in one hand, travel coffee mug in the other, tapping out posts to the forum on her phone before jumping into her car and rushing downtown to her fiftieth-floor corner office. Scrolling further, he saw another post from her, this one directly responding to SoNotWicked's question.

Tuesday, April 5 @ 9:15 a.m.
SNW, I have to say I've been thinking a lot about that myself. I think it's pretty clear MotorCity's the all-in type. Same with FosterFranny, though that situation might be a little different – I know FF is planning to adopt those kids out of foster care. I'm interested in hearing from you on this, MotorCity. I know it must be tough to think/write about. But I'm hoping discussing it with us will make your

upcoming goodbye easier somehow? Or not *easy* but
at least more tolerable?

Scott scrolled further and found a message from another
friend, flightpath:

Tuesday, April 5 @ 4:20 p.m.
Also interested in hearing from MotorCity on this – and
FF. You all know I think the foster/guardians among the
group are the true heroes. I don't have it in me – too
selfish.

Flightpath had joined the forum to find moral support
and advice for living with an aging parent after her
dementia-suffering mother moved in. She became so close
to the regular members, though, that even after her mother
died, she still checked in every day. Hers was a voice of
reason among the sometimes helicopter-parentish questions
posed by the younger members, even if her responses were
sprinkled with the tiniest bit of acid. When someone asked
a few weeks ago how to help a child finish a third-grade
science project, flightpath answered, 'Tell him you've already
passed third grade, then leave the room and let him do it
himself.'

She had chided plenty of them off the ledge when they
were twisting themselves into knots about something they
were unable to offer their children, whether fancy vacations
or college educations or, in Scott's case, a permanent father
figure, after Curtis returned to LaDania.

'Knock it off, MotorCity,' flightpath ordered. 'You can
control one thing here, and that's what you offer that child
while he's with you. And since you seem to have forgotten

75

what that is, I'll remind you: a whole year with the best father figure he could ever hope to have. Beyond that, you can't control anything. Stop pretending you can.'

Another of Scott's closest forum friends was the brash-talking, sports-loving 2boys. He never married the mother of his son, who left them both shortly after the boy was born. Several years later, he married a woman with a child of her own. A year into their marriage, she was diagnosed with leukemia, and two years after that he was a widower and the single father of two young boys.

He joined the forum shortly after his wife's death, declaring himself a bachelor for life ('they either take off on me or they die on me; one way or the other, i appear to repel women'). Scott and 2boys bonded quickly over sports, often filling the message board with so many posts about team records and player statistics and draft picks that one of the others would lightly tell them to take it over to a sports blog so everyone else could get a word in. Scrolling a little further on the page, Scott saw a note from 2boys from later in the day.

Tuesday, April 5 @ 4:33 p.m.

@flight – not sure i could do it either. hell, half the time i resent all the time i spend on my 2, and they're attached to me by blood and law. if it weren't for the tax break they provide, i swear i might try to unload 'em.

@motor – first things first, you hear about the missiles pettitte threw in the first 2 innings last night? the guy's on fire; yanks're gonna take the series this year, i'm tellin ya right now. nah, first thing is l-man, i know that. you know i'm in awe, i've said it before. and i'm as interested as the others are in hearing how you're handling it.

Scott hovered over the keyboard for a moment while he composed his thoughts, and then began to type.

Tuesday, April 5 @ 6:53 p.m.
@SoVERYWicked – that's what you should be called, for raising this issue right now! j/k – it's a fair topic, and I know others on the forum are/have been in a similar position and may want to discuss it. Seconds before I logged in, I was listening to LMan reading aloud and thinking how much I'll miss having that sound in the background as I grade papers or write out basketball plays or chat with all of you. I can't believe I only have 5 days left with his whispered, stuttered reading.

But to answer your Q, I don't think of it in terms of what I've poured into him and won't get back. I think of it in terms of what he's poured into me this past year, and how much it's gonna hurt to live without it. I'm trying to focus on being happy about what he and I have in store – he's going to be reunited with his mom, and I'm going to have my own new family.

As I'm sure my wife would attest, though, I'm not doing all that well at keeping the positive focus. I've been told I act too much like a man who's about to lose a child, and not enough like a man who's about to gain one.

@LaksMama – you're the virtual sister I never had. You know that. But you can't know how much your morning shout outs help, or how much I'll be counting on those for the next few weeks (well, now you know).

@boys – Post something when you can contribute intelligently. Yanks r done. Tigers alllll the way.

He hit 'post' and angled his head toward Curtis, listening.

'You . . . can . . . sit . . . in . . . that . . . care.'

Music to his ears. He logged off the forum and shut down his laptop. 'LMan, try that sentence again. I think you mean "chair," not "care."'

'*LMan?* Since when do you call me *LMan?*'

He flicked the side of Curtis's head. 'I meant Little Man. "Chair." Try it again.' He flopped onto the couch, a few inches from Curtis, who wriggled closer, pressing himself against Scott's side.

'You can . . . sit in . . . that . . . chair.'

'Awesome. How about five more pages, then some math.'

'Five *more?* I've already *done* five. Laurie only said I had to *do* five. And we might not have time to shoot if I do a whole ten.'

'Well, if five is good, then ten is great. And you want to be great, right?'

Curtis huffed, and Scott shot him a warning look. '*Fine*. But only two math pages would be great, right? Anything more would be *not* so great, I think.'

Scott laughed. 'Yeah, two math pages would be great.'

The trifecta of torture – reading practice, math practice and a shower – took too long to allow for a game of hoops. Curtis stood in front of his bedroom closet, sighing as he pulled on his pajamas. 'I *told* you it should've been *five* pages.' He made a show of looking wistfully at the basketball posters that plastered his wall, then at the indoor hoop Scott had hung near his closet. Finally, he dragged a set of sad eyes to Scott, who leaned against the door frame and tried not to show his amusement at the melodrama and self-pity the kid had perfected.

Crossing the room, Scott grabbed the well-worn copy of

Stuart Little from the bookshelf under the window and sat on the bed, stretching his long legs in front of him. He patted the space beside him. 'How about we read an extra chapter about the mouse tonight? Or would you rather waste all of our tuck-in time pouting? Because we can do that instead, if you want.' He stuck his lower lip out, exaggerating the child's expression.

Curtis tried to maintain his pout but was unable to prevent his lips from curling into a smile. 'Extra *Stuart*!'

As the boy got settled, Scott pretended to study the cover of the book as he allowed himself a few moments to enjoy the contented silence, the feeling of the warm little body against his, the narrow arm resting on his leg. Curtis didn't appear eager to interrupt the moment, so Scott rested his chin on the boy's head and let his gaze move slowly around the room.

It was the ultimate little boy's room: sports posters on the walls, an assortment of race cars, Legos and army men scattered on the wooden floor. Two large rubber dinosaurs lay on their sides on a large area rug designed to replicate a city map. Scott and Laurie had listened from their room as the dinosaurs decimated the city before school that morning. The brutes sent the city's Lego occupants fleeing over the rug and under the bookshelf. A few made it as far as the closet, whose open door revealed an overflowing hamper and some very poorly hung clothes. A unit of the army had evidently tried, and failed, to protect the city; green limbs poked out from under one of the dinosaurs and Scott noticed a few deserters cowering among the books on the bookshelf.

The wiggling beside him told him it was time to read. He opened the book, gingerly retrieving the wrinkled photograph that marked the place where they had left off last night. The picture showed Scott and Curtis, huddled together on the bed as they were now, the then-brand-new *Stuart Little* in the boy's hand. It was Curtis's first night with them and Laurie had taken a million pictures to mail to LaDania and Bray, to show them Curtis was doing fine in his new, temporary residence. Curtis had asked for a copy, and it had served as their bookmark ever since.

As Scott was turning to set the picture on the bedside table, a small hand reached out to stop him. 'Can I see it?'

Scott handed the picture over and the boy held it gingerly in both hands for a few seconds before tracing a finger slowly around the outline of the two images. 'I'm gonna miss you, too,' he said. An answer to what Scott had said in the driveway hours earlier. 'I love my mom, but . . .' He ran a pajama sleeve across his nose and mouth.

'Of course you do,' Scott said, kissing the boy's head. 'And the fact that you'll miss me doesn't mean you don't love her, or you love her less. You can love both of us, the same way I love you and Laurie. And Bray. You're not doing anything wrong.' He pulled Curtis closer. 'I'm going to miss you more than I can tell you. But I'll always be right here. And you can come over anytime. I'm counting on it. Who else am I going to wipe the court with?' He nudged the boy in the ribs and smiled.

Curtis giggled, nudging Scott back. 'Yeah, but if I bring Bray with me, *you'll* be the one being wiped *all over* the court.'

'Well, you got me there. But bring him anyway. You two are always welcome here.' He gave the boy's shoulder a squeeze. 'Always.'

Curtis sniffed and dragged his sleeve across his nose

again before handing the picture over. While Scott was reaching to put it on the table, he felt fingers poking his armpit. He whipped around, grabbing the mischievous hand in his.

'Are you . . . tickling me? Are you saying, basically, that it's tickling time? Because you know if you tickle me, that's the message you're sending.'

The boy shrieked and tried to move off the bed, but Scott grabbed him, flipped onto his knees and pinned the boy underneath. He held two wriggling arms with one hand and used the other to tickle until the shrieking grew to its usual deafening level. After a few final armpit pokes for good measure, he delivered the fake punch to the gut that always signaled the end of their matches, and sat against the headboard.

'*Awwwww!*'

Scott grabbed the hands that were poking his armpit again, trying to goad him into more tickling. 'I know, I know. But it's time to quiet things down, not torque them up.'

He turned to the book, not open to further negotiation about whether they would settle down or not. 'Now, where did we leave the mouse last night?'

10

Mara

Mara crossed the kitchen to the sliding glass doors and peered into the nighttime sky. Something moved in her peripheral vision and she drew back; it was the suncatcher, swinging from its fixture above the door frame. She touched it with a fingertip and watched it spin slowly, a miniature replica of Montreal's Notre-Dame Basilica. She and Tom had bought it when they were there four years ago, visiting the city where they'd fallen in love in hopes of rekindling those feelings.

They met at McGill during their sophomore year, Mara having grown up mere blocks away, Tom across the border in upstate New York. She was planning to go to law school in the States; her parents were eager to move to warmer weather when they retired and wanted to live near their only child. Thanks to Pori's work as a chemical engineer for a company with business on both sides of the border, he had dual citizenship in addition to an Indian passport, making life someplace warmer than Quebec a real possibility. Tom was thinking vaguely of medical school, though he made his plans sound a little less vague when he realized how serious his exotic, raven-haired companion was about her future.

She talked about her intended legal career on their first date, as they sat on the front steps of the church, drinking coffee from paper cups and pretending it was the cold that forced them to huddle closely together. She described in detail the high-powered litigation practice she planned to have, the fast track to partnership she intended to jump on, the long career that would last well past normal retirement age. And she teased him that if he was looking for an MRS to go with his MD, someone who would stay home all day and leave the working world to him, they had better part ways right then.

Tom laughed that night, but two years later, at the start of their senior year, he took her back to Notre-Dame. And as they stood on the steps where they had spent their first date, he told her he was looking for an MRS after all. He had always imagined he would end up with the kind of wife who stayed home and cooked meals, he confessed, but had come to realize that the only woman for him was one who would be as married to her career as she was to her husband. Who would infuriate him by bringing work home on weekends and away on vacation and everywhere in between.

That's the kind of MRS he wanted, he told her, as he dropped to one knee, held out the ring he admitted wasn't good enough for her and asked: Did she know anyone who fit that description? Mara tapped the suncatcher again and as it twirled faster, she spun her engagement ring on her finger. Tom had begged her many times to let him replace it with a better one. An expensive one, with the huge diamond he had wanted to give her then and could afford to give her now. She told him he had better not ever dare.

Mara eyed the church as it slowed once more. He had surprised her with the trip four years ago, a few months after their visit to Dr Misner. Tom hadn't mentioned Huntington's again in those few months, and Mara had taken better care to keep her moodiness in check. As a result, some of the wall of tension between them had crumbled a little, but it was still there, and she had been shocked when Tom had sprung the idea of a weekend away.

The trip was ostensibly for their anniversary, but on the morning of their second day, Tom sat Mara on the couch in their hotel room and confessed the real purpose for the getaway was for him to make a renewed effort at convincing her that all was not right with her. He desperately wanted her to reconsider seeing Dr Thiry at the Huntington's clinic. She could tell from the rigid way he held his shoulders that he was prepared for her to react aggressively at the mention of Huntington's. Instead, she folded forward, head in her lap, and sobbed – about the symptoms she finally admitted she had, the diagnosis she conceded Tom was likely right about. She told him she'd been thinking about it since the night they'd seen Dr Misner. She had thought about every-thing the doctor had told her about the disease, and she had done some research on her own. Eventually, she found a website with hundreds of comments written by early-stage Huntington's patients themselves, or by the spouses, chil-dren and other family members who were caring for them. Mara recognized herself in the list of symptoms and in some of the early-stage testimonials she had read online, and she had decided, finally, that she wanted to be tested, to confirm the suspicion she now shared with Tom and his former classmate.

'If I have Huntington's, I want to know,' she told Tom, as they gripped each other's hands in their Montreal hotel room. 'I need certainty, like you said. I want to prepare. And I want to find a way to explain it to Laks – maybe not the gory details, but at least the fact that it's going to take me from her. She's already been abandoned by one mother without explanation. I don't want her to go through that a second time. If she's going to lose a second one, I want her to know why.'

Tom pushed her, explaining the staff at Dr Thiry's clinic would do the same. Was she sure she was ready to find out? Did she know how she would feel, what she would do, if she tested positive?

She told him she was ready. 'If it's positive, I'll feel relieved, more than anything,' she said, still bent forward, arms hugging her sides. 'I've known something isn't right with me. And I've felt us slipping apart because of it. I know you have, too. The stress of not knowing, for both of us, has been excruciating. Even if the answer is terrifying, it'll be an answer.' Looking at him nervously, she said, 'I hope if we can name it, know what we're dealing with, then maybe we can find our way back to each other again?'

'We can,' he said, taking her shoulders in his hands and gently raising her back to sitting. He put an arm around her and pulled her close. 'We can absolutely find our way back to each other. We've already started.'

She pressed her cheek against the warm skin of his hand. 'I'm going to die,' she whispered. 'Before our grandchildren are born. Before Laks even gets married, graduates from college—'

'Love, let's find out first, before you—'

'I have it,' she said. 'I know I do. And so do you.'

As she spun the suncatcher again, Mara felt a tear slide down her cheek, then another, then a stream as she remembered how she had doubled over again, this time with her head in Tom's lap, her arms clutched desperately around his waist, her shoulders heaving as the force of it hit her. What she'd be leaving behind.

'I won't be there for her,' she cried. 'She won't have a mother. I won't get to see her grow up. I'm going to miss it all.'

'Oh, Mara,' he said, and she could hear the agony in his voice even now, almost four years later. Feel the weight of him as he folded himself on top of her, trying to shield her from danger. But the threat wasn't coming at her from the outside, and no matter how closely he pulled her into him, no matter how completely he covered her body with his, she knew he couldn't protect her from the attack she was under by her own body.

11

Mara

They spent almost six hours at the Huntington's clinic on their first visit, and it was a blur of interviews, meetings, tests and exams that Mara hardly recalled now. What she remembered most vividly were the little things. The kindness of the team leader, Betty, who coordinated all of Mara's tests and interviews for the day and held her hand as she walked her and Tom from exam room to office to conference room.

The way Dr Thiry greeted her, taking her hand in both of his and holding it for a long time. It was a gesture that made her feel instantly cared for and safe, the way she still felt every time she set foot in the clinic. How Tom reached for her hand a million times, rubbed her shoulders every few seconds, kissed her cheek, her temple, her forehead, told her he loved her.

Or maybe those weren't little things at all.

The various members of Dr Thiry's staff spent ages explaining the disease in great detail, but Mara had read so many things about Huntington's disease, or 'HD,' on her own, it was hard to remember now what information she had learned from where. She knew before she arrived at the clinic that HD is a genetic stutter, a higher-than-normal repeat of a certain protein sequence – the 'C-A-G sequence,' or 'CAG' – at the end of a specific DNA strand.

She knew the blood test that confirmed whether a person had HD or not did so by showing the number of CAG repeats in the person's DNA. Below 35 repeats and you were fine – no HD gene in your DNA, no future symptoms to worry about. Above 40 and you were positive for HD, and would develop symptoms at some point, assuming you lived long enough. Between 36 and 39 and you were in no-man's-land, and you had to wait and see; maybe you'd develop the symptoms, maybe you'd skate free.

Mara stopped the church from spinning and traced her index finger along its outer edges as a few details of that first appointment came into focus. In their hour-long session with Betty, Mara had asked if it was true that someone who had a higher CAG score – 45, say – would decline faster than someone with a score of 40. She had read online that a higher score was worse; it meant HD would anni-hilate your neurons faster, cutting off the communication between your brain and muscles with greater haste, so you lost control over your limbs sooner. It meant it would kill you quicker. The kids with juvenile HD, for example, had CAG scores in the 60s, and only about five years between HD's first appearance and its final, fatal blow.

She remembered Betty saying no, there wasn't a scientifi-cally proven correlation between high CAG score and rate of progression. And that was the first, but not the last, time Mara realized she might not be able to rely on the clinic, or the medical profession in general, for her information. There was still so much they didn't know, Betty said, and by 'they' she meant the MDs buried in labs, trying to sort out the why and how of it all.

But meanwhile, in the real world, there were plenty of people living with the disease and sharing their experiences online. And even if the guys in the white lab coats hadn't caught up, Mara knew what she had read: dozens of testimonials from HD patients and their spouses talking about how a person with a CAG score of 45 had gone downhill so much faster than their uncle or brother or grandfather who'd had only a 41.

And she also knew what she'd seen: a video of a woman with a count of 46 who only eight months earlier had scored two goals in a parents-versus-kids soccer match with her daughter, and now stood grimacing in front of a camcorder, her upper body lurching so dramatically it looked like she'd topple over any second. The woman's arms flailed uncontrollably and she reminded Mara of the brightly colored, people-shaped wind socks that stood in the parking lots of car dealerships, their torsos and limbs bending and twisting and waving spastically with each new gust of wind.

Another thing Mara remembered distinctly from their first visit to the clinic was that when Dr Thiry asked about her chorea – the involuntary limb movements Dr Misner had noticed and explained to her – she was once again surprised to look down at her hands and see them moving rapidly over her lap. She looked wildly at Tom and he shrugged apologetically. 'It's usually pretty mild. It only gets this bad when you're under a lot of stress.' Mara clasped her hands together to stop them from moving and Tom leaned over and kissed her. 'This is pretty damn stressful, love,' he said.

Dr Thiry explained it wasn't uncommon for people with HD to have a marked misperception of their own movements. Someone who fidgets constantly because of chorea might not realize they're moving at all, he said. Or they might have an extremely irregular gait, but believe they're walking perfectly normally.

'It's called anosognosia,' Dr Thiry said.

'Anosognosia,' Mara repeated, thinking it was a strange-sounding word. But then, it was a strange phenomenon – how could someone's arms be moving without them knowing? How could someone's entire gait change without their awareness? Implausible as it sounded, it appeared to be her reality now.

'Anosognosia,' she whispered to herself, staring at her still-moving hands. It was like they were attached to someone else's body.

Speaking to Tom, Dr Thiry asked, 'So, there's been chorea for some time, I take it? Any other physical symptoms?'

Tom glanced furtively at Mara before turning back to Dr Thiry and nodding once. 'She drops things,' he said quietly, and Mara knew he was torn between trying to spare his wife from hearing more distressing news about herself and giving Dr Thiry the information he needed.

'It's fine,' she told him, smiling to show she was no longer on the defensive. 'Tell him everything.'

Tom shifted uncomfortably. 'She runs into things, too,' he said. 'End tables, the kitchen counter. And . . .' He paused as though gathering the courage to say the next words. 'She falls now and then.'

'You've talked to Steph?' Mara asked, remembering her Drop Dead Dogs in yoga. There'd been many more of them since the first.

Tom cocked his head. 'No. I've seen you fall. Why? Have you fallen in front of Steph?'

'Not very many times,' she whispered. He moved his chair closer and put an arm around her.

Later, in the car, Tom brought up the issue of her anosognosia. It explained why he had noticed her fidgeting before, even though she hadn't. 'I thought about telling you when it first started,' he said, 'but you didn't seem all that open to hearing about it. And I can't say I blame you. Do you want me to tell you when you're doing it, from now on? Or if it gets worse?'

Mara thought about the wind-sock-looking woman she'd seen online, the one with the CAG of 46. Who would want to know they looked like that? She shook her head. 'No,' she said.

The rest of the details of that first appointment, the other five or more hours of discussions and prodding and nodding and note taking by various professionals whose names and faces were lost to her now, she didn't recall. She didn't remember much about the second appointment, either, a month later, when they went back for the blood test.

But she remembered every detail of the third appointment, when they met briefly with Betty and Dr Thiry to hear the results. The appointment started and ended with a number:

Forty-eight.

Her CAG score.

Forty-eight.

48.

Four, eight.

Dr Thiry handed the paper to her and Mara held it for only a second before dropping it like she'd been stung. She squeezed her eyes shut and told herself she would never again look at that number without feeling bone-splitting rage. She would avoid the winter weather report. She would ignore her birthday the year after forty-seven, if she even got that far. She opened her eyes and realized, from the expressions on the others' faces, that she'd been saying it all out loud.

She tried to stand, to leave the room, but she was suddenly unable to support her own weight. Tom stood quickly and reached for her, helping her up. Wrapping his arms around her, he pressed his cheek, his chest, his legs, the entire length of his body tight against hers as he kissed her cheeks, her eyes, her hair and told her he loved her. She wasn't sure how long they stood that way.

After a while, Tom turned and spoke quietly to Betty and Dr Thiry and they left the room, but he didn't move, and Mara couldn't. She wasn't sure how he got her from the office to the car but she imagined he must have carried her most of the way, or at least supported the majority of her weight. They cried all the way home, she remembered that, squeezing each other's hands so tightly they both lost feeling and had to release their grip and open and shut their hands a few times to get the feeling back before grasping on to each other again.

When they were home, they pushed through the garage door into the family room and collapsed together on the couch, too spent to make it one step farther. They lay there, a mass of tangled arms and legs and tears, until well past dark. Finally, Tom carried her into their room, helped her put on a nightgown and slide under the covers. Stripping off everything but his boxers, he climbed in beside her. He wrapped his arms around her, draped one of his legs over both of hers, buried his wet face in the back of her neck and rocked them both to sleep.

The rest of the week went by in a blur, although there were parts of it that stood out: Neerja's keening wail when Tom gave them the news; her parents taking Laks out of the house the night Those Ladies came over; Steph cursing a blue streak and Gina sobbing, then getting right to work organizing a schedule for people at the firm to bring meals for the next several weeks; other friends (former friends, now) coming once, looking pale at Tom's description of what was to come and then disappearing for good.

Her parents were a constant presence that week, of course, her father returning to the house every half hour with more groceries, her mother in the kitchen, cooking, despite Gina's gentle reminders that she had assigned the night's meal to someone else already. Mara remembered sitting in the living room one night with her mother, Steph and Gina, having drinks and talking quietly while Tom and Pori tucked Laks in. Mara told the other women she wasn't sure why she was in such shock. She'd known for some time, intellectually, that there could only be one explanation for her symptoms. She'd known, logically, that this would be the result. Gina nodded and Neerja clucked in sympathy while Steph poured them all another drink and said, 'I guess intellect and logic don't know shit about being diagnosed with incurable diseases.'

12

Mara

Mara left the sliding glass doors and took her seat at the kitchen table, opening her laptop. The computer's clock read two fifteen in the morning, over two hours since she'd crept out of Tom's bed and into Laks's. She shook her head, amazed at how upended her sleep cycle had become since her diagnosis. Constantly worried about what she might face the next month, or week, she hadn't slept a full night in over a year. Nights like this were common now, the rest of the house sound asleep while Mara sat in the dark kitchen, reliving. Worrying. Planning.

She lifted her laptop and peeled off the sticky note she'd hidden on its underside earlier: her list of people to say goodbye to, things to accomplish in the next five days. With a pen, she struck through the names of two McGill friends she had called after lunch, using the pretense of updating her contacts list. She also crossed out the name of one of her closest mom friends from Laks's school, whom she had e-mailed before Laks arrived home. The e-mail began with a fabricated question about the school's upcoming Field Day before moving into the thank-you-for-your-friendship

94

paragraph Mara had rewritten four times until she was satisfied it didn't sound suspicious. Not bad progress, she told herself. She'd chickened out on the forum, but she still had time. She stuck the note back onto the bottom of her laptop, opened her Internet browser and clicked the forum open, scanning the entries that had been posted since the last time she had been on. She smiled to see MotorCity's post about considering her like a sister, and smiled wider when she saw how many people had chimed in to offer their support during his final days with his little man. She wasn't religious, but she closed her eyes and made a fervent wish into the atmosphere that her friend would be okay after the boy moved home. Thank goodness he had his own new baby to look forward to. While she was at it, she added a plea that Dr Thiry's staff would call tomorrow and practically laugh at her notion that one incidence of incontinence meant anything.

Her wish on its way into the atmosphere, she opened the HD research website she had bookmarked four years ago and reached for a legal pad and a pen to make notes. In the first few months after her diagnosis, she had scoured the site every day, thrilled to read about the various research teams around the world who were making 'substantial progress' or receiving 'significant new funding' to support their quest to discover the cause and cure of the disorder.

Several times, she'd caught Tom doing the same, though he always denied it, claiming to be looking up something about a patient and never adequately explaining why he felt the need to snap his laptop closed before she could see the screen. She hadn't caught him in some time, and she herself had given it up. The 'positive starts' and 'exciting possibilities' never led to anything conclusive, and after a while, it felt like searching for money under her pillow in a house that didn't believe in the tooth fairy. It had been ages since she'd opened the site.

Now, buoyed by the news she hoped to hear on the phone the next day, she held her pen over the pad and clicked it a few times, a NASCAR note-taker revving up her engine, ready to record details about the latest break-throughs so she could tell Tom all about them in the morning, make a different plan for how to spend her birthday. She read through the headlines on the home page, clicking through to scour the details of each animal model study that had recently been wrapped up or was currently in progress, each patient trial offering hope.

After twenty minutes, she gave her pen a final anemic click before letting it fall to the table.

There was nothing.

There had been plenty of effort since her last visit – pages' and pages' worth – but nothing to show for it. A drug company had discontinued its long-standing research study after 'disappointing results' were found in animal models. A lab had delayed the kickoff of its work to examine how neurons die in HD patients, with the first phase now sched-uled for completion in eighteen months, not six. The end product of the project was, the team hoped, development of a drug that could slow the progression. Not a cure, then, just a governor. And not for three phases, each six to eighteen months long. There would be no elixir at Mara's pharmacy anytime soon.

She should have known. The answers to the disease, the secret to how it worked, how it could be stopped, were as elusive as ever. She had been lured once again into checking under the pillow. All she'd found was her rotten, bloody tooth, no shiny coins in its place.

Mara looked from her laptop to the phone on the counter and wished she hadn't left the message for Dr Thiry's clinic. They wouldn't dare confirm her grocery store incident was the beginning of the end. No way would they predict impending doom based on one event.

But neither would they be able to promise her the incident wasn't the start of her slide down the slippery slope toward her ultimate demise. That it wasn't the signal of more humiliation to come, of greater decline. That she still had plenty of time before she lost enough physical control that she would no longer be able to command her own exit. That she could wait another year, or even another month. The only thing talking to them would accomplish for certain was having more people know about her embarrassing public spectacle.

When the clinic returned her call the next day, she'd let the phone ring.

PART II

Wednesday, April 6

Four Days Left

13

Scott

Scott woke late, having spent much of the night staring at the ceiling. He was surprised to smell coffee as he made his way downstairs, since lately the smell made Laurie nauseous. He had started buying a cup at a drive-through place on the way to work.

She was dressed for work and sitting in the kitchen, finishing a piece of toast. He pointed to the coffeemaker as he walked toward it. 'You drinking coffee?'

She made a face. 'I'm not sure I ever will again. It's the ultimate rip-off of pregnancy, you know. You hear all the time about all these cravings pregnant women have. They don't tell you about all the sudden aversions to things you used to love. I made it for you. I wasn't sure you'd make it to the coffee shop this morning. Did you sleep at all?'

'A little.'

'Can I take a wild guess at what was keeping you awake?'

He eyed her carefully as he debated whether he should make something up – staff cuts at school, maybe.

She stood, set her plate in the sink and put a hand on his chest. 'You know, I was awake myself for a while.

And I was thinking, if you're this devoted to a boy who's not even ours, then this baby is going to have the most devoted father on the planet.' She moved her hand from his chest to his cheek. 'I feel like maybe I haven't been as sympathetic about it as I should be. I forget sometimes that as close as he and I are, you two are a hundred times closer. As hard as it's going to be for me to see him go, as much as I'm going to miss him, it's going to be so much worse for you. I'm sorry if I haven't acknowledged that enough.'

The understanding in her voice, in her eyes, was so unexpected he couldn't speak. He closed his eyes and pressed his cheek into her hand.

'You need me to get him from school today?' she asked.

'No. I only have a few more chances to drive him home. I'm not letting anything get in the way of that. I could kick myself for letting it happen last night. You were right – I turned practice over to Pete this week so I could spend more time with him, and then I let that woman—'

'Good for you,' she said. Her voice was soothing. He waited for a mild reproach about always putting the school first and decided he wouldn't argue when it came.

It didn't, and grateful, he turned his head to kiss her palm, then her cheek. 'Thanks for the coffee.'

When she left for work, he was fifteen minutes behind in an already packed schedule. Curtis would have to hightail it, but there was a prize in it for him if he was in the mood to cooperate, and it was one of his favorites: pick the radio station on the way to school.

Scott grabbed their lunch bags from the fridge and tossed them onto the counter, setting a banana and a granola bar on top of one – a 'to go' breakfast for his passenger. He set his cup in the sink, peeled a banana for himself and downed it in four bites as he took the stairs three at a time. 'Little Man! We've got to be in the car in six minutes! Let's go!'

Curtis was out of bed like a shot and easily earned his prize. 'I'm not gonna bother with sports talk today,' he told Scott as he climbed into the backseat. 'All they talk about is *baseball* now and I don't care about it so much.' Quickly he added, 'But I love the *Tigers*. Tigers *allll* the way!'

'Tigers allll the way,' Scott agreed. 'So what'll it be, then? Rock? Jazz? Blues? A little Motown?'

'My mom *loves* Motown.'

'A little Motown, to celebrate seeing her again on Monday? Moving home?'

He bit his lip the instant the words left him. Sending the boy to school with a weight on his mind was never wise. Scott kicked himself and composed an e-mail in his mind to Miss Keller: *Sorry if Curtis is a pain today – all my fault. . . .*

But true to his young age, Curtis was as excited about the news today as he had been upset about it the night before.

'Yeah! Motown to celebrate moving home with my *mom*!'

'Motown it is.'

He found the station and backed out of the driveway, joining Smokey in the off-key voice Laurie always begged him not to reveal in public.

*'So take a good look at my face
You'll see my smile looks out of place.'*

103

Curtis folded forward, hands over his ears in a show of being deafened. 'Aaaaaah! Please! Make it stop!'

'C'mon, you expect this Detroit boy to hear Smokey and not sing along? And what's your excuse? Sitting there complaining when you should be belting it out. Let's hear it.'

'I only know the "good look at my face" part. I don't know the rest.'

'Well, mister, you'd better learn it if you intend to keep living in this town.'

They drove the rest of the way in companionable silence. Despite Curtis's impossibly high energy level the rest of the day, he wasn't a morning person. Scott reached behind and patted the knee of the quiet child now gazing blankly out the window at the buildings and trees whipping past him. Their morning drives often played out this way, sports talk or music on the radio, the two of them content to be together but lost in their own thoughts.

Scott was happy to dial up the excitement when the boy was in the mood, but he was also happy to spend the commute quietly, thinking about what new plays to try at practice, what new novel to introduce to his eighth graders. Today, he let his mind go blank as he watched the tony sections of Royal Oak give way to the blighted streets of Detroit.

After ten years of working at Franklin Middle, Scott had seen it all a million times. But there were small changes from time to time, and he watched for them when he could. Usually, the changes were depressing – another boarded-up house, another smear of graffiti on a building whose owner had cleaned the last paint off a week earlier. Another square paper nailed to another front door, its size and color announcing it was an eviction notice even if the words weren't readable from the car.

From time to time, though, there were encouraging signs. Lights on again in a small machine shop that hadn't operated for years, a few cars in the employee parking lot. A 'Now Open – New Management' sign in the window of a produce store that had gone out of business a year ago. Laundry hanging in the yard of a house that had been abandoned but now showed new curtains in the windows, children's toys on the peeling, slanted front porch.

It was these changes that kept Scott hopeful. Things could get better here. Families could reclaim houses and apartment buildings. Honest businessmen could reopen stores and small factories. A kid like Brayden Jackson could get a college scholarship. A degree. A real job. A life away from here.

Franklin, where Scott spent his days, was a microcosm of Detroit, at once depressing and beautiful, a has-been and a might-be. It must have been majestic once, Scott imagined, when it was new. Three stories of red brick with tall windows and huge double front doors. The front lawn would have been lush green, the outdoor basketball court flat and black under solid white court lines, the fence around it straight and proud. The marble hallway floors shone then, he bet, the wooden classroom doors smooth and clean.

He wondered how many people who had attended Franklin in its first days had studied it lately, and how they felt when they did. The brick was faded now, gray in some places and black in others, the discoloration a remnant of the now closed row of factories down the street. Several windows lacked a complete pane of glass, and the different solutions teachers had come up with to fill the gaps – duct tape in varying colors, squares of cardboard – had turned the façade from impressive to clownish.

The front 'lawn' was no more than a brown patch of dirt now, with sparse clumps of weeds and grass struggling to lift themselves. The lines no longer showed on the basket-ball court, and much of its surface had heaved into cracked waves by the force of decades of Michigan winters. The fence had been cut or torn in multiple locations; no longer straight and proud, now it was bent and twisted into a drooping, sad thing.

And inside. The hallway floors were dull, scuffed. The walls were a putrid pale green that might once have been a cheerful shade but now reminded Scott of the sixties-era psych wards he had seen in movies. The classroom doors were barely recognizable as wood, covered now with kids' initials and curse words, some scrawled in ink, some etched by knives.

They arrived at Logan Elementary, Curtis's school, located a few blocks from Franklin, and Scott pulled into the parking lot. Logan hadn't started out looking as majestic as Franklin. It was one story of pale yellow brick and green metal doors. But it also didn't appear to have fallen as far as Franklin. The brick was blackened in fewer spots and not as dark. The windows were still in one piece. There was no graffiti. The classroom doors, Scott had pointed out to Laurie on parent-teacher conference night, bore no curse-word tattoos.

Scott put the car in park. 'Your stop, Little Man.'

The boy jumped out, hoisted his backpack onto his

shoulder, grabbed his lunch bag and walked around the car to Scott's open window.

'Fist,' Scott said, holding his own out.

Curtis bumped his fist to Scott's.

'Cheek,' Scott said.

Curtis feigned embarrassment, but smiled as he leaned his cheek closer for Scott to kiss.

'Promise,' Scott said.

'Promise.'

'Nope, not good enough. I want to hear the whole thing.'

Curtis sighed. 'I *promise* to do what Miss Keller *tells* me.'

'For how long?'

'For the *whole entire day.*'

'Nice. Go get 'em, Albert Einstein.'

Scott reached his classroom with ten minutes to spare before his first-hour class. Enough time for a quick forum check. As he opened his laptop, he thought how odd someone might find it that during a week when he was trying to cram in as many experiences with Curtis as possible, he was thinking about the forum at all, let alone making time to post there. And it might seem equally odd, if not more so, that at a time of such devastation, most of his shoring up was coming not from his best friend, Pete, or even his wife, but instead from a group of people he wouldn't recognize if they stepped into his classroom this second. Not that Pete and Laurie weren't comforting – or at least, they tried to be. But, as oxymoronic as it sounded, when it came to revealing his most intimate feelings, nothing beat the total anonymity of the Internet. Unlike the people who knew him in 'real life,' LaksMom, flightpath, 2boys and the others had no context in which to put his posts, no history – good or bad – against which to measure the things he said. To Laurie, the phrase 'It's going to kill me to live without him' was hurtful, offensive, because of all the implied meaning she heard along with it: 'Curtis is more important than the baby. Curtis is more important than you.'

Pete didn't read the same hurtfulness into it, but he couldn't escape the big picture any more than Laurie could: 'But, dude, you'll see him again, when he's a student at Franklin. Three solid years with the kid. And in the meantime, you'll have your own baby to focus on, not to mention the twenty kids on the team and the three hundred others you walk past in the halls every day.' It was an attempt to be helpful, Scott knew. But it didn't help.

Scott's friends on the forum didn't know his big picture. They read a phrase like 'It's going to kill me to live without him' for its precise meaning, and nothing else. They didn't read more than those nine words into the message. They didn't take offense, didn't try to talk him out of it. Didn't resent it for its presumed relativity.

'Of course it is,' they said. And it was the same way they'd responded to every other thing he'd told them about himself: his thoughts on parenting, on marriage and sex, on education and race. They read what he wrote, and only what he wrote, and they responded. Not always in agreement – he'd had plenty of heated discussions over the past year on this issue or that. But he didn't need yes-men any more than he needed someone to read twenty-one extra words into the nine he'd written.

As for this week, he didn't need Laurie to make him feel guilty on top of feeling heartbroken. He didn't need Pete to try to cheer him up, to make him see things in a shinier light. Curtis was leaving in four days: there was no cheer to be found, no silver lining. He didn't need anyone to fix the problem – there was no fixing it. He needed someone to acknowledge his feelings. Accept his pain. Agree that his heart was broken, and that it should be. And that it might stay broken for a long, long time.

And that's precisely what he got when he talked to his nameless, faceless friends on the forum: pure, unadulterated acknowledgment. That's why he was making time for the forum today. And that's why he would keep making time for it, when he had three days left, then two, then one, and after the boy was gone.

When he found the prior day's conversation, he was touched to see how many people had commented about his situation. There were more than thirty new posts. These weren't mere strangers at unknown IP addresses. They were friends, and they cared about him as much as he cared about them. He couldn't help smiling as one member after another came forward to wish him good luck in the next few days.

There was a reminder from SoNotWicked that it's okay for men to cry, and he laughed. He had tiptoed into Curtis's room the last few nights after Laurie drifted off, eased himself into the rocking chair and let the tears pool in the corners of his eyes, one or two slipping down his cheeks and neck, under the collar of his T-shirt, as he watched the flickering eyelids and twitching lips of the boy who was no doubt sassing and complaining to some dreamworld creature.

Scanning further, Scott stopped at a post he was hoping to see, by a now-and-then poster who called herself FosterFranny and had, along with her husband, fostered almost a dozen children over the past decade or so.

109

Tuesday, April 5 @ 8:41 p.m.
I'm afraid I'm of less help than you might expect. The best advice my husband and I were given before we started fostering was this: don't let yourself get too attached. We have followed that advice from the start, and while the children we have cared for have made a real imprint on our hearts, we have always used caution to maintain substantial emotional distance.

Consequently, when it's been time to return them to their parents, we haven't felt like we're having our innards ripped out, the way we would if we were being forced to give up one of our own children. From all you've said about your relationship with LMan, I have to surmise that what LaksMom said about you earlier is accurate: you have gone all-in, and instead of reserving some part of your heart for safekeeping, you have given it all to the boy.

If this is true, I suppose the only thing for you to do is to keep reminding yourself what's best for the child. As you and I have discussed at length via personal messaging in the past, in most cases, the best thing for a child is to be with their parent(s). If LMan's mom has kicked her habits while serving time – and you informed me some months ago you believed this to be the case – then indeed, the best thing for him is to return to her. Focusing on that will lessen the pain of letting him go. Not by much, perhaps, given how you care for him, but hopefully by some. Good luck, my friend.

Scott checked his watch. Six minutes till his first-hour class arrived. Time for him to post a reply to Franny.

Wednesday, April 6 @ 7:54 a.m.
@Frans – I guess I should've asked you for advice *before* LMan moved in. You and LaksMom are right about how much of my heart I kept sequestered from him: 0%. Not sure I could've done it differently even if I'd set out to, though – this is a kid who gets right in your bloodstream.

Good advice to focus on what's best for the boy, and your wisdom on that score, from our PM chats a few months ago, has stayed with me. More than that – it's what's getting me through this. To the extent I'm getting through it, that is; I definitely feel like my guts are being ripped out. But it's easier to take when I'm doing it for him.

@2boys – how're your Yanks looking after last night's drubbing by the Orioles, you think? ;) Tigers alllll the way. I'd offer a big money bet on this if I knew I'd be able to track you down to collect. Wonder if SNWicked would make an exception to the anonymity rule for that?

Thinking about last night, and how he had been unable to sleep, he added:

@SNW – how about extending our membership into Asia? I've got insomnia these days and it'd be nice to have someone to chat w/ in the middle of the night. I've seen all the classic games ESPN replays in the wee hours and am dangerously close to switching to infomercials to keep myself company. I need to sock away every spare cent I have for all the baby paraphernalia my wife's been talking about – the last thing I need is to be tempted to call in a 2 a.m. order for a collection of ceremonial plates depicting all of the presidents. . . .

He shut down his laptop, stuck it in his briefcase and checked his watch. Two minutes. He thought about Franny's too-late advice to avoid becoming too attached. And how, even if he'd heard it in time, he couldn't have kept the little man out of his system if he'd tried. The minute he said yes to Bray last year was the minute he signed up for having his guts ripped out next week.

Bray had shown up on Scott and Laurie's front porch, Curtis in tow, almost a year ago. The brothers were a long way from home – the apartment they lived in with their mother was a few ugly blocks from Logan Elementary, in a squalid beige cinder-block complex unrivaled for the past decade in the number of reports of domestic violence and drug dealing. The boys had different fathers and their mother never appeared quite up to the task of raising two boys on her own.

Scott had tried to talk to LaDania many times during his tenure as Bray's coach at Franklin Middle, and he had worried out loud to his wife about LaDania's level of sobriety after every attempt. LaDania had this vacant look about her whenever he saw her, and she always seemed distracted and unfocused. She didn't seem to grasp the things he tried to tell her, about how talented her older son was on the court, what a future he had ahead of him. So, although Scott was surprised to see Bray and Curtis on his front porch that cold April night, he was not entirely shocked when, after he ushered them into the house, Bray whispered that he needed to talk to the Coffmans privately about a drug-related complication his mother was having.

Once Curtis was occupied in the family room with paper and crayons, Scott led Bray and Laurie to the living room, where Bray confessed that 'complication' might have been a bit of an understatement: LaDania had been arrested that morning for drug possession and she faced a twelve-month sentence – eleven months in jail, followed by a monthlong stay in a halfway house. The public defender told Bray there would be no leniency, since this was her third possession charge. Arrangements would need to be made – for her belongings, her mail and her seven-year-old son, Curtis.

Bray had driven in from Ann Arbor that morning in a car borrowed from a teammate, and spent the day talking with the Wayne County public defender and trying to sort out what to do with his younger half brother. One option was to take Curtis with him to Ann Arbor. But he couldn't very well move a child into student housing. The apartment he shared with three of his fellow teammates was crowded as it was, and hardly the kind of environment suitable for a first grader. And given his packed schedule of classes, practices and games, Bray didn't have the time to play father for the next year.

Plus, he had talked to Curtis's teacher at Logan that afternoon, and that conversation added another complication: despite fairly significant behavioral issues, Curtis was beginning to show some progress. Progress that might be undone if he were uprooted to a new school in a new city. The boy would return to Logan when their mother was released, and pulling him out for a year, only to return him again later, seemed unwise.

Another option was for Bray to drop out of Michigan for the year and move home. He could try to re-earn his spot on the varsity roster the following year, once LaDania was released. As much as he loved his kid brother, Bray wasn't thrilled about this option. He'd just begun living his dream and he wanted to follow it to the end if he could.

But he wasn't ruling the alternative out. He couldn't promise to be happy about it, but if there was no other way, he was prepared to move back.

The public defender was as keen as Bray to find a different solution. He had seen too many kids throw away their potential by getting caught up in trouble and never finding their way out of the inner city, and he urged Bray to consider every possible alternative. Wasn't there anyone, the defender asked, who could help out? Someone Bray trusted, who could serve as limited guardian for the boy until LaDania was free? Someone who could step in for the year so Bray didn't have to ruin his future?

Bray had never known his own father or Curtis's, and in his nineteen years, the only relative he'd ever met was LaDania's mother, who died soon after Curtis was born. The Johnsons, live-in superintendents at the housing complex, had been good to the boys over the years, but they were older, Mrs Johnson was sick a lot, and Bray didn't want to trouble them. Their neighbors, and the crowd his mother ran with, weren't worth considering.

Desperate, Bray turned to the person who had already done more for him, and shown more interest in him, than anyone else, including his mother. The one person in the world who he was sure would want him to stay at Michigan as badly as he wanted to stay there: Scott Coffman.

A year was a long time, Bray acknowledged, looking nervously from Scott to Laurie. It was a lot to ask, he knew that. But at least he could guarantee it wouldn't be a day more. LaDania would spend eleven months in prison, the twelfth in a halfway house, and then she could return to her apartment and reclaim her son. Twelve months, and they would be done.

It was an easy decision for Scott, who had known within the first few minutes of seeing Bray on the court eight years earlier that there was something special about him. After one week of practice, Scott announced to Pete, and later, at home, to his wife, that Brayden Jackson was the best player he would ever coach. He had never seen such talent or work ethic in such a young player, and the kid's height – six feet in sixth grade – made him that much more impressive.

Equally impressive was Bray's personality. He was a natural leader on the court and in the classroom and he was mature and responsible far beyond his years. Part of that, Scott knew, was Bray's home situation. At her best, his mother wasn't the world's most attentive parent. At her worst, she wasn't even lucid. She wasn't an excessive drug user, Bray said – at least, not relative to the people she hung around. And he wasn't sure he'd call her an alcoholic, either, based, again, on relativity. But she 'had too many feelings' from time to time, and she had taken to smoking or drinking them away.

From what Bray had reluctantly revealed to Scott, the boy was more of a parent to his younger brother than their mother was, bathing and dressing and feeding Curtis while his mother was out, or passed out. He was a caregiver at school, too, always watching out for the younger kids, both on the team and in the hallways. When Bray approached Scott at the end of sixth grade and asked for Scott's help in improving his game, Scott was more than happy to help the kid who was always helping everyone around him.

All summer long, Scott met Bray at Franklin the minute Scott's summer school classes let out. They spent hours working out on the school court or, when that was occupied, in the Coffmans' driveway. Bray's dream was to make the Parker High varsity team, and he hoped that if he worked hard for the next two years, he'd have a shot at it. Scott thought Bray had more than a shot at it, whether he kept up the rigorous extra practice or not, but he preferred that Bray spend time on a basketball court rather than on the streets. Like the public defender, Scott had seen plenty of kids with potential blow it by getting involved with the wrong crowd. So he kept his opinion about Bray's chances to himself and offered to keep up the extra coaching for as long as Bray wanted.

Two years later, Bray made the Parker team and quickly became a starter, and then a star. Scott and Pete went to every game during Bray's first season, and Scott posted on his classroom bulletin board every newspaper article that mentioned Bray. There were plenty. When the season ended, Scott was bursting with happiness and pride for Bray. He was also consumed by a level of sadness that surprised him when he realized his time with this talented, dedicated, amazing boy, whom he had come to love, would now be over. Bray had secured his spot on the Parker team; he wouldn't need Scott anymore.

But Bray had no intention of resting on his freshman success, and the day after the season ended, he called Scott to ask if they could resume their workouts that weekend. His season as a star had been great, he told Scott, but he wanted more. He wanted to be the best player Parker High had ever had. And then he wanted to get a basketball scholarship. He had dreams of being a businessman, of making a better life for himself, his brother and his mother. And he knew there would be no college in his future unless he paid his way himself, with his talent on the court.

They continued their sessions at Franklin and in Scott and Laurie's driveway, week in, week out, for another year. And Scott and Pete, who were at every game of Bray's sophomore season, saw him blast through his goal by the end of the next year; the local papers declared him to be not just the best player Parker High had ever seen, but the best the city of Detroit had seen. Scott cut out the articles and headed for his bulletin board, carefully setting the prior year's clippings in a file folder in his desk drawer to make room for the new ones.

Bray broke scoring records that had been held for decades by players two years his senior. Letters of interest started pouring in from colleges. Scouts started appearing at his games. He didn't want to ease up, though, so they kept up their driveway sessions, and by the end of Bray's junior year, the articles on Scott's bulletin board reported that Brayden Jackson was considered one of the top high school players in the nation. Bray narrowed his many scholarship offers down to Michigan; he wanted to be close to home so he could check in on Curtis and his mother.

By the end of Bray's senior year, Scott and Pete, who hadn't missed a game in four years, along with the reporters who continued to provide material for Scott's bulletin board, predicted that college ball would not be the stopping point for this player. They'd be seeing Brayden Jackson in the NBA.

Scott's devotion to Bray had cost him hundreds of hours over several years, but he had loved every minute of it. He considered it a small price to pay for the enormous future Bray had created for himself through his determination and hard work. The young man whose long limbs were folded awkwardly on Scott and Laurie's living room couch that

April night the year before, his leg shaking with nerves, was mere weeks from finishing his first year of college. If his exams went as he expected, he told them proudly, he would finish the year with a good enough grade point average to get him into the business school sophomore year.

What Bray didn't tell them, though Scott knew it, was that more and more, Bray's business degree was starting to become a nice backup plan. Rumor was that a handful of NBA scouts had already made a few trips to Ann Arbor to see the freshman phenom at work.

For Scott, despite the suddenness of Bray's request that they take in Curtis, not to mention the unfathomable magnitude of it, the answer was simple: he would do anything to keep Bray at Michigan, playing basketball, working toward a degree and quite possibly the pros. It wasn't so simple for Laurie, and she said this to Scott in hushed tones after they excused themselves to confer in their bedroom about how to respond to Bray's request.

Laurie's relationship with Bray wasn't at all the same as Scott's, her investment in the boy's future not nearly as great. The idea of having her life turned upside down wasn't so quickly minimized by the lure of having Bray realize his dreams. The work involved in caring for someone else's child – a child with behavioral issues, no less – wasn't as easily waved away for her by the vision of seeing Bray in a business suit, or even an NBA jersey, as it was for Scott. They had seen Curtis from time to time over the years, at Bray's games, or when he tagged along to the training sessions in their driveway, and they had seen what a handful he could be. An afternoon with him was one thing. An entire year was something else.

Plus, she reminded him, she had dreams, too, and one

in particular: to have a family of her own. They had spent the past three years trying to get pregnant – years that involved a considerable amount of heartbreak, frustration and tense moments between them, not to mention countless doctor's appointments, fertility tests and IVF. The first IVF round hadn't worked, and they had recently concluded they had the financial and emotional capacity to try only one more round, in the fall.

All of Laurie's energy and attention was directed toward the baby of their own they were hoping for. She didn't see how she could direct that attention toward someone else's child.

Seizing on her singular obsession with starting their own family, Scott tried to sound casual as he suggested having Curtis there while they waited to start the second IVF round, and then waited to see if it had been successful, might be exactly what they needed. Busying themselves with a child would distract them from the crazy-making process of waiting, hoping, wondering, worrying. And a child with a few minor behavioral challenges? All the better to distract them, right?

And the timing was perfect, he pointed out. It would be a relief to spend the summer months entertaining a seven-year-old instead of fretting about their impending 'last chance' at IVF. If they were lucky enough to get pregnant this time, they would still have an entire school year of pregnancy. By the time their little bundle was born, their temporary charge would have gone back to LaDania.

Laurie wasn't entirely convinced that taking on a yearlong babysitting job was a good idea. She could think of any number of ways she'd rather spend their hopefully final child-free year. But it was true their journey to parenthood had been fraught with worry and tension, and more impatient waiting didn't appeal to her. The distraction of having a child in the house had its allure. And she knew how important Bray was to her husband. So she reluctantly agreed.

Curtis could stay for the twelve months of LaDania's sentence, she told Scott. He couldn't stay longer – by that time the next year, Laurie fully expected to be making preparations for a baby – but he could stay for twelve months.

The following morning, Scott, Laurie and Bray met with Janice, the social worker appointed to the Jackson family case. Ideally, Janice told Scott and Laurie, they would keep Curtis for one year and one week. That would allow LaDania a week after her release from the halfway house to apply for a job and to get herself and her apartment ready for her son's return.

Scott looked pleadingly at his wife, who sighed, but agreed Janice's plan made sense. That afternoon, with LaDania's blessing, along with her signature on the limited-guardianship placement plan form, the four of them appeared before the judge to request the Coffmans be made Curtis's limited guardians for twelve months and one week. A few statements by Janice, a half dozen questions from the judge to the Coffmans and Bray and one rap of the gavel later, Scott and Laurie were Curtis's guardians.

LaDania had moved out of the halfway house and back to her own apartment the previous Sunday night. She was looking for jobs, Janice had reported to Scott and Laurie, and she was fixing up the apartment in preparation for having Curtis move back on Monday, after the court formally dissolved the Coffmans' limited guardianship at the hearing set for Monday morning. And now, Scott only had until Sunday with the little man, four days left with the boy who had made him feel more like a father than a 'limited guardian.'

The fact that LaDania hadn't called Curtis more than a handful of times all year, or even responded to half the letters he'd sent her in jail, wouldn't be relevant to the court. Nor would the fact that Scott and the boy were connected by so much more than a one-page legal form.

LaDania was Curtis's mother, and Scott was merely a man who'd looked after him temporarily.

14

Scott

The joke was on Scott. Curtis had played his role of distractor as well as Scott had promised Laurie he would do. He had occupied so much of their mental energy, in fact, that Laurie credited the boy for her pregnancy. Her doctor had been telling her to try to stop obsessing about getting pregnant, to occupy her brain with other things so she could go into the next IVF round with a body that wasn't taut from anxiety about conception.

Curtis arrived on the scene in April, and by September, Laurie was so embroiled in behavior charts and reward systems, so consumed with getting his reading level up and his visits to the principal's office down, that she had little time during the day to perseverate about fertility, and no energy at night to do anything but fall soundly asleep. When they found out the IVF had worked, her first statement was, 'This is because of Curtis.'

Her gratefulness for the boy's distracting qualities didn't translate into her wanting him around longer than the agreed-upon twelve months, though. Scott didn't blame her for this at all. He was the one who had gone off script, letting himself get closer and closer to the little man with each passing month so that now, when it was time to say goodbye, he couldn't bear the thought.

For the past several weeks, they had reversed roles, and Laurie had been the one trying to convince Scott to seek distraction elsewhere, starting with the child she was carrying.

'*Our* child,' she liked to emphasize, in a tone that made it clear she wasn't happy to have to remind a father-to-be that he was, in fact, a father-to-be, and that such title was (in her mind) far more important than that of limited guardian to someone else's boy. So far, Scott had managed to refrain from saying out loud, 'How can I get excited about a child I haven't even met yet, when I'm so upset about losing the child I already have?' But the looks his wife had given him over the past few weeks suggested his general mood had conveyed the same message.

Like his wife, Scott had dreamed of having a family, his mind swirling with images of father-son games of catch in the front yard, hockey and HORSE in the driveway, family cookouts in the back. He had been overjoyed about the pink lines on the white stick in October, and he'd felt his own heart might burst when he heard his baby's heartbeat for the first time, saw her shadowy image on the ultrasound.

He was excited. Beyond excited. Who wouldn't be? But feelings were relative, so he had learned, and the fact was, he hadn't been able to maintain the same level of giddiness as his wife. He had tried; man, had he tried. And then he'd beaten himself up over the fact that something so easy should require such an effort – as had his wife.

But their baby girl was still over three months from

arriving. And there was a boy here, now, who needed him. A boy who would be returning to a world of skipped meals and grimy clothes and a not-always-lucid mother. And while Scott had mostly come to terms with the concept that being with his mother was better for Curtis than being separated from her, it still tore him apart when he thought about the kind of life his little man was leaving, and the kind he'd be returning to. And it was just so goddamn hard to think about anything else.

Scott was startled out of his reverie by the clanging of the bell announcing first hour. Moments later, muffled voices in the hallway turned into louder ones inside his classroom as a herd of eighth graders made their way to their seats for Mr Coffman's first-hour English class. Scott lowered the hand that had been clutching his stomach at the thought of the little man's future after next Monday.

Next Monday. It was too soon.

Don't think about it, he told himself. There's plenty of space between now and then. Time to cram in plenty more memories. Spaghetti and cookies and cake and burgers and movie night.

And monster trucks – the crazy-looking vehicles made of regular-sized pickup truck bodies and oversized, heavy-duty tires that competed to see which one could drive over the biggest pile of dirt or jump the longest row of old car chassis while an arena full of rabid fans cheered on their favorite. Curtis had watched monster trucks on TV, he told Scott once, and he had dreamed of seeing them in person his 'whole entire life long.' It was soon after he had moved in. They were, not surprisingly, playing Would You Rather, and Scott had asked if Curtis would rather be the first kid on the moon or the first seven-year-old president.

'Well, if we're talking about best things in the world,' Curtis said, 'then neither. I'd rather see monster trucks.'

'Monster trucks?' Scott laughed. 'The best thing in the world is seeing monster trucks? Better than being in space or running the country or . . . what about playing for Michigan with Bray?'

'Nope. Monster trucks.'

'Playing in the NBA with Bray?' Scott tried. 'Having a lifetime supply of bubble gum? Or ice cream? A lifetime pass on homework? Or—'

'Monster trucks,' Curtis said firmly. 'Seeing monster trucks would be the best thing in the *entire world*, of all the things you can mention. You can go on *all day*. But there's nothing I'd rather do than that.'

At dinnertime two months earlier, Scott had casually slid the tickets across the table and waited as Curtis whispered the words out loud as he read. 'Mon. Ster. Truck. No, trucks. Mon. Ster. Trucks. Monster. *Monster!* Monster trucks! *Monster trucks!*' Raising the tickets above his head, he jumped out of his chair, sending it crashing against the wall behind him, and ran laps around the first floor of the house, shrieking as he went. 'I'm seeing monster trucks! I'm seeing monster trucks!'

Scott, laughing, had to retrieve the tickets so the boy didn't crush them in his grip. He stuck them in the top corner of the bulletin board in the kitchen, afraid to leave them anywhere Curtis might be able to reach them. 'Can't have you drooling all over them, reducing them to a wet mass of unreadable paper.' The tickets were for this Sunday, for Scott and Curtis's last day together.

It took Laurie one day to realize she needed to give Curtis a Monster Trucks Countdown Calendar so he wouldn't drive her insane asking, 'How much longer?' every half hour. Since then, the last thing he did each night was mark a big red X through that day's date, and announce the number of days left until 'the *very* best day I'll *ever* have in my whole *entire* life no matter what else I ever do for the next *hundred* years.'

Half a dozen times since that night, Curtis had asked Scott to lift him up to touch the tickets pinned out of his reach. Each time, he ran a finger slowly over each word, sounding them aloud in the whisper Scott loved so much. A few nights ago, Curtis went through his whisper-reading routine twice. As Scott set him down, the boy put a small, cool hand on Scott's cheek and, in the same quiet whisper, said, 'This is the *very best thing* anyone will ever do for me.'

Scott swiped a knuckle across each eye as he walked to the front of the classroom and waited for the din to fade. There wasn't a last-day-together extravaganza big enough to show the child how deeply Scott loved him, how terribly he would miss him, how much a part of his very fiber the boy had become. But Monster Trucks was pretty close.

15

Mara

Laks and Tom were standing at the front door, ready to walk out to the bus, when Mara dragged herself into the living room. 'I can't believe I almost missed you!' she said, making her way to them. 'Sorry I slept so late.'

She kissed Laks and laid her hand against Tom's cheek. 'You should've woken me, darling. I could've handled the morning routine.'

'No problem. Breakfast with one of my two beautiful girls is never a chore.'

She could tell from the way he said it, from the way he was grinning at her, that he was pleased with himself. She could picture him standing over her sleeping form earlier, reaching first to brush a strand of hair off her face or touch her cheek, then to turn off the alarm she had set, smiling to himself as he did her this 'favor' of letting her sleep in after she was up so late.

Mara did a poor job of returning his smile. She had so few mornings left with Laks, and it destroyed her that she had wasted one of them. She would have to remember to set a second alarm tomorrow, one he didn't know about.

She wondered if she still had her running watch. Had she given that to Goodwill with all her other gear, or was it around somewhere, in a drawer she hadn't looked in for a while? She hoped she would remember to look for it as soon as Tom left for work.

'Are you walking out with us?' Laks asked. She crinkled her nose as she assessed her mother, still in her nightgown, robe hanging open, one end of its belt dragging on the floor. Mara bent to look at her reflection in the glass of a picture frame that hung beside the front door. A clump of her short black hair stood straight up at the top of her head and deep lines crisscrossed one cheek. She tried to smooth down the disobedient hair with one hand while she rubbed her cheek with the other to erase the lines. It didn't work.

Backing away from the picture, she made a funny face at her daughter, pretending not to care about how mortified Laks seemed. 'Of course not! I'd never let anyone but you and Daddy see me this way! I'm a total mess!' She walked to the front window and stood behind the drapes, one hand holding them open an inch or so to allow her to peek outside without being seen. 'Get going, you two. The bus'll be here any minute. I'll hide here, behind the curtains, and wave, invisible to everyone but you.'

The little girl smiled her relief and skipped out the door with her father, calling over her shoulder, 'Bye, Mama! See you after school!'

'Bye, sweetie! I promise I'll be presentable by then!'

Mara was at the kitchen counter, wrestling with the Wednesday compartment on her pill container, when Tom came in. 'She didn't mean to hurt your feelings.' He reached for the container but she pretended not to notice, continuing to fight with it until the lid finally flipped open. She popped her daily mood-leveling pill into her mouth frantically and reached for a glass of water to wash it down. If ever there was a day her emotions threatened to overcome her without pharmaceutical soothing, this was the one.

Tom waited for her to swallow the pill before running a finger over her cheek. 'You're beautiful, even right out of bed.'

She lifted her hand, batting his away, and covered her cheek to hide the lines. 'Liar.'

'You. Are. Beautiful.' He moved her hand. 'You didn't need to hide behind the curtain. She was only being—'

'Honest,' she said. 'She was only being honest.' She glanced down at her robe, which had fallen open again, and shook her head with disgust. She cinched the belt tight enough to hurt.

'I don't want you to think—' Tom started, and she knew what he was going to say. That he didn't want her to think she had done what she had so clearly just done: embarrassed her daughter.

'Well, of course I think that, Tom. And if she's embarrassed now, when I'm still walking, talking, able to at least recognize when I need to hide behind the curtains, how will she feel in a few years, or sooner, when those things go, too?'

'Stop.' He took her chin in his hand and turned her face to his. 'Stop.'

'Stop what? Stop it from happening? Because nobody can—'

'Stop assuming how she'll feel at any point in this process,' he said, his voice stern. 'You don't know how—'

'I think this morning gave us a pretty good idea how she'll feel, don't you?'

He exhaled slowly and wrapped his arms around her, pressing his lips against the top of her head. They had had this debate before, Mara fretting there was no way Laks could emerge unscathed from this kind of childhood, Tom insisting their daughter was a lot stronger than Mara gave her credit for, a lot more willing to deal with even the ugliest aspects of Mara's illness.

She let herself relax against his chest, let his arms keep her upright. He released her after a while and leaned down to kiss her. 'New topic of conversation?'

She smiled at him gratefully. 'Please.'

'Last night. What got into you? And how can we arrange more of it?'

She called up a casual expression and asked, 'What? Can't a woman express appreciation for her gorgeous husband and his beautiful body?'

'She most certainly can. As often as she wants.' An arm still around her, he reached across her to pour two cups of coffee. He filled hers only a quarter high and she nodded for him to keep pouring, then reached for the cup greedily when he was finished.

'You might want to reduce your caffeine intake a little,' he said as he handed it to her. 'I get the feeling you're having more trouble sleeping than usual these days.'

She shrugged.

'You need more rest, love,' he said. 'You know that. Should Thiry up your Ativan dose, do you think? Or are you forgetting to take it some nights? Should I be reminding you?'

Her heart knocked into her rib cage as she pictured him standing in front of her, pills in one hand, a glass of water in the other, smiling sweetly as he watched her swallow.

An unknowing prison guard standing between her and the escape tunnel she had painstakingly dug.

Or worse, accompanying her to the Huntington's clinic to ask for a stronger dose and hearing she had made the same request a few months ago, unbeknownst to him. And that the new dose she had been prescribed was the strongest amount anyone would order for someone her size. There was no way it wasn't working, Dr Thiry would say. If she wasn't sleeping, she must not be taking it.

'Oh, no,' she said, waving him off. 'Not necessary. I've got a whole routine going, and thanks to all my sticky notes, I never miss a step. Brush, floss, take an Ativan, finish my water, climb into bed. Kiss my husband goodnight. Thankfully, no sticky note required for that last one yet.'

She stared into her cup, unable to look at him as she lied. When she had put the 'Ativan!' sticky on their bathroom mirror months ago, it was to remind her to add to her secret stash regularly, to make sure it was still concealed at the back of the bathroom drawer, behind the hand towels. Tom didn't look convinced, so she reached for his keys and pressed them into his hand while she turned to the clock on the stove. 'Look at the time!'

It worked. He disappeared to find his briefcase, his mind on the office now, on patients, not on his wife's sleeping pills and why the dose he believed she was obediently taking wasn't keeping her asleep.

He returned moments later, briefcase in hand, suit jacket over his shoulder, the taste of mint toothpaste in his kiss. For the first time that morning, Mara noticed how his eyes shone. Her closet-arranging strategy had worked; he was wearing a blue shirt. Her favorite, an Italian cut with a subtle herringbone pattern. Her eyes fell to the wedding band on his left hand and she imagined, not for the first time, how much excitement he would stir in the women who caught sight of him once he finally took the ring off.

And, not for the first time, she fought to keep the warm spread of jealousy from rising above her collarbone and reddening her cheeks. The thing about suicide, she reminded herself, is that the price, at least for the actor, must be paid in advance. There was no 'later' over which she could parcel out her loss. The thought of Tom with another woman, the pain of everything she would miss in Laks's life, would all pile up on her in these four days.

Stop feeling sorry for yourself, she thought. It's four days for you. It'll be a lifetime for them.

'Plans for today?' Tom asked, and she was grateful for him interrupting, halting her on the path of self-loathing she'd started down.

'A few errands later,' she told him. 'I called a cab to come around two thirty.'

'Great,' he said. 'Listen, I want you to leave the laundry. I'll do it tonight, when I get home.'

'Tom Nichols,' she said sternly, 'I am perfectly capable of doing laundry.'

'But a lot of it's my running gear and it's really rank—'

'Nice try,' she said. 'But I know what you're up to, and you can knock it off. I've washed your rank running clothes for over twenty years. It hasn't killed me yet.'

'Fine,' he said, holding his hands up in surrender. 'But at least let me pick up dinner on my way home, spare you from having to cook. You could take an afternoon nap instead.'

She rolled her eyes. 'Oh yes, please. How will I ever manage to make dinner and fit in a rest, all in a mere seven hours?' He flinched, and she instantly regretted her sarcasm. Smiling an apology, she touched a few fingers to his temple, grazed them over his sideburns. 'You spoil me. I can make dinner.'

'Let me spoil you. Please. If I can't bring dinner home, what about groceries? Need anything?'

They both turned at the same time to the half-dozen pink sticky notes on the fridge door. It was part of Gina's master system, and she had come over herself to explain it to Mara and Tom: pink sticky notes listing the groceries they needed, yellow ones telling Mara what she planned to cook that night, green ones signaling she needed to take something out of the freezer, blue ones reminding her to make Laks's lunch each night. Tom walked to the fridge to retrieve the pink squares. 'I'll get this stuff on the way home.' He held one hand in front of him, a sticky note on each finger, as he walked to the garage. 'Love you,' he called over his shoulder. 'Take a nap, please.'

'Yes, Dr Nichols.'

The phone lit up as Mara set her coffee cup in the sink. A few months ago, loud noises had started to make her flinch, and Tom had immediately switched their regular kitchen phone for one with lights that flashed to announce a call. It wasn't something she had read about in any of the lists of Huntington's symptoms or side effects from her medications, but she had knocked more things off the counter, the table, her dresser, because of a ringing phone, a knock on the door, Laks or Tom calling her name.

It didn't seem to make a difference if she knew the noises were coming. There was a certain game Laks had, one involving quacking ducks, that Mara had finally given up playing. Even when Laks warned her mother a duck was about to sound, the quack would make Mara fling her cards across the room, or knock the pieces off the board.

Mara leaned over the sink and read the caller ID screen: Thiry clinic. As the lights continued to flash, she thought about the results of her desperate Internet research the night before: there was no new medical discovery that might halt the slide she had started down with the grocery store incident on Monday. The clinic would have no promises for her, no assurance that she need not worry about the incident. No guarantee that she could let Sunday's deadline pass and still retain control over her own ending.

At best, they would utter sympathetic clucks and tsks while they shook their heads on the other end of the line and thanked God they weren't as pitiful as Mara Nichols. At worst, they'd alert Dr Thiry that given the humiliation Mara had undergone, he had better alert her husband to be extra vigilant about her, lest she do something reckless in response.

Mara glared at the phone until its lights stopped flashing and the screen went dark.

16

Mara

Mara checked her watch. One fifteen – enough time to check the forum before the cab arrived. She'd pass over whatever new topic SoNotWicked had posted for the day's discussion, she decided, and focus on the posts from yesterday's thread about MotorCity and his little man.

She scanned through the posts added since her last visit, stopping when she saw an entry by MotorCity from earlier that morning. His comment about opening membership to Asia made her smile; there was something she could offer him after all, more than the vague commiseration she knew wasn't enough.

Wednesday, April 6 @ 1:20 p.m.
MotorCity, I've been doing a detailed analysis of which middle-of-the-night infomercials are most effective (the answer is 'none,' though I will confess I've considered the juicer more than a few times) and which newspapers get delivered earliest in my neighborhood (Wall Street Journal wins – 4:30 a.m.). I had no idea that all this time you were up too and available for late-night chatting.

Want to meet me online tonight – say, midnight (Central time)? We can switch to personal messaging so the rest of the crowd need not parse through our drivel on the main board tomorrow morning.

The instant she saw her message post, she thought how annoyed Tom would be that she had made a commitment to talk late into the night about someone else's problems instead of getting the sleep she needed. She thought of the to-do list hidden underneath her laptop, and everything she needed to accomplish in the next four days. Was she crazy to spend another second talking online to people she'd never met in person, when she had so little time to organize her departure from the 'real life' people who mattered most?

Maybe she was a little crazy, she thought. Then, smiling, she told herself that without the forum, she'd be even crazier. Her 'real life' family and friends mattered most, of course, but it was her virtual friends who had, by treating her like a normal person all this time, kept her sane enough to enjoy her real life for as long as she had.

And maybe for that reason, or maybe because she was feeling sentimental, she was reluctant to cut the forum loose this week, no matter how pressed she was for time. She would find a way to check in with her online friends and still check off all the items on her to-do list. And anyway, it wasn't like she'd be working on the list through the night for the next four nights if she wasn't chatting online. And she certainly wouldn't be sleeping. So she might as well be helping one of her friends from the group.

Mara logged off, slipped on the flip-flops she had kicked under the table and reached for her purse. She was organizing its contents when the doorbell rang. The noise made her fling her wallet across the kitchen.

'Shit.'

She swore again when she saw it had landed in the narrow space between the fridge and the wall. Her arm would fit in the space easily enough, but she was worried that given her questionable balance, bending so low might be her undoing. With the cab about to arrive, this was not the time to end up splayed out on the floor, unable to get up. Maybe she could slide the wallet out with the broom. But it wasn't in its usual spot and she had no idea where she had put it. By the time she remembered, or made her way around the house to look for it, the cab would be here.

'Goddamn it.'

The doorbell chimed again.

'For Christ's sake. Leave your flyer and go.'

Another chime. Whoever it was, they weren't going to leave. And she didn't want them there when the cab arrived, an audience to wonder why the fortysomething woman was being carted around in a taxi instead of driving herself.

'Coming!'

Annoyed, she opened the door a crack and was about to bark something to scare her visitor off when she found herself staring at the fleshy red face of the cabbie. He was a slightly destitute version of Santa with his red flannel shirt stretched taut over his belly, greasy gray hair slicked off his forehead. His scent was a mixture of mothballs, mouthwash and aftershave. Cologne, she corrected herself, noticing the few days' worth of gray growth on his face.

'Afternoon, ma'am. Thought I'd come a little early. Give ya . . . Give us . . . Leave us time ta . . .' He ran a thick hand through his hair and tried again. 'I know ya want ta leave by two sharp.'

'Oh. Thank you, but you didn't have to walk up. Don't you usually wait in the car? I was going to meet you out front, at the curb.'

''S no problem. I thought ya might . . .' He looked at Mara anxiously, like he was afraid of saying the wrong thing. 'I thought I might . . .' he tried again. 'I saw how long the front walk is . . .'

'Oh.' Her face grew hot.

After humiliating herself in the cereal aisle Monday morning, and once she had recovered enough to drive, Mara had raced out of the grocery store parking lot and sped down the street, desperate to get out of her smelly wet pants and into a hot shower. But in her agitation, she took a wrong turn. When she finally realized she was headed away from home and not toward it, she yanked hard on the steering wheel to turn her northbound car in the opposite direction. The erratic maneuver set off a cacophony of honking horns and squealing brakes as Mara's car bumped over the median and into the south-facing lanes. Her right hand reacted to the sudden noise by pulling on the steering wheel, moving her car halfway into the next lane.

'Shit!'

A pickup truck blared its horn behind her before the driver gunned the engine and raced past her, middle finger in the air, his angry expression mouthing, 'What the fuck?'

Frazzled, Mara spotted a side street half a block away, on the other side of a small bank that sat on the corner. In her eagerness to get off the main road, she cranked her steering wheel too forcefully to the right. She wasn't able to correct the oversteering fast enough, and her car crossed two lanes of traffic before bouncing over the curb, across the sidewalk and into the large metal sign on the bank's front lawn.

Something made a terrible crunching noise as the airbag slammed into her, pushing the breath out of her lungs in one large gasp. The engine hissed, and when she batted the airbag out of the way, she saw the entire right side of the car was wrapped around the sign pole.

'Goddamn it!'

Slowly, methodically, she assessed every limb, wiggled her fingers and toes, and moved her ankles and wrists in circles. Nothing seemed broken, though from the way her ribs felt, she could swear she must have belly flopped from the roof of the bank onto the parking lot below. The growing noise of people startled her. When she saw the size of the crowd gathering, she wished she could sink down in her seat until her bones and skin melted and she dripped through the floor and out of sight.

A knock sounded in her left ear and a woman wearing too much makeup and a bank name tag appeared in her window. Mara tried to lower it but it didn't work, so she pushed her door open.

'You okay, hon?' the woman said. 'You about gave us all a heart attack just now. Thank God for airbags, huh? You don't seem to have a scratch.' She peered over the hood of the car, toward the front, before leaning in to speak again. 'Can't say the same for your car, I'm afraid. It looks pretty messed up.'

She bent toward Mara, her lips parted as though she were about to say something else. But suddenly she pressed them together, twisting them a little. She ducked her head a little lower, leaned close to Mara's ear and whispered, 'You got something to cover yourself with?'

Glancing down, Mara saw the blotting she'd done hadn't helped; her pants were still visibly stained. She put a hand over her face and wished again she could disappear.

'One sec, hon,' the woman's voice said in her ear. She jogged to the passenger side, reached in for Mara's jacket, and seconds later she was back, holding the jacket appraisingly before she handed it over. 'Looks maybe a little too fancy for . . . this. But, desperate times, I guess, right?' She patted Mara's shoulder. Mara managed to wrap the jacket around her waist and the woman said, 'There, that's better. I can't smell it, to be honest, so as long as no one sees, no one but you and I have to know.'

Mara stole a quick glance at the tree-shaped air freshener sitting in the cup holder beside her. In the grocery store parking lot, she had torn the tree from its string on the rearview mirror and rubbed it over her pants. Amazingly, it had done the trick. Quietly, she thanked the woman, who clucked sympathetically and moved away to make room for the paramedics and tow truck driver who had arrived on the scene. Mara eased herself out of the car, waving off the assistance of the first responders.

'I'm fine, really,' she said.

'You musta been in some hurry,' the tow truck driver called from the front of her car. 'No time to park and go in, so you thought you'd make your own drive-through ATM, huh?' He guffawed and she gave him a limp smile before moving out of earshot of his laughter.

She managed not to cry on the tow truck ride to the repair shop. But when the car mechanic gave a long whistle and told her it was amazing she wasn't hurt, the thought that she could have seriously injured someone, or even killed them, was a punch in the gut. What if Laks had been in the car?

Her chin dropped to her chest as sobs worked their way loose. Out of the corner of one eye, she saw the mechanic take a quick step away from her. His body shifted from one foot to the other while he cleared his throat and told her, without conviction, 'No need to be upset there, ma'am. You're fine.'

The manager told her it would be Friday before they could return her car, and he wasn't sure he had a loaner available. He was fretting about calling a rental company for her when she finally told him not to worry about it. She wouldn't be driving anymore, she said flatly. She didn't need a loaner or a rental. After they were finished with her car on Friday, it would only sit in her garage until her husband had it taken away.

The manager cocked his head, waiting for her to explain. But the one sentence had taken too much from her, and she stood, mute, tears and snot running over her lip and into her mouth, until the receptionist pushed the manager aside, reached across the counter for Mara's hand and said, 'Here, honey, let me call you a cab.'

She stood at the front door of the repair shop, leaning against the glass. The taxi pulled up and she held up her hand. The driver waved back from the front seat, waiting for her to walk out. But after she pushed open the door and took a few steps, suddenly the cabbie was leaping out of the car and running to her side, a panicked look on his face.

He thrust an arm toward her and she glared at his unnecessary show of drama. The tow truck driver and car mechanic had recoiled, too, after seeing her take a few

141

steps. What was with these men? She had growled at the tow truck operator and the mechanic and she hissed at the cabbie now, telling him he should get back in his cab and wait, the same way he did for everyone else.

Because she didn't need his help. And she didn't need his pity. And she could walk. Perfectly well. By herself. As he could damn well see.

He lowered his arm but the look on his face showed he didn't completely agree, and he stayed by her side all the way to the cab. As he walked, he whistled aimlessly and made a show of glancing around casually. He opened the door for her, telling her quickly he did that for everyone. Then he took a step back and waved her inside with the pretense that he was happy to stand there, holding the door while she got in. But when she lost her balance and began catapulting headfirst into the cab, he uttered a quick apology and reached both arms out to her.

Once seated, Mara started to glare at him again, but stopped herself. He might have overstepped, but he had also prevented her from cracking her forehead on the cab door. She smiled at him apologetically and instructed herself not to sneer when she saw the mixture of pity and self-satisfaction she knew would be on his face. The self-congratulating expression that said, 'Well, aren't I the man, helping the poor rag doll of a woman who couldn't even get herself into a car. If it weren't for me, she'd have knocked herself unconscious.'

But that's not what she saw when she raised her eyes to his. There was no pity in his expression, no self-satisfaction. Instead, the gaze that met hers spoke the best thing she could have hoped to hear: *I've got my own problems, lady. I'm not about to spend any time wondering about yours.*

She asked for his card.

And now, here he was standing in her doorway, the same look of impassiveness on his large, weathered face. And here she was, eyeing him as though he had pointed at her and laughed. She instructed the color to recede from her cheeks.

'I'm sorry,' she said. 'It was nice of you to think of me. I was getting ready to walk out. But I dropped my wallet in the kitchen and I can't reach it. Would you mind?'

Surprise at the help she had asked this stranger for, no matter how unassuming he was, caused her cheeks to catch fire again, and she was thinking of how to retract her request when he answered.

'Happy ta.'

She regretted having asked him but what could she do now, tell him she hadn't really dropped anything? Didn't really need his help? She couldn't pay him if she didn't have her wallet. And she needed to get to the pharmacy.

'Thank you.'

She led him to the kitchen and pointed to her wallet, which he retrieved in a second and held out to her. She grasped it and promptly dropped it. She shook her head, disgusted. The kitchen floor was like a magnet, sucking things out of her hand.

But the cabbie's expression gave nothing away as he bent to pick it up. 'Here,' he said. 'Why don't I just . . .' Slowly, one eye trained on her face as though he thought she might snap forward and bite him, he opened the purse that hung over her arm and dropped the wallet inside.

'Thank you.'

'Pleasure,' he said. 'Should I go outside again, wait for ya by the car?'

'I think we're past that now, um . . . ?'

'Harry.'

'I think we're past that, Harry.'

As they made their way to the front door, he edged an arm toward her and viewed her with a wary squint. She heard him exhale as she placed her hand on the soft flannel of his sleeve. She smiled. He was clearly a southern gentleman, preferring a woman walk on his arm. And he had been so gallant about the wallet, it seemed only right to reward him with a hand on his elbow.

'Thank you. I'm Mara Nichols, by the way.'

'Pleased ta meet ya, Mrs Nichols.'

She laughed. 'I can't imagine. So far I've done little more than glare and hiss at you.'

He led her out of the house and down the walk. 'I've got a feelin' there's more to ya than glare an' hiss,' he said. He was silent for a bit. When he spoke again, he tilted his head away from her slightly, as though preparing for her to smack him. 'I get the feelin' maybe you're used ta bein' in control. Not all that keen on . . .' He hesitated, looking nervous again. 'Help,' he said finally.

Mara threw her head back in a loud laugh. The sudden movement caused her to tip backward, and Harry took a quick step to the right, behind her, catching her against him. He gently pushed her upright and took his place at her side again, casting his attention intently in every direction but hers. She looked gratefully at his profile but he wouldn't look at her, so she nudged him in the side until he finally turned his head toward her. She flashed him a conspiratorial smile and laughed again, and this time he laughed with her, a low, rumbling chuckle that she sensed he cut short on purpose.

As he called in his status to the dispatcher, Mara looked

around the interior of the cab. She had been too upset on Monday to notice that, unlike the overworn appearance of its operator, the car itself was pristine. The seats and floor were spotless, and the various piles of maps, receipt books and business cards on the console were each bundled together neatly, fastened by black binder clips. A small cooler sat on the passenger side floor in front – his lunch, she guessed – and a neatly folded jacket lay on the seat.

His sun visor was down and in the bottom right corner was a small, faded and slightly creased picture. Mara leaned forward to get a closer look. It was a school photo of a young girl not much older than Laks. She sat primly as kids in school photos do, shoulders straight, hands clasped together in her lap, a small, slightly forced smile on her face.

'Granddaughter?' she asked.

But even as she asked it, she knew the answer was no. The photo was too old, the girl's hairstyle and clothes too dated. The photo must be ten years old at least, making the girl a teenager now, or older. Mara studied Harry's profile and tried to estimate his age. Mid-fifties at the most. He had the look of someone who had lived a tough life, but he didn't appear old enough to have a granddaughter who was now a teenager.

Harry looked up from the notes he was making in his driver's log. 'What's that?'

'I was asking about the photo on your visor. Is that your granddaughter or . . . ?'

'Oh. Uh. No.' He shot a hand to the visor and snapped it shut, concealing the girl. Mara was about to apologize for upsetting him when he turned and smiled. 'So. Errands, ya said on the phone. Where ta first?'

He pressed the button to start the meter. He wasn't upset, then. But there would be no more discussion about the photo.

'Pharmacy,' Mara said. 'Then there's a clothing store a few blocks from there. I've already called ahead and they're holding some things for me. I have to try them on but it shouldn't take long.'

He nodded and pulled away from the curb.

17

Mara

Mara told herself this was no big deal, people bought these things all the time. The cashier wouldn't think twice, other shoppers wouldn't even notice. It was no more embarrassing than buying tampons, which she used to bury under a dozen bottles of lotion, shampoo and sunscreen when she was a teenager but now had no problem carrying in plain sight through a crowded store. The same way she'd seen middle-aged men standing unapologetically in line, a tube of hemorrhoid cream in hand. Nothing to it.

Harry had offered to go into the pharmacy with her. Carry the basket while she shopped, tote the bags out to the car, but she told him she didn't want to trouble him. It wouldn't have been any trouble, she knew, but he backed off. He must have sensed she wanted to be alone.

Inside, she grabbed a handbasket from the stack near the door and took a confident step toward the aisle marked 'Walkers/Adult Undergarments/Misc. Aids.' It was a generous phrase, she thought: 'Adult undergarments.' She would never be able to think of them as anything but diapers.

And that did it: diapers.

She was forty-two, and she was buying diapers.

Not the cute kind with little yellow ducks on the cloth that signaled a perfectly normal phase of life, but large, ugly pieces of cloth that screamed, 'I can no longer control my bladder any better than an infant.' And though the write-ups on the Internet swore the new designs were discreet, some even stitched in pretty patterns to look less like the exact thing they were, there was no getting past the big, bulky, plastic packaging that alerted everyone in the store that the purchaser was 'having difficulties,' like the Internet ads said. Incontinent, like everyone would think.

Her second step wasn't confident. It wasn't a quick walk from door to aisle to cashier anymore, but a treacherous journey to the end of a plank and into the perilous waters of the diseased, the decrepit. She was a failure. Her body had failed her, and the fact that this was happening in her forties instead of her eighties made her failure that much more pathetic. She felt like a thirteen-year-old boy buying condoms, a fourteen-year-old girl buying a pregnancy test. There was an age range in which certain drugstore purchases were innocent, unremarkable. Outside that range, the same purchases were despicable, suspicious.

Humiliating.

Mara felt her skin warm from her collarbone to her chin as she made her walk of shame to the aisle. When she reached it, she did a slow circle, looking in 360 degrees to make sure no one was following. Watching. Noticing. No one was, and she took a breath and told herself to act now, while she had a narrow window of privacy. Move quickly down the aisle, she heard her voice sound in her head. Grab two packages, race to the cashier, make the purchase, run for the cover of the cab. Do it fast and maybe it won't be so bad. Three . . . two . . . one: rip off the Band-Aid.

But she couldn't make her feet move down the aisle. And while she stood, shoes cemented to the linoleum, she concocted a new theory: if she refused to walk the remaining steps, refused to touch the packages, maybe the problem would simply go away.

She had started down that course that morning, though, before deciding it was too risky. Standing in the bathroom, a maxi pad in her hand, she had convinced herself if she didn't wear it, if she didn't concede there was a reason to guard against another accident, then one wouldn't occur. Preparing for it was tantamount to inviting it to happen. She tossed the pad back into the box, which she then pushed into the deep recesses of the cupboard.

But minutes later, when she was pulling on her freshly laundered yoga pants, she saw the boy from the grocery store in her mind, the surprised 'O' of his mouth as he stared at the stains on her pants, and she stammered and stuttered and tried to explain that there was a reasonable explanation for why she was standing in a public place, covered in pee stains and shrouded in the revolting stench of urine. She marched back into the bathroom, retrieved the box and put on a pad, praying it would do the trick until she made it to the pharmacy for the real thing.

Stalling for time, Mara glanced left and right, in front and behind, another check to make sure no other shoppers were nearby. An end-cap display offered a stack of Dallas Cowboys beach towels, and although in her twenty-plus years as a Texan she had never cared one lick about football, she decided that now was the time for her to own some local team merchandise. Holding up one towel, then another, she debated the merits of blue background with white helmet versus the opposite, ignoring the snide voice in her head that said for $4.99 per, she needed to just buy both damn designs and go about the business she had come in the store to conduct.

She heard a man's voice in the next aisle over and remembered Harry. If she delayed any longer, his southern gentility would demand he come in and find her, make sure she was all right. She put two towels in her basket and faced the aisle, warily eyeing the shelves halfway down. She had chosen a brand last night after doing some Internet research and now she narrowed her eyes and inspected the packages until she spotted the one from the website.

She shot another furtive look in each direction. All clear. Taking a deep breath, she clamped her mouth closed and walked as fast as she could down the aisle. Without a break in her forward motion and without breathing, she snapped an arm out sideways, snatched two packages from the shelf, crammed them into her basket under the towels and kept up her pace to the end of the aisle. Only when she had rounded the corner into 'Household Items/Paper Products' did she open her mouth, letting the trapped air out in a rush before doubling over and sucking in a deep breath, then another, and another.

When she recovered, she stood upright, gazed at the square shapes pushing out from under the towels and let the edges of her lips rise ever so slightly. Done. She had done it.

She was about to let herself smile fully when a woman appeared at her elbow from nowhere. Quickly, Mara spun away, swinging the basket to the other side of her body and out of the woman's sight, pretending to examine the laundry detergent options in front of her while she waited for the woman to make her way past. The woman slowly moved out of the aisle and Mara, smiling broadly now with relief, headed to the front door of the store and the waiting safety of the cab.

And then she remembered she had to pay.

Goddamn it. How could she have forgotten that? And now she was walking the plank again, or down the long green hallway to the execution chamber, or along the Trail of Tears or whatever other passage of misery man had traveled before her. She stepped reluctantly toward the register and prepared to reveal the contents of her basket to the twenty-something clerk whose mouth would surely form the same horrified 'O' Mara had seen in the grocery store on Monday.

She eyed the cashier closely, and taking in the blue streak in the girl's hair, the pierced eyebrow, the ring on every finger, she decided the woman was precisely the right age and personality to hold up the package and say something like, 'Ewww, these. My granny has to wear these.'

Mara decided if she could pull off a cool shrug and say, 'Oh, yes, they're for my mom,' she might be able to make it out of the store with her dignity intact. But she could feel the warmth on her neck and cheeks and she knew her humiliation was showing in bright red. Her palms were sweating and her throat felt thick, and if anyone could pull off a casual, innocent remark to convince a cashier that 'these aren't for me,' it was not Mara Nichols.

There was a line at the register and she hovered nearby, one eye on the line and the other on the door in case Harry appeared. The cashier prattled on to each shopper, and the litany of Texas cheer Mara had always found endearing before – How are you today, ma'am? Did you find everything you came in for? I sure hope you'll have a great day! You come back! – now felt like sharp nails against her inflamed skin.

When the last customer had gone, Mara stepped closer, feeling dizzy now, and with her remaining strength, hoisted the basket up onto the counter. She braced herself with one hand and promised her body it could collapse in the cab if only it would stay upright another few minutes. As the clerk raised her eyes in greeting, Mara reached for one of the gossip magazines on display near the register and snapped it open in front of her face, a barricade between her and the 'Ewww, my granny wears these' comment, the anticipation of which was making Mara's breakfast threaten to make an appearance.

'How are you today, ma'am?'

'Fine.' Mara felt her lips move but didn't hear the word come out. She tried again, but again it came out as nothing more than a small push of air.

There was silence for a few seconds, and Mara guessed the cashier was waiting for her to look out from behind the magazine and respond more politely. Like a civilized person, she thought, and shame rose in another hot wave from her collarbone to her neck to her cheeks.

'And did you find everything you came in for? Oh, what on earth?'

The words clenched Mara's heart and it stopped for a full few seconds before kick-starting itself and revving into high gear, beating in her throat more than her chest. Holding her breath, she lowered the magazine a fraction and saw the cashier carrying one of the glaring white plastic packages, frowning as she turned it over in her hands. The woman looked at Mara, a puzzled expression on her face, and Mara wondered if a human's skin could get so hot from humiliation that it broke out in blisters. Panicked, she eyed the door and tried to estimate how long it would take her to make it outside, and whether if she made a run for it, the cashier would chase her down, waving the diapers for everyone in the parking lot, including Harry, to see.

'Oh, here it is! Pesky bar codes can be so hard to find sometimes.' The girl held the package up to Mara to show the elusive symbol and Mara raised a hand, lowering it quickly, to indicate the girl should lower the package. But the girl stood motionless, smiling to herself for having located the bar code and not, evidently, in any rush to ring up the sale. From the corner of her eye, Mara saw an elderly man making his way from the end of an aisle to the register.

'I'm in a terrible hurry,' she said, in a voice she didn't recognize.

The salesgirl jolted into action, running the scanner over the towels and the two packages. 'Oh, yes, ma'am, no problem. That'll be fifty-two ninety-five. Oh, wait – I think the undergarments had a coupon this week. In the circular? They're at the front, near the baskets.' She pointed as the old man took a shuffling step closer. 'Do you want to look—'

'I'll just pay the full price,' Mara said, her eyes on the man now.

'Or I can, if you want me—'

'Just ring it up! Please, just ring up the fifty-two ninety-five. I really must go.' Mara thrust her credit card at the woman and buried her face in the gossip rag again before their eyes could meet.

'Certainly. Now, if you'll look online when you get home, there may be a way to claim the value of the coupon as a rebate. You just go to www—'

'No!' Mara shot her hand up, smacked the magazine onto the counter and reached for the bags. 'Just let me go!'

The cashier flinched. Wordlessly, she handed over the bags and receipt to Mara, who, too embarrassed by her behavior to speak, tried to fit a thank-you and an apology into a nod of her head.

'Well, I sure hope you'll have a great day,' the cashier said mechanically. 'Come back soon,' she added without feeling, at the same time Mara was thanking God she'd never have to come back again.

18

Scott

Scott was in the middle of assigning homework to his fourth-hour students when the classroom intercom buzzed and a fairly frantic-sounding Mrs Bevel, the school secretary, asked him to come to the office immediately. She had already arranged for the school's guidance counselor, Miss Styles, to supervise Scott's classroom until he returned. Scott glanced from the intercom to the clock to the hopeful-looking eighth-graders in front of him, who were, he could tell, wondering if he'd finish assigning the homework first.

'You got lucky this time,' he said, and turned toward the door. 'Maddie,' he called over his shoulder to a girl in the front row, 'you're in charge until Ms Styles gets here.' He walked into the hall, smiling as he heard a small cheer erupt behind him. He was still smiling when he reached Mrs Bevel, and even when Janice, the Jackson family's social worker, rose from a chair in front of Mrs Bevel's desk.

'Hello, Scott,' Janice said, and as usual her voice was as stiff as her body. She looked at her shoes as though she were uncertain what to do next. The niceties of human interaction always seemed to elude her. For a social worker, Scott had remarked to Laurie a few times, Janice didn't seem all that social. He had always given her the benefit of the doubt, assuming she cared about the children and families on her caseload more than her outward conduct would indicate.

But the rigid way she carried herself, the vacant way she seemed to look at people, the dullness in her voice, made it seem like she was only going through the motions. Had she been different when she first started? he wondered. Was it only that decades of overwork had drained the feeling out of her? Or had she gone into the job this cold and distant? Maybe she had received the same advice as FosterFranny: don't get too attached.

'Janice! I didn't expect to see you here.' Scott extended a hand and Janice reached hers out, barely touching him before pulling her hand back.

'I thought Mrs Bevel called me down to chastise me about leaving my classroom lights on or being late with grading or any number of other things,' he said, turning to Mrs Bevel and flashing her a grin. 'I have a long list of sins, don't I, Mrs B?'

Mrs Bevel looked nervously from Scott to Janice, then stood, mumbled something about needing to check on a file and disappeared into the hallway that led to the inner offices. 'Well,' Scott said to Janice, still grinning, 'I seem to have scared her away. I hope you—'

It was then that he noticed the look on Janice's face. Her lips were pressed so firmly together they were more white than pink, and her eyes seemed to be boring a hole into the side of Mrs Bevel's desk. He couldn't discern her emotion. Anger? Anxiety? It was something under the umbrella of 'very upset,' that much was certain. No wonder Mrs Bevel had hightailed it down the hallway. Scott wished he could follow.

'I'm afraid I have some disturbing news,' Janice said. She sat and absently patted the chair beside her. Scott read the gesture as an order and regarded her carefully as he lowered himself beside her. As he waited for her to explain, his mind raced with possibilities about what the news could be. Curtis in trouble at school again? But Miss Keller had his cell number and she had always texted or called before. Something about Bray? But Bray would call himself.

Unless he couldn't.

'Is Bray okay?' he asked, suddenly feeling ill.

Janice didn't answer at first and Scott felt his stomach lurch. 'Janice, is Bray—?'

'It's LaDania. She came by my office this morning. She told me she intends to get Curtis from school this afternoon. And take him home.'

'*What?*' He jumped up from his chair as though it were on fire. 'But the hearing's not until Monday!'

'That's just a formality, as you're aware. She says she's ready for him to come home now. Today. And legally, she has every right to take him now. The guardianship order grants rights to you and Mrs Coffman, but removes none from her. And of course, technically, the order grants you such rights only until her release, which occurred last week. She agreed Curtis would stay with you for this extra week because I convinced her that the extra time between her release and the formal hearing terminating your guardianship would be a benefit to her. She is no longer convinced she benefits from this agreement. She says she's lonely living on her own. And she wants her child with her.'

Scott clutched both sides of his head with his hands and squeezed, but the words he had heard wouldn't go away. Curtis was leaving today.

There would be no spaghetti and homemade cookies tonight. There would be no more reading in bed. No final game of HORSE in the driveway. No more tuck-ins. No movie night on Friday.

No Monster Trucks on Sunday.

No goodbye.

He leaned against Mrs Bevel's desk and ground his knuckles into his eyes. He put a hand on his gut and willed himself not to throw up.

After a few minutes, he spoke quietly. 'But I still have a few days. *We*,' he corrected himself. '*We* still have a few days. We've got a whole big thing planned. Extra reading every night, special dinners, a final hoops game. We've got movie night on Friday. And Monster Trucks on Sunday. We were counting on—'

'I know,' Janice said, and Scott was surprised by the softness in her voice. 'I know you were counting on having this final week together.' She smiled, but it was a sad smile. 'I assumed you'd have something special lined up, and I told her so.'

The tone of Janice's voice changed then and Scott could feel her anger as much as hear it. He took his fists out of his eyes and looked at her. She was leaning forward now, and the eyes that met his were bright with emotion. He could see the long, thready muscles in her thin forearms working as she twisted her fingers together in her lap. 'I also told her the boy needs to end his time at your house the right way. He needs to be allowed to have a proper goodbye, and so do you and Laurie. And after everything you've done, you more than deserve it. I told her all of this,' she said, 'very clearly and in ten different ways. It didn't make one bit of difference.'

Her emotion startled him. She had been to the house several times over the past year, but she had remained as distant and reserved after the tenth visit as she was after the first. Seemingly against her will, she accepted coffee or lemonade each time, but left it untouched as she sat ramrod straight at the kitchen table and made cramped notes about Curtis's eating and sleeping habits, his behavior, his school-work. She took down pages of data about the boy but it always seemed to Scott and Laurie that it was more about putting words in her notebook than about getting to know the child, or his guardians.

She asked Curtis questions, too, sometimes, and when he gave silly answers, she didn't crack a smile or show any hint of amusement, but simply repeated her question until she received an answer worthy of recording. Other times, she sat alone in a corner of the room to 'observe,' asking them to go about their business and pretend she wasn't there.

Scott and Curtis were able to do just that, and continue whatever wrestling match or checkers game or other activity, but Laurie remained on edge each time, hovering too close to Janice, offering to refill the glass or mug Janice hadn't yet taken a sip from. 'It's like the Grim Reaper telling you to go about sleeping while he's sitting at the foot of your bed,' Laurie told Scott after the first 'observation' session.

'I told her there's no justification for separating the two of you one day earlier than you were planning, let alone several,' Janice continued. 'It will be hard enough, I told her, for him to leave you. And for you to let him go. I

159

told her I have never seen . . .' She leaned back in her chair, almost collapsing, as though the effort to sustain such feeling had tired her. 'Well, I told her it was the wrong thing to do. She is very aware of my position on this. But I'm afraid she is very firm on hers.'

'So,' Scott said. 'That's it. She just . . . gets to take him. She gets to ignore what we've all been counting on. Because she's lonely. And she changed her mind. That's . . . incredible. That is just . . .' He paused, trying to find the right word. 'It's just fucking. Incredible.' Janice did a double take at the curse word and he considered apologizing, but the most he could bring himself to do was shrug.

'Could I fight it?' he asked.

'You mean in court?'

He nodded.

Janice twisted her lips. 'You don't really have a legal basis. I'm not sure the court would even entertain it. I suppose you could speak with a lawyer.'

Scott thought about whom he could call. Pete's neighbor was a lawyer; maybe he could help. Sure, he didn't have legal rights to the boy but he had to try something. It was ridiculous, what LaDania was doing, and unbelievably selfish. Did she have no regard for him and Laurie, and what they had done for her son for the past year – for both of her sons? What they had done for her? Did it not occur to her that they might want these last days with Curtis to say a proper goodbye? Did she think about them at all?

But then he thought about what FosterFranny had said: *focus on what's best for the child*. He lifted his palms waist high in a gesture of helplessness. He didn't have a choice here. If he fought this, it would be for himself, not Curtis. 'Never mind,' he told Janice. 'She's his mother. I won't stand between him and his mom, no matter how much I disagree with this. I wouldn't want to end our year together by arguing over him. That wouldn't be any better for him than what she's doing.'

Janice nodded. 'I must say it's refreshing to deal with one adult today who's willing to put the child's interests ahead of his own.'

'So, now what?' Scott asked. 'She just shows up at Logan at three o'clock, says, "Surprise!" and takes him?'

'She does,' Janice said, 'though I've convinced her to let me go with her, so I can ensure Curtis hears some explanation about what's happening. I'm hoping my presence there will help ease him into the sudden transition more effectively than if I weren't there.'

'What about his things?' Scott asked. 'He's got clothes at our place. Toys. Books.' He thought about *Stuart Little* and felt his throat close.

'She asked me to take those to him later tonight. I considered telling her you'd deliver it all yourself, to give you a chance to see him. But I think that might make things harder on Curtis – to see you so soon, before he's had a chance to adjust to the new . . . situation.'

'So I don't even get to say goodbye?' Scott whispered. He swallowed hard and struggled to fit air around the lump in his throat.

'Like I said, I guessed you'd have some plan in mind for your last weekend,' Janice said. 'And I asked her to consider allowing you to go ahead with at least some of that plan. She said she would.' Janice made a bitter sound then, and she scowled.

'We were going to go see Monster Trucks on Sunday,' Scott said. 'It'll kill him to miss it. He's been talking about it for months. He's been marking the days off on his calendar. He—'

He couldn't go on. He walked slowly to Mrs Bevel's chair and sat. Leaning forward, he put his arms on the desk and let his head, which suddenly felt very heavy, fall on top of them. The tears he'd been holding in found their way out and he didn't bother trying to stop them.

An unrecognizable sound came from Janice, and seconds later he felt her beside him, her arms around him so tightly he had to gasp for his next breath. He started to pull away but he didn't have the strength to move. Or so he told himself as he relaxed into her arms and let her press herself against him, her voice soft and comforting in his ear, murmuring, 'There now.'

After a time, she relaxed her grip slightly and he felt her hand making slow circles on his back, soothing. 'When I see her at Logan later today, I'll ask about Monster Trucks.' She patted him gently. 'I'll *insist* about Monster Trucks.'

19

Mara

Harry offered to put the pharmacy bags in the trunk, but Mara declined. As he drove, she reached a hand into one and carefully eased a 'discreet female undergarment' out of its package and into her purse. Every crinkle of the plastic was a trumpet sounding in her head and she prepared herself for his curious gaze in the mirror, or over his shoulder. But he was focused on the road in front. Or pretending to be.

The clothing store was one of the trendy, casual-chic places Steph had been urging her to shop at for ages. 'You can't dress like a high-powered attorney when you're helping in art class,' Steph said. 'And you can't dress like that.' She indicated Mara's yoga pants, her baggy T-shirt. 'You've got to look . . .' She paused. 'You know, hipper.'

Steph would be so proud to learn she'd finally stepped inside the store, Mara thought. Though Steph wouldn't be impressed to find out her friend had shopped online and put in a 'store pickup' order rather than browsing the racks, comparing colors and cuts, trying things on for hours on end as Steph loved to do. They were holding three black

163

cotton skirts for her at the cash register, along with three tops – all in different colors but the same brand and style.

'If they fit,' Mara asked the salesclerk, 'would you mind if I wore one outfit out today? I'm about to volunteer in my daughter's class and my friend tells me I need to show up in something a little nicer than workout clothes.' She gave a self-deprecating smile as she gestured to the black Neiman Marcus yoga pants she was wearing, two times as expensive as the three skirts and blouses put together.

'No problem. We get a lot of moms in here looking for these.' The clerk, no more than twenty, handed over one of each item. 'You ordered three of the same thing, so you only need to try on one set.'

Mara could hear the mild disapproval in the girl's voice. Who spent two minutes looking online, then called the store and asked them to hold three of the exact same thing?

'I know,' Mara said. 'I should have my "woman" badge taken away. My friend tells me that all the time. But I confess I hate to shop. At least the tops are different colors, though, right?'

The girl eyed Mara as though she were a rare animal and shook her head in an exaggerated fashion. 'We get your kind in here from time to time,' she joked. 'I don't understand it myself. I live to shop.' Leaning closer, she dropped her voice. 'The trying-on part, I do not live for. So, your strategy of getting the same brand and size for everything makes a little sense to me. Anything to spend less time in the dressing room. All those floor-length mirrors, right? And those lights! They're the enemy.'

'Exactly,' Mara agreed, pretending that had been the reason she ordered everything the same. As she headed for the dressing room, the skirt and top over her arm, she turned

164

to smile at the clerk and found the girl watching her, a puzzled look on her face. Caught, the girl gave an embarrassed smile and turned quickly to the front of the store as if she'd just heard someone walk in. Mara frowned, but told herself to cut the girl some slack. It was odd of Mara to have ordered all the same things, and the salesgirl had been far less judgmental about it than others her age would likely have been. There was nothing to be upset about.

In the cramped cubicle, she wrestled out of her yoga pants and removed her expensive silk bikini-fit underwear. Holding the 'adult undergarment' up for inspection, she saw with relief that it was a lot slimmer than the ungainly product she had been expecting. But when she slid it on and felt its cold, rough bulk against her skin, the bridge of her nose stung and her throat thickened. Slimmer material and curlicue stitching or not, she was wearing a diaper.

She stood under the unflattering glare of the dressing room light and gawked in the mirror at the rectangle of disposable fabric and the two pale, toneless legs that reached gracelessly from the white cloth to her flip-flops. She ran her eyes up and down the mirror and praised herself for never having a full-length one installed at home. She had always been so proud of her body. Years of dedicated exercise and healthy eating had given her the perfect blend of lean muscle and feminine curve. Tom had murmured his appreciation a million times while Mara's friends had confessed their envy.

But over the past four years, the caloric demands of a disease that came with ever-moving limbs had robbed her of every spare ounce of muscle, every last hint of feminine curve. She had pretended not to notice when her hands grazed over protruding hip bones in the shower, or when an inadvertent glance at herself in a windowpane or mirror showed bony shoulders jutting under her T-shirt, a too-prominent clavicle stealing attention from her necklace. Slowly, her body had gone from bronze and muscular to . . . this.

The dressing room mirror delivered a harsh message: the fact that Mara had refused to watch her body morph from healthy-looking woman into anorexic-looking hadn't stopped it from happening. She never changed in front of Tom anymore but, God, even in the dark, even under the sheets . . .

She lifted her head and found her dark eyes staring back at her from the glass, tiny pools of liquid forming in the corners, betraying her. Pressing the tips of her fingers into her eyelids, Mara counted to five slowly while she told herself to get it together. She didn't want the salesgirl to see her crying when she walked out – or Harry, for that matter.

It took her until a count of thirty, but she managed to calm herself down. She pulled on the skirt, smoothed it flat and turned slowly from side to side, inspecting herself from every angle to ensure no one would be able to detect the secret underneath. Satisfied, she put on the top. It wasn't a bad look, and she could see why the young moms at the school favored this over yoga pants and T-shirts.

'Nice!' the girl said when Mara walked out of the dressing room, and Mara was glad she'd stopped herself from being upset about the staring episode earlier. 'Do a spin for me!'

Mara held her breath as she spun in a slow, nervous circle, waiting for the quick intake of breath when the salesclerk saw the outline of the diaper. Or, given her similar age to the pharmacy cashier, squealed, 'Ewww, you're wearing paper panties, like my granny!'

But the mirror hadn't lied. 'Fantastic!' the girl said, clapping her hands. Quieter, she added, 'If you don't mind my saying, this makes you look a little younger.'

Of all the responses Mara feared she might hear, that one was more than fine.

'I don't mind one bit,' she said.

Harry raised a brow in the rearview mirror. 'Can't help but notice the outfit change. Looks real nice. We goin' somewhere special next?'

'Actually, these were my only errands for today. But would you mind taking a quick detour on the way home? My daughter's class should be out for afternoon recess about now, and I thought maybe we'd catch a glimpse of them.'

'She forget somethin'?'

'No. I just . . .' Mara paused for a second. 'I just wanted to see her. It's close by – only a few blocks out of the way. But if you're in a hurry—'

'All the time in the world.'

She gave him directions to the school and as they drove, she noticed, not for the first time, how much newer and more colorful Plano was compared to the northern world of gray in which she and Tom had grown up. The manicured lawns flying past her window seemed artificial, they were so green and flawless. The houses were cartoonishly large, each one looking newer and grander than the last. Even the public spaces were beautiful here, the medians along the road a cheerful spray of colorful gardens.

It was a Disney movie set, Tom had said the first time they drove through. They were house-hunting in the northern Dallas suburbs, his offer letter from the dermatology practice folded neatly on the console between them.

Mara was a third-year lawyer then, and in twenty-four hours her husband had gone from underpaid chief resident to princely paid dermatologist, outearning her a few times over.

'I feel as though any second now all the store owners are going to burst onto the sidewalk and break into song,' he laughed. 'And is it me, or is the sun a little brighter here, the sky a little bluer? I think the city of Plano has big fans that blow all the clouds south to Dallas.'

Harry and Mara arrived at the school as a crowd of children poured out the doors in a shrieking wave, spilling onto the playground.

'See her?' Harry slowed the cab to a crawl and they both turned to scan the schoolyard.

'Not yet . . . Oh! There! The one with the dark black hair? With the pink shorts and the pink-and-white shirt? Climbing up the slide? Third rung from the top.'

'Ah. Looks exactly like ya.'

She smiled. He wasn't the first to say it. All Indians look the same, after all. No matter that she and Laks shared no DNA whatsoever, the same way it hadn't mattered that she and her parents shared none. Everyone thought she was the spitting image of them, too. Tom was the only genetically unrelated one of the group, in the minds (and comments) of strangers who saw them all together – the handsome American tour guide leading around the elderly Indian couple, their daughter and granddaughter.

'Ya wanna park here and watch for a while,' Harry asked, 'or do ya need ta be home?'

'I don't really need to be anywhere anymore,' Mara said.

Harry nodded, put the cab into park and turned off the engine. Shifting in his seat, he turned toward the playground and watched, a look of contentment on his face as though he, too, had nowhere else to be. Must be nice to be so relaxed, Mara thought, as reflexively she reached into her purse and pulled out her phone to check her work e-mails.

There were none. Of course there were none. In fact, the small 'KL' icon she used to click to show her work in-box was gone from the phone's screen, as it had been for weeks now. The firm had let her keep the phone but it removed her from the Katon Locke network immediately, as a matter of policy. She cursed under her breath for having forgotten. Her personal account was still there, but she wasn't in the mood to check it now.

Mara leaned her head against the tinted black car window and closed her eyes against the realization, still new to her, that she was no longer a high-powered lawyer with an ever-filling e-mail in-box. She was no more pressed for time than Harry – and likely less so than he was, since he still had a job.

Her head still against the window, she opened her eyes and clicked open her text messaging program. It was separate from the e-mail system, so her long string of texts hadn't been wiped clean when the firm removed her from the network. She scrolled through several inconsequential exchanges with Gina about the logistics of packing up her files and cleaning out her office, while she searched for something substantial. A message that would restore her fractured ego, even for a minute, by reminding her that she was, not so long ago, someone who had important places to be, urgent things to do.

And there it was, finally. A text from Steph: 'Need to talk to u re: Baker appeal – research on evidentiary argument.'

Mara closed her eyes again and smiled, allowing herself to ignore, for a second, how long ago it was that she had worked on the Baker appeal, and how it had all ended.

It had started out as the Baker case. Mara's client, Mara's case. Four and a half weeks in the courtroom. Twenty-two witnesses, 209 exhibits. An associate and paralegal had lugged the trial notebooks to the defense table every morning and kept all the documents straight. But it was Mara who examined all the witnesses, offered all the exhibits into evidence, argued all the evidentiary motions. Won the case.

That was almost five years ago, when all was right with the world. When Tom thought his wife was working too hard but didn't suspect anything more. When the only reason they ever said the word 'Huntington' was because it was the name of an avenue five blocks away and they sometimes turned there if traffic was backed up on the main street.

The plaintiff had appealed, and the case worked its way through the appellate system over the following few years – first briefing, then oral argument, then a retrial of the damages issue, then more briefing – at almost the same rate the disease worked its way through Mara, first obliterating her short-term memory, then wreaking havoc on her concentration and judgment.

It crushed her to have to do it, but she brought Steph in on the case before the retrial. 'Just as a backup,' Steph assured her friend. But by the end of the retrial, the backup had become lead counsel as Mara found herself increasingly unable to keep straight which exhibits went with which witness, which legal argument applied to which motion.

Typical Gina, she had come in on a weekend to spare

Mara from watching as an entire file drawer in her office was emptied of its contents. Over time, as knowledge of Mara's condition became public at the firm, the rest of her file drawers would eventually be relieved of their bulging case folders, too, as they were distributed to the other litigation partners – all under Gina's watchful eye at times she knew Mara wouldn't be there to witness it. Seventeen years of her life hauled away in a mail cart. Not having to watch it happen hadn't made it any easier.

Gina. If not for her, Mara's retirement would have come far earlier. Gina had run interference for Mara since the beginning, working overtime to lessen the effects of each symptom as it appeared, delaying the inevitable day when Mara finally had to concede she could no longer effectively represent her clients. Gina became Mara's external memory when her internal one was at its worst – a walking sticky note, reminding her not only about briefing deadlines and hearings, but also Neerja and Pori's anniversary, Steph's children's birthdays.

Later, after the disease shifted its assault from Mara's memory to her emotions, turning her from unflappable to erratic almost overnight, Gina vigilantly kept watch over Mara's office door. Drawing from a litany of excuses, she managed to keep everyone away but Steph, so that no one else would witness what was happening to the once-brilliant lawyer who could no longer control her cases, or her temper.

Mara thought about the hundreds of sticky notes and to-do lists Gina painstakingly maintained for her, frequently skipping lunch to keep the files in up-to-the-minute order, now that her boss was incapable of remembering the status or next steps for any case unless it had been written down.

The extra workload must have almost killed the woman, Mara told Tom and Steph much later.

As Mara got sicker and routine tasks started to take her five times as long, Gina spent more and more time in Mara's office helping, and less and less time at her own desk. As a result, she had to stay later and later, to finish the regular administrative tasks she was responsible for but no longer had time for during the day. Mara's pleas that Gina enlist help from the temp pool went unheeded; Gina didn't want to tip people off that she was falling behind because her boss could no longer think straight.

This time last year, at Dr Thiry's insistence that she must fit more rest days into her schedule, Mara had dropped down to four days a week at the firm. It killed her to do it. It killed her to admit the reason to Kent, the managing partner, too. And she almost hadn't. It was so tempting, and it would have been so easy, to claim working-mother guilt as the reason for the request and hide the truth from him for as long as possible. But she hadn't felt right about it, so she'd let him in on her condition, and the fact that her doctor had advised she would be more productive if she reduced her schedule to four days and allowed her body and brain to recharge on the fifth.

Kent had been remarkably supportive about it, telling her if she could handle four days, the firm would love to have her for those days. He'd scoffed and waved a hand when she told him she would cover Gina's overtime out of her own paycheck, since the reason for it was her condition. He'd refused to agree to her request that he change her title on the firm's masthead from 'partner' to the lesser 'of counsel,' too, telling her in his view, and that of everyone else at Katon Locke, she would always be a full partner.

With Kent's support and Gina's help, Mara gushed to Tom that night, she would be able to pull off a four-day schedule indefinitely.

And then, overnight it seemed (although it hadn't actually happened until last fall), she was suddenly so exhausted by her four days of work that Dr Thiry ordered her to downgrade to three. Three shorter days, at that – three 'baby days,' as she called them – eight to five only, a fraction of the dawn-to-dusk hours she was used to putting in. Not surprisingly, Tom didn't even want her to do three short days. 'Just stop altogether,' he urged. But he knew even as he said it that she would never give up that easily. She talked to Kent again and they agreed she would squeeze out the three-day schedule for as long as her condition would allow.

It allowed six months, until February of this year. At which time, with appalling speed, the woman who used to go for long runs with her husband on weekend mornings could no longer do a simple Downward Dog pose without falling over, could barely hold a coffee cup without spilling, had clumsily allowed a dozen dishes to meet their fate on the kitchen tile. The woman who used to be able to pull off three good days in the office was, without warning, a distant memory.

It was the high CAG score, Mara told Those Ladies. But she didn't say it to Tom; he didn't like hearing her talk about it. 'It just bloody figures, doesn't it?' she said to Steph over drinks one night. 'Wouldn't you know that of all people, I'd be the one to get the overachieving, Type A version of the disease. For once in my life, I'd love to know what it's like to do something the slow way.'

By the beginning of February, just two months ago, she was struggling to put in one productive day each week.

And that's when Kent cried uncle. He sidled into her office one afternoon, closed the door behind him and said, 'Mara, we need to talk.'

It was beyond impressive, how long she'd managed to work, he told her. He would forever consider her the bravest person he'd ever had the honor of knowing. 'But I have an entire firm to consider,' he said, his arms waist-high, palms turned to the ceiling. Pleading with her to understand his position. Begging her to forgive him. 'I have to think about our clients.'

He couldn't risk that her condition, which seemed to be racing along much faster suddenly, might cause her to overlook an important deadline on a case, or forget to include a vital argument in a legal brief. 'And I know you wouldn't want that to happen, either,' he said, and his expression showed he believed he was thinking of her, too, and not just the bottom line. 'I know you'd never forgive yourself if it did.' If they were in another line of work, he said, one that didn't rely so heavily on mental acuity . . .

And Mara had stood then, nodding and forcing her lips into a smile and letting him think she did understand, she did think he was considering her in addition to the firm's profits, she did forgive him, while she gently pushed him out of her office. 'I'll make arrangements with Gina to clear out my things,' she said, before closing the door behind him, locking it, falling to the carpet, curling into the fetal position and crying.

That was it, then. Her career was over. The life she had dreamed of since she was a child, had worked tirelessly toward for four years of undergrad and three years of law school, had screeched to a halt. The titles – lawyer, litigator, partner – she had acted humbly about but felt so proud of no longer applied to her.

It took her two hours to gather the strength to pick herself up off the floor, walk to her desk and call Tom to come to get her. It took her a week to muster up the emotional strength to call Kent and talk through logistics. They agreed she'd stick with her one-day-a-week schedule for as long as it took her to pack up her office, send any old case files to the storage room, and give any still-relevant research files to Steph or her other partners.

At the end of February, she boxed up the last of her personal belongings and said her final goodbye – to her colleagues, to her office, to the career she had lovingly devoted almost twenty years of her life to, and had intended to thrive at for at least that many more. On her final day, she gazed out over Dallas from her window on the thirty-third floor, admiring for the last time the view that had kept her company through endless hours of trial prep, brief writing and research. She studied the thick metal window frame and the latches that held it closed. In under a minute, she thought, she could release the casement, push it free, fit herself through the opening. But she reminded herself of her promise, and told herself she still had more time.

She held it together as she pulled her office door closed behind her for the last time. Smiled through the retirement dinner they threw for her at a swanky restaurant downtown. Nodded graciously at the speeches Kent and the other partners made about her, signaling the inglorious and premature end to a brilliant career. It was only at home that she lost it, first in Tom's arms, and then weeks later, when it was clearly upsetting him that she was still distraught, in the shower whose thunderous blast, she had gratefully come to realize, drowned out even the loudest weeping.

20

Scott

Later, Scott wouldn't remember what he taught his classes for the rest of the day, or what homework he assigned. He had a vague recollection that Pete had come into the classroom for lunch, as he always did, and asked a torrent of questions to elicit the reason why Scott was staring catatonically at the floor. He recalled Pete swearing in a long stream of choice expletives, so he was certain he must have relayed his conversation with Janice, but he couldn't remember saying the words out loud: 'Curtis is gone.'

After school, he walked to his car on autopilot and headed, as was his habit, to Logan. Only when he turned the corner and the school came into view, its masses of children swarming around the playground equipment, lining up for school buses, greeting parents, did he remember he wasn't picking Curtis up today. Or any day.

He pulled over and watched the little bodies spill from the door to waiting cars and buses and swing sets, scanning each small form for Curtis, each larger one for Janice or LaDania. He didn't spot them, and he waited awhile longer for them to come out later, maybe with the principal or

Miss Keller to accompany them, keep Curtis in line. The playground equipment blurred a little in his vision as he realized he had missed them. Not that seeing the boy from two hundred feet away would have made up for not taking him home. But it would have been something.

He hit the radio button and a Motown song came on. He wasn't a crier, but hearing Smokey again so soon might be the thing that set off the tracks of his own tears. He hit the button again and drove the rest of the way in silence.

Laurie was waiting for him in the front hall when he walked in and she threw herself at him. 'Janice called me. She told me everything. I'm so angry with LaDania I could—' She shook her head, evidently not willing to vocalize what she was tempted to do to Curtis's mother. 'She said she was going to come later for his things, and I told her to come right away instead. So you didn't have to be here. She left a few minutes ago. What can I do?'

Bring him back, Scott wanted to say. But there was what he wanted her to do, and what she wanted him to say. And a vast chasm between the two. 'Maybe a drink?' he said.

'A beer, or something stronger?' She looked at him closely. 'Something stronger coming up,' she said. 'Why don't you sit in the family room and I'll bring it to you?'

Moments later, she lowered herself to the couch beside him, handing the glass over with one hand and patting his knee with the other. 'One bit of good news. Janice told me LaDania said yes to Monster Trucks. You can get him early on Sunday morning, drop him back off whenever. At least you two will have your last big day, right?'

He gave her the slight smile she was waiting for and took a sip.

'I thought I'd order in,' she said. 'Thai? I figure the last thing you'll want is the spaghetti we were—'

'Thai would be good. Thanks. You want to sit, let me call it in?'

'I already called. It'll be here in an hour. Want me to turn on the TV?'

'I might take a nap upstairs, if you don't mind.'

'Sure.'

'You want to come?'

She shook her head and reached for a book sitting on the coffee table. He recognized it from the tall stack of baby books in the corner. 'I want to read a little. I'll call you when it's here.'

Upstairs, he fought and quickly lost the bet with himself that he could walk past Curtis's room without looking in. The room hadn't looked this tidy since before Curtis moved in, and despite the many times Scott had nagged the boy to pick up the clothes and toys that constantly littered the floor, the lack of little-boy detritus made him feel sick. The closet door was closed, and he guessed Laurie had done that on purpose, to spare him from seeing the empty shelves and hangers inside. She had sent Janice away with two overstuffed duffel bags, she'd told him. She focused on clothes first but filled any leftover space with as many toys as she could.

Flopping onto the bed, he leaned against the headboard and slowly swiveled his head around the room. Commit it to memory now, he thought, before Laurie makes her way inside with cans of paint and fabric for curtains suitable for a baby girl. Take it all in. This is what the room looked like when you had a son.

Every item in the room came with a memory. *Stuart Little*, which had surprisingly not been crammed into a

179

duffel but faced him from the bookshelf, came with a thousand. A section of the shelf was empty, so it was clear Laurie had sent some books. Had she kept this one on purpose, given how much sentimental value she knew it held for him? It was nice of her, he thought, but the little man should have the book, and the photo inside. He would mail it to LaDania's address tomorrow.

On the windowsill above the bookshelf he spotted a few green army men, detached now from the rest of the infantry, which had been piled in a heap on the city-map rug earlier today but must have been packed into a duffel. He'd mail those guys, too. Maybe he should take a more thorough inventory of the remaining contents of the room; maybe send a pretty large package to the kid.

He'd spare the boy a long, emotional letter about how much he missed him, but he'd tape a note to the army men, something to let Curtis know Scott was thinking about him. Smiling, he thought of the perfect thing to write: *Would you rather shove these army guys up your nose or melt them into liquid and drink them?*

As he stared at the green plastic toys, he heard Curtis's voice announcing their next mission, which always involved rescuing the area-rug city from its latest invaders – the toy dinosaurs, or some Lego monster he had built for the purpose, or the most dreaded enemy of all: Scott, aka the Giant Shoes. 'Now, listen up, men, I've got bad news. I know you *thought* you were going to have a little more R&R tonight, but the fact *is*, the Giant Shoes just showed up, and we're all probably going to be ordered to go to a *lights-out* situation. You know I've got a plan, though, like I always do. And let's face it, the Giant Shoes aren't the smartest enemy on the planet.'

But the commander had fallen pretty quickly that night, Scott recalled, as, faux-offended, the Giant Shoes stepped gently on half the green unit and pretended their next landing place would be the commander's hand. The commander jumped up and onto the safety of his bed, where the Giant Hands, evil companion of the Giant Shoes, proceeded with the Tickle Torture until the commander shrieked his surrender and agreed to go to sleep.

Standing, Scott went to the window and picked up the three army men, turning them over in his hand and hearing Curtis's voice bark commands, reports from 'the front,' strategies for attacking or retreating. On the other hand, Scott thought, sticking the plastic toys in his pocket, how many soldiers did the boy need? He wouldn't miss three. But in case he asked about them, Scott would keep them in his bedside table drawer for a while. He could always mail them later if requested, and if not, he thought Commander Jackson would approve of his installing a small armed unit in the drawer to protect his watch and pocket change.

For that matter, he wondered, stooping to lift *Stuart Little* from the shelf, did it make sense to mail the book? What if the boy lost interest in the mouse, as surely he would? What if it sat unread in some closet at LaDania's, only to be tossed unsentimentally into a garbage bag one day, either by a mother who was unaware of its significance or by a boy who was suddenly too cool for such an immature story? What if the photo met a similar fate? And it would, of course.

He slid the paper out and, as Curtis had done only the night before, traced an index finger along the outline of the two subjects. It was more like one two-headed subject;

they were pressed so close together in their nightly tuck-in pose that where one ended and the other began wasn't readily discernible. He thought about the somber expression on Curtis's face when he'd held the photo the night before, then imagined the look of embarrassment the boy might wear a year from now, on seeing how he used to cuddle at bedtime with a man he wasn't even related to. Of course, the picture would find its way into a refuse bin if he were to mail it.

The thought made Scott queasy but he chastised himself to cut the drama. How long could a child be expected to remember his ninth year? Closing his eyes, he tried to remember one thing he'd done when he was that age. There was the time he received a Detroit Lions jersey for Christmas and insisted on wearing it over the suit his mother made him wear to church. Or was he nine then, or ten? He pictured his elementary school and struggled to remember where his second-grade classroom was. Top floor, toward the front – or was that the year he was on the ground floor, near the office? He stopped the exercise without putting himself through the paces of trying to recall his teacher or the names of any of his friends.

This year had been unforgettable for Scott, but that didn't guarantee it would be the same for the boy. In fact, the better bet was that this year wouldn't carry a fraction of the importance to Curtis. Sure, Scott was a hero figure right now, but what about five years from now? He would still be deeply affected by the boy's absence from this Royal Oak bedroom then, but over in Detroit, would the name Scott Coffman evoke hero worship, or just a cloudy memory?

He tucked the book in his back pocket. It would join the army unit in his bedside table drawer.

Deciding it was best not to push himself, he left the closet door closed and took in the rest of the room. Laurie would keep the rocker in here for the baby, and that was fine with him. It was there he had honed his nurturing skills – rocking Curtis one night when a painful earache kept him up. 'I'm too old to be rocked to sleep,' the child complained weakly before resting his head on Scott's shoulder and nudging the man's arm until Scott wrapped it around the boy and pulled him close.

'I won't tell anyone,' Scott whispered.

He couldn't guess how many hours he'd spent in the chair over the past twelve months, holding spelling lists while Curtis stood on the city rug, trying to say the right letters in the right order, or listening to some wild tale the boy was telling about what he'd done at school. Most of the time, the stories needed to be acted out, with the bed, the floor underneath it, the interior of the closet and Scott's lap all composing the stage. A few times Curtis had been sick, or homesick for his mother, or inexplicably sad, and had asked Scott to 'just be with me until I fall asleep.' On those nights, Scott balanced classroom papers on his knee or chatted with LaksMom and the others on the forum, often describing the sight and sounds of the boy dozing a few feet away.

'You're a born father,' 2boys had commented once, in an uncharacteristic display of sincerity. It was before Scott and Laurie had seen the positive sign on the pregnancy test. 'I know it's gonna happen for you someday,' 2boys wrote. 'The universe can't waste a guy like you.'

That was the night Scott suggested the idea of an older-child adoption to Laurie. LaksMom had warned him that the cost of baby adoption wasn't unlike that of a European sports car. They'd spent their sports car money on IVF by then, though, with another installment left to go. If it didn't work, they wouldn't have the option of holding out for adopting a baby.

But aside from the money, it was a no-brainer to adopt an older boy or girl, in Scott's view, a local kid from the local foster care organization. Rescue a kid who might otherwise languish in the system, and in return you have an instant family, no waiting. Win-win. After all, the point was to be parents, right? The point wasn't how the child came to them in the first place.

It turned out being a parent wasn't the only point for Laurie. She wanted to be the parent of her own child. Adoption wasn't Plan B for her, she told him – it was Plan Z. All stops needed to have been pulled, and pulled again, before she'd consider adopting. Adopting a baby, that is. One too young to come with any significant emotional baggage. Once a child was past a year or two, in her view, it was too late – the emotional bags had been packed, and often to the point of bursting.

'They don't take those kids out of happy homes, you know,' she told him. She had heard horror stories about foster care kids with attachment issues, emotional walls, night terrors. About lying, stealing. Kids constantly testing rules, pushing boundaries.

And she had dreamed of babies. Pictured them, planned for them, designed a nursery for them in her mind. One after another in the little room at the top of the stairs, until they were big enough for a toddler bed in one of the other rooms. And that's where she was keeping her sights set – on chubby, pink babies.

He should have left it at that. That's what Pete told him

later, when Scott described the crying, the slamming doors, the week he spent sleeping on the couch. The things that could never be unsaid.

Think of all the disappointment she had been through, Pete said, and how amazing she had been about it. Did Scott have any idea how fortunate he was? Hadn't he heard about the potential infertility fallout – wives blaming husbands, sex lives coming to a complete standstill, marriages falling apart? Why, Pete asked, would Scott push his astoundingly good luck by continuing to pressure her on this?

But he couldn't help himself. He saw kids in his head, five and ten years old and never knowing what it is to feel wanted, to belong. And he saw what became of those kids later – he drove past them every day on his way home from work. Rough kids with vacant expressions, eyeing him at the stoplight, casting up and down the street for cops, calculating whether they had time to hit him up for some money, sell him a sack of weed, knock his head into his steering wheel and take his wallet, his car. Kids who could have turned out so differently.

So he had pushed, long after he should have stopped. Even if IVF worked this time, he argued, maybe they should adopt an older child as well, or start taking in foster children. She'd have her baby, and they'd also be helping some kids who had no one.

It hadn't led anywhere good. He was the one who felt responsible for saving every neglected child in Detroit, she told him. Not her. And she resented the implication that she should feel the way he did. That she was somehow wrong, selfish, for wanting what she wanted. For not sharing his savior complex. 'Goddamn savior complex' was actually how she put it.

She was already sacrificing her husband to the cause of the children of Detroit, she spat at him, and her bitterness was a living thing. He spent more time at Franklin than he did at home, more time planning practices than he did date nights. She had given enough. She was allowed to keep her dream for herself.

Even after she had let him come back to their bed, it had been another two weeks before she would let him touch her.

21

Mara

Mara wiped a hand over her eyes, put her phone back in her purse and looked out at the playground. There was a whirring sound as the tinted window beside her head started to lower. 'No!' She ducked forward, head on her knees. 'I mean, no, thanks. I don't want her to see—'

She heard Harry turn in his seat and she imagined he must be staring at her, wondering what was the matter with her. All the glaring and hissing and now this, complete insanity. But he said nothing, and she heard his seat creak as he turned to the front, another whir as he slid her window closed.

For fifteen minutes, they sat quietly, watching the kids at play.

The kid at play.

Laks climbed up the stairs to the top of the slide, zoomed to the bottom, climbed up again, over and over. The seat of her pink shorts was brown by the time she and Susan moved on to the tetherball pole. They shrieked as they swung for the ball and missed, swung and missed again. Next, they ran races from the pole to the climbing structure at the other end of the playground.

Mara wanted to call out, 'Don't run in flip-flops!' Remarkably, Laks managed to keep from nose-diving into the ground as she ran full tilt with the flimsy pieces of rubber barely attached to her feet. Mara shook her head; she had tripped in hers several times today, walking slowly.

Minutes later, the little girls were on the slide again. Next, running to the monkey bars. And over to the swings, where they lay on their bellies and pretended to be Superman. And now the front of the girl's shirt would match the seat of her pants, Mara thought. She could only imagine how the bottoms of the child's feet looked. She had let Laks talk her out of a bath the night before, and far too many other nights recently, because it had gotten more difficult for Mara to change position from standing to kneeling and back to standing without losing her balance. And she hadn't wanted to admit it to Tom. She would find an excuse to have him give Laks a bath tonight; those feet couldn't go another day without warm water and soap. Really, after the start of April, a nightly bath should be nonnegotiable. Should she write that down, for Tom?

She had already dictated a long letter to him, and one to Laks. They were filed away on a locked drive on her laptop, ready to be printed on Sunday and placed on Tom's pillow for him to find when he came home from his morning run. She had considered leaving them a number of letters, one to read on each birthday, maybe. But then she heard a program on public radio about a mother who had done that very thing, leaving her daughter a letter to read each year, with various bits of motherly advice, and it had been more of a burden for the daughter than a gift. Each year, the daughter would read about what kind of life her mother had envisioned for her, what college major, what career, what kind of husband. If the mother's proscription differed from the daughter's reality, the girl would spend weeks in a guilty depression, worried she was letting her mother down. Or worse, resentful that her mother had burdened her with expectations based on who the girl was years ago, and not on who she had become. There was no room in the letters for her daughter to grow into her own person.

Mara wouldn't do that to her daughter, or her husband. She would leave them each one letter to tell them how much she loved them, how lucky she was to have been part of their lives for a brief, glorious time, how happy she would be for them no matter what they did next. And she wouldn't write out too many instructions for Tom, she decided now, as Laks and Susan performed dramatic dismounts from their swings, faces red, hair matted with sweat, clothes and skin dusted with sand. She'd leave him a few tips, just as she might if she were leaving for a business trip – little logistical things that would make his life easier. But the big things, the Care and Feeding of Lakshmi, she would leave up to him. Let him give in to the bath-avoidance negotiations in early April or even mid-July. He would learn, when the girl's morning body bowled him over the next day and her gritty feet left tracks in her sheets.

He would be fine, Mara told herself. He would mess up in the same ways she had, and maybe in some new ones. But he would be fine.

A whistle shrieked and the noise made Mara's hand wave into the hard plastic door beside her. She swore under her breath as the swarm of kindergartners moved its way from the playground equipment over to the door of the school, where a playground attendant stood, arms directing them

189

into a line. An airport worker on a runway. Rubbing her hand, she cursed silently again at her nervous system's inability to deal with loud noises.

'That was fast,' Harry said. 'Recess used ta be thirty minutes when I was a kid.'

'Same here,' she said, craning to find the clock on the dashboard. 'Um, the meter stopped when you turned the car off. Could you put the fifteen minutes back on?'

'Yuh, I could.' But he didn't.

'Harry, don't you make your living by driving a cab?'

'Yuh, I do.'

'Well, here's the thing, my friend. Cabdrivers make money by running the meter.'

'Huh.' He pretended to think about that for a bit. 'Excellent tip. But this little detour ain't gonna make or break me.'

'Well,' she said, 'what if I wanted you to drive me straight here one day? Not as a detour, but a final destination? You'd let it run then, wouldn't you? Or do I need to call someone else, if I want to do that? Someone who'll let me pay.'

'You'd call another cabbie?' He stabbed an imaginary knife into his heart.

'Not unless I have to. I won't have you driving me here for free.'

'When?'

'Tomorrow?'

'Done.'

'You'll run the meter?' She pointed to the machine.

'You'll only call me?'

'Deal.' She smiled, extending a hand toward him.

'Deal.' They shook. Harry started the car, gave her a thumbs-up sign and a broad smile in the mirror and pulled away.

Harry stabbed a thick finger at his window as he pulled up in front of the house. 'Looks like ya got some callers.'

Mara set cash for the fare on the console beside him before looking out her window to see her parents standing at the front door, Neerja holding a casserole dish, Pori a plastic bag with the telltale markings of Agarwal's Indian Grocery.

'Ya havin' a cover-dish party? Looks like you've got company and they brung dinner.'

'Nope, no cover-dish party. That's my parents. They often find they've inadvertently made too much food. Always, conveniently, in an amount precisely enough for my family. I'm guessing they also mistakenly bought entirely too much at the grocery store again, too.'

He shook his head and chuckled. 'Shoo, they got the wrong daughter, didn't they? They sure enough did not get the bring-me-dinner kinda daughter.'

Mara laughed. 'You're right about that. Only for some reason, they haven't figured out in forty-two years what you figured out in twenty-four hours.'

'Want me ta keep goin'?' He put his hand on the gearshift, ready to put the car into drive and pull away.

'Oh, no! And I shouldn't have sounded so rude. They're wonderful, and they mean well. But I was going to make dinner tonight. I am perfectly.' She brought a hand down hard on the seat. 'Capable.' Another slam of her hand. 'Of making. Dinner.' She aimed a determined look through the glass, making the silent point to her parents: she was not helpless. They needed to stop treating her like she was.

They needed to stop treating her like she was made of glass, too, Mara thought, remembering what had transpired after their last visit to the house. It was a few days earlier, on the weekend. Pori and Neerja had come for lunch (which they had brought with them), and later they took Laks out for ice cream and a walk. Not an hour after they had dropped their granddaughter back at home, Mara asked the girl to put away her Barbies and the answer was a cheerful, 'Sure, Mama.'

Mara rolled her eyes and marched straight to their room to find her husband and complain. He looked at her curiously and she reminded him that if Laks were responding according to her true nature, the answer would have been 'Can't I do it later, Mama?' Or 'But I'm going to play with them again in a minute.' Responses that were completely normal and expected from a child her age, and especially that particular child. 'Sure, Mama' wasn't normal.

Little Miss Perfect was in the house, Mara said to Tom, and she knew who was behind it. Coincidentally, her daughter's Little Miss Perfect routine always seemed to start just after she had spent time with her grandparents. The girl couldn't sustain it, of course, and Mara was thankful for that. Laks was incapable of lasting more than half a day in 'Yes, ma'am' mode before she broke script and acted like herself again, fighting with her mother about the most ridiculous of things.

But those half days with Little Miss Perfect were infuriating, and when they occurred, Mara barely recognized her daughter in the phony, solicitous child standing before her, asking if there was anything she could do to help, offering to carry this or reach for that. Tom had shrugged, unwilling to concede there was cause for concern. Laks was growing up, he said. Kids don't argue all their lives. But Mara was on to him, she warned, and she was on to her parents. It wasn't that Laks had miraculously matured fifteen years in a few months, and everyone knew it. It was that she was under strict orders from her grandparents, with the obvious consent of her father, to never talk back to her sick mother. And those were orders that needed to be rescinded immediately.

Mara was not helpless, and she was not made of glass. She didn't need to be propped up on soft pillows while her parents ran her household for her, and she wouldn't shatter if someone argued with her. And Pori and Neerja, whether they wanted to or not, needed to get that through their heads.

Mara was stirred from the noiseless lecture she was making to her parents by the sound of Harry unclipping his seat belt.

When he put his hand on the door, she said, 'Don't help me out, Harry. Please.'

'Oh, yer dad'll wanna come, I s'pose. Walk ya to the door.'

'He will, but he knows better about that, at least.'

She unfastened her seat belt, but didn't move to get out. 'I suppose you think I'm insane, letting you help me when no one's around but not when someone is. Maybe even selfish, letting a perfect stranger walk me into the house on Monday, the way I let you, but not my own father.'

Harry cleared his throat and she looked up to find him in the rearview mirror.

'I wasn't always a cabbie,' he said. 'I used ta be . . .' He paused. 'Somethin' more. Years ago, in Tulsa.' He turned away from the mirror then and looked out the windshield for a moment. Mara thought she saw wistfulness in his profile, and she wondered if he was imagining how things were then, when he was 'somethin' more.' He found her eyes again in the mirror and continued. 'When I had ta

193

slide down a peg or two and take this job, I didn't wanna do it there, where people'd known me as . . . someone else. Someone better. So I came here, where people never knew me any different than I am now.

'People here, they don't look at me the way they used ta know me then, when I was . . . so much more. They don't get this . . . thing in their eyes, this look that shows it's so sad for 'em ta see how far I've fallen.' He frowned as though picturing the looks of pity he was seeking to avoid. ''Cause they don't know that about me. If I had ta do this in Tulsa, see those looks in people's faces all the time?'

He shook his head. 'So, no. I don't think you're insane. Or selfish. I think you'd rather deal with someone from Tulsa, who never knew ya when, and doesn't always look at ya like he did.'

'Jesus,' Mara said, incredulous. 'Were you a shrink in Tulsa? Bartender? Priest? Mind reader?'

'Ha,' he laughed. 'Nah.'

'Harry?'

'Yuh?'

'I'm sorry about whatever brought you from Tulsa to here.'

'Huh,' he said, looking away from the mirror again for a second before looking back. ''S no big thing.'

'Oh, don't you dare try to fake a faker.' She winked at him, then shoved her door open and fought her way out of the car.

She knocked on his window from outside the car and he put it down.

'You know,' she said, 'I'm throwing a little caution to the wind this week. You saw how I was on Monday, the first time you tried to help me. I don't usually stop hissing, the way I did with you. So it's not as if I let strangers help me all the time, and not my own parents.'

He smiled. 'I'm the lucky one, I guess.'

'Ha,' she laughed. 'That's one way to look at it.'

'Well, it's the way I'm lookin' at it.' He lifted a driving log and pen from the console and poised to write something down. 'Same time tomorrow?'

'Actually, does ten forty-five work? Morning recess is at eleven.'

He nodded, making a note. 'I'll ring the doorbell. Take advantage of the chance ta help while you're still throwin' yer caution around.'

'I know you will.'

'It's possible I'm about as stubborn as ya are.'

'Oh, more probable, I'd say, than possible.' She smiled. 'But it might explain why we're so . . .' She shrugged and looked over the top of his cab, uncertain whether to send her thoughts about him into the air where he could hear them. It was preposterous for her to feel so close to someone she barely knew. More preposterous still to say it out loud.

'Yuh,' he said. 'I s'pose it might.'

'Marabeti!' Neerja called from the front door.

Mara turned to wave at them while Neerja reached to hold Pori back as he made an instinctive move toward his daughter.

'Hello, daughter,' he called. 'Your mother and I were hoping you could take some food off our hands before it spoils.'

Mara turned to Harry, who gave her a knowing smile, then thrust his arm out the window and up to the sky in a high salute before pulling away.

22

Mara

Her parents were a pair. They were precisely the same height, and as usual, they were dressed for a cocktail party rather than a quick meal delivery. Pori wore pressed khakis, dress sandals and a silk shirt, and Neerja wore a linen dress. Her dress was the same lilac as his shirt; it was a funny thing she had started years ago and couldn't be talked out of. She had stopped short of fastening her hair with a lilac tie, at least – this time, anyway. And that was the only place they didn't match; Pori's remaining fringe of hair was now completely gray, where his wife's long braid was still at least a quarter dark black.

'We've only stopped by for a moment,' Neerja said. 'To bring you some moorgh and rice and some of the extra samosas we bought at Agarwal's.' She held the grocery bag aloft. 'We won't stay long. Although I'm dying to get at this garden. I see a few stray weeds I'd like to get my hands on . . .' She let her sentence fade as she studied the garden, no doubt making a mental plan of attack.

Mara frowned. This was not how they had intended to spend their retirement years. As long as she could remember, they had talked about traveling. They were always bringing brochures to show her and Tom – of the Aztec ruins they wanted to see, the boat ride in Venice they'd always dreamed of going on, the Norwegian fjords they couldn't wait to photograph. They had pored over travel guides at the library, made lists of their top twenty destination choices, spent hours reordering the list, refining it.

And then Mara learned her CAG repeat was 48, and they stopped bringing brochures around. And started bringing casseroles and groceries, tools for the garden and cleaning supplies for the bathroom. Mara had been stubbornly shooing away her parents' help since elementary school, insisting they let her 'do it myself,' no matter what it was. She was as opposed to being treated like an incapable child again as she was to watching them sacrifice their golden years for her. So she made mild suggestions that they need not do all of her cooking and cleaning and gardening for her; she could still manage it herself. When that didn't work, she turned to pleas, and when those failed, too, she finally resorted to giving strict orders that they knock it off, stop treating her like she wasn't capable of running her own house.

They promised they'd stop, but all they did was change their approach. It wasn't that they considered her incapable, they told her; it was simply that they missed being able to vacuum a real house now that they lived in the small condo they'd moved to in retirement. It was such a pleasure to run the machine over a few rugs at her place, for old times' sake. Also, it was good for them to keep moving at their age, and what better exercise than stooping to pull weeds in her garden? As for the food, everyone knew how difficult it was to cook for only two – easier to make a larger meal and share it.

And this, Mara knew, is how it would be from now on. Because they would never, not even for a week, leave their sick daughter. And by the time she died, the Aztec ruins would need to be struck from the list because they would no longer be able to climb that far. The gondola trip in Venice would be out, too; they'd be far too unsteady on their feet by then to manage stepping down into a rocking boat. If there was a degree in Making Sacrifices for Loved Ones Without Complaint, the two people standing on her porch this moment would be the best-qualified professors on the planet.

Mara hoped it wouldn't occur to them later that in modeling such selflessness to their daughter, they had inspired the promise she made to herself four years ago. She hoped they would find her actions selfish, cowardly. She hoped they would never realize that as much as she didn't want to have to live with HD anymore, she didn't want them to have to live with it, either.

Hanging on to the bitter end, which was of course what they wanted her to do, wouldn't change the fact that they were going to outlive their own child. The only thing her hanging on would accomplish would be to annihilate any chance they had of living the rest of their years the way they had dreamed. The way they deserved, after everything they had done for her.

No way in hell was she going to take that from them.

On the porch, she kissed them both before fishing in her purse for keys. The key refused to steady itself long enough to slip into its spot on the door, and before she could object, her father broke free from his wife's hold and helped Mara guide it into the lock. He stepped into the house first and extended a hand to usher first Mara, then her mother, through the doorway.

'Oh, stop that, Pori,' Neerja hissed, rolling her eyes at Mara in an exaggerated and entirely fake display of disgust in her husband. She held the casserole dish out, forcing him to leave Mara's side. 'Take this, please, set it on the counter and let the woman walk into her own house. Leave the bag here and I'll bring it in later.' Her mother was trying to make her voice sound cross but Mara caught the affection in the older woman's eyes, and before Pori turned, Neerja crinkled her face into a smile. 'Thank you, Puppa.'

Turning to Mara, Neerja clapped her hands together, placing them under her chin as she surveyed the living room. 'The house looks lovely, as usual, Beti.' It was a total lie, of course, and Mara knew the second she left the room, her mother would be doing a quick once-over with a duster, one eye on the doorway to be sure she wasn't caught.

'What's in the bag, Mom?' Mara asked, frowning. She had told her mother to stop wasting her afternoons cooking for Mara's family.

'Oh, just some samosas,' Neerja said, looking guilty. Quickly she added, 'Store-bought, obviously. I only made the casserole.' Mara arched a brow and her mother said, 'I'm sorry. But it's Laks's favorite and your father insisted we bring—'

'Fine,' Mara sighed. Store-bought samosas were a compromise, at least. 'Let's put them in the kitchen, and I'll pour you and Dad a glass of wine.'

Before Neerja could suggest they have Pori pour the wine to avoid certain disaster if Mara tried wielding the heavy bottle, Steph's voice rang from the doorway. 'Did someone just offer drinks?' She looked askance at Neerja. 'And did people not answer in the affirmative?'

Gina trailed behind Steph, a full foot shorter, and possibly a foot wider, than long, lithe Steph. They were like a cartoon pairing, Mara thought: tall, blond, confident Steph and her squat, dark-haired, timid sidekick.

She'd known Steph almost twenty years, starting on the first day of law school orientation at SMU, when by fluke they ended up in neighboring seats in the auditorium for the dean's welcome speech. From that moment on, they had been almost inseparable, to the amusement, and sometimes mild annoyance, of their husbands. They'd spent hours together in the law school library, bent over casebooks and outlines. They'd freaked out together over final exams. Celebrated together when they made law review. Shopped together for interview suits when it was time to trade their sweats and backpacks for heels and briefcases.

They had summer-interned together at Katon Locke at the end of second year, and that August they'd sat together on Steph's balcony with a pitcher of Long Island iced tea, reading each other's offer letters from the firm, only 'consulting with' their husbands after they had already decided, together, that they'd accept. Over their almost twenty years together at the firm, they'd held countless 'meetings' in the ladies' room or in each other's office to gripe about caustic opposing counsel and micromanaging clients. Or to complain about incompetent secretaries, Mara always patiently trying a 'make it work' strategy before gently returning them to the secretary pool, Steph generally jumping pretty quickly to a 'show 'em the door' solution.

They had tried cases together. They had made faces at each other over the table at dull Bar Association meetings and litigation practice group 'lunch and learn' sessions. They were godmother to each other's children. Mara was in the delivery room when Steph had Christopher and then, two years later, Sheila. Steph was waiting at Tom and Mara's house at three in the morning, a pot of coffee on, a freezer full of casseroles and a table covered in baby supplies, when they arrived home from India with baby Laks.

'Hi, Mrs Sahay,' Gina said politely, extending a hand to Neerja as Steph grabbed the woman firmly, kissed her cheek and said, 'Mummy! Where's that handsome husband of yours?'

'Hello, you two!' Neerja said. She clapped her hands once and held them together under her chin as she watched them both greet Mara with hugs and kisses. 'I always love to see Those Ladies together.' She turned, worried, to Mara. 'I keep forgetting I'm not supposed to use that term anymore. Lakshmi isn't home yet, is she?'

Mara shook her head. 'Tom picked her up from school and took her to get new ballet shoes. She was almost expelled last Saturday, or so she says, for having "falling-apart shoes." But she doesn't mind us saying "Those Ladies," anyway, remember? It's "Dose Yadies" she was in such a huff about.'

'Oh, that's right,' her mother said. 'I knew that. Anyway, let me get your father and we'll get out from underfoot so you can visit with your friends.'

'Please stay,' Mara said, gesturing to Steph and Gina. 'They want to see you as much as they want to see me, anyway. I think Steph probably followed the scent of samosas.'

'Samosas?' Steph asked, her face brightening. 'Where?'

Neerja held up the bag proudly and Mara's heart broke to see how delighted her mother was to be praised, not criticized, for bringing food.

23

Scott

After the hearing the previous April, Scott had taken Bray and Curtis to LaDania's apartment to pack Curtis's things. Graffiti covered almost every inch of brick at the complex, and parts of the doors and windows. There appeared to be only one functioning car in the parking lot. The others were missing a wheel or two, their bare axles propped up on two-by-fours and cinder blocks.

A few rusted grocery carts took up one parking space and a picnic table sat in another, three rough-looking teenagers sitting on top of it, their feet on the benches, bottles wrapped in brown paper in their hands. They called 'Hey' to Bray as he, Scott and Curtis got out of the car. Bray called 'Hey' to them, and under his breath said to Scott, 'Lock the car.'

The smell in the hallway made Scott gag: a combination of sweat, vomit and urine. The graffiti continued on the inside walls and up the stairwell. The stench carried into the stairwell, too, the confined space making it even stronger. He was glad Laurie hadn't come. Over the years, he had dropped Bray off outside many times, but had never been inside. He always offered to walk Bray in, but the boy always quickly declined. Scott had guessed why, but never guessed it was this bad.

When Bray unlocked his mother's apartment, the smell of spoiled milk hit Scott before he could see anything. It was worse than the vomit and urine in the hallway. When Bray turned on the light, Scott saw at least a dozen roaches scurrying across the counter and floors.

'Visitors,' Curtis announced casually, as he gingerly stepped over them.

'He doesn't ever want to kill anything,' Bray said to Scott. 'But you can't let them stay, Curtis. Where are those traps I got you?'

The boy shrugged and Bray brushed the roaches off the counter and stepped on as many as he could. Some escaped into the space between the counter and the small grime-covered stove. Curtis watched them go, looking pleased they had dodged the stomping. Scott took in the rest of the kitchen, which overflowed with dirty dishes. There was a cereal box on the counter, tipped over, its contents spilled out. A blackened, oozing banana sat nearby and beside that, the source of the offensive odor, a half-full container of milk.

Bray shook his head in disgust but put a gentle hand on his brother's head. 'Curtis, you've got to put stuff away. Remember how I showed you?'

He picked up the milk, shoved some dirty dishes to one side of the sink and poured the liquid down the drain. But when he turned the tap to wash it down, only a clanging noise came out of the faucet. He turned to his brother, a confused look on his face.

'*That's* why I couldn't wash the dishes,' Curtis said. 'We haven't had water in a while.'

Bray sighed and turned to Scott. 'This is the reason I picked Michigan over all those other schools. So I could stay close by. And I still wasn't close enough. I never knew they didn't have water.' Turning to Curtis, he asked, 'What about the money I made Ma promise to set aside for water and heat and electric?'

Curtis looked at the floor, plainly unhappy about telling on his own mother. 'Think she used it for something else.'

'Where've you been taking showers?' Bray asked.

'Johnsons'.'

'Have they been feeding you, too?'

Curtis shrugged. 'Sometimes. They don't always have a lot of food at their place, though. So I usually tell them I already ate.'

Scott tried to conceal his shock but Bray caught his expression. 'You don't get fat living here,' he said, flashing a quick smile and patting his lean stomach. 'Those rich kids from the suburbs, they're all too heavy to keep up on the court. Eight Mile diet, that's what every athlete needs.'

'Maybe Pete should move in, once your mom gets back,' Scott said. He and Bray had been chiding Pete about his weight since Scott and Pete started coaching Bray at Franklin.

Bray laughed, and Scott handed Curtis the duffel bag he had brought from home. 'Little Man, why don't you grab your things? Then we've got to let your brother get on his way to school.'

'Little Man,' Curtis giggled. 'I like that.' He grabbed the duffel and disappeared as Scott and Bray stepped into the living room. Scott noticed only one door leading from the room and guessed the place had only one bedroom.

A glance at the couch confirmed it; there was a pillow on one end, a sheet crumpled up on the other.

Bray followed Scott's gaze. 'My mom sleeps there,' he said. 'She used to sleep in the bedroom, and Curtis was out here. But I made her switch with him. She gets home too late, I told her. She needs to let him sleep in there so she doesn't wake him when she gets in.'

Scott couldn't hide his surprise.

'She goes out after he's asleep,' Bray said, clearly not happy about it. 'I've told her a hundred times, you can't leave a kid that age on his own, but she says the Johnsons are right here if he needs them. Only Mr Johnson's asleep by eight, and Mrs Johnson can't really get up the stairs anymore. Those kinds of details don't really interest my mom, though. So I've been having a friend down the hall check in every night, to make sure Curtis is okay, gets to bed on time.' He shrugged. 'Best I know to do. Should've told him to check on the water, too, I guess.'

He looked at the couch again and shook his head, as though his mother were sitting there. 'I was thinking last night that her going to jail might be the best thing that's happened to him, you know? I know it isn't great for you and Laurie. But it'll be better for him. When she gets out, he'll be one year older, more ready to take care of himself. I can find a way to get him a cell phone, so he can let me know when this sort of thing goes down.' He gestured to the kitchen sink and shook his head again. 'I can't wait to get him out of here for good. He shouldn't have to live this way.'

Scott was about to speak when Curtis ran into the room. 'Done!' he said, holding up what appeared to be an empty duffel bag. Scott motioned for him to hand it over, and he looked inside. There was one T-shirt and a pair of socks. Scott opened the bag toward Bray so he could peer inside. 'You don't have more clothes than that?' Bray asked.

'Nuh-uh.'

'What about that stuff I bought you over Christmas break?'

'Ma sold it to a lady.'

Bray knelt, a big hand on each of the boy's small shoulders. He hung his head and shook it slowly from side to side, and Scott knew Bray was blaming himself for the conditions in which his younger brother had been living. Bray leaned forward until his forehead rested against his brother's. 'Why didn't you tell me?' he whispered.

'Ma said not to.'

The muscles in Bray's jaw flexed and he turned to the couch again. He took a few deep breaths to control himself before he stood, picked up the bag and walked toward the door, a hand on Curtis's shoulder. 'Let's get you some clothes before I head back to Ann Arbor.'

'Please don't,' Scott said. 'Laurie loves kids' clothes. She'll be ticked if you deprive her of the chance to shop.'

Bray looked at him skeptically.

'Really. She'll love it. Don't take that away from her.'

'Sorry, Coach,' Bray said. 'It's more of a mess than I thought.'

Scott had told his online friends about the apartment a few weeks before, when he was listing for them all the reasons he was struggling with the thought of sending Curtis home. 'Dude,' 2boys had written, 'you've gotta keep the kid away from that. Permanently.' Which was the same thing Scott had told himself countless times beginning that day a year ago, when he drove Curtis from Detroit to Royal

Oak and allowed himself to think about how much better off the boy would be, living in the Coffmans' large, clean house, with all the running water and clean clothes and extra food he wanted, and all the parental supervision and guidance he needed.

But it wasn't that simple. Scott suspected it then and he knew it with certainty now, after a year's worth of discussing the issue with Janice, of personal messaging about it with FosterFranny and reading about it in every book and article he could find on the subject. Children were better off with their parents – that was the bottom line.

There were exceptions, of course – abuse, neglect. But while LaDania may have been exceptionally careless about her young son in the final weeks leading up to her incarceration, she hadn't always been that way. According to Bray, she had always kept it to the 'light stuff' and always had it under control, able to pick it up and set it down again without an issue. Last year, she had hit a streak of bad luck – a lost job, a breakup – and feeling lonely without the comforting presence of her elder son, she had turned to something 'more serious' to get her over the rough spot.

It was bad judgment on her part, but Bray felt confident she had learned her lesson and wouldn't repeat it. She had promised him as much. And despite his anger at her over getting herself locked up and upending her sons' lives for the year, he admitted to Scott and Laurie that for the most part, LaDania had made an effort to be a good mother. A good enough one, anyway – he didn't think she had set out to win any awards. She was a little selfish at times, choosing to sleep late over getting up in time to see her children off to school, to make sure they ate breakfast before they left or had money in their pockets for lunch.

She was a little careless with money, and the fairly frequent sight of an empty fridge for the last few days of the month, and two hungry boys standing in front of it, hadn't done anything to make her more responsible. She was a little too willing to leave the boys to their own devices for long periods of time while she went out with her questionable friends. She wasn't the best at holding down a job, wasn't the most nutrition-minded cook and had never been particularly interested in keeping her apartment clean. As for setting rules and making her children follow them, she saw no point; they knew soon enough if they'd stepped out of line.

But exercising poor judgment didn't disqualify a person from raising her own child. If it did, Janice told Scott, many parents would be disqualified. And if having roaches in the kitchen, being a poor disciplinarian or staying out a little too late now and then with shady people while neighbors looked in on her child meant LaDania didn't deserve to get her son back, then there were plenty of people in Michigan and beyond who had better hand their children over.

FosterFranny told him the same thing in a series of late-night PMs last fall, adding that LMan's story wasn't all that different from that of any number of kids in Detroit, Cleveland, Houston or a hundred other cities around the country. There were plenty of parents who could do better, plenty of children who might get more to eat, more attention, more help with homework if they were sent to live with different families than their own. But that didn't mean taking them out of their homes was the right thing to do. There wasn't a child psychologist in America who would say that a nicer house, better meals and more regimented discipline were better for a child than the love of his own parent.

'The state has no right to require perfection from parents,' Janice told Scott. 'We always hope people will strive to be the best they can be for their children. But if they love them, and want them, and aren't putting them in danger, then we have to consider that to be enough, and move on to the next case.'

Scott wished it could be enough for him, too, to know Curtis was with a parent who loved him and wanted him. He told himself it was – he repeated it every day in the words he'd said to Laurie the day before. But despite the self-talk, he hadn't been able to stop his stomach from burning every time he thought of Curtis living in his old apartment. It tore him apart to think of the boy's potential, and how it would be wasted when he took up his old life again. The homework that would go back to being undone, the reading level that would surely nose-dive at the same rate the boy's visits to the principal's office would skyrocket.

The high school diploma that might never get earned. Never mind about college, and getting out of the crummy neighborhood that had trapped so many, LaDania included, in a downward cycle of drugs and booze and poverty. Bray had fought his way out, but Bray was unique, a one-in-a-million kind of kid with an unusual combination of talent, height, work ethic and intelligence that didn't come from straight DNA, which Curtis didn't completely share with him anyway. Scott hoped eight was too young to tell, but so far it didn't seem like Curtis had the same drive as his brother, the same physical prowess or even the same potential for height. In the Coffmans' house, he could achieve something, make a good life for himself. Scott and

Laurie would have seen to it. Without them? It made Scott's stomach hurt to imagine where the boy would stall out.

He lowered himself into the rocking chair and let his eyes take one more tour around Curtis's abandoned room. 'It's going to be okay,' he said, recalling his mantra, but it came out weak and thin and unconvincing. 'He's going to be okay,' he tried again. But it didn't sound any more true, and as he spoke the words he wasn't sure he believed, he thought the city-map rug, the low bookshelf and the basketball posters all seemed washed out suddenly, as though their vibrancy, their usefulness, their very colors had seeped out of the house now that the boy wasn't coming back.

24

Mara

Mara took in the group of people in her living room and realized that in a few-foot radius sat the four people who, besides Tom and Laks, were most important to her in the entire world. A loud cackle erupted from Steph, and Mara turned to study her friend's profile. As usual, Steph's face was a dichotomy of fast-moving lips and still, intense eyes. She was the first person Tom had called, after Mara's parents, the day they received Mara's CAG score. She'd been waiting by the phone at home; she took the day off, she told Tom, because she knew whatever the news, her response would be loud and obscene.

Sure enough, he'd had to hold the receiver away from his ear as she shouted, 'Goddamn sonofabitch! I'll be there in ten minutes.' She'd repeated the phrase, not quietly, countless times over the next week until Pori was repeating it, too, much to his wife's disapproval. And much to Gina's disapproval, Mara thought, as her eyes moved from one friend to the other. Gina was all southern gentility and conducting oneself appropriately; Steph had no interest in any of that.

Before HD, only Mara's constant refereeing had kept the two women from coming to blows. Kept Steph from coming to blows, that is – Gina would never have participated in such unladylike behavior. But after the bad news came, the relationship between them shifted and the differences that used to annoy them about each other were now sources of good-natured teasing.

It was one of the few positives from the before HD/after HD list, Mara thought, grinning now as Gina put a hand on Steph's forearm in an effort to get her to ratchet down the foul language in front of Mara's parents. Steph shook off Gina's hand and said, in response to a statement Mara hadn't heard, 'I know, that's what I thought! I mean, what the fuck, right, Pori?'

Mara stifled a laugh as Gina shuddered and Neerja pursed her lips. But at least Gina didn't storm out like she might have done before Mara's diagnosis. Although she would never condone the cursing, over the past four years, Gina had learned to appreciate Steph's directness because of the obvious relief Mara felt in having at least one person who could always be counted on to call it as she saw it.

'Yep,' Steph had said to Mara once, after Mara had complained about how the disease was making her face look too angular, 'I can see how you'd think you were looking a bit skeletal. The gray in your hair's not doing much for you, either. Nothing a little color and foundation can't fix, though. I'll get us both on the schedule at the salon. And after, we're going to stop at the makeup counter at Saks, see about getting better foundation.'

And Steph soon saw there was more to Gina than a rotund repository for rules of decorum. She was as loyal and tireless a friend as she had been a secretary, forever culling through the stacks of mail on Mara's kitchen counter and labeling them 'M' or 'T,' and then following up with Mara to make sure she'd gone through hers. She spent a weekend overhauling their laundry room, pantry and front hall closets to make it easier for Mara to keep things in a certain place – all the easier to remember where she'd put something last.

'You're the most organized person I've ever known,' Steph told Gina once. 'You're better than every secretary at the firm, combined.' Mara and Those Ladies were sitting in lawn chairs in Steph's backyard, drinking wine and discussing their own, and each other's, greatest strengths and faults.

'And you're the most direct person I've ever met,' said Gina, quickly adding it was meant as a compliment. 'I wish I could tell more people what I really thought.' It was then that Steph had made the suggestion that between the two of them, Those Ladies would be able to cover every topic Laks would ever need help with. 'So true,' Gina said, laughing. 'You've got me on organizing school supplies and schedules, along with manners, how to write a proper thank-you note, all of that. And Steph on everything no one else wants to face head-on: getting a period, masturbation, oral sex, birth control.' Mara had laughed along with Gina and glanced over at Steph, waiting for her to join in on the joke she'd given wings to.

But Steph's lips were turned down, not up, and Mara saw tears on her friend's cheeks. 'Steph?' Mara asked. 'What's wrong?'

They had been sitting in a loose circle, and Steph picked up her chair, moved it closer to Mara and took Mara's hand in hers. 'I know you worry about how she's going to be when you're—' She choked on a sob and couldn't finish. Mara squeezed her friend's hand and Gina moved her chair closer to the other two and put a hand on Steph's knee. 'When you're gone,' Steph finished, choking out the words. 'But I want you to know' – she looked at Gina – '*we* want you to know—' Steph choked again.

Gina patted Steph's knee and finished the sentence Steph had begun. 'We want you to know,' Gina said, tears streaming down her cheeks, too, 'that we'll be here for Laks. For whatever she needs. Whatever she has questions about. Needs help with. Wants to talk about. Forever.' She reached for each of the other two women's free hands. And then Mara was crying, too, and the three of them sat that way, holding hands and weeping, until Gina finally wiped her eyes and sniffed and asked Mara, 'Was it wrong of us to bring it up now? Too early, I mean? Because it's not like Laks will need us for years—'

'Not wrong,' Mara interrupted. 'Wonderful. I worry all the time how she'll be without a mother to turn to. She might not need you right now, but I needed to hear this now. Tom is incredible, you know that. But can you imagine him talking to her about choosing her first bra, or getting her period for the first time, or having her heart broken? These are the kinds of things that keep me up at night. And even though I've always known you two would see her, spend time with her, I would never have asked you to sign on for this kind of thing.'

She looked at each of them in turn, her dark eyes telling them how thankful she was. 'I feel like the two of you have just relieved me of the greatest sorrow I've been carrying. She won't have a mother. She'll have—'

'Two,' they finished with her.

Mara's eyes spilled over again and as a single unit, Those Ladies leaned forward and wrapped their arms around her, a three-person, sobbing huddle of women. Mara's friends had just made a promise that, until ten minutes earlier, she hadn't dreamed of asking of them. Now it seemed to her to be the most important thing she could do for her daughter. For all her lists and plans, she had left out the biggest one. Leave it to Those Ladies to identify and resolve it in the span of half a glass of merlot.

Steph raised her wineglass and the others clinked theirs against it. 'To Those Ladies. The two of us together will never come close to being half the mom Mara is. But we'll damn sure do our best.'

Since that night, Mara had talked to them individually about their respective lists of responsibilities. At yoga one day, Mara told Steph, 'You're on nutrition, fitness, eating disorders, all that sort of thing – you know that, right?' Gina openly admitted to her love/hate relationship with food and her hate/hate relationship with exercise. Tom would lecture on essential amino acids and complete proteins, but what did he know about avoiding the teenage peer pressure to starve yourself? Steph tilted her head as if to say there couldn't possibly be a different choice.

Another time, Gina was updating the various sticky notes around Mara's kitchen, putting things back in their proper place as she went. Mara was peering in the pantry for something to make for dinner. 'You'll tell her things like, figure out your husband's favorite meal and make it for him often, won't you? I'm afraid she'll get so much women's lib blather from Steph she'll end up thinking that doing something nice for your spouse will lead to the complete disenfranchisement of women. I want her to feel free – and generous – in expressing her love, whether it's politically in vogue or not.

'And not just with her spouse, but with everyone. Calling her grandparents to check in, instead of waiting for them to call. I want her to keep all those thoughtful little things in mind, you know? All those extra-mile things that so many people don't bother with, but that can be so important. Calling Tom on his birthday is easy but—'

'She should call him on your anniversary,' Gina said softly.

'Exactly.'

'Already on my list,' Gina said, tapping her temple. 'All of them.'

25

Mara

Laks flew into the living room, shrieking with delight as she discovered her favorite people in the world – her grand-parents, her mother and Those Ladies – sitting together. She hugged her grandparents first, then Mara, Steph and Gina. She settled on Gina's lap, and Mara could hear the two of them whispering about the new ballet shoes. Moments later, Tom walked in and planted kisses on the cheeks of three women, the lips of the fourth. He clasped hands with Pori as he held a small bag out to Laks.

'Right into your closet, please, Miss Messykins, like we discussed.'

'Dadeeeee,' Laks said, angling her eyes at the others. 'Not that name in front of Those—'

'Apologies,' he said. 'Lakshmibeti.'

Gina did a double take and Tom shrugged. 'I only know nicknames. Haven't mastered the rest of it yet. Give me another twenty-two years.' Neerja patted her son-in-law fondly on the arm and smiled knowingly at Mara. It was less about learning a second language for Tom, Mara and her mother knew, than it was about feeling like he belonged in a family. There were no pet names in his childhood, unless 'little asshole, just like your father' counted.

Laks grabbed the bag and ran to her room. 'Mission accomplished,' Tom said to his wife when the girl was out of earshot. 'I believe she'll narrowly avoid death by hanging at Saturday's class. Not sure how she'll fare at the recital, though – I had to give up on the pink tights. They were all either "too strangly" or "too clutchy" or "too" something else I've forgotten, but which seemed to involve the cutting off of her circulation to the point where an amputation was almost required.'

'Well,' Steph said, 'she was with the right parent, then. You could've performed the amputation in the store.'

'Derm, Steph, not surgery. A zit, I could've popped in the store. A leg amp would've been more problematic.'

'What's a zit?' Laks asked, back from her room. 'And what's a leg lamp?'

'Did you put your shoes away?' Mara asked.

'I hung the bag on my door—'

'Please put them where they belong, and where your father told you to put them – on your ballet shelf in your closet.'

'But Maaamaaaa. I want to see Those Ladies before they leave.'

'They'll still be here in two minutes, which is how long it will take you to obey your parents.'

The girl stomped off as loudly as she could, leaving six adults behind who had to fight not to laugh. Thirty seconds later, she was back again, rounding Steph's chair on the way to the kitchen. Steph pulled the child onto her knee, waggling a finger in the small face. 'Lakshmi Nichols. What did I tell you was going to happen the next time you talked back to your mother instead of behaving all "yes, ma'am"-ish like the world's most perfect five-year-old child?'

Laks squeezed her eyes to think. Smiling, she stuck a finger in the air to show she'd remembered. 'Money!'

'That's right.' Steph pulled a dollar out of her purse. 'Remember, there's lots more where that came from. Now, go look in the kitchen to see if there are any more samosas for Auntie Steph.' She set the girl on the floor and gave her bottom a swat. 'Away with you!' Laks, giggling, ran into the kitchen, waving her money.

'Steph,' Gina and Mara said at the same time, in the same stern tone.

'What?' Steph said, shrugging innocently. 'You had a problem with Little Miss Perfect treating you like you're too fragile to be sulked at or argued with. I simply found a way to solve the problem. This is what they pay me for.'

After Steph and Gina left, Mara insisted her parents stay for dinner. They conceded, but on condition Mara let them heat the casserole and set the table while she relaxed in the living room with Tom. Reluctantly, she agreed to their terms, and half an hour later they were all sitting at the dining room table. Pori had set out the good china and silver and Laks clapped her hands once in delight. If she'd only put them a little closer to her chin, Mara thought, she'd be a miniature Neerja.

'Fancy!' Laks said.

'Oh,' Pori said, looking to his daughter, 'was I supposed to save this for a special occasion?'

Mara was ashamed of how worried he was that he'd broken one of her rules.

'This is a special occasion,' she told him. 'My four favorite people together for dinner.'

Laks giggled. 'We're together all the time, Mama. But since we're being fancy, can we say grace? Susan's family says it every single night.'

Mara regarded her daughter in surprise. 'Grace?'

The girl nodded. 'It's something you say before—'

'I know what it is,' Mara said, laughing. 'I'm just surprised to hear you ask about it. But sure. Why not? Let's say grace.'

'Oh, goody!' Laks clapped again and looked around the table, waiting for one of the adults to begin. But three of them weren't Christian and the one who was, Tom, appeared to be at a loss.

'Let me think,' he said. 'It's been a while.'

'What does Susan's family say when they pray, Lakshmibeti?' Neerja asked her granddaughter.

'Only about how they're happy and thankful to be together.'

'There's nothing "only" about being together,' Pori said. 'Isn't that right, Mummy?' He was looking at Neerja. His mouth was curled into a smile but Mara caught the sorrow in his dark eyes. Neerja nodded before brushing a finger across her own eyes.

The reason for their shared sadness hit Mara so heavily she felt her body sag under its weight. Their daughter was dying.

How often had she considered that – really, deeply considered it? She didn't want to admit the answer. Or the fact that when she did think of it, it was only in a context that made clear she was the victim, not them.

'I don't care if their preferred method of dealing with their daughter's incurable disease is to attack the news with a broom and a vacuum and a dish of curry,' she had vented to Tom countless times. 'I am the daughter in question, and I don't want them treating me like I can't look after my own house or feed my own family.'

When was she going to admit they were victims here, too?

Their daughter was dying.

Mara looked at her own daughter and felt the familiar burning pain of incomprehensible loss sear through her body, from her core to the ends of her fingers and toes. How could she have spent her last few days consumed by the scorching agony of facing her last moments with her own child, and not have spent one second acknowledging that her parents had been shrouded in the same pain? She was not the only parent at this table who was losing her baby.

Mara took her mother's hand and Neerja, assuming her daughter's gesture was the start of grace, dutifully took her granddaughter's.

'Only Susan's family doesn't hold hands,' Laks said, but she reached for her father's hand nonetheless, and he reached for Pori's.

Pori took Mara's, then smiled at his granddaughter. 'We won't tell her.'

As the others bowed their heads and Pori said a few words about love and family and new ballet shoes, Mara swiveled her head slowly around the table, letting her eyes rest for a few seconds on each bent head.

Then she closed her eyes, bent her own head and made a silent wish that she had a god to believe in, like Susan's family did. It would be a comfort to think there was something, someplace, after this. That there was a reason for her illness, that it wasn't merely the result of a random

221

lottery drawing she'd lost at birth. That there would be some lesson in it all for Laks.

And, she thought, even if believing didn't bring her comfort, at least it would be nice to have someone to blame.

26

Scott

Wednesday, April 6 @ 11:47 p.m.
MotorCity sent this private message:

This has been great, LaksMama. Thanks for staying up to message me.

I was trying to remember when the last time was that we did this for so long. Seven months ago? When we'd gotten bad IVF results and I was starting to broach the subject of adoption with my wife. There was a window in there where she seemed keen on the baby adoption route and you were the best resource we had about it all. To this day, when I mention you, she gets this smile on her face. I'm surprised she hasn't suggested naming the baby 'LaksMom.' ;) She wanted you to write a book, remember?

Wednesday, April 6 @ 11:49 p.m.
LaksMom sent this private message:

I do. I actually considered it, briefly. But then, as they say, life happened . . .

Wednesday, April 6 @ 11:50 p.m.
MotorCity sent this private message:

It always does.

So. We've been talking about me for too long. I don't know about you, but I'm sick of me. Your turn. What's keeping you up these nights?

Wednesday, April 6 @ 11:51 p.m.
LaksMom sent this private message:

Honestly, I'm in my own head so much these days I've been happy for the chance to get out of it for a while. Can we chalk it up to middle-aged insomnia and move on?

I'm not sick of you at all. I've been thinking so much about you, and feeling bad. I'm not able to help nearly as much as I want to. I wish there was something more I could do. Something more meaningful than PMs.

Wednesday, April 6 @ 11:54 p.m.
MotorCity sent this private message:

Believe me, this past hour has been exactly what I needed. Sometimes, things that seem small end up being the most meaningful, you know?

Thursday, April 7 @ 12:01 a.m.
LaksMom sent this private message:

I absolutely do know that.

Thursday, April 7 @ 12:03 a.m.
MotorCity sent this private message:

Hey, here's something we've sort of danced around a little tonight, but haven't hit right on:

In terms of my lying awake tonight, worrying about how LMan's doing with the sudden turn of events, do you think it's possible he's not as busted up as I am, because as close as we are, he's still got this invisible but unbreakable thread pulling him toward his mom?

Does the bio relationship trump all, do you think?

I'm hoping that's a fair question to ask an adoptive mom, and not a 2boys-type question. If I'm wrong, tell me to F off and we can change the subject.

Thursday, April 7 @ 12:05 a.m.
LaksMom sent this private message:

LOL. You could never ask a 2boys question – you have tact. He has none. ;)

It's a perfectly fair question – to me, anyway. Not sure how other adoptive parents feel, but this is something I think about all the time.

I don't know if you'll love or loathe my latest conclusion, but what I've come to believe is that as much as adults are capable of loving someone else's child as though they were our own, children don't have quite the same ability. They'll always feel the strongest pull toward their biological parents.

I bristled at this in the beginning. Who wants to think that our children aren't as attached to us as we are to them? I wanted to believe what so many adoption advocates say, what so much of the literature claims: an adoptive relationship can be as complete as a biological one. It was heartwrenching for me, to be honest, to think that after five years of raising my daughter from infancy, giving her every ounce of love in my body, she could possibly have a drop of affection left inside her that she's not directing toward me.

225

I'm sure the adoption advocates would take me to task for reaching this conclusion. But as my friend Steph would say, 'Fuck 'em.' Plus, you've seen all the Oprah episodes, just like I have: Kid is given up for adoption at one day old. Kid lives with adoptive parents for 18 years and they do every single thing for her. Kid turns 18 and presto! Kid is on journey to find her bio mom. No one can deny the reality – the bio pull is like those high-powered magnets they use at NASA.

But I have come to love this reality instead of bristling at it. It means losing me won't be as hard on my daughter as losing her will be on me. She won't miss me as much, or for as long, as if I were her bio mom. It means if my husband were to remarry, she'd be quicker to accept his new wife as 'Mom,' quicker to bond with her, because she wouldn't be a non-bio mom trying to replace a real one; she'd just be a newer, likely younger, version of non-bio me.

I hope the thought will comfort you, too. As broken apart as you are about being without your LMan, perhaps it can be a solace to you to know that all year, he was broken apart about being without his real mother. He's been feeling the pull toward her all this time. Now that he's with her again, he's no longer fractured.

Of course he misses you. But none of us wants our children to feel sad, right? The fact that he may not feel quite as sad as you do, given the lack of shared DNA, will maybe make it easier for you to sleep. Yes?

Thursday, April 7 @ 12:06 a.m.
MotorCity sent this private message:

Wait! Back up! What do you mean, 'losing you'?! Why is your daughter losing you?!

Thursday, April 7 @ 12:13 a.m.
LaksMom sent this private message:

Oh, I meant hypothetically of course. I'm a professional imagineer of bad things happening. How will my client get screwed in this contract? How will my client get pummeled in this lawsuit? How will my husband and daughter survive if I crash my car en route home from the office? It's the gift of lawyers and mothers – we worry not only about the things that are and the things that will be, but also the things that might potentially possibly occur, no matter how low the probability, how slim the chance . . . you get the point. Sorry to alarm you.

Thursday, April 7 @ 12:16 a.m.
MotorCity sent this private message:

Don't scare a guy like that, please! Now that my heart has resumed beating, let me reread what you wrote.

. . .

Okay, got it. And yes, it makes me feel better, and I can see how it would for you, too, in the event your low-probability, highly doubtful and pretty-much-crazy hypothetical car crash were to occur.

We're as tied to them, emotionally, as if they were our own. But no matter how open they are to receiving our love, there's some small part of them that they don't fully give to us. They reserve it for their real parents. So when something terrible happens – they get yanked out of our houses a few days early, or we pretend-crash our pretend cars in our insane heads ;) – they don't mourn us like we do them.

Helps. You're right – I don't want the kid to be a fraction as sad about losing me as I am about losing him.

227

But let me ask you. I know you were adopted yourself. And maybe this one really does cross the line into 2boys territory: Does everything you've said mean you don't view your adoptive mom as a 'real' mom? You've been holding back all these years, wishing you could find your bio mom?

Thursday, April 7 @ 12:18 a.m.
LaksMom sent this private message:

What I've told myself is that I'm more attached to my adoptive mother than my daughter is to me because mine was home with me full-time. As long as my daughter's been with us, she's spent as much time with my parents as she has with me. This used to break me up a little – working mom guilt and all that – but now (when I'm running through my car accident hypo) I find it a relief. Even if she might've gotten as attached to me as I did to my mom, the logistics of our family life never permitted it to happen.

So, same on this end – she won't be a fraction as sad to lose me as I would be to lose her.

Thursday, April 7 @ 12:19 a.m.
MotorCity sent this private message:

Only, your kid is NOT losing you, thank God. Except in the crazy recesses of your mind, which would likely think more rationally if your whining friend would stop his sniveling and let you get to bed.

G'night, LMama. And thanks.

PART III

Thursday, April 7

Three Days Left

27

Mara

Mara woke to the beeping of her running watch hidden under her pillow. A glance at her bedside clock showed the alarm had been turned off. Tom. In the bathroom, she stripped off her paper underwear and shoved them into a plastic shopping bag, then another, and finally a third bag before she'd pressed them all down into the bottom of the wastebasket. She made a face at the new pair and pulled it on fast, wrapping a towel around her waist quickly in case Tom walked in.

She put on a skirt and top – bright fuchsia this time and as far outside her comfort zone as the bright purple one she'd worn yesterday. Steph would be impressed with this one, too, another step on what she assumed was Mara's long-awaited foray into the world of stylish dressing. She ran a hand through her hair, splashed water on her face and compared her reflection to the one she'd seen in the picture frame yesterday morning, the one that had her daughter curling her lip and worrying about what the kids on the bus would think. 'Better,' she breathed, before following the sounds of talking into the kitchen. Tom was leaning against the counter, listening attentively as Laks chatted to him from her tall stool across from him, a bowl of cereal before her.

'Good morning!' Mara said.

'Mama!' Laks climbed down and threw milky hands around her mother while Mara wondered how Tom had failed to notice the girl was eating cereal with her fingers.

'Only three more days!' Laks said, hugging her mother's legs.

In a second, ice filled Mara's veins and she staggered backward, out of the girl's grasp. Had they found the sticky note under her laptop? She stole a furtive glance at Tom, but his back was turned to them as he put away the milk and cereal. But if they'd found her note, why would Laks be so cheerful?

'What are you talking about?' Mara asked, trying to keep the panic out of her voice.

'Till your birthday!' Laks said, clapping. 'Only three more days till your birthday!'

'Oh, that!' Mara said, her body warming with relief. 'Yes, of course.'

And before her relief could change to guilt about what she had planned for that day, Laks was speaking again. 'Are you walking me out to the curb today?'

'I absolutely am,' Mara said, happy for the change of subject.

'Yay! And then you're coming to library class later, right? Because it's your turn to be the parent helper this week, remember?'

She had signed up weeks ago, at Laks's request, but she'd assumed the girl wouldn't want her there after the reaction she drew from her yesterday morning. But now the little face tilted up at her expectantly. 'You want me to go?' Mara asked.

The child squinted as though the question had been posed in Latin.

'What a treat, having Mama available for things like this, huh?' Tom was facing them now. His question was directed at his daughter but his eyes were trained on his wife, silently reminding her what he'd told her the night of her retirement dinner, when she had sobbed about how without the law, her life would have so much less meaning. How she would add such less value to the world, to their family.

'I completely disagree,' he had said. 'You're going to add a lot more value. Think of what it's going to mean to Laks to have you available during the day. You'll be able to go on field trips, help with class parties, be the library lady. Those things are so much more important to our family than a second income. And they're so much more important to our little girl than having a big-shot litigator for a mom. Retirement doesn't have to feel good to you – I'm not saying it should. But one person's loss is another's gain, as the saying goes, and I can't think of a better illustration of that than Lakshmi Nichols having her retired mother around during the day.'

Mara kissed her daughter before lifting a strand of hair out of the little face and tucking it behind her ear. 'Yes,' she said. 'Of course I'm coming to library class today.'

Laks hopped back onto her stool. 'Happy is a library lady mom!'

Mara and Tom laughed. Mara had read *Happiness Is a Warm Puppy* to Laks at bedtime a few weeks earlier, and the girl had been announcing the things that made her happy ever since, although she hadn't managed to get the phrasing quite right. Happy is when Mama reads an extra book to me! Happy is noodles and sauce for dinner! They had given up trying to get her to say it properly – it seemed at cross-purposes to correct a child when she was talking about happiness.

Mara headed for the coffeemaker and Tom trapped her in his arms as she reached past him for a mug. 'Notice how excited she is to have you walk her to the bus?' he whispered. 'Yesterday morning was only—'

'I know. I overreacted. I'm sorry, darling.' She held her mug out to him. He poured it half full, and she thrust it toward him again.

'You're cutting down, remember?' But he poured a little more and motioned for her to sit at the table, where he delivered the coffee to her. 'How late were you up last night?'

'Not too late. Relatively speaking.'

'On the forum? Or reconsidering that juicer?'

She laughed. 'Forum. I've decided the juicer's not for us after all.'

They both turned to look at Laks, who was occupied with squeezing pieces of cereal between her thumb and forefinger. Tom reached an arm out and held his daughter's wrist. 'All right, Miss Messykins, enough of that. Two more bites – with a spoon – then it's time to wash those goopy hands, brush your teeth and walk out to the curb with this week's extra-special library helper.'

As soon as Mara heard the garage door lower after Tom pulled out, she lifted her laptop and peeled off her to-do list. She spent two hours dictating e-mails to a few more friends from undergrad and calling three more classmates from law school, striking a pen stroke through each name as she went. She studied the rest of her shrinking list and smiled. Three days left, and she had gotten it down to a manageable length.

When Harry arrived an hour later, Mara was waiting for him at the window, and opened the door before he could ring the bell.

'Mornin', Mrs Nichols.'

'Harry, please. It's Mara.'

'A woman who's ready early. Not sure I've ever seen such a creature.' He extended his arm and they moved slowly together toward the cab.

They walked without talking and, glancing sideways at him, Mara asked herself how it could be that after a lifetime of practically biting the head off anyone who had ever offered help, here she was, so naturally taking the arm of this man. Thanking him, rather than barking at him, when he held out his arm to her, opened doors for her, put out a hand to protect her head as she lowered herself into his cab. She hadn't yet known him for a week and already this denim-and-plaid-clad man with his southern drawl and his own secrets had managed to make her see that it wasn't always so terrible, after all, to let people help.

She had never been sure what to believe in terms of higher powers. Her parents weren't religious, as last night's hesitation about what to say for grace had demonstrated, and Tom's Catholic upbringing, which he wasn't particularly good at discerning from his alcoholic upbringing, had turned him off church for good. But the idea of a higher being of some kind, whether a deity or a grander scheme of the universe, had always held some appeal for her.

For over twenty years, she had described meeting Tom as something dictated by some omniscient force, never conceding something so significant could have been solely the result of chance: she was hiding from the rain in the lobby of a building she had no classes in; he was on his way to interview for a volunteer position in the health center and, distracted, stepped inside the wrong door. Someone, or something, had wanted them to meet. She was sure of it.

As Harry stooped to open the cab door for her, she wondered if the same someone or something that had sent her Tom then also sent her Harry now. In the past few days, an idea had started to creep its way out of the recesses of her mind, nagging at her until she had no choice but to think about it before it scurried away again, into the shadows: If she could let a stranger open a car door for her, was it such a big step to let her husband help her? Or to let her parents?

Look at the progress she had made last night alone, allowing her mother to organize dinner, her father to set the table. Maybe she could work her way up to smiling, rather than fuming, the next time they offered to weed the garden. From there, was it that great a leap to let a home health nurse comb her hair, help her dress? Last week, she would have said those ideas were far too impossible for her to consider. Now she wasn't so sure.

But then, anything was easy when you only had to do it for a few days. If she knew she would have to take Harry's elbow for another few years, let her parents make and serve dinners a few times a week for the foreseeable future, would she be so gracious? Could she allow a nurse to brush her hair, her teeth, wash her naked body, if she knew it would happen for a thousand more days, not just a few?

She lowered herself carefully onto the seat while Harry held a protective hand between her head and the top of the door frame. Inside the car, he busied himself with his trip log for a minute, studiously avoiding the rearview mirror.

'Thank you,' she said softly.

He nodded as he started the car, but didn't look up. 'Okay, then. Off we go.'

He flipped his visor down and she saw the photo of the little girl again. At an earlier time, she might have pushed a little. Come on, tell me a bit about her. How old is she? Who is she? Why don't you want to talk about her? It'll make you feel better to get it off your chest, out in the open.

But that was a lifetime ago. Back when she was oblivious about how lucky she was to have nothing in her life that was unfit for public consumption. No dark, twisted vines of truth not fit for sharing with others. She turned her face to the window and watched the Disney Channel streets of Plano flash by.

Mara assessed the long hallway that led to the school library, then glanced at her watch and pursed her lips. It was eleven twenty-eight; library class started at eleven thirty. It had taken her longer to walk into the school than she had allotted for when she'd told Harry what time to get her. And now she had cut it too close – the bell would ring in two minutes. She picked up her pace, hoping to get to the safety of the unpopulated library before the noise set off a reaction in her limbs.

At the same time, she tried to calm herself. Stress had

an even more pronounced effect on her body than noise – that one was most definitely an HD thing. She'd read about it in a pile of articles. Avoid stressful situations, especially in public. Being watched by multiple sets of strangers' eyes made things worse for everyone, even those without excessive CAG repeats.

Think happy thoughts, she ordered herself. Think how delighted your daughter is to have you here today, how excited she was to learn you were coming. Think about what Tom said, about retirement being the worst news for you but the best for her. Think how much more time she's had with her mother in the past few months – time for afternoon snacks and arts-and-crafts projects and stuffed-animal tea parties in the backyard. Time that she never had before, with a mother always in too much of a rush, too preoccupied with briefs and discovery and trial prep. The greatest loss of the mother's life to date – forced retirement – had led to the greatest gain in the daughter's.

Which went to show how a different vantage point led to such dramatically different interpretations of the same situation. Here Mara was, determined to remove herself from the planet ASAP to spare Laks from having a mother who was so much less than what Mara wanted to be for her daughter. But wasn't it possible that just being here – here at school, here at home, here, instead of in the office, or in the ground – was all the girl needed? When it came to parenting, wasn't here much better than gone?

And wasn't that true even if being here ultimately meant walking down this hallway looking like a wind-sock figure, then gliding down it in a wheelchair? Even if it meant, finally, not being able to come to library class at all, but being propped up in bed when Laks got home, and listening to how her day had gone? Was the requisite skill for mother-hood coordinated movement? Or was it love – enough love that you'd let the chance to escape go by so you could be here for your child, in whatever condition?

The hint of a smile appeared on Mara's lips and then grew wider as she quickened her pace down the hall. Had she just convinced herself it was better for Laks if she stuck around longer? Talk about win-win.

She was halfway down the hall when the two classroom doors closest to her opened at the same time. The nearest door was to room 112, Laks's classroom. She could hear a young voice instructing the class. There must be a substitute today; Laks's teacher was an older woman. As she moved closer, Mara could hear the sub calling out instructions about lining up in single file inside the classroom so today's line leader, Samantha, could lead everyone to the library. Slightly farther down the hall, a woman Mara recognized as a fourth-grade teacher leaned against the door frame of her classroom, her mouth giving orders Mara couldn't quite make out.

She moved past room 112 quickly. But as she neared the fourth-grade classroom, the teacher disappeared inside and a throng of ten-year-olds spilled out the door, jostling and chiding one another as they filled the hallway, blocking her passage. From the other direction, a clear voice spoke. 'Okay, then, Samantha, you may lead everyone into the hall. Please stand quietly until the bell rings, though.'

Mara heard the kindergartners shuffling behind her. Short of physically pushing fourth graders out of her path, she couldn't see a way past them. She looked back quickly and saw Samantha's single-file line had already fallen apart; the five-year-olds spanned the width of the corridor. She heard the loud rush of her own heartbeat in her head as she

239

stood, trapped, a group of rowdy ten-year-olds on one side of her, a cluster of five-year-olds, including her daughter, on the other.

And then the bell rang.

The clanging rolled past Mara's ears in slow, undulating waves, and for a horrifying sixty seconds, everything occurred in stop-frame before her:

Her torso lurched sideways as the noise knocked the balance out of her. Her reaction time being HD-dampened, she couldn't respond fast enough to counterbalance the sideways movement of her body and the momentum took the rest of her with it, causing her to take two quick steps forward before she crashed loudly into a locker.

A group of fourth graders turned to stare, as did most of the kindergartners.

The mouths of the children closest to her, Laks among them, opened in shock as Mara struggled to pull herself upright but lost her grip on the locker and fell to the floor. Trying again, she pushed up but the fourth graders' loud cackles seemed to slide right into her muscles and paralyze them, and she fell again.

A fourth-grade boy yelled, 'Hey, look, that lady's drunk!'

A dozen fourth-grade voices laughed, followed by as many kindergarten ones.

A girl screamed, 'Someone needs to call nine-one-one! What's a drunk person doing in the school?'

Another said, 'Don't laugh, you guys! Don't laugh! You're being mean!'

A few stopped laughing. Others laughed louder.

The substitute teacher, hand over her mouth, told her class to get inside the room as fast as they could. But the kindergartners were frozen, gaping at Mara.

'I said, get in the classroom this instant!' the teacher said. 'Samantha! Lead everyone into the room, right now! Samantha! Children! Everyone! Come quick!'

All but one of them obeyed, and Mara could hear the buzzing of voices inside room 112. 'Freaky' and 'crazy' wafted out the door and into the hall, ringing in her ears along with the echo of the bell and the murmurs and laughter of the fourth graders.

'You!' the substitute hissed to the one kindergartner who hadn't followed Samantha into the class. 'You!' the teacher called again. 'I said to come in this instant!'

From her hands and knees, Mara raised her head and locked eyes with the child standing motionless and wide-eyed in front of her.

'Mama!' Laks scolded, her voice in a low whisper as she cast her eyes from her mother to her teacher to the fourth graders and back to her mother again. 'Stand up! You need to stand up right now!'

The look of humiliation on her daughter's face, the accusation in her voice, brought hot tears to Mara's eyes. She willed herself to tune out the older kids gawking and laughing at her, willed her arms to obey as she tried another time to push up from the floor. It worked, and she stood tall, a proud smile on her face until she realized what a pathetic thing it was for her to feel proud of, and ordered her mouth to straighten into a line.

'I'm so sorry,' she whispered. 'The bell went off, and the noise . . . and for some reason it's so much worse today. I lost my balance, and then . . . I wouldn't have come if I'd known it would be this bad. I didn't know. I'm so sorry.'

She took a few tentative steps toward Laks, and as she

241

did, another fourth-grade boy yelled, 'She's really drunk! Look at her walk!'

Mara frowned, confused and annoyed by the fourth graders and their drama. What was the kid talking about? The Falling Lady Show was over, and she was walking perfectly fine. Why didn't he find something else to exaggerate about?

As her mother inched closer, the girl took a step away. 'Mama, they're laughing at you! The big kids are laughing at you! And the kids in my class are calling you names!'

Mara's entire body was on fire with shame. This was so much worse than the cereal aisle. 'I'm so sorry,' she croaked, the lump in her throat leaving little room for words to escape. 'Mama is so sorry. I don't know why my body's behaving so badly today.'

'You can't go to library now! Please don't go to library!' Tears slipped down the girl's cheeks and she swiped at them angrily.

'Of course not. I'll go home.'

Laks nodded, still swiping at her tears. The fourth graders fell quiet as their teacher finally appeared. Mara heard one of the boys start to recite what had happened, but the woman's voice cut him off, announcing they were late, it was time to get to the gym, he could tell her later.

'Should I walk out with you, Mama?' It was plain in the girl's tone what she hoped the answer would be.

'No, sweetie, that's okay. I'm fine now, see?'

She reached to touch her daughter's hair, but Laks retreated a step, then another. 'I have to go,' she whispered, stealing another furtive glance down the hall. 'Teacher said.' She made a move toward her classroom and looked at her mother impatiently, waiting to be released.

'Of course,' Mara said, waving the girl toward the classroom. 'You go. I'll be fine. The cab will be here soon. I'll wait out front—'

'Can you wait over behind that one tree? So no one can see you from the windows?'

Mara nodded quickly and turned away.

She was slumped at the base of the tree, head in her arms, when she heard the cab pull up. Harry leaped out and ran to her, his door wide open, car still running.

'What on earth? Ya look like you're tryin' ta disappear.'

She raised her puffy red face to his and opened her mouth to speak. No sound came out, and she shook her head slowly, looking past him toward the car.

'Sure,' he said gently. 'We'll go home.' Without another word, he part-led, part-carried her to the car, helped her in and fastened her seat belt.

As he drove, Mara stared blankly out the window, not seeing the bright colors of Plano but only the dark, angry, tearful eyes of her daughter as the girl, humiliated, pleaded with her own mother to hide out of sight of the other children. She stopped trying to wipe away the tears that streaked her face, stopped holding a tissue to her running nose, stopped pressing her fingers against her puffy eyes to try to restore them to their normal size. She'd let Harry see her like this if he looked at her in the mirror, let him see her ugly, splotchy, puffy, snot-streaked face when he helped her out of the car at home. She deserved it. She deserved that embarrassment, and so much more, after what she had put her daughter through.

She let out a grunt of disgust at her idiocy in the hallway, when she had almost convinced herself that being here, under any conditions, would be better for Laks than being gone. Her eyes still closed, she sensed Harry shift in his seat at the sound of her voice and she could picture him looking back at her, concerned, eager for an explanation. She turned her head toward the window and pressed her forehead against the cool glass, letting his questions go unanswered as she chastised herself for her foolishness.

Of course the girl wouldn't be better off having her around under these conditions. There was no justification for exposing Laks to more of this. Mara could imagine the shrieks of laughter on the bus as the child's wind-sock figure of a mother teetered on the curb waiting for her school bus. The gawking as, later, they noticed the girl's mother was now in a wheelchair. The whispering as the rumor got around that now the woman was confined to her bed. Now, if you went to Lakshmi Nichols's house for a playdate, you didn't see a mom standing at the counter with freshly baked brownies; you saw a closed bedroom door. Or worse, an open one, beyond which a sickly, wasted woman lay staring out at you, or through you.

At five, Laks was too young to hide her disgust about how her mother had acted. She was too instinctively open about her feelings to pretend everything was fine, that her mother's behavior wasn't embarrassing. One day, though, she'd learn to filter her emotions. She'd figure out that it upset her mother, and her father, if she said anything negative about Mara. She'd learn to keep her feelings to herself, and they would roil away inside her, a toxic blend of humiliation and revulsion, bitterness and anger. How could anyone say that would be better for a child than having her mother simply die?

Mara had witnessed it, a glimpse of what was to come,

when she was first diagnosed. She'd overheard one of Dr Thiry's nurses mention the name of a nursing home where one of their patients lived, and she'd driven there herself, lying her way into a tour with a tale about her failing mother. It had taken her no time to spot the HD patient; the woman sat in the corner of the 'activity room,' a thin blanket lying in a heap on the footrests of her wheelchair while she gyrated wildly from the waist, bending forward, then to the side, then forward again, her face in a stiff grimace.

A man stood beside her and two teenage children, a boy and a girl, sat slumped in plastic chairs to the side. The woman's gaze was fixed on an empty chair several feet away, and though the man's mouth moved constantly, the woman gave no indication that she heard him, or that she was even aware he was there. The children might have been waiting for a train, Mara thought, as unengaged as they were with their mother. Their heads were bent over phones and they each wore headphones and moved their heads to a beat only they could hear.

But then, it was hard to blame them, since their mother was so devastatingly unengaged with them. It was easy to imagine the kids trying, on earlier visits, to talk to her, to fill her in on what they'd been up to since they'd seen her last – what they'd done in school, on the sports field, with friends. And being met with the vacant stare Mara saw on the woman's face now. A stare that told them she hadn't truly heard them. She no longer even knew them. As Mara's tour leader droned on about activity nights and field trips and meal plans, Mara watched as the man picked up the blanket and spread it over the woman's legs, tucking it snugly behind her waist. Within a few seconds, it was at her feet again, and he smiled patiently as he bent to retrieve it again. He patted the woman's shoulder and resumed his patter.

The woman dislodged the blanket again, and as the man stooped again to retrieve it, Mara saw the boy nudge his sister with his foot. The girl looked up from her phone and her brother indicated with his chin the pickup game their parents were playing. He glanced briefly at his father before rolling his eyes dramatically at his sister. She rolled hers back and shook her head, her upper lip curled in disgust. Their father stood, bringing them back into his peripheral vision, and quickly they dropped their chins back to their phones and resumed their rhythmic nodding, pretending they hadn't noticed a thing.

Mara never told anyone she'd gone to the nursing home, but she intimated a few times to Tom that she knew what the end stages of HD would be like for her, and how hard it would be on Laks. And on him. Tom claimed it would be perfectly fine. Not ideal, perhaps, but they would find a way to deal with it, and they would be just fine. But he was only speaking wishfully, Mara knew. She had seen reality. She had glimpsed their future.

She stole a glance at Harry and considered what she'd been debating as they walked to the cab earlier, about whether she might be able to let go of her independence, accept help from Tom and her parents and home health care workers and, ultimately, nursing home staff, for the sake of having more time with Laks. But all that would do, she saw now, is lead to more days like today. More snickering, more gawking, more whispering. More humiliation for Laks. Until Mara was in a wheelchair in the corner of some activity room, kicking off her blanket for the tenth time while her daughter pretended not to notice how pathetic her mother had become.

At the house, Harry rushed to Mara's door to help her out of the cab, but she waved him away and pulled herself out. She let him follow closely behind her as she made her way up the walk, but when he reached out to help her up the front step, she shook her head firmly and he quickly dropped his hand. At the door, she handed him cash for the fare before fumbling with her keys.

He shoved his hands in his pockets and waited wordlessly until finally she sighed and handed him the key. He unlocked the door and pushed it open. She opened her mouth to thank him, but he raised a finger to his lips and shook his head. Then he turned and walked to his cab, raising a hand high in salute as he went.

28

Scott

Scott was showered and changed and waiting for Laurie when she arrived home.

'Wow,' she said. 'Sport coat and dress shirt. And those shoes I love. What's the occasion?'

'I'm taking my wife to dinner. Some would call it a date.'

'Twice in a row?'

'Pffft. Takeout hardly counts as a date. And even if it did, why not? You deserve a break. You need anything before we go? Our reservation is for six.'

'Absolutely not,' she said, turning to walk back out the door. She seemed to prance down the porch steps and into his car. 'Oh my gosh, I can't remember the last time we did something spur-of-the-moment like this! I love it! It's been at least . . .' She paused. 'Never mind.'

'You can say it, Laur.'

'No. It's insensitive. You're still—'

'Laur. It's okay. You can say it.' He waited, but she refused to speak. 'Fine, I'll say it,' he said. 'It's been at least a year. Since Curtis moved in. We haven't been able to do anything so last-minute since then. You're allowed to be excited about it.' He kissed her, and started the car. 'You're allowed to tell me how you feel. You don't have to pretend not to be relieved to have our lives to ourselves again, when we both know you've been looking forward to it.

'And so have I, for that matter. It's not like if we refuse to find a silver lining to the situation, it'll change, right? He's gone. We can be morose or we can find a way to look on the bright side. Either way, he's still gone.'

She nodded, but she didn't add to what he'd said. They held hands and sang to the radio, and when he looked at her, he saw a new radiance he hadn't noticed before. Whether it was the late stages of pregnancy or the fact that he'd gone to the trouble of planning a date night or the peacefulness of having time without the four-foot-high third wheel who'd been with them every minute for the past twelve months, he couldn't say. But she looked beautiful.

'You look beautiful,' he told her, raising her hand to his lips. 'You look . . . content.'

'That's exactly how I feel.' She closed her eyes, and they stayed that way for the last ten minutes of the drive – holding hands, Scott glancing from the road to his wife and the two of them singing along softly with Elton as he mourned Daniel's departure and the red taillights.

Midway through dinner, she set her knife and fork down. 'Okay, I'll admit it. I'm relieved.'

He lifted his eyes from his steak and found her looking uncertainly at him, as if wondering whether she'd made a mistake in taking him at his word. He gestured for her to continue. Not so much because he wanted to hear what he knew she was going to say, but because he felt he owed it to her. She hadn't been wild about the idea of taking the boy in, but she had done it anyway, for an entire year, for

Scott's sake. The least he could do was let her express how she felt about it.

'I am,' she said. 'Relieved. Content, like you said in the car. Utterly, completely relaxed for the first time in forever. I mean, oh my God, Scott. Remember how easy last night was? Dinner on the couch, our feet up? Remember the quiet? No arguments about table manners or talking back? And after, while you were grading your papers, I read six chapters of that book and started another, all in glorious, uninterrupted silence. No pausing to negotiate about homework or showers or bedtimes or whether someone could have seconds on dessert when he didn't finish firsts on vegetables. It was heaven.'

She regarded him closely, a tentative look on her face. He knew she was waiting for him to tell her she could keep going. He felt a pang of disloyalty to Curtis in listening to her list all the ways in which they were 'free' of the boy, and he almost raised a hand to stop her. But letting her say it out loud didn't mean he had to agree with her. He waved his fork, granting permission.

'Okay,' she said. 'Well, after I got to bed and then you went – where'd you go, anyway? Downstairs, I think? Were you on that forum of yours? Anyway, I was lying there thinking that for the next three months, every single night will be like that. Just you and me and enough quiet we'll actually be able to hear our thoughts.'

She paused again, and he nodded. 'It was definitely quiet,' he said.

'Was it ever,' she said, missing, or maybe ignoring, the fact that his tone was more wistful than grateful. 'So quiet, I couldn't get over it,' she said. 'And you know what else?' He raised his eyebrows, inviting her to tell him. 'The idea of all this time,' she said. 'It's incredible to me. Time together, time alone. Time to take afternoon naps! Or to sleep in on weekends without being woken at six by stage-whispering, "TROOPS, FALL OUT! BUT STAY IN THE HALLWAY! NO GOING INTO THE ADULTS' ROOM AND WAKING THEM UP!"' Scott laughed. The kid never had gotten the idea. Or maybe he had, since the stage whispers were always followed by Laurie nudging Scott until he dragged himself out of bed and went downstairs with the noisy boy so Laurie could keep sleeping.

Laurie laughed, too, her relief evident in the lightness of her voice. She reached for his hand, grazed a thumb across his knuckles and gave him one of her dazzling smiles, the kind that made him feel more liquid than solid. 'We've had . . . not the easiest few years, you and I, is that fair?' she said. He nodded and she grazed her thumb in the other direction.

'And I'm not saying we can repair in three months all the strain we've built up in that many years,' she continued. 'But we can repair a lot of it, don't you think? With all this time alone before the baby comes, think of all the date nights, the movie nights on the couch with no little body between us, keeping us from cuddling. All the lazy mornings in bed.' She flashed him a seductive look and now he was more vapor than liquid.

'Three months,' she said. 'It's enough time to get ourselves back on track before we have a third body in the house again. Enough to get ourselves melded more solidly together, like we used to be, before this little one comes and adds sleepless nights and anxiety and all the things that can pull people apart. And I guess, although I'm furious with LaDania and heartsick that we didn't get to say goodbye to our little man like we wanted to, I see these few extra days as a gift, because it's that much more time for us.' She looked at him nervously. 'Is that . . . okay?'

'Of course it's okay,' he said.

Because really, what other choice did he have?

After dinner, she asked if they could stop by her favorite baby store, Bundles of Joy, and pick out a few things for the registry. He called up an imitation of the most excited voice he could think of, and even though it rang hollow to him, she ran with it, either because of her own excitement about their mission or because she was letting him coast awhile longer on his date-night win.

She did not, however, run with it when she was trying to show him 0-3-month dresses and he was looking the other way at infant-sized baseball gloves and glaringly boyish Tigers uniforms. Taking him by the arm, she pulled him to the dresses. 'I need you to look at these,' she said. She took one off the rack – pink gingham with a butterfly on the stomach – and held it toward him, her eyes instructing him to remark about how cute it was.

He smiled wanly and she shook her head.

'Not good enough,' she said. 'I need you to be excited about this.' She shook the dress toward him. 'I need you to point out the adorable butterfly on this one. And' – she reached for a yellow dress with a big daisy on the front – 'the cute flower on this one,' she said, holding it toward him.

She set the dresses back on the shelf and put a hand on each of his shoulders.

'I need you to act and feel over the moon about the fact that we're having a daughter. I need you to convince me that the most important thing in your life is not the family living in an apartment in Detroit, but the one you and I are creating in Royal Oak. I need to see it in your eyes and hear it in your voice and feel it in your kiss that this family, our little family of three, is your priority. I don't think that's too much for me to ask. I don't think it's too much for you to give. But if I'm wrong about that, this would be the time for you to tell me.'

She let go of his shoulders and turned back to the dresses. Scott examined the floor. Could he really promise, right here, right now, that as of this minute, he would get over the loss of his little man and move on? Just like that, be excited about the baby and not show another bit of lamentation about the boy?

He raised his eyes and took in his wife's legs, her bulging belly, her face. Even annoyed, she still glowed. God, she was gorgeous. And there was something about her, about the two of them together, that was nothing short of electric. How many times had she reduced him to non-solids tonight alone with a mere swing of her hair or a flash of her eyes? For him, she was it. The only woman he would ever love.

What she had asked of him right now was, as she had said, eminently reasonable. And paled in comparison to what he had asked of her that night last April when Bray showed up on their porch, younger brother in tow. He could imagine what Pete would say – 2boys, too, for that matter – if they were witness to his internal debate about whether he should promise the love of his life that he would act from this moment on as though she were exactly that: 'Uh, what the fuck is the dilemma here?'

'You're not wrong,' he said, reaching for the pink dress with the butterfly and holding it up away from them, appraising. 'So what – do they make miniature clothes hangers for all this stuff? Because no way is this kind of thing going to fit on the ones from our closet.' He held the registry scanner toward the tag, waiting for her go-ahead before he added the dress to their list.

'Thank you,' she said quietly.

29

Mara

Mara waited on the porch for the school bus to arrive. There would be no standing at the curb anymore.

'Laks, sweetie,' she said when the girl reached her. Mara bent unsteadily, bringing her face to the level of her daughter's so she could look in the girl's eyes. 'I can't tell you how sorry I am about what happened today.'

'It's okay, Mama.' The girl studied her shoes. 'Can I have a snack?'

Mara's breath came easily for the first time in hours. 'Sure.'

'I told you,' Tom said when he arrived home and Mara relayed Laks's behavior after school. Mara had called him right after Harry left, sobbing, telling him she was certain Laks would never speak to her again after what had happened. 'Nonsense,' he said. 'She's far more resilient than you've ever given her credit for.'

But later, Mara was carrying clean bath towels to Laks's linen closet – only two at a time, since carrying a large pile of laundry had become too difficult – and Tom, she thought, was on the couch, reading a magazine. But as she neared her daughter's doorway, she heard his voice asking, 'Laks? What's wrong?'

Mara peeked through the small opening between the door and the frame. The child was facedown, sobbing into her pillow. Her father was sitting on her bed, stroking her hair.

'Laks, talk to me,' he said.

He was answered with more sobs, and Mara watched as he studied the crease of his pants. After a moment, he asked, 'Is this about what happened today at school?'

Mara took a sharp breath as the dark head on the pillow moved up and down.

'I see. I want you to talk to me about it. When you have big feelings, it's best to get them out. Not keep them inside.'

Laks turned, her face scrunched and red with anger. 'I am not friends with Lisa,' she sobbed. 'Anymore. I am never talking to her again.'

'Oh!' he said, and Mara shared the relief she heard in his voice. 'This is about Lisa? What happened with Lisa?'

'She said' – Laks paused to catch her breath – 'mean things,' she choked, before breaking into more sobs.

'What mean things?'

The small face turned to the wall.

'Lakshmi. Answer me. What mean things?'

Still facing the wall, she mumbled, 'She called Mama a "drunken lady."'

'Drunken lady?' Tom said, and Mara heard the strain in his voice as he tried to make it light, forcing a half laugh. A feeling of dread crept into her chest. 'Well, that's a silly name,' he said, 'and a strange one for a kindergartner to come up with, but I don't know if she meant it to be mean—'

Laks looked sharply at her father. 'She got it from the fourth graders. And she meant it mean.' And in an instant, her sharp look collapsed into a pained one and fresh tears spilled onto her cheeks. Her tiny shoulders started to shake and her voice took on the choking, gasping sound of someone trying to fit words around sobs. 'They all. Said it,' she panted. 'Everyone but Susan.'

She took another breath. 'She's the only one. I'm still friends with.' She paused again to let more sobs out. 'And they all. Meant it mean. The big kids. Too.' She gulped in more air and sniffed. 'They all started calling her that. "Drunken lady." Because she was. Walking. All funny,' she panted. 'And the big kids said. She looked. Drunk. And I asked. Teacher. What "drunk" means and she. Said it's. Bad.' The little body convulsed and she threw her arms around her father's waist, burying her head in his lap.

Drunk. Mara looked down; the towels she was holding were moving back and forth, up and down. She hadn't noticed her arms moving.

Anosognosia. The complete lack of awareness some HD patients have about the way their bodies are moving. She remembered Dr Misner explaining it to her. Then Tom. Then Dr Thiry.

She'd heard of HD patients being arrested for public drunkenness because of their awkward, listing, bent-over gait and arguing that they were walking just fine – which never helped their case with the police. And now Mara had done the same. Only instead of embarrassing herself in front of the police, she had humiliated her daughter in front of a hallway full of children. Had it only started today, at the school, she wondered, or had she been walking strangely for longer?

Suddenly it hit her: the boy and his mother in the grocery store had looked at her like there was something wrong with her – more, even, than the fact she'd wet herself. Harry had fairly jumped out of his car and sprinted to her after he watched her take a few steps at the car repair shop. And the salesgirl at the clothing store seemed to be staring at her, too. She had written it off at the time – she was acting oddly herself at each of those times – and assumed everyone's puzzled looks were a reaction to that.

Now she knew what all the gawking was about. She'd been walking like a drunk all week long.

Only her family and friends had acted like nothing had changed. She knew she was supposed to love them for that, but the sound and sight of her daughter bawling made it difficult not to feel the opposite.

'I'm so sorry,' Tom said to Laks. 'And Mama is so sorry. But it's not her fault. Remember when Mama and I told you about how she wasn't feeling well? How she had something called Huntington's, and that's why she stopped working? That's why she used to be a little angry sometimes, until she started taking medicine? Remember that? Remember how we talked about how when people have a disease, they can't help it? So when the disease makes them act in ways we might not really like all that much, we need to try hard not to be mad at them, because it's the disease's fault, and not theirs? Do you remember all of that?'

They hadn't said much to Laks about Mara's condition. It wouldn't be unusual if they decided to keep it from her completely, given her age, the social worker at Dr Thiry's clinic had told them. But that's not how they did things in their family, Mara said. They were straight shooters. Tell-it-like-it-is types. The kind of parents who referred to body parts by their real names. So, last summer, when Laks, then four, asked her mother, 'Why do you take all those pills every morning?' they sat her down and told her why.

Against Mara's wishes, Tom had added the piece about being understanding, not being upset with Mara for acting out, dropping things, falling. Mara wanted the girl to be able to express anger, frustration, at her mother, if that's what she was feeling. Burying it because of some promise she'd made to her father was the exact opposite of what Mara wanted for her daughter. It was lucky Tom hadn't been in the hallway at school today, Mara thought; Laks might have felt pressured to walk Mara out to the curb even though what she'd really wanted was to pretend she didn't know her.

Laks nodded. 'I remember.'

'Good,' Tom said, running a hand over the top of her head. 'So you remember we need to be sure not to be mad at Mama for what happened, since it's not her fault, right?' Laks didn't answer. 'Right, Lakshmi?' Tom said, his voice stern now, instructing her to agree.

But the girl didn't nod in agreement. Mara didn't blame her.

And Tom didn't push again, but sat quietly, letting her cry in his lap while he rubbed the shoulders that rose jerkily up and down with sobs. And now Mara saw the glistening trail on her husband's cheek. She raised a hand to her mouth to cover her own sob and stepped sideways, leaning against the wall as the towels slid from her hand and dropped to the floor.

She had spent hours ruminating with worry that one day her condition might embarrass her daughter. That dealing with the effects of her illness, helping their daughter try to deal with it, might become too much for her husband. But she had not, in any of those hours, come close to realizing how she would feel if either of those things actually came true.

She heard Laks's voice, loud now, and sharp. 'I don't want her to come to school anymore, Daddy!'

Mara felt a momentary flash of pride in her daughter for expressing how she felt before a vise grip locked down on her chest. She could feel the pain in her child's voice, could picture her tiny face screwed up with dismay at the words she heard herself say about her own mother. 'I don't want her to stand at the curb, either. I don't even want her waiting on the porch! I don't want the kids making fun of her. Or me.'

'Now, hold on a second,' Tom said. 'I don't want to hear you say—'

'I want her to stay in the house forever and never come out again!'

Mara braced herself weakly against the wall. As painful as it was to think of Laks having to hide her true feelings about her mother's illness, it was excruciating to hear her say them out loud. A scorching pain seared from Mara's ears to her feet, filling her, clawing into her organs, wrapping around her bones, pushing against the inside of her skin. And then she felt hollow. Her legs threatened to give out and she thrust her shoulders up high, forcing her body to stay upright. Taking deep, slow breaths, she begged her body not to betray her this once.

'There, there,' Tom was saying now. 'There, there,' he said again. And then something low and stern, but gentle.

'You don't understand me, Daddy,' she heard the small voice say, and he responded, low and stern and gentle again.

And Mara stopped hearing Laks's words, and Tom's, and was only vaguely aware of his low murmurs, her high-pitched protests, until finally their voices faded into nothing and she heard nothing and saw nothing but this:

Tom and Laks are driving silently. She's sullen; he's steeling himself, trying to ignore her. They park, enter the building, sign in. Laks covers her ears as the buzzer sounds and the interior doors open. It's an ugly, annoying sound and she has grown to despise it. They walk to the end of the hallway, into the common room. The nurses call it a living room but come on, Laks thinks, who are they trying to kid?

Mara sits by the window. Staring, but not seeing. An old, worn blanket covers her, although it's ninety degrees outside.

Laks blanches. The smell of the place turns her stomach. But she has learned that complaining about it to her father will land her in her room for the afternoon. When her dad's not looking, she covers her nose with a hand.

Tom walks to Mara and gently picks up one of her hands, kisses the top of her head. Her hair is lifeless, unbrushed. Her scalp is dry. He ignores this, kisses her anyway.

Watching his lips touch her mother's head makes Laks retch. She's careful to do it soundlessly. She flops onto a chair, folds her arms across her chest and pouts. This is stupid. She doesn't want to be here. She wants to be on the Internet, on the phone, texting her friends. Hell, even homework would be better than this.

She has no use for this woman. She has already said goodbye to her mother, in her mind. The mother she used to have. The mother who read to her, pushed her on the swing, put little notes in her school lunches each day: 'I will always love you. xox, Mama.' The mother she used to look up to, brag to friends about. Was excited to see every day as the bus drove her closer to home.

She takes in her dad's profile and her mouth turns downward in disgust. He used to be so handsome, so alive. Now his hair has gone completely gray. His face is too thin and it's always drawn tight. The blue in his eyes has faded – she didn't think that was possible, but she swore it was true. His mouth is permanently set in a straight, serious line. Except for here, when he forces his lips to curl up and pretends there's no place he'd rather be. Nothing he'd rather be doing than chatting mindlessly to this woman who isn't even listening, who can't even understand what he's saying.

She used to admire him for this. His loyalty. His faithfulness.

Now she thinks he's pathetic.

She hates herself for thinking this way about him, as much as she hates herself for thinking this way about her mother. But what's she supposed to think? She wants a life. She wants a dad whose eyes haven't gone out.

Why won't the woman die already?

In a second, Mara was in the guest bathroom near the kitchen, kneeling in front of the toilet as everything she had eaten for dinner came out in a rush. She heaved several more times until finally there was nothing left. She splashed cold water on her face and looked sternly at her reflection in the mirror. Then she walked resolutely to the kitchen, picked up the phone and hit the speed dial for Dr Thiry's office. When the answering service picked up, she announced her name and asked to leave a message for the doctor.

'I'm not sleeping.'

30

Mara

In the living room, Tom sat at the end of the couch, his laptop open on his knee, an intense look on his face. Mara cleared her throat and he snapped the computer shut and set it on the coffee table. 'Oh, there you are,' he said, patting the space beside him.

'There's no new research,' she said as she sat. 'I checked last night. And again this morning.'

'What are you talking about?'

She gave him a daring look and reached for his laptop. As she expected, he grabbed her hand before she could lift the screen and see what site he'd been on. She smiled victoriously. 'You don't think I know about this nightly obsession of yours?'

He regarded her blandly, still pretending he wasn't following. She would get back to that, she decided. 'Why didn't you tell me I look like a drunk when I walk?'

'What? Oh, did you overhear—?'

'Difficult not to, when the girl was bawling, "Don't let Mama ever leave the house again!"'

Tom grimaced. 'I'm so sorry—'

'Don't. You've got to be sick of saying that. I know I'm sick of hearing you say it. That's your hundredth "I'm so sorry" in one night. Why did you let me leave the house, walking like that? Did you tell Laks not to say anything about it? Because normally she isn't gentle.'

'Laks probably didn't realize it,' he said. 'You're Mama. It's how Mama walks. It was only when—'

'Only when she became the laughingstock of Plano Parkway Elementary that she figured out Mama walks like a drunk?' He shook his head but she didn't let him speak. 'Why didn't you tell me?' she asked again, louder.

He frowned. 'You told me not to.'

She started to argue, and then she remembered: the windsock woman. The day Dr Thiry explained anosognosia, she had instructed Tom not to tell her when she was moving strangely. She hadn't wanted to know. 'Oh.'

She pointed to the laptop he'd closed so quickly. 'Seriously,' she said. 'Aren't you sick of it?'

'Of what?'

It was no surprise he was acting obtuse about it; she'd stopped expecting him to act otherwise.

'Sick of scouring the Internet for news,' she said. 'Sick of crossing your fingers that there'll be a new drug today, a new trial, when there wasn't one yesterday. Sick of hoping for a new ending to this story, hoping for that alleged cure that's always "just around the corner" but in reality is still in the next town over. The next state. The next continent. The most brilliant minds in research still can't say how the disease even works – they are not "just around the corner" from figuring out how to stop it. Aren't you sick of holding your breath, opening your laptop and telling yourself, "Maybe this time"?'

He lifted a shoulder. 'I'm not all that anxious about the research. They're making advances. And we've got time.'

'The hell we do. I've gone from Super Mom to "Don't Let Mom Leave the House" in two months flat.' She snapped her fingers. 'Maybe the lucky ones with CAGs in the low forties have time. Not me.'

'Not this again, Mara,' he said. His voice was strained; she could tell he was trying to control his frustration. 'I've told you, Dr Thiry's told you, every member of his staff has now told you – there's no proof there's a correlation between CAG score and speed of progression,' he said.

'Well, I've read plenty of things online about people with high CAGs deteriorating more quickly than—'

He held up a hand. 'Please. Stop letting yourself get carried away based on random anecdata from the Internet. I think we need to rely on the medical profession—'

'Ha!' she scoffed. 'You want me to rely on the medical profession? You mean the profession that hasn't discovered one new clue about this disease since the day I was diagnosed? I'd be just as safe to rely on Laks's Magic Eight-Ball.'

He didn't respond, and they sat silently for a few moments. He was thinking of ways to calm her down, she knew, and before the knowledge could anger her, she took a deep breath and counted to three before letting it out. It would be nicer to avoid an argument. 'Honestly, though, Tom,' she said quietly, 'aren't you sick of pretending you're okay with the shitty future you've been handed?'

'But I am okay with it,' he said gently, lifting one of her hands in his. 'I mean, sure, I wish things were different for your sake, but—'

'Oh, come on,' she said, coaxing, trying to get him to

confess. 'Don't give me that old line of BS again. You wish it were different for your sake, too.'

'I don't.'

'Of course you do,' she said, nodding slowly, indicating he should follow suit and nod in agreement. 'You wish you hadn't lost so big in the wife-choosing lottery.'

He recoiled, shocked and angry, as though she had slapped him. 'Mara! Of course I don't—'

'You do. I know you do. You wish you didn't have to pick up all the slack all the time. You wish you weren't saddled with this pathetic—'

He jumped up, wrenching his hand from hers, and stood, feet planted wide, hands in fists at his sides. 'Don't tell me what I wish. Don't assume you know what I wish, what I think, how I feel—'

'Well, I can guess,' she said, 'since I'm going through the same thing. And I know I'd rather have it just finish me off already, be over with now, rather than drag out for years to come. I know how much better off Laks would be with me in an urn on the mantel, rather than as an object of ridicule in the school hallways. I know how much better life would be for you with me out of the way, and room for some young, healthy bombshell to sweep in and take my place. Someone you can look at with pride rather than pity. And if I know those things with certainty, then I know you know them, too—'

'Goddamn it, Mara!' She flinched. He never swore or yelled. She was the foulmouthed screamer of the family. 'What did I just say? You don't know what I know! You don't know what Laks knows! Quit trying to—'

'Fine. I know what *I* know. And what *I* know is that you'd be better off—'

'For Christ's sake!' He was pacing now. His face was red and she could see him clenching and opening his fists, trying to control his anger. He was failing. 'You're wrong. When are you going to get that? You're flat-out wrong. We would *not* be better off—'

'Well, forgive me if that's a little hard to believe.' She waved a hand, indicating his pacing, his red face, his clenched fists. 'You're not in the best position to tell me you're doing just fine.'

'I get to be upset, Mara, just like you do. I get to be enraged. About what HD is doing to my wife, to my daughter, to our family. I get to hate it as much as you do. So does Laks. I get to pace and swear and get red in the face and shout about it all I want. We all do. Laks and I haven't done a lot of it so far, and tonight may signal a change, or it may be a onetime thing. I don't know, and I don't care. Because getting upset is perfectly normal when things are upsetting! And I want her to know that. But just because we might be upset now and then doesn't mean we can't deal with it, or don't want to.'

He sat again and took one of her hands in both of his. 'Think about it, love,' he said softly, pleading, all anger gone from his tone now. 'I'm a doctor. If I didn't want anything to do with sick people, I wouldn't have become one.'

'You're a dermatologist,' she said acidly. 'It's hardly oncology.'

He started to respond, but stopped himself. He took a measured breath, then raised her hand to his lips and pressed it there. It made her resent him, how he had managed to force himself to regain his calm so quickly, how able he was to pull himself away from the emotional brink like that, ignore her insult and try another tack to get them back on the right track. It was something she was no longer capable of doing.

Then again, she told herself, he wasn't the one under assault. Who couldn't manage to keep it together when they were only a witness to the destruction? You didn't see people losing their shit when they watched war coverage on TV news. The only ones losing their shit were the ones actually in the goddamn war.

'Please don't tell me we'd be better off without you around,' he said softly. 'It's simply not true. And it hurts me that you'd ever think it. It would hurt Laks, too, I think—'

'Fine.' She shrugged. 'I'll leave you two out of it. *I'd* be better off if this ended now. I'd be better off not having to stick around any longer, knowing I'm making my child the brunt of jokes at school, knowing I'm dragging down my husband—'

He didn't jump this time, but he dropped her hand, let out an annoyed groan and stood. He took a step to the other side of the coffee table and flopped into one of the armchairs that faced the couch. From the expression on his face, his brief stint at controlling his anger was officially over. She couldn't help feeling a small flash of satisfaction about that.

'What?' she said. 'Why are you angry now? I wasn't talking about what was best for you two. I was saying what *I* want—'

'Because this isn't all about you! It isn't all about what you want, or how you feel!' He leaned forward. 'Did you ever think of that? Has that ever, even once in the past four years, occurred to you?' He spread his hands. 'You've read the websites, the brochures from Thiry's office. Thirty thousand people in the USA *have HD*. A far greater number *are affected by HD*. You might get to claim the gene but you do not get to claim the goddamn disease. Sure, HD is in your body. But it's in this family. And you are one of three people in this family. One of two people in this marriage. And yes, you're the one with HD and I will never pretend I know how it feels to be the one with the disease. But I'm the one who's *married to* the woman with HD. And that little girl' – he stuck his arm out toward Laks's room – 'is the *daughter* of the woman with HD. And we love that woman. More than anything.

'I know this disease has knocked the crap out of you. But you seem to forget it's knocked the crap out of us, too. You seem to forget that as much as you need us to help you get through this, we need you to help us get through it. I need the love and comfort of my wife. Laks needs those things from her mother. We need you here, with us. We would not be better off with you in a goddamn box on the goddamn mantel. Don't ever say that again!'

'Well, sure,' Mara said, rolling her eyes, 'that's what you have to say. But in your heart—'

'For fuck's sake, Mara!' He was on his feet again. 'Stop it!'

She watched, her mouth open, as he walked toward their room and disappeared inside. Moments later, he was back with her pillow, nightgown and the comforter from their bed. 'You want me to stop treating you with kid gloves?' he asked. 'You want me to stop feeling sorry for you and cutting you slack and doting too much?' he choked.

He tossed the items on the end of the couch. 'This is what I'd do if you didn't have HD and you'd spent the last fifteen minutes telling me I don't love you enough to want to be with you for every last fucking minute I can be, no matter what that means. This is what I'd do if you were perfectly healthy and accused me of preferring the easy route over looking after the love of my life. This is what I'd do if you'd never been diagnosed, if we'd never mentioned the word "Huntington's" in this house, and you confessed to me that you want out because, evidently, there are some downsides of living that, for you, outweigh the upside of being with me.'

He turned, walked back to their room and slammed the door behind him.

Mara looked dumbly from the pillow and comforter on the floor to the closed bedroom door and back again.

Good strategy, she told herself wryly – piss him off so much that maybe now he'll be happy when you're gone.

She crossed her arms and tried to scoff, but the noise came out as a wounded moan and tears clouded her view of the closed door between them.

She sat in the dark for over an hour, trying to work up the courage to go to him. She couldn't sleep in the living room, not when they had so few nights left together. He would never forgive himself, after, if she stayed on the couch because of his command. Finally, she stood and gathered the things he'd tossed to the couch. At their door, she paused, then pushed it one tentative inch, and another, until she was able to squeeze through. Squinting, she made out his form in the dark. He was lying on his back, head resting on folded arms, eyes open – and on her.

'I'd like to sleep in here, if it's okay with you,' she said softly, her voice thin.

He didn't respond.

It was better than a no, she decided, and climbed in beside him. She edged toward him and put a tentative hand on his thigh. He remained on his back, staring at the ceiling now, not acknowledging her.

'I'm sorry,' she whispered.

Still no response. She turned toward him and studied the firm line of his mouth, the way his jaw clenched as though he were working to keep himself from speaking. Or crying? She drew a quick breath in as she saw his tears. She had hurt him.

The thought made her own eyes sting, and for the first time she allowed herself to consider that the so-called I'm-fine-with-your-HD spiel (her name for it) he'd given her just now in the living room, the same one he'd given her so many times since the diagnosis, might not be a spiel at all, but the truth. Maybe he did want to look after her. Maybe it truly hurt him to think she didn't believe it. Maybe he really did want her with him, not out of the way. Maybe, for the second time in as many days, she had been wrong to leave the message she'd left for Dr Thiry.

'I'm sorry,' she said again. 'Tom, please talk to me.'

'It breaks my heart when you talk like that,' he whispered, still staring overhead, 'like you don't believe me when I say I want to be with you to the bitter end.'

'Oh, Tom.' Gently, she turned his chin to make him face her. His eyes had overflowed now and her lips parted in surprise but he shrugged unapologetically. Mara swiped a thumb under each of his eyes, then pressed it to her lips.

'I'm not going to be able to drive anymore,' she whispered. 'You'll be stuck with all the errands.'

'I don't care,' he whispered back. He locked his eyes

271

resolutely on hers, daring her to tell him he didn't mean it with everything in his body.

'I'm going to be ugly and pale and thin and covered in spit, sooner than you think. You're going to have to push me around in a wheelchair.'

'I don't care.'

'If you want to take me anywhere, that is. You'll be so embarrassed of me, it'll be such a hassle to cart me around, that you'll want to just stay in the house, hiding.'

'I won't.'

'I'm going to forget who you are. Who Laks is. I'm going to stop talking. I'm going to have to move into a nursing home, and you won't want to come see me. You'll make yourself come out of duty. You'll make Laks. And she'll hate me.' She scowled at the thought and turned away, but he put a hand on her chin, forcing her to turn her face back to his.

'She won't,' he said, his gaze steady.

'You'll never be able to retire. Nursing homes cost a fortune. You'll have to work till you're seventy. Laks will end up in some community college.'

He laughed softly. 'Do you pay attention to the investment statements I show you? I could retire tomorrow and we'd be fine.'

She squinted at him and he laughed again, and this time he was the one to lean over and kiss her. 'I could,' he said. 'And I will want to see you. Of course I will. And so will Laks. It won't be a duty for either of us. And she could never hate you.'

'She will. And you will, too. You'll end up lonely and miserable, visiting some old husk of a person who doesn't even know you. When you could be out. Meeting someone else. Marrying someone young and healthy, starting a new life.'

He shook his head. 'I don't want a new life. I want this life. With you.'

'But I'll be—'

'You'll be the love of my life. For the rest of my life.'

She sighed and closed her eyes. She felt him shift beside her until he was on his side, facing her. He slid an arm underneath her, draped the other across her and pulled her close. Soon, she heard his breathing slow, felt his grip around her slacken. Carefully, she eased herself out of his arms and sat watching him sleep. He really was a work of art. 'You mean a piece of work,' he always answered, laughing. And she'd reply, 'No, I mean a work of art.'

Lightly, she ran her fingers through his hair, from the top of his forehead to the crown of his head, then let them drift over his sideburns and along his jaw. It was unforgivable to let this beautiful man waste his years playing caretaker to a woman whose looks and body and sex appeal were draining away in a fast-moving torrent while his were only rising.

She traced the laugh lines at the edges of his eyes. He was such a kind, generous man. Of course he would take care of her until the end. He was right about what he'd said in the living room earlier: he was trained for this. He was a professional nurturer. He would care for her better than any patient had ever been cared for, if she let him.

She would have many more years at home, because of him, than HD would normally allow. She could imagine him saying, 'Not quite yet, love,' each time she suggested maybe now was the time for them to look into nursing homes. She could picture him pushing her wheelchair, carrying her from the couch to their bed, blending her food. Brushing her hair. Lifting her into the tub and bathing her tenderly, being overly cautious about the water temperature, the pressure of the washcloth on her skin, the nearness of the shampoo to her eyes.

He was her ticket to more time with Laks, with her parents, with Those Ladies.

But he was right, too, about something else he had said in the living room earlier: there were two people in this marriage, not just one.

Two people who loved the other to the edges of the universe and back.

Leaning closer, she inhaled deeply, taking in the manly, stirring, intoxicating scent of him. She pressed her lips gently against the lovely warmth of his cheek, the sexy coarseness of his nighttime beard. She let her tongue peek out softly and tasted the saltiness of his skin.

Two people motivated so strongly by love for the other that either of them would do anything for the other's sake.

She pressed her face hard into his neck and let her tears glue her skin to his as she considered all she would be giving up by refusing to let him look after her for as long as he could.

And all he would be giving up if she didn't refuse.

PART IV

Friday, April 8

Two Days Left

31

Scott

Scott was aware that his adjective/adverb refresher lecture wasn't exactly riveting, but when the entire class of seventh graders turned their heads to the doorway, he knew it must be more than uninspired teaching on his part. He followed their collective gaze and was surprised to see his wife in the doorway. Her eyes were puffy and red, as though she had been crying recently, and her lips were quivering now as though she was about to restart.

Oh my God, he thought: the baby. Turning to the class, his face suddenly clammy, he said, 'Give me a minute, will you? I'll send Mr Conner over.' Pete's classroom was next door.

He stepped into the hall, shutting the classroom door behind him, and put trembling hands on Laurie's shoulders. 'Is it the baby?'

She seemed surprised at the question, and shook her head, a protective hand moving to her round belly. 'It's LaDania,' she said. 'She's dead.'

'What?' He stepped backward, almost bumping up against the classroom door. '*Dead?* How?'

'She overdosed. Last night, they think. Janice called me at work. The police found her around four this morning. I tried calling you earlier, but the office didn't pick up. And I figured we should go get Bray anyway, so I might as well drive straight here and tell you in person. And then when I got here and signed in at the office, Mrs Bevel took one look at me and told me I could come right up. I don't think she wanted to be alone with me while she waited for you to come down to the office. Anyway, I'm rambling. Can you leave?'

'Yeah, yeah. Sure, I can leave. Wait here one sec.'

He walked a few feet down the hall and stuck his head into Pete's classroom. The student chairs were empty and Pete was at his desk looking at a stack of papers, a red pen in his hand. Scott cleared his throat and Pete looked up. Seeing his friend's expression, he dropped his pen. Before Scott could speak, Pete was out of his chair and walking to the door, his face pale.

'What happened?' Pete asked, before he noticed Laurie. 'Oh! Laurie, I didn't see you there. Hey, are you crying? What's wrong? Is it the baby?'

'LaDania,' Scott told him. 'She's dead. She overdosed—' He looked at Laurie. 'Last night, did you say?'

She nodded. 'Yes. Well, technically, early this morning, I guess. Or late last night, however you want to look at it.' She shrugged and fluttered a hand near her face. 'I'm rambling again.'

'Holy man!' said Pete. 'Shit!' He put an arm around Laurie's shoulders. 'I mean shit. I mean sorry. I mean – I'm rambling, too, I guess. I don't know what to say. I'm shocked. She was doing okay, wasn't she? Moved back in, the little man with her? Didn't you tell me she was

278

interviewing for jobs this week? Talking to Janice like she had her shit together?'

'She was,' said Scott.

They stood for a minute, none of them knowing what to say next.

Finally, Scott turned to Laurie. 'We should go. Track Bray down before Janice calls him. And, oh no—' He clapped a hand to his forehead. 'What about Curtis?'

'Still at school,' Laurie said. 'We'll get him on the way back from Ann Arbor. He doesn't know yet. Only Bray does. Janice called him before she called me. I told her we'd break it to him and she said since he's the next of kin, she had to tell him first. But I called him on my way here to say we'll pick him up, take him to get Curtis from school so he can be there to tell him. He seemed happy about that. So we can do that for him, at least.'

Scott looked at Pete. 'I can fill you in later, once we know more.' He pointed to his classroom. 'Can you?'

'I've got it,' Pete said. 'No worries at all.'

Bray's eyes were bloodshot and puffy, and he slumped in the backseat as Scott drove, Laurie beside him. Janice had called earlier and offered to pick him up and take him to his brother. 'But I told her I was pretty sure I'd be hearing from one of you, and you'd come get me.'

Scott and Laurie exchanged a glance and he mouthed the words 'thank you' to her. It was clear who operated best in a crisis.

As if proving his point, Laurie turned to Bray and said, 'I hope it's okay, but I called Pastor John on my way to Franklin.' Pastor John served a church that LaDania had attended on a fairly irregular basis. He had stayed in touch with her while she was in prison and had called the Coffmans several times to check on Curtis.

'No, that's good,' Bray said. 'Thanks for doing that. I guess I need to talk to him. Arrange a service.' His voice broke and he put a hand across his face, slumping lower.

'I did,' Laurie said, reaching her hand back and resting it on his knee. 'He can do it tomorrow at ten, he said. It's really soon, but he thought that might be better, for you and Curtis. But if you want to wait—'

'No,' Bray said quickly. 'Rather do it fast as possible.' He made a grunting noise and looked away, and Scott had the feeling the boy was chastising himself for wanting to get his mother's funeral over as fast as possible.

'I completely understand,' Laurie said softly, apparently picking up on Bray's guilt, too. 'Pastor John said he'd contact some of her friends from church. And the Johnsons. He'll ask the Johnsons to spread the word at the apartments. Other than that, I think it's just us, right? No other relatives you know of? He didn't know of any.'

'No. Other than my grandma, there wasn't anyone else. That I knew of, anyway.'

'Okay,' she said. 'We're all set, then. We can call him later about the details, if you want. Music, readings, that kind of thing. Or I can do it, if you want.'

'Thank you,' Bray said quietly.

'Yeah, Laur, thanks,' Scott said. He put a hand on her knee and tried to think of something he could do to help, and she covered it with hers. She was covering all the bases while he followed behind, lost. 'You can stay with us for the weekend, of course,' he said to Bray. 'And I can get you back to Ann Arbor on Sunday.'

Bray cleared his throat. 'Uh, I was hoping I could stay

over on Sunday night, if that's all right. I've got to be in Detroit Monday anyway, for the hearing.'

'What?' Scott asked. 'Why? What's the point of ending our guardianship now, if there's no one else to take over?'

At the same moment he realized he shouldn't have said that out loud before discussing it with his wife, her hand drew away from his. He tried to make eye contact, but she shifted her body away from him and stared intently out her window, her shoulders rigid.

'I talked to Janice about that,' Bray said. 'And I could put it off, considering everything. But it seems to me it's better for Curtis if he knows as soon as possible what's gonna happen to him. So I told her I want to go ahead with it. Tell the judge my decision, get it all formalized and let Curtis get on with his life.'

'What decision?' Scott asked.

'She said my choices are to either be guardian myself, or turn him over to the foster care system.'

'What?' Scott said. 'She told *a college kid* he should consider becoming guardian to an *eight-year-old*?' He couldn't believe what he was hearing. '*That's* one of the choices she suggested? Where does she think he's going to sleep, on the floor of your room? Is he going to do home-work in the locker room while you practice? Sleep on the bus on the way to your away games?' He banged the steering wheel as he spoke and he could feel the heat rise from his chest to his neck and into his face. He knew without looking in the mirror that the veins in his neck were bulging.

Laurie spoke without taking her eyes off her window. 'Calm down. Bray's not the one making the suggestion. He's telling you what Janice said.'

'Sorry,' Scott said, looking at her apologetically. But her gaze was still trained out her window and she didn't see the gesture. He cast a sheepish glance at Bray in the rear-view mirror.

'Nah, it's okay,' Bray said, dismissing Scott's apology with the wave of a giant hand. 'I was pretty blown away at first myself. But I've been thinking about it all morning. And I talked to a couple of the guys about it. And it makes sense, if you think about it. I'm his only family. I'm the one who should be guardian. And why wait? You two have your own family to get ready for. I can't leave him with you any longer—'

'So you're going to drop out, just like that?' Scott snapped his fingers. 'Give up your degree? Your entire future?'

He stared at his wife as he spoke, willing her to tell Bray to hold off, let them keep Curtis for a while so Bray could take more time to make such a huge decision. This time she met his gaze, but her eyes were dark and narrow. 'Scott,' she hissed. 'Let. Him. Finish.'

Scott took a deep breath. 'Sorry, Bray. I'm . . . I'm . . . Go ahead.'

Laurie shot him another dark look before turning once more to her window.

Bray waved a hand again. 'It's fine. I mean, it's not exactly fine. It's crazy, the whole thing. But I don't want to put it off, make him wait, wondering what his life is gonna be while I take my sweet time deciding what to do. He needs an answer. Deserves one.' Bray took a long breath in. Letting it out slowly, he found Scott in the rearview mirror. 'And my answer is, I'm going to be his guardian. I'm gonna quit school, move home. My mom had a little money – some life insurance policy from a job she had one time. Janice told me. It's not much, but it'll get us by till I find a job.'

He held a hand up to Scott, who had resumed panting and sputtering, waiting to jump in and protest. 'I know everything you're thinking,' Bray said. 'Everything you're going to say. But yeah, I've thought about it. And yeah, it's going to suck to quit. College, basketball, all of it.' He gazed out the window and shook his head slowly as though imagining the demise of his future career, the death of his dreams. Turning back to Scott, he said, 'But I wanted the big NBA career, the business degree, mostly to make a better life for my family. You know that. And Curtis is my family. What kind of guy am I if I turn him over to foster care and go on and make a better life just for me?' Scott opened his mouth to answer but Bray shook his head and Scott let him go on. 'I can understand if you're mad,' Bray said, 'if you think you wasted all that time, all those years, helping me reach a level where I could get into college and might even have a shot at the pros. And you should be mad at me for throwing all that away. I'm mad I have to do it.'

He turned to the window again, scowling, and Scott could hear the bitterness in his voice. 'I'm furious with my mom for putting me in this position. For leaving Curtis without a parent.' Bray glared out the window for a moment before taking a deep breath and turning back to Scott. 'But it is what it is,' he said. He shrugged, his expression passive now, calm. 'And I don't see any other way. So that's what I'm doing.

'I can go to night school later, once I have some money saved. Get a degree, a better job. Won't be Michigan, and it won't be the NBA. But those are done for me now, and

I'm okay with it.' Scott started to interrupt again, and Bray put his hand on Scott's shoulder, silently asking him to hold his protests a moment longer. 'And what I need now is for you to be okay with it, too, Coach. And get behind me on this. Not tell me what I already know, about how this is a crying shame and it's not fair and all that. I know it. But I can't think about that now, and I don't want to hear about it. Please.'

Scott forced himself to stop sputtering. He followed Bray's example and took a deep breath. Then another. And another. He commanded the color to leave his cheeks and the veins in his neck to retreat. He drove several miles taking long breaths in, letting them out slowly, until he was sure he could speak calmly.

Finding Bray in the mirror again, he said, 'I'll support you. If you're sure about it. Absolutely, one hundred percent sure that this is what you want to do. But . . . and I'm not arguing here, only trying to talk you through it. And I want to say that nobody would blame you for not being sure about wanting to sign up for this. Anybody would under-stand if you said you wanted to wait a little while, put the hearing off for a bit, so you can think about it a little longer. Decide if this is really the right answer. See if there's another alternative. And anyone would understand if, ulti-mately, you decide it's too much for you, and not something you're ready for, after all.'

Scott looked sideways at his wife again. Her shoulders stiffened and he knew she could feel his gaze on her. But she kept her body turned away from him, pretended to be focused on the scenery out her window, and said nothing. Scott sighed and turned his attention to the road.

'Appreciate that, Coach,' Bray said. 'But I'm a hundred

percent sure about it, right now. Bottom line is, I'd blame myself every day if I put my own brother in foster care, sent him to live with strangers, because it's "too much." That's not me. I don't shy away from things because they're too much.'

'No,' Scott said, 'you don't. You never have.'

32

Mara

Mara was about to review the to-do list she'd peeled from the bottom of her laptop when the phone lit up. It was Dr Thiry's clinic, and this time she answered, knowing they were calling to discuss the message she'd left with the service the night before, about her need for more sleeping pills.

They had checked the date of her last refill and they were clear to call in another, the receptionist said. Mara could pick it up from the pharmacy anytime. Mara grimaced at the thought of walking back in there. Maybe this time she'd make Harry's day by sending him in for her.

'While I've got you,' the receptionist said, 'should we schedule your next follow-up? I don't see that we have you down here.'

'Oh, yes, that's a great idea,' Mara said, feeling her cheeks heat with the lie. 'But I don't have my calendar with me. Can I get back to you later?'

'Of course. But try not to leave it too late – you know how he schedules out a few weeks in advance. Although it's nothing like the pediatrician, right? I don't know about you, but I have to book my kids' appointments months ahead of time now. Their dentist, too. Everyone's so busy these days, soon the hairdresser will be on a months-out schedule.' She laughed and Mara joined in halfheartedly while quickly she reached for her to-do list and added, 'Schedule L appts.'

She hung up with Dr Thiry's office and immediately dialed Laks's pediatrician. 'Just for the five-year shots?' the receptionist asked. 'Or do you want to get the well child lined up, too? In fact, that only gets us to December, and the system lets me go out twelve months. I could get the six-year-old shots in the system, too, if you'd like. Nothing like planning ahead!'

'Perfect,' Mara said. 'And you'll send postcards to the house, right, reminding them – I mean, reminding me – a few weeks in advance?'

'Always do.'

She called the dentist next. 'I thought I'd just line up her next three half-year cleanings, while I'm thinking of it,' she said. 'I'm about to have a very busy work schedule and I thought I'd take care of it now, while I have a little time.'

'Oh, sorry,' the receptionist said, 'but I can only log in one cleaning at a time. Maybe you could put a place marker in your calendar to call me back in six months? No mom is too busy for a quick phone call, right?'

No, Mara wanted to tell her. But some mothers are too dead.

Mara watched the phone fall from her hand. It hit the counter, bounced once and clattered onto the floor. The rectangular piece that covered the battery flew off with the impact. She could hear a tinny voice wafting up from the tile, and though she couldn't make out the words, she could imagine what the voice was saying. She stared at it, paralyzed, until the tinny voice turned into a dial tone.

Lifting her gaze from the floor, she swept it around the kitchen and family room and pictured Laks and Tom moving stiffly, sadly, through their days. Laks sitting at the counter, head hung over her cereal but making no move to lift it to her mouth with her spoon. Too upset, even, to pick it up and crush it between her thumb and fingers. Tom standing on the other side of the counter, barely sipping his coffee while he urged the girl to eat. The two of them walking to the curb together, the child clinging to his arm and begging to stay home from school.

And it would be the same in the evenings, the two of them picking at their dinner until Tom finally gave up and let them both get away with only one or two bites. Perfunctory bath time, neither of them in the mood to play pirate ship or any of Laks's other silly made-up games. And finally bedtime, the most painful time of day for anyone who misses someone. Mara could imagine them clinging to each other on the girl's bed, Tom trying to hold himself together as Laks bawled, a stack of books beside them, untouched yet another night.

Because of her. Because of what she was doing. The dial tone coming from the phone sounded to Mara now like the flat line on an EKG machine – the one-note dirge that announces someone has gone, and someone has been left behind. What sound could cause more grief? How could she voluntarily join that particular chorus?

How could she? Mara imagined that phrase ringing out in a choir, too, a sea of voices – the moms at school, the lawyers at the firm, their neighbors. Steph, Gina, her parents. And Tom, loudest of all. How could she do this to us?

Using a stool for balance, Mara bent to retrieve the phone and shut it off. She needed the noise to stop, and with it the images of what these rooms would look like once the sound of her own flat line joined the chorus of those that had gone before, ruining lives as it rang out.

It's *for* them, she reminded herself. She was doing this *for* them. Not *to* them. She had to focus on that. She sat at the kitchen table and regarded her to-do list. If she distracted herself with the pain she would cause, and lost sight of the pain she was trying to prevent, she wouldn't get through her list of tasks. And she would never be able to go through with the final one.

'It's *for* them,' she whispered, and then, louder, she said it again. 'It's *for* them.' She lifted a pen and wrote 'FOR THEM' on the top of her sticky note, and made herself say it again, even louder this time. 'It's *for* them.'

She cleared her throat, straightened her shoulders and struck through the item she'd added to her list a few moments ago: 'Schedule L appts.' Scanning the rest of the sticky note, she gave a determined nod. With two days to go, she was nearly finished with her calls and e-mails, but there were other important items she still needed to complete. 'Tom – advice' was at the top of the note and still unfinished. Sticking the note to the table, Mara turned to her laptop and opened the document she had started weeks before – a bulleted list of advice she had been compiling for Tom as new ideas came to her. She typed the information about scheduling appointments months in advance below her admonition to be sure to buy Laks's shoes one size too big so she had room to grow.

Above the shoe-buying tip: buy the pants with the hidden elastic and buttons in the waistband, so they'll be long enough for her legs but still able to cinch tightly enough to fit her tiny waist; don't be shy about playing the widower card when the PTA starts hassling you to help with the gift-wrap fund-raiser in December and whatever else they come up with – those things are huge time sucks, and though the women will try to convince you otherwise, it's more about their needing something to do than the school needing money; for that matter, play the widower card to get Laks whatever teacher she wants most – the office will tell you they don't take requests, but they take them from the PTA and they won't be able to say no to the widowed doctor; always, always ask for Elizabeth at the hair salon – Marian drags her comb too roughly over Laks's scalp and she will scream bloody murder for the entire appointment and all the way home.

Sixty minutes later, Mara struck a line through the 'Tom – advice' item on her list and sighed. What to do now? She'd sent e-mails to everyone she'd written down and suffered through a frustrating, passive-aggressive call with Tom's mother, who was already drunk enough, at nine fifteen in the morning, that she'd never remember to mention the call to Tom. She'd checked the forum for word from MotorCity. There was none, and unable to fake her way through the topic SoNotWicked had posted today – fitting exercise into a busy schedule – she had signed off quickly. She assessed the stack of magazines beside her laptop, lifted one and scanned the cover, tossed it back on the pile.

It was only nine-thirty. Harry wouldn't be there until eleven, and she had already showered and dressed. Sticking her bottom lip out, she blew a long stream of air upward, making her short bangs ruffle against her forehead. She peered at the remaining items on her list. Her letters to

Tom and Laks were finished; she would allow herself one last review tomorrow before printing them, but there were no more big changes to make. She lifted a pen and struck through that item, and the next: last night, she had gone through the two plastic boxes she kept under the guest room bed, one of cards Tom had given her over the years – for her birthday, their anniversary, Valentine's Day – the other of artwork Laks had brought home from school: a handprint turkey for Thanksgiving, with seven googly eyes and three feet, but only one tail feather; a snowman whose head was bigger than his body, and who wore a ball cap like the one Tom ran in, rather than a stovepipe one; a pink heart, much bigger on the left side than the right ('Medically accurate, even if not all that artistic,' Tom had said).

It was risky, she knew, rereading all Tom's love notes, running her hand over the shirts in his closet. Going through all of Laks's drawings, her first printed words. Burying her nose in the girl's stuffed animals. Sex with Tom. It was picking her way through land mines – any one of them could explode in her face, shatter her resolve. But it would feel cowardly not to meet the sights and smells and all of it. Like apologizing in the dark.

There was a selfish reason, too. She wanted to absorb it all, let it seep through the layers of her skin and drip into her bones. Take it all with her.

She glanced at the list again and realized she had missed one thing: looking at all the paintings and other art they had acquired over the years. Starting in the living room, she ran her hand the length of the mantel and over the expensive ceramics their overpriced decorator had insisted they buy right after they moved in. There were four in all, whimsical,

Chihuly-looking pieces whose bright colors matched perfectly the intricate custom tile work around the fireplace. Tom had remarked that the pieces would make great vases and the decorator almost hit him. Not one drop of water was to go in them, on them or anywhere near them, she admonished; they had cost more than many people spent on their first car. They were to admire, not to use.

By then, Tom was days away from firing the decorator. The two of them had practically come to blows over Tom's decision to change the custom fireplace from gas to wood burning. A quaint, old-fashioned idea, having a real fire, the decorator had condescended in her moneyed Texas drawl, but they needed to think about resale. No one with the means to buy this kind of house would be willing to kneel on the hearth and fuss with dirty logs and ashes. Mara had to stop Tom from filling the ceramic pieces with flowers before the woman's next (and final) visit. She smiled now, thinking how proud he would be to see her holding one of the pretentious objects in her clumsy hands, risking a fatal fall to the tile below. She placed it beside the others and moved on, running her fingers over the etchings in a cut-glass picture frame. This, she wouldn't take risks with.

It was a picture of her and Laks, taken last Thanksgiving. Mara is sitting on the floor of the family room, legs spread wide, while the girl reclines between her mother's knees. Laks is pitched at a wild sideways angle and she is peering up at her mother, her mouth open, mid-laugh. Mara's head is tilted toward her daughter, her mouth as wide as the girl's. Her arms are draped over the small shoulders and the girl is gripping one of her mother's elbows in each small hand. They had sat that way for an hour, chatting and cuddling, while Tom snuck off for the camera.

The bridge of Mara's nose began to burn.

'No.' She said it firmly, pressing fingers into her eyelids as she looked away from the photograph. 'No.'

For them, she reminded herself. She was doing Laks a favor. Tom, too. And she was almost there. This was not the time to start questioning her plan.

Or was it the very time?

Mara made herself look at the picture again. Mother and child, cuddling and chatting. Was there anything better? On winter days in Montreal, Mara would trudge home from school in the bitter cold to find Neerja waiting in the kitchen with hot chocolate and cookies. Mara would climb into her mother's lap and feel warm arms around her as she chatted away about what she had learned, or who had been sent to the office, or what games they had played at recess.

As she got older, she sat in the chair across the table from her mother but she never outgrew the routine of chatting with Neerja about her day. And although she stopped telling her mother everything, she still confided in her. Not because Neerja always had the best advice – their generations and upbringing were different enough, in fact, that Mara sometimes had to stifle a laugh at the solutions her mother proposed about boys and friendships.

But Neerja always listened as though what Mara had to say was the most interesting thing in the world. She always nodded along, and Mara always felt understood, and like her mother was on her side, even when she was telling her about how she'd gotten in trouble in class or received a bad grade on a test or forgotten to hand in her homework.

At the end of high school, when Mara had an after-school job, they moved their chats to the evenings, before bed. Throughout college, when Mara lived on campus and then in apartments with friends, they couldn't sustain daily visits but they called each other. And here they were still, dropping by each other's house a few times each week, though lately it was Neerja coming to Mara. Mara still didn't tell her mother everything, and she still had to hide a smile from time to time over the advice her mother gave. But they were still talking. Mara still confided in her. Neerja still listened as though hearing what her daughter had to say was more important than anything else she could do.

Mara listened to Laks the way Neerja listened to Mara. It was the greatest gift she knew how to give the girl, the loudest expression of her love. And even if she couldn't keep it up for a few decades like her own mother had, she could make it last past Sunday. Long after she stopped being able to greet Laks with after-school snacks, or play tea party in the backyard, she would still be able to listen.

And maybe the dozens of things, hundreds even, that Mara wouldn't be able to do for Laks anymore wouldn't matter as much, as long as she could still do that. Because looking back on it, it wasn't the hot chocolate or the cookies or even Neerja lifting Mara onto her lap and holding her tightly around the waist that had meant so much to Mara. It was the listening.

Mara touched a finger to the glass frame, to the middle of the girl's small chest. What was it Laks had been telling her that day? She tried to remember. Something about a dream, or a trip, or was it—

Out of nowhere, she felt a desperate need to go to the bathroom. Realizing she had forgotten to put on a diaper after her shower, she quickly drew her hand away from the frame and turned –

Too late.

She clapped both hands over her mouth.

'No.'

She had hidden the damn things in the back of the vanity drawer the night before and in doing so had made it more difficult to remember them. Thank God she was home and not in the back of the cab. She waited for it to stop, but it seemed every drop she'd had to drink in the past twelve hours was on its way out, snaking a disgusting yellow trail down the insides of her legs, over her bare ankles and onto the white living room carpet, where it left a stain five times brighter than it looked against her skin.

The circle of reeking urine crept out from her feet and, without thinking, she bent quickly and cupped her right hand at the outer edge, as if she might hold it in, keep it from widening. The movement threw off her balance and she toppled forward. Her reaction time was miles too slow; her arms didn't come close to breaking her fall and she landed face-first in the puddle.

'No!'

Instantly, she regretted opening her mouth. Her lips were planted on the carpet, and now the warm, wretched-tasting liquid found its way between them, covering her tongue and teeth. She gagged, and part of her breakfast rushed onto the carpet along with her urine.

'Goddamn it!'

Slowly, and with no choice but to put her hands in the mess to push herself up, she managed to ease herself to standing. Stiffly, her underwear and skirt drenched, she made her way to the bathroom, every step a sticky, smelly pronouncement. Stepping out of her skirt, then her under-wear, she stuffed both into the wastebasket, peeled off her shirt and bra, considered both, and dropped them into the basket after the others.

Naked, and cursing, she stomped to the kitchen for a bucket, cloth and carpet-cleaning solvent and carefully knelt beside the puddle, spraying and blotting and spraying and blotting again until she was satisfied the stain wasn't identifiable.

Back in the bathroom, she knew better than to look in the mirror but she did it anyway and saw a clump of vomit on her cheek, a larger one in the hair above her ear. She felt her gut clench, threatening to send out more of the remnants of her breakfast in whatever way was quicker. Trained now to always worry about choking, she sat quickly on the toilet and stayed there until she couldn't imagine there was anything left in her bowels.

She tore reams of paper from the roll and tried to clean herself but her arms had gone into highly uncooperative mode because of the trauma and she ended up with a revolting brown smear on the insides of her legs, the bottom of her stomach, under her fingernails. She lifted a wad of toilet paper to wipe her nose but the stench from her hand made her gag, so she lowered the paper and let her nose run down her chin, onto her neck.

She remembered the look of disgust on the little boy's face in the grocery store. The way the mechanic in the car repair shop stepped away from her. How her daughter's voice sounded when she asked Mara to hide behind the tree at school so no one could see her, then later, begged her father not to ever let her mother leave the house again. And she realized that as lovely as it was to imagine a future where Laks raced home after school, sat beside her mother and told her everything about her day, that wasn't ever going to be their reality.

The reality was, if Mara stayed around longer, this terrorist of a disease would put her in filthy situations like this again and again, and it was only a matter of time before it happened in front of her daughter. And after that, Laks wouldn't be running to Mara's bedside to talk – she'd be sneaking past her mother's door and out of the house, where she could be free from the disgusting woman who at the best of times walked like a drunk and at the worst of times, peed and shit herself.

And after a while, even on rare days when Laks did grudgingly sit by Mara's bedside – by order of her father and grandparents – it wouldn't be to gain insightful advice from a mother who listened carefully to her troubles. But only to stare wordlessly into the vacant eyes of a woman who didn't even register her existence.

When she had cleaned herself as well as she thought she could on the toilet, she slid off, onto the floor. Kneeling, she pressed her mouth firmly closed and tried not to breathe as she ran wet towels over the splattered toilet and the floor in front, then tossed them into the garbage.

She turned on the shower and while she waited for the water to heat, she washed her hands in the sink, over and over, scrubbing as hard as she could until her skin was red and burning. Only when no more soap would come out of the dispenser did she shut off the faucet and step into the shower. She slathered body wash all over herself and scoured every inch of skin she could reach, scratching and scraping more than washing. Punishing more than cleaning.

When her expensive soap was gone, she switched to her

even more expensive shampoo. Then her conditioner. Then Tom's body wash. When every container in the shower was empty, she stood with her back to the faucet, her body prickling with the sting of hot water against raw skin.

Her skin screamed but she wouldn't let herself step away from the stream. She deserved this. For what she was thinking of doing to them, she deserved this. She extended her arms, palms facing in, and examined her hands. Even after all the hand soap, the body wash, the shampoo, she could still smell it. She would always be able to smell it. Turning her hands slowly, she noticed the fine line of brown under her nails and let out a bitter cackle. Was there a more fitting symbol of her failure than this?

Turning toward the faucet, she slanted her face upward. 'Please,' she spoke into the streaming water. 'Please. Go away. You win. I lose. Leave me alone now. Please, I beg you. Not for me – for Laks. I beg you. She needs me. Please.'

The only response was the hissing of the shower, the hollow sound of water against the hard plastic casing. And then this: a movement in her left arm. One she might not have noticed were it not for the confines of the space, but which was impossible to ignore when her wrist collided with the hard plastic outer limit of the enclosure. It hurt; the stress was causing her arm to move with a lot more speed and force than she was aware of it doing before. Bang! Bang!

'Please stop. Please.'

Bang!

'Plea—'

Bang!

'Fuck you!'

Roughly, she grabbed her left wrist with her right hand and yanked it toward her body, gripping it hard. It was like trying to hold on to a fish. Her arm came out of the slippery hold and hit the wall again.

'Stop it! Stop! Fucking! Moving!'

The showerhead hung in front of her like a microphone. She reached a hand up, grabbed the slick metal to hold herself steady and yelled as loud as she could into the makeshift mic.

'You evil! Sonofabitch! You fucking! Devil! You bastard! Goddamn. Cocksucking. Asshole of a disease! I hate you! With every! Fucking! Diseased cell in my goddamn body! Haven't you done enough? Haven't you made things bad enough already? For me? For Laks? She's a fucking! Kindergartner! Do you really. Fucking. Need. To destroy. A kindergartner? Do you really. Fucking. Need. To keep. This. Up?'

Out of breath, she let go of the metal and put her arm on the wall to brace herself. Panting, she hung her head and concentrated on regulating her breathing. She looked up again and began to raise her hand once more but her arm was too tired. She let it fall to her side as she hung her head lower.

Cranking the water hotter, she stepped away from the faucet until she could feel the shower wall behind her. Slowly, she slid down the wall until she was sitting on the floor, the now painfully hot water assaulting her legs. She breathed deeply, letting the steam fill her lungs. Enjoying a respite from—

Bang!

A sob came loose from deep in her chest and after it, another. She tried to bend her legs, put her elbows on her knees and her head in her hands. But her left arm wouldn't obey. And her right leg wouldn't stay bent.

'Fuck it!'

Right hand in her lap, she let the scalding water pound the top of her head, her shoulders, as her left wrist continued to fling itself, a little weaker now, against the shower wall. Bang! Bang! Bang!

'I. Give. Up.'

The dull sound of water raining against the shower floor was punctuated by the knocking of her wrist against the wall, the erratic gasping of her breath as she tried to suck in air past her sobs, and the steady rhythm of two words she repeated over and over until the water ran cold.

'Forgive me.'

33

Mara

By ten thirty, Mara was dressed again, and this time she
hadn't forgotten her padded underwear. In the kitchen, she
made a sour face at the half cup of coffee she had poured,
dumped it in the sink and turned to unload the dishwasher.
She lifted a glass from the top rack of the machine, and as
she reached to set it in the cupboard, it slipped from her
grip, bounced off the counter and hit the floor, shattering.
Small fragments of glass flew in every direction.

She bent to pick up the pieces closest to her but then,
thinking twice, she straightened. Slowly, deliberately, she
lifted a china cup out of the rack and held it up admiringly
before raising it high above her head. She extended her
arm as far as she could reach and then, in one fast motion,
brought it down like the flag girl at a car race, releasing
the cup on the downward stroke. She watched, transfixed,
as the cup splintered on the tile.

As she stared at the shards of china and glass on the
floor, her lips curved into a satisfied smile.

She lifted another cup from the top rack and held it aloft
before quickly dropping her arm, releasing the cup to its

301

fate. She reached for another glass. And another. Another cup, another glass, until she had cleared the top rack. She was standing in a pile of broken china and glass when the front door opened and Harry's voice sounded.

'Mara! Are ya okay? I heard a noise. Did ya fall—?'

He rounded the corner from the living room to the kitchen, stopping abruptly when he saw the floor. He raised huge, questioning eyes to Mara's. She met his gaze and held it for a few seconds before she turned, took in the empty rack of the dishwasher and reached into the cupboard.

As the next cup hurtled toward the floor, Harry took a quick step to the side, out of the way of the shrapnel. He opened his mouth to speak. Closed it. And then he planted his feet wide, thrust his hands in his pockets and watched, wordlessly, a mixture of concern and admiration on his face, as Mara reached for another cup, then another glass, then another, and another. When she had made it through all the glasses and cups in the cupboard, she eyed the stack of plates.

Harry followed her gaze. 'Plates might crack the tile.'

She nodded and stared at the sea of fragments around her. Gingerly, Harry stepped into the kitchen and grabbed the broom leaning against the wall. He swept the broken pieces into a large pile in the middle of the floor, and when he was finished, she pointed to the pantry. He found the dustpan inside, and some garbage bags.

When he had filled two bags, she tilted her head toward the door leading to the garage and listened to the loud thud as he tossed around ten pounds of broken cups and glasses into the garbage container. Returning, he ran water over some paper towels and, on his hands and knees, slid the towels slowly over the floor, collecting tiny shards that had evaded the broom.

'Can't have that sprite cuttin' her little feet in here later,' he said.

She opened her mouth to thank him but her words were missing, and he bent again to his task before she could find them. She rested a hand on his shoulder briefly and he paused in his work for a second – his way, she knew, of letting her know it was enough. When he was finished, he carried the paper towels into the garage.

In the kitchen doorway, he asked, 'Should we go shoppin' for cups and glasses?'

She shook her head. Tom had put a box of extras in the garage. She pointed them out to Harry and leaned against the counter while he took each item out of the box, rinsed it, dried it and set it in the cupboard. He carried the empty box into the garage, stepped into the kitchen and smiled as though he had only just arrived at the house that second.

'Ready ta go watch recess?' he asked.

She nodded.

'Okay, then.' He thrust his elbow toward her. 'Let's go watch recess.'

When they were most of the way down the front walk, he asked, 'Wanna tell me what was behind that?'

'Not worth bothering you about,' she said quietly.

'Maybe ya oughta let me be the judge of that.'

She looked at him briefly before turning away. 'Honestly, Harry, if I told you half the things that are true about me, you'd never show up at my door again.'

'Shame,' he said. 'It's one powerful emotion.'

'Indeed.'

'Ain't no stranger ta it myself, y'know. Don't imagine there are many among us who are.'

She regarded him thoughtfully, remembering what he'd

303

said about having been someone once, back in Tulsa. 'I'm sure you're right. But all the same, as cathartic as it might feel to dump it all in your lap, or in the backseat of your cab, I think I'll pass.'

'Understood.'

He helped her into the car, clicked the meter on and pulled away. 'Been lookin' forward ta seein' the tiny thing on the slide today, I gotta say.'

She smiled out her window. 'You are something else, Harry. I'm sure you do your best to make every customer feel special. And I'm sure I shouldn't take it so seriously. But somehow, you've got me believing you really mean it.'

'Only one reason for ya to believe it, I'd guess.'

'Yes, I suppose that's true.'

'Same reason I get this feelin' ya truly care about me.'

She looked at him in the mirror. 'Well, I do.'

'I know,' he said, smiling at her reflection. 'And if I were gonna tell anyone the sad story of my life, it'd be ya. Shame and all.'

She smiled back. 'You don't have to go that far.'

He parked in the school lot, tucking the cab in the middle of a row of teachers' cars. While he busied himself calling the dispatcher, Mara found Laks, this time in pink shorts and a white T-shirt. White for now. They sat in silence for a few minutes, and then Harry cleared his throat.

'I'm a recoverin' alcoholic,' he said. 'Sober thirteen years now. But drunk twenty-five before that, and I did a whole lotta damage in them twenty-five years.'

'What made you—?'

He held up a thick hand. 'No questions. No comments. No sympathy. No judgment. Deal?'

She arched an eyebrow. It was a fair enough request,

though. God knew she was sick of sympathy. And she sure as hell wouldn't stand up to anyone's judgment. 'Deal.'

She waited for him to continue, but he was staring into the dashboard now, waiting. She took a breath and focused on her daughter as she spoke. 'It's Huntington's,' she said quietly. 'HD, they call it. The only thing my birth mother left me with when she dumped me at the orphanage two weeks after I was born was this fatal, genetic, incurable monster of a disease.'

Harry shifted his gaze quickly to the playground and the little sprite she knew he had grown fond of, if only from a distance. His lips were pressed tightly together and his cheeks were taut, as though he were holding his breath.

'Oh, no,' she said quickly, realizing his concern. 'No need to worry about her. She was adopted, too. And, thank God, she actually came with medical records. No history of HD on either side. She's fine.'

A hiss of air escaped his lips.

'Ironically enough, my husband was relieved I wanted to adopt because he has' – she paused – 'certain genes in his family he didn't want to pass on to a child. And meanwhile, it was my DNA that hid the ticking time bomb. If she were ours, and I had passed on that risk to her . . . But we don't have that worry, at least. I don't have to carry that particular guilt. My greatest sin, or at least my longest-lasting one, will be depriving her of a second mother far too soon.'

Harry whipped his head around sharply and she could see a hundred questions flash across his face, as many sympathies play over his lips as he struggled to obey his own rule. He turned to his spot on the dashboard and was quiet for so long she wondered if he had fallen asleep. But when she peered closely at his face, she saw his lips were moving slightly, and realized he was saying a silent prayer. She regretted having only met him now. She wondered if his confessional was over and breathed a sigh of relief that perhaps she wouldn't have to say more herself.

'I have a daughter,' he said finally. 'Caroline. I ain't seen her in seventeen years. And it ain't no one's fault but mine.' He flipped his sun visor down to reveal the photo of the young girl Mara had been wondering about. Caroline.

'I had my own diner in Tulsa,' he went on. 'Harry's Hash. Maybe not the best name for someone who turned out ta be an addict.' He chuckled quietly. 'Whole town came on weekend mornin's. Everyone knew me, I knew everyone. Caroline always said she was gonna work there, alongside her old pops. She was gonna be head waitress while I did all the cookin'. But I lost it – lost the diner. Spent mosta my money on booze, a little on blow. Started stiffin' my suppliers so I could buy my fix and still make the mortgage on the restaurant.

'I gave up the house first. Moved my wife – her name was Lucy – and Caroline into a crappy little apartment. All so I could keep the diner, keep up appearances. And also keep up my drinkin' and druggin'. I was all about me.' He hung his head and sniffed, then made a fist with one hand and brought it down hard on his leg. 'I was such a bastard. A selfish, self-centered bastard.'

It took everything she had not to reach out, touch his shoulder, his arm. But rules were rules. And now it was her turn again.

'I was terrible to my husband,' she said. 'When the symptoms started, and before we knew what was wrong with me. My entire personality changed. I turned into a

terror, almost overnight. Completely irrational. A little paranoid. Moody, oh, you can't imagine. It's part of the disease,
or can be. So is denial. It's not the best combination for a
marriage.'

She caught Harry's expression in the mirror. 'Believe it,'
she said. 'I was crueler than you can imagine. Remember
when we first met? The glare? The hiss? That was nothing
compared to what I'm talking about. I was horrible to him
for well over a year. Rejected him. Said things to him I
wish I didn't remember. But HD doesn't get your long-term
memory, unfortunately. Or your husband's. After everything
I've put him through, there's nothing I wouldn't give, or
do, to spare him from pain.'

She folded her hands in her lap and waited. Harry had
said no judgment, but it was hard to imagine he would be
able to keep from judging her now.

He sighed. 'Lucy was so sweet about havin' ta leave all
her friends in our neighborhood, our nice house, move into
the tiny apartment. Anyone could fall on hard times, she
told me. 'Cause of course I lied ta her, told her business
was slow and that's why I couldn't make the house payment.
Never mentioned I'd brought the hard times on myself – on
my family – by snortin' and drinkin' away all our savin's.

''Bout two weeks before I knew they were gonna take
the diner from me, I left. Couldn't face her knowin' the
truth about what I'd done. Couldn't live up ta what my
life had become. So I told 'em I was goin' out ta buy more
milk. And I never went back. I left them there. My own
wife and daughter. Left Lucy ta deal with the mess at the
diner and the mess I'd made of our family.

'I called her a few years ago. Lucy, that is. Cried like a
baby for almost half an hour while she sat there on the

other end of the line, lettin' me sob and sniff my way ta finally calmin' down enough so I could tell her how sorry I was. I asked her ta forgive me, and she said she'd already done it. Can you believe that? I never deserved that woman. Caroline was already moved out then, and Lucy said she'd better ask Caroline about it first, before she gave me her number. Said if Caroline said yes, she'd call me back.'

He stared at his thick hands, folded in his lap. 'But I never heard from her again. And that was my answer about whether my daughter wants ta hear from me. I'd give anythin' ta be able ta talk ta her, beg her for forgiveness, see if maybe she could see her way ta wantin' somethin' ta do with me. But I can't imagine she would. She's all grown up now. Twenty-three. She don't need nothin' from me now.' He gestured to the photo on his visor. 'This is the only picture I have of her. It was in my wallet the night I left.'

Mara bit her lip.

Harry went on. 'The idea that I might never see her again, never get a chance ta tell her how sorry I am, makes me wanna get drunk enough so I don't know my own name. Leastways what I done ta her, ta her mother, with my foolishness.' He sniffed and she saw a tear roll a thin, shining track down his face. To her surprise, he took a carefully folded cloth handkerchief out of the pocket of his plaid shirt and touched it to his cheeks, then the corners of his eyes. He took a long look at Caroline's picture, then gently closed the visor.

Mara felt the sting of her own tears and quickly turned to the window. She found Laks again and took deep breaths as she followed her around the playground. 'Yesterday was my last day to help in the library,' she said. She put a hand on the window, wishing she could touch Laks through the glass. Stroke her hair. Tell her again how sorry she was. 'She's so ashamed of me. Tom thinks she'll get over it,' she said. 'I don't think she should have to.'

She spread her fingers wide on the glass. Goodbye.

At her front door, Mara fumbled in her purse for her keys and Harry turned to study the planter, pretending to be too intrigued by the flowers to notice the trouble she was having. But a minute later, when she was still trying to force her key into the lock, Harry's big hand covered hers.

'How long?' he asked.

'Not long enough.' She regarded her left arm, which was moving slightly, and remembered what had happened in the shower. 'Or too long. Depends how you look at it.'

'And how do ya look at it?'

She let out a long breath. 'I'm forty-two years old and I'm already retired. I thought I'd work till seventy. I can't drive anymore. I can't remember anything unless it's written on a sticky note. And when I want to watch my daughter play with her friends, I have to do it on the sly from behind the tinted windows of a cab so I won't humiliate her. In a year, maybe less, I'll be in a wheelchair.

'I'll have to take one of those special vans to spy on her at school. If I even have my wits about me enough to remember when recess is. Or the fact that I have a daughter. I might not even live here anymore.' She jerked her head toward the house. 'I might be in a nursing home by then, sitting in a corner, staring at the ceiling, blissfully unaware of this house, my family inside it and the fact that you and I ever had this conversation.'

'I'd visit ya there.'

She put a hand on his cheek. 'I wouldn't want you to.'

'Yuh, I guess I knew that. Don't want anyone seein' ya . . . like that.'

'Don't want to be like that. All those people doing all the things I should be doing for myself? Feeding me? Brushing my hair? Giving me a bath?' She shuddered. 'I don't even want to think about it.'

'Not ta pry, but I gotta say. You've relaxed so much around me, don'tcha think? And in a couple days only. Lettin' me help ya into the car, lettin' me get yer wallet that one day? And today . . . with the, ya know . . . dishes. Don'tcha think ya could keep doin' that, a little more at a time, until it didn't bother ya so much for other people ta do that stuff for ya? Yer parents even? Yer husband? People at a . . . nursin' home?'

'Honestly, Harry, I think you must have some kind of super power. I've been thinking that exact thing, how being around you this week has . . . changed me so much. But I'm not sure it's enough. I'm afraid what you've seen may be about the limit of what I can allow.'

'Too old a dog for those kinda new tricks?' he asked.

She smiled. 'Something like that.'

'Right.'

'So let me ask you a question,' she said. 'You know, to even the score a little.'

He laughed. 'Fair enough.'

'What about writing Caroline a letter, letting her know how you feel? How sorry you are, how badly you want to make things up to her. I'm not sure someone in her position will reach out to you first, but it doesn't mean she doesn't want to hear from you. She may be waiting for you to make the first move.'

'Yuh, I've thoughta that. Even tried writin' a time or two, but ended up tearin' up the pages. I ain't got yer gift for words, not that it ain't obvious by now. My heart knows what I wanna say but my head can't order the words right.'

'I see. If you could write a letter, would you say anything more to her than what you told me in the car?'

He thought for a second. 'Nope. I think what I told ya about sums it up. Not a lot ta say other than I messed up and I'm sorry and I'd love ta see her if she'd let me. Love ta make it up ta her if she'd give me another chance. I mean, I'd say it in a longer, better way than that if I could. But that's the basic message.'

They stood quietly for a few minutes, and then Harry spoke. 'So when ya called me on Tuesday, ya said ya needed someone for the week. And now the week's over. But you'll still call me, whenever ya need me.' He said the last part as more of a command than a question.

'I will,' she said. 'In fact, I have a few errands to run tomorrow, and then a lunch date with my girlfriends, while Tom's at ballet with Laks. I usually take her, but . . .'

'So you'll do errands instead,' he said. 'With me. And then I'll take ya to yer lunch.'

He leaned forward and kissed her cheek. Before she could react, he turned and headed down the walk, sticking an arm up in a high salute as he went.

34

Scott

Having Scott, Laurie and Bray come to his school in the middle of the day couldn't mean anything good. Curtis's lips were quivering before he even got the words out.

'What's wrong?'

He folded to the hallway floor in a crumpled heap of limbs and tears when he heard the answer.

LaDania hadn't been a great mother. She left Curtis with Bray more often than she should have. She let him go hungry, dirty. She sold half the contents of his home to support her on-again, off-again habit. She had only responded to a fraction of the letters and artwork he sent her in jail, her responses not usually longer than one or two sentences. But she was his mother. And he had been counting on her to keep herself together, for his sake.

When he finally stopped crying long enough to look up at them, Bray held his arms out. But Curtis reached up to Scott, who lifted him into his arms and held him, Curtis clinging around Scott's neck as though he were drowning and Scott was a life buoy. Scott looked at Bray apologetically and started to hand Curtis to him, but Bray shook his head. 'He counts on you more than anyone,' Bray said quietly. 'You should feel good about that, not bad.'

At home, Curtis lay on the family room couch in the fetal position, a throw pillow clutched tightly to his chest. Bray sat beside him, murmuring to him softly and stroking his head. After a while, the little boy edged his way closer to the big one until his small head was on his brother's legs. When Scott went in to tell them dinner was ready, the boy's entire body was curled in Bray's lap. He was facing Bray now and had his arms wrapped around his waist.

'Do you want to?' Bray asked him.

The small head lifted, moved from side to side, then lowered.

Bray looked up at Scott helplessly and shrugged. 'Think we'll sit here a while longer, Coach, if that's okay with you.'

'No problem.'

They were still in the same position an hour later, when Scott and Laurie had finished dinner and cleaned up.

'You've gotta be starved,' Scott said to Bray.

Bray nodded, then gestured to his lap and shrugged.

'Curtis,' Scott said, 'what do you say we get you to bed? I'll take you up – unless you want your brother.'

Wordlessly, Curtis slid off the couch and went to Scott, a hand out. 'No *Stuart* tonight,' he said.

'No,' Scott said, squeezing the small hand. 'This isn't a night for *Stuart*, is it?' Looking at Bray, he said, 'Laurie put a plate for you in the fridge. Help yourself.'

'Should I come upstairs after? You know, to check on him?'

Scott looked at Curtis, who was listing a little as he stood, his eyelids half closed with exhaustion. He reached down and lifted the boy into his arms. 'Don't think there'll be anyone awake for you to check on.'

Upstairs, Scott found an old T-shirt for Curtis to wear to bed and got him settled under the covers. Being tucked in seemed to rouse the boy a little and he started to sob big, gasping sobs that shook his entire body. Scott felt his own tears start to come and he stretched himself out on the bed, wrapping his arms tightly around the heaving little body. This was not how he'd imagined his first reunion with the boy would go. 'I know, Little Man,' he whispered. 'I know. It's a raw deal. I'm so sorry.'

He stayed long after the boy's sobs gave way to rhythmic breathing and the sky through the windows turned from the light bluish gray of early evening to darker gray and then finally to the deep black of nighttime. A little after ten, Laurie peeked in on her way to bed and said she had set Bray up to sleep on the family room couch. 'I wish we had one of the other spare rooms set up for him to stay in,' she said. 'He's about three feet longer than the couch.'

But they had put off outfitting the other upstairs rooms with beds in an effort to spare their limited decorating funds for the rooms they had a regular use for.

'He's fine,' Scott told her. 'I've offered to get one of those blow-up mattresses for him a million times and he always says he'd rather be on the couch. I think he likes being near all the action.'

After twelve lonely years living with an often-gone mother, followed by another six with a brother who needed comfort more than he provided, Bray seemed to migrate toward people. He had laughed at Scott and Pete's suggestion that he live in a private dorm at Michigan so he could focus on schoolwork when he wasn't on the court. 'I feel better in a crowd,' he told them, and accepted the invitation to live in tight quarters with a handful of teammates who went everywhere he did, and not quietly.

Life in LaDania's old apartment, with no one but a child for company, would kill him. Long fingers of dread spread through Scott's chest.

'Come to bed,' his wife said gently.

He raised himself to sitting and stole another glance at the sleeping boy. He was about to stand when Curtis flinched suddenly and let out a small whimper.

'He's only dreaming,' Laurie said.

But Scott had already lain down again, edging his body close to the boy and draping an arm around him. 'I know. But I'll stay a few more minutes. Just in case.'

Later, Scott eased himself into bed beside his sleeping wife. He turned onto his stomach, head in his arms. Lying motionless in the quiet darkness, he became acutely aware that the hard knot of tension that had formed in the bottom of his stomach earlier in the day hadn't gone away. Neither had the dull throbbing below his skull. He had taken something for his headache after dinner, but it hadn't worked. And the glass of scotch Laurie had poured for him hadn't untied the knot.

He tried taking deep breaths, but it didn't help and he wondered if the knot in his stomach, the throbbing in his head, would ever go away. He felt Laurie shift beside him, and a second later her warm hand was on the back of his neck, her thumb and fingers massaging below his skull in exactly the right spot. He closed his eyes and tried to let the gentle pressure lull him to sleep, or at least relieve the tension in his neck.

Neither happened, and finally he turned to face her. 'I can't stand this.'

She moved her head closer until they were sharing his pillow, their foreheads almost touching. She stroked his cheek. 'I know.' Her voice was low, soothing.

'He has no idea what he's getting himself into.'

'I'd give him more credit than that.' Her thumb rubbed his temple. 'You promised you'd support him.'

'But this is crazy. How do I stand by and let him do this when it's so crazy?'

'I don't know that you have a choice. Not if you want to keep them in our lives. If you're planning on telling him every time you see him that what he's doing is crazy, he's not going to come around much.'

'I didn't mean that,' he said. He took a breath and asked himself if he should go on. But if not now, when? 'I meant . . . what if . . . we stop it from happening in the first place?'

She drew her hand away. 'What do you mean?'

But he could hear the strain in her voice, and her eyes were suddenly flitting everywhere.

'I mean, maybe we should offer to keep him?'

She rolled onto her back, letting out a long breath, and stared at the ceiling. He reached for her hand but she folded her arms across her chest and tucked her hands underneath, out of his reach. 'Offer to keep Curtis,' she said.

Propping himself on an elbow, he tried meeting her gaze but she took another long breath and tilted her face away from his, toward the bathroom door. The skin around her mouth was taut; it wasn't a good sign, he knew, and he prepared himself for a lecture on all the reasons he was wrong to ask this of her, after everything. But when she turned to face him again, her mouth was soft. For a second, he thought she was going to say yes.

'Don't you think it's a little, I don't know, insulting?' she asked. 'For you to suggest he's not capable, so we need to do this for him?'

'It's not about him being capable. It's not about him at all. I'd say the same thing to anyone his age. He's twenty years old. How can he raise a kid? He's only a kid himself.'

'He's not, though. He's a twenty-year-old man. People become parents at that age all the time. Kids you know – friends of his – already have kids. Do you want to tell him he can't handle what they're doing? After he asked you to stop challenging him and stand behind him?'

She had a point. He couldn't sweep in, cape flying behind him, and rescue someone who didn't want to be rescued. He flopped onto his back, and now it was his wife who propped herself on an elbow, leaning over him. She kissed his temple. 'I'm not saying it's going to be easy. I'm only saying you promised him you'd do it.'

'What about his future?' he said. 'His degree, the draft. Everything.'

'This is his future,' she said. 'This is what he wants.'

'But—'

'He asked for your support, Scott. You promised to give it.'

He felt her shift beside him, edging closer, pressing against him. She put a hand on his chest and moved it in slow circles and her touch calmed him a little. But after a while, the hand on his chest slowed, then stopped, and her breathing grew deep and steady. He lay still for a few minutes more, talking himself into falling asleep. It didn't work and he lifted himself out of bed, crept into the hall and eased the bedroom door closed behind him.

35

Mara

Mara's parents appeared at the front door minutes before Laks's afternoon bus was scheduled to arrive. A pale yellow silk dress for her mother today, light green shirt with pale yellow stripes for her father. Phone against her ear, Mara smiled and gestured for them to come in, raising an index finger to tell them she'd only be another second. She was in the middle of convincing the second of her two best friends that she didn't need a ride to the restaurant the next day.

'Yes, Gina, I'm positive. Like I told Steph, I've got some errands downtown and I'd rather get them done and not have to go out again. I've already arranged for the cab. He'll drop me at the restaurant and come back and get me after. . . . Yes, the same guy. . . . Yes, I am, a torrid affair in the back of the car. Look, my parents are here. Can we talk tomorrow? . . . Great, see you then. Love you, too.'

It wasn't until she'd hung up the phone and started in on an apology to her parents that she realized only her mother had walked inside. She poked her head out. 'Dad? You coming?'

'Why don't we let your father wait for Lakshmi while you and I put these things away?' Neerja held up another Agarwal's bag.

'Did Tom ask you to come?' Mara directed her question at her father, knowing her mother would never confess.

'I'm going to pull up a few weeds while I wait,' he said, walking away. 'You know how I can't stand to sit here with nothing to do.'

'I'm going to wring his neck when he gets home,' Mara said. 'I don't need him arranging things for me like this. Interfering. Protecting me.'

But it hit her: she wasn't the one he was trying to protect. It was Laks who said she didn't want her mother outside the house.

'What's that?' Neerja asked.

'Nothing, it's fine. It was a misunderstanding.' Her mother of all people would never understand, she thought, frowning. And then she caught herself – no more than forty-eight hours ago she had chastised herself for unfairly criticizing her parents and here she was, doing it again. She turned to her mother and put a hand on her arm. 'Stay for dinner.'

Neerja clapped her hands, holding them under her chin. 'We'd love to!'

Soon, Laks arrived home and cajoled her grandfather into pushing her on the swing set in the backyard. 'Mama does a big push for every year I am,' she told him as she led him by the hand out the back door. 'That's five big pushes. I'm lucky, because Susan's mom won't even do one anymore. She says it's too much work, and sometimes Susan smacks right into her when the swing comes back, and her mom doesn't like that.' Mara heard her father tsking about Susan's misfortune in having such a mother, and promising he wouldn't hear of his granddaughter suffering such an injustice.

She watched them through the sliding glass door for a few minutes and when she turned away, she found her mother in the family room, examining a photo on the wall: the five of them, last Halloween. Laks was dressed like the Tin Man because Tom had been in charge of the costume, and he was in the garage one day, putting gas in the lawn mower through a funnel, when Laks asked what she should dress up as. He spray-painted the funnel silver, and he and Pori spent an hour wrapping the girl in foil on Halloween night, then rewrapping her each time she bent a limb and ripped their handiwork. They finally deemed her costume good enough to head outside, but even then, they sent the women a few paces in front while they followed behind, each carrying a roll of foil and carefully examining the child after every step. She spent more time being repaired than asking for candy.

When Neerja realized she was being watched, she swung her head away from the picture and made a very poor effort at wiping her eyes without detection. 'Don't mind me,' she said. 'I'm just a sentimental old woman.' She laughed. 'It's just seeing that girl in her costume—'

'It's not that, and we both know it.' Mara crossed to her mother, hugged her. 'You get to be upset, Mom. And you get to be upset in front of me.'

Her mother didn't respond and Mara led her to the couch. When they were seated, she took her mother's wrinkled hand in hers, turning it over and running her fingers along the older woman's veins, as she used to do as a child. 'I know what we should do. Come with me.' She led Neerja to the guest room and pointed to the narrow bookshelf in the closet that held the family photo albums. Neerja clapped her hands and reached for the five thick albums on the top shelf, carrying four of them back to the family room while Mara trailed behind her with the last one.

They sat on the couch and Mara indicated the stack of albums on the coffee table in front of them. 'The complete life of Mara Nichols, volumes one through five, ages three months through forty-two years.'

'Are you sure you want to do this?' Neerja asked, a hand on Mara's knee.

Laks had asked about looking through the albums recently and Mara declined. When Laks pushed, Neerja ushered her away, distracting her with toys in her room. 'I understand, Beti,' Neerja told Mara later. Mara nodded, and they said nothing more about it.

It was too painful to watch herself growing up on Kodak paper, knowing what was waiting for the girl blowing out the candles, opening her presents, graduating from college, walking down the aisle, making law review, making partner. Knowing that in each moment, the girl wasn't enjoying the occasion as much as she might have had she realized how finite the cakes and ceremonies and celebrations would be. Instead, she was thinking ahead to the next big goal, telling herself she was one step closer, telling herself not to bask too long in the moment but push harder. If she'd had some warning . . .

Mara shook the thought away, put her hand on her mother's and nodded toward the stack. 'In order, or random?' she asked, reaching toward the books. 'In order, I think.' She took Volume 1 from the pile as Neerja laughed. Mara joined her. As if random had been a legitimate option for Mara.

They had made it to her junior high prom when Tom

came home. He took one look at the weeping pair on the couch and said, 'Not sure any man is safe in here.' He bent to kiss them both, then spotted his father-in-law and daughter in the backyard, took two beers out of the fridge and escaped out the door to join them.

By the time they were into her McGill days, he was back inside, asking about dinner. 'Laks says your parents are staying, which is wonderful. Want me to just come up with something, or do you two ladies have a plan?'

Mara and Neerja stared blankly at him before Neerja blew her nose and Mara wiped her eyes.

'Right,' he said. 'I'll grill some chicken.' After rooting in the freezer and fridge for a minute, he left again, with an armful of white packages from the butcher and bottles of marinade. 'I suggest we take our time out here,' Mara heard him say before the glass door sealed off his voice.

'So many memories,' Neerja said, smiling through her tears. She took a fresh tissue and wiped her nose again.

Mara considered all they'd seen – trips to the Rockies, the Maritimes, the Grand Canyon. Birthday cakes in the shape of castles, dragons, books. New bikes, roller skates, record players. Sleepovers with ten or more giggling girls in their small Montreal living room. 'Did you and Dad get any sleep those nights?' she asked her mother.

'Not one minute,' her mother confessed. Yet they'd allowed her to do it countless times, from sixth grade through twelfth.

'You've done so much for me, you and Dad,' Mara said, taking her mother's hand again. 'Without a thought about yourselves. You've put me first since the day you brought me home from Hyderabad. Before then, even. Since the day you decided to go rescue me.'

'It's nothing, for someone you love.'

'It's everything, Mom. I've had a lovely, lovely life because of the two of you. How can I ever thank you for everything you've given me? Everything you've done for me? And now for Tom and Laks, too?'

'You just did.'

'No. I mean *really* thank you. How can I *really* thank you for all of that? How can I *really* show you how much you mean to me, how much I love you, how lucky I feel to be your daughter?'

'I don't need *really*. I need this.' Neerja patted Mara's leg, which was pressed against her mother's, then nodded toward the albums. 'Only this.' She tilted her head and rested it on Mara's shoulder, and in that moment Mara felt like something between them opened up. For her entire life, her mother had looked after her. Even more since the diagnosis. Never once had her mother revealed uncertainty or anxiety about any aspect of parenthood.

Neerja had cried about the diagnosis, of course, but other than that, she'd never shown fear or vulnerability or weakness where her daughter was concerned. She had been Mara's capable, self-assured mother. She had everything under control at all times, including her emotions, because she never wanted her daughter to worry about her. And here she sat, head on her daughter's comforting shoulder while she allowed her own to quake with noiseless sobs. Allowed Mara to put an arm around her, pull her close and say, 'I know. It's okay. I'm right here. Let it out,' as she had done for Mara so many times.

Mara kissed her mother's soft, dark hair before tucking it behind her ear the way she did for Laks each morning. 'I love you.' She spoke into the top of her mother's head, where her lips remained. 'I love you.'

They sat that way, while outside, on the other side of the glass doors, Tom marinated and grilled the chicken and Pori pushed Laks on the swing, then watched her show off her 'spider guy' method of climbing up the slide. They sat that way while Laks climbed the monkey bars and called to her father and grandfather, who sat in lawn chairs, lazily sipping their bottles of beer. They sat that way until the sliding glass doors finally whooshed open and a 'starving-sostarvingsostarving' Laks raced through to her bathroom to wash her hands for dinner, calling as she ran that she'd decided on the pink plate and the yellow cup, please.

'Photo albums!' Pori leaned over to flip one open. 'I haven't seen these pictures in years.' He turned hopefully to the women on the couch, widening his eyes in surprise when he realized they were both crying.

'Not tonight,' Neerja said, sniffling. 'We've just been through them all, and you know it's not Mara's favorite thing. Wait for another time, Puppa.'

Mara kissed her mother again, then gently nudged her a few inches to the left to make room on her right. She smiled at her father, patted the space beside her and reached for the first album.

36

Mara

At two thirty in the morning, Mara gave up the pretense of waiting for sleep to come and slid out of bed. In the doorway, she turned back to regard her husband. A bit of moonlight shone through a gap in the blinds, illuminating a strip of Tom's sleeping form. Another contented slumber after another lovely session in bed together – that was one thing she hadn't stopped being able to do.

He had to be a little suspicious about that, she thought. Not since their thirties, twenties maybe, had she been this assertive. She took in the rest of the bed; the sheets were a tangled mess and her pillow was missing. He didn't seem to have been pretending. But then, when someone's eyes were closed, they could be thinking anything. She turned quickly, picking her way carefully through the dark living room to Laks's room. The girl had thrown her covers off and they lay in a heap on the floor. Mara covered her and reached to the foot of the bed for BunnyBunny, the large white stuffed rabbit Laks had slept with every night since she was two. She must have kicked it away with the sheets. Mara lifted the furry toy to her face, pressed it close and breathed in deeply. Morning body.

With BunnyBunny tucked under one arm, Mara tiptoed around the room, running her free hand over everything she could reach – the smooth wood of the gliding chair, the cold ceramic piggy bank on the bookshelf, the silver-framed picture of infant Laks in proud Pori's lap. She traced her fingers slowly over the edges of everything, trying to commit the contents of her daughter's room to memory.

Her throat closed when she saw the music box Tom had brought home a week after they returned from Hyderabad. 'I have a little girl,' he announced to Mara, 'and every little girl needs a music box.' Mara longed to pick up the box, feel the weight of it in her hands, but she didn't trust herself not to send it crashing to the floor. She slid a palm over the smooth surface of the lid, hearing its melody in her head. 'Beautiful Dreamer.'

She lifted a small ball cap from its hook beside the closet and ran her finger along the embroidered red *R*. The cap was a prized souvenir from the Rangers game Pori and Neerja had taken their granddaughter to one weekend. Smiling, Mara thought about 2boys and MotorCity and their ongoing debate about the Tigers and Yankees. She wondered what they thought of the Rangers. She would ask them tomorrow, if she remembered.

She held the inside of the cap to her face and inhaled, then returned it to its hook and opened the closet. The door creaked and she turned to the bed quickly, worried, but the sleeping form didn't stir. Mara looked from side to side, a burglar checking to see if neighbors were watching, then stepped into the closet, closed the door behind her and pulled the thin chain to switch on the light.

The mayhem on the closet floor made her suck in a breath and let it out in a noiseless laugh. Ever organized, she had set up a system of plastic bins in the closet and trained her daughter to store her toys in an orderly fashion. Each container was meant to hold a different category of toys: dollhouse furniture, puzzles, Barbies, dress-up clothes, plastic kitchen utensils. But Mara hadn't supervised a room-cleaning day in a long time, and the potpourri of toys in each bin defied any single category or unifying theme. Barbies were folded into plastic pots for the kitchen. A miniature cradle held a handful of puzzle pieces. Inside a purple dress-up purse was a collection of pocket-sized soft plastic dolls.

An old doll stroller held, of all things, schoolwork, and Mara shook her head as she leafed through it. There were counting worksheets, a classroom newsletter, crumpled bits of artwork whose glitter had long since trickled off and now lined the bottom of the stroller. A colored folder caught Mara's eye and she lifted it out. 'Poems – by Lakshmi Nichols – Kindergarten.' Laks had talked about their poetry unit and had shown some barely legible and largely nonsensical poems to her parents. It was an ambitious project, Tom commented, teaching poetry to kids who could barely read or write on their own.

Mara flipped through the first few pages, taking in the careful printing, pressed so hard in some places the letters went through the page. She could picture Laks taking her time to make each letter perfect and she felt a pang of sadness. She didn't want her daughter to be as intense as she was. Maybe she should arrange for Laks to spend time each week with Harry. The thought made her throat burn.

'Mara?'

Her heart thudded to a temporary halt as the door opened

and a drowsy Tom stood in the opening in boxer shorts, his head cocked to one side. 'Love?' Tom whispered. 'What on earth—?'

'Oh. Um, hi,' Mara whispered back, struggling for an explanation as to why she would be in her daughter's closet in the middle of the night. 'I, uh . . . couldn't sleep . . . and I thought maybe I . . . could get a head start cleaning in here. I was going to do it on Sunday morning when she's at my parents'. Get rid of some things while she's not here to protest, you know? And I thought I'd come in and see what lay ahead—'

'At three in the morning?' He leaned into the closet. 'Are you—? Why are you crying?'

She slid fingers over her cheeks to erase her tears. 'Oh, it's nothing. I—'

He pointed to the folder in her hand. 'What?'

She held it out to him.

'Oh, I remember this,' he said, still speaking softly. He flipped to the last page and held it up to her.

A Haiku by Lakshmi Nichols
No one is as strong.
My mom will never give up.
I'm a proud daughter.

He nodded, as though agreeing with the sentiment in the poem. 'Nice portrait,' he whispered, pointing. There was a picture beside the haiku: Laks and Mara, holding hands, Mara a female Popeye with giant, bulging muscles. 'Good haiku, too,' he added. 'I always loved that one.'

'You've read this before? I found the folder in the stroller she's using as a filing cabinet.'

328

He shrugged. 'I helped her work on it. Although mostly I counted syllables and fixed spelling. "Daughter" was d-o-t-r for the first few drafts, until I convinced her my way was correct. The idea was all hers, though. You were . . . I don't know where you were that night. Out with Those Ladies, maybe? She had to do a haiku about a characteristic – you know, honesty or strength or loyalty. She settled on strength, and I asked her what she thought of when she thought of strength. She didn't even think, she immediately said, "Mama."'

Mara sniffed and dragged the sleeve of her robe across her face. 'She thought of me for strength?'

Tom knit his brows together. 'Who else would she think of?'

'Oh, I don't know . . . *you*? The marathon man who logs twenty miles before breakfast and can still chase her around the yard all afternoon?'

'Pffft. Not the same kind of strength. Nothing I've ever done is the same kind of strength. You don't know that?' He tilted his head toward the bed. 'Your "proud daughter" over there is smart enough to know it.'

'She's not so proud anymore. Not after the fiasco at school.'

'She'll get over it. Remember how embarrassed you were of your parents' accent? "Mortified" is how you described it, as I recall. And how long did that last? Not even a school year, right? And then you decided "different" didn't mean anything but different.'

'This is a little worse than a thick Indian accent.'

'No, it isn't. It's being embarrassed by your parents. Accent for you. Public drunkenness for me. Huntington's for Laks. It's all the same. We all go through it, we all get over it.' He held a hand out to her. 'Come to bed.'

329

PART V

Saturday, April 9

One Day Left

37

Mara

When Mara walked into the family room early Saturday morning, she found her five-year-old curled on the couch, staring catatonically at the TV.

'Good morning, sweetie,' Mara said.

Laks, engrossed, didn't respond. Shaking her head, Mara regarded the girl and wondered if Tom was right: Was Mara's condition no heavier an albatross for Laks than Pori and Neerja's accent had been for Mara, or Tom's parents' alcoholism had been for him? Lying on the couch, ignoring her mother in favor of the asinine show on TV, Laks certainly seemed like any other child in America.

If her mother hung around, and got sicker by the year, or even the month, there would be disadvantages to Laks's life, the same as there were in the lives of every other child in the country. Every other child on this very street, for that matter. Right now, down the block and throughout Plano and in every state, kids were lying on couches, engrossed in cartoons while their parents yelled at each other, or one of them moved out. While their older brothers moved home, having flunked out of college, or their teenage sisters confessed to being pregnant. Did Laks's particular disadvantages really stack up so much higher than every other child's?

Mara took one last look at her daughter and sat at the table, peeling the sticky note from the bottom of her laptop. She could continue this debate while she attended to her task list. There was no harm in getting through the rest of the items, even if she decided to abort the mission.

She put a fingertip on one of the items not yet struck through: letters to Tom and Laks. It was the perfect chance for her to finalize them. Tom was running and wouldn't return for another hour. It appeared the walls could fall down around her daughter and she would remain glued to the screen.

Mara clicked open the letters, reminding herself she was permitted to scan them only. She had no time this morning for the kind of wholesale rewrites she had done so many times the last few nights. She still needed to get herself ready to meet Those Ladies for lunch, feed Laks breakfast and supervise her getting ready for dance class. The ponytail alone – a requirement of the teacher – could take thirty minutes of negotiating and rearranging. And anyway, she would never be satisfied with the letters, no matter how many more times she revised them. How do you sum up the contents of your heart in a single document?

She read each letter twice and re-saved them. She would print them tomorrow, put each in its own envelope and set them on Tom's pillow after he left for his run. She would leave a third envelope for him, too – the list of helpful tips she'd compiled to assist him in the task of raising their daughter. She opened that list now, scanning it to see if there was anything she had left out.

She had added a section about the promise Those Ladies had made, letting him know he could punt any subject he wanted to Steph or Gina. She'd also added a paragraph about how she'd been warning her parents for several weeks that once Laks was in first grade, Mara thought it best for the child to attend after-school care until Tom could pick her up on the way home from work.

It would allow the girl a chance to socialize more, Mara had told them. But what she really wanted was to make it easier for Tom to extricate her parents from his daily life, in case their constant presence was too painful. She knew they would insist on resuming their afternoon babysitting, and she knew he would never be able to tell them no. Unless they all knew it was one of Mara's last wishes.

And she'd added a line or two telling him she'd paid her Neiman's balance and canceled the account, so he needn't worry about it. She didn't want to think about him opening the statement, reading down the list of her last purchases. She'd canceled everything else she could think of, too – law school mailings, catalogs, anything that might show up at the house with her name on it.

Finally, on a separate page he could throw out if it angered him, she had written down the names and numbers of some Unitarian ministers who would perform a memorial service, even for someone who had never set foot in the place. Even for a family who would make no promises they would ever attend a service again. For all the lack of connection to the church Tom claimed, she wouldn't be shocked if he wanted a real funeral service. It was about ritual, perhaps, more than belief. And there wasn't a ritual older than gathering people together to say a few words about the dead.

Even if the words Tom wanted to say were 'Fuck you.'
She read over the list of names, unsure. Was it fair, providing
these names and numbers? Once he considered the idea,
she knew he wouldn't be able to ignore it. And if there
was a service, he wouldn't be able to say 'Fuck you.' Not
out loud, anyway. Out loud, he would be forced to say
nice things about her. He would make himself talk about
all the good things she had done, for him and for Laks,
before she had done this terrible thing.

He would have to nod and smile and agree with her
parents and Those Ladies and others who came that yes,
it was a dreadful thing to do to a child, to a husband, to
such caring parents and friends, but really, who were any
of them to judge? How could they ever truly know what
she had gone through? Who were any of them to say they
wouldn't have at least considered the same thing?

And he would, in saying those things out loud, nodding
as others said them, have to allow to himself that maybe
some of them were true. He might still whisper, 'Fuck you,
Mara,' when he was alone in their room, or driving to
work, exhausted by the demands of juggling a career and
a child on his own. But the funeral service would have
planted the seeds of empathy and understanding, and now
and then, she hoped, those seeds would sprout and rise up
through the curse words. Maybe those seeds would never
be enough to crowd out all of the resentment and bitterness. But maybe they would be enough to push away some.

'Mama!' Laks was peeking over the arm of the couch,
looking like she'd discovered a pony standing in the kitchen.

Mara laughed, and swiveled around to face her daughter.
'Yes. Mama. Mama who said good morning to you thirty
minutes ago and has been sitting here, five feet away, ever

since.' She smiled and shook her head. 'You and those cartoons.'

'Watch with me!' Laks scrambled to a sitting position and patted the couch beside her. 'Mama, watch with me!'

Was there a worse form of torture for a parent than half an hour of SpongeBob's maniacal laugh? Mara glanced at her laptop, scrambling for one of her stock excuses for why she couldn't possibly spare the time, why sitting in front of mindless cartoons would have to wait for another day.

What other day?

'I'd love to.'

She sat carefully beside the girl, leaving a few inches between them. Since the library incident, she'd been more self-conscious about her body, especially in front of her daughter. But Laks inched toward Mara until the space she had so carefully left was gone, and then tipped over sideways from the waist so her upper body lay across her mother's lap, her cheek on her mother's knee. Mara stroked her daughter's hair with her left hand and with her right she traced small circles on the fabric of the girl's pajamas, above her bony hip.

Laks wiggled, pressing her body tightly into her mother's lap. Two little hands reached out to grab Mara's right, bringing it into the girl's chest and clutching it tightly. She wiggled once more to reposition herself, then lay still and let out a long, contented sigh. Mara let out a similar sigh and the girl giggled.

Mara had been wondering how to say goodbye to Laks, deliberating over what she could say or do that would be significant enough to bring meaning to the child later, but not momentous enough to make her worry now. She felt the hot sting of tears as she realized: this was it. Tom would drive Laks to Mara's parents' house after dance class, while Mara was at lunch with Those Ladies. This was goodbye.

The closest box of tissues was on the table, out of reach, so she let the tears flow and counted on the girl being so engrossed in the ridiculous cartoon she wouldn't notice. Her right hand was trapped, and she couldn't bring herself to stop her left from stroking Laks's hair, so she turned to wipe her nose on her own shoulder. As she turned, her laptop came into view and it struck her that she knew exactly what 2boys would say if he could see her now, and if he knew everything she hadn't been telling: 'On the upside, this is the last thirty minutes you'll ever have to spend watching SpongeBob.'

Mara let out a strangled half sob, half laugh at the thought, and Laks, who was already laughing at the screen, laughed harder.

38

Mara

Mara and Those Ladies settled into their booth at the
Wooden Table, Mara's favorite restaurant. As they adjusted
themselves, arranged napkins, found places to store their
purses, Mara turned to Gina.

'Would you take Laks to church sometime?' she asked.
'If she wants to go, I mean? And maybe even if she doesn't?
Maybe around middle school, or late elementary, when you
get the sense she's old enough to take in what they're
saying? Tom won't mind. I told him I was going to ask
you about it.'

'I'd be honored to,' Gina said.

'Thank you,' Mara said. 'Oh, and remember we talked
once about you reminding her to call Tom on our anniversary? And I think you said you'd have her do it on Mother's
Day, too? I was thinking, you should tell her to stop if he
remarries. And Steph, you're going to have to be the one
to talk to my parents about being nice to any new girlfriend
or wife – you know that, right? I mean, I can't imagine
them being anything but kind to anyone, but in that case,
I don't know—'

'Where's all this coming from?' Steph asked, her eyes narrowed suspiciously. 'What aren't you telling us? Did Thiry give you some news that things are moving faster, or—'

'Oh, no,' Mara said, backpedaling. 'I just . . . think about these things, you know? Laks was talking the other night about how Susan's family always says grace, and she wanted us to try it, and it made me think about how she might enjoy church. Or at least benefit from going a few times, seeing what it's all about. And the other things just, I don't know, came to me, I guess, at various times. And since you're both here, and I actually remember them . . .' She didn't mention she had written each down on a sticky note and reviewed them surreptitiously as they took their seats.

Steph twisted her lips as though she didn't quite buy her friend's explanation. Mara lifted her menu and before Steph could interrogate her further, Mara smacked her lips loudly and read a few items out loud. 'They have the best filet mignon here. They wrap it in the thickest bacon. And the creamiest tiramisu. Oooh, but the chocolate brownie with warm fudge is so tempting.'

'I wish,' Gina said, looking down at her protruding waistline. 'It's going to be another house salad for me, with cottage cheese and fruit for dessert.' She put finger quotes around 'dessert' and made a face.

'Well,' said Steph, 'since we began the meal with all the maudlin talk about messages we all need to pass on to Laks from the one who'll be beyond the grave' – she hiked a thumb at Mara – 'I'd say this is as good a time as any to order something decadent enough to qualify as a last meal.'

Gina opened her mouth to chastise Steph but Mara put a hand on Gina's arm and shook her head. 'She's right. I mean, why wait until the absolute last meal? Especially since my last meal will be through a tube. That's not the way I want to savor my last bite of chocolate fudge!' As she spoke, she rooted through her purse for the small notebook Gina had given her ages ago to record things she didn't want to forget. Gina smiled as Mara produced it.

Flipping through the pages, Mara said, 'Here it is. I can't remember where I found this – big surprise – but I knew at least one of you' – she slid her eyes toward Steph – 'would appreciate it. And this is the perfect occasion for it. It's something Nora Ephron wrote, or said in an interview or something. Here goes: "*When you are actually going to have your last meal, you'll either be too sick to have it or you aren't gonna know it's your last meal and you could squander it on something like a tuna melt and that would be ironic. So it's important . . . I feel it's important to have that last meal today, tomorrow, soon.*"'

'Perfect indeed!' Steph said, clapping her hands once and then holding them under her chin, Neerja-like. They all laughed and Mara winked at Steph, a silent thank-you for keeping the moment from becoming depressing.

'No tuna melt for me, ladies,' Mara said. She handed the book to Gina, who was wiping her eyes, having not fully escaped the depressing angle. Pointing to the quote, Mara smiled at Gina. 'No house salad, either. It's filet mignon and brownie time. Bacon and chocolate are the two essential ingredients in any last meal. And I'm having a martini, too. Dirty. What the hell, I'm not driving.'

'I'll have the tiramisu,' Gina announced proudly. 'That way, you can have some of each. What's your next choice for entrée?'

Mara read through the menu again and chose the

lowest-fat option she could find for her weight-conscious friend. 'Um, I think the salmon with vegetables.'

'Bullshit,' Steph said.

'Eggplant Parm,' Mara admitted.

'One eggplant Parm, one tiramisu,' Gina said. 'Done.'

'And after that?' Steph asked.

'Butternut squash ravioli with sausage. Extra sausage. And lemon meringue pie.'

Gina smiled and handed the book back. 'It all sounds so much better than a house salad.'

As they ordered, Steph and Gina sounding proud when they announced their lunch choices to the waiter, each adding a fancy drink, Mara silently rehearsed the speech she'd come up with in the cab earlier. It was part goodbye, part thank-you, part spoken love letter to two women who had been like sisters to her. It wasn't adequate, the few words she'd come up with. But nothing would be.

When the waiter was gone, Mara took a breath and launched into her oration. She spoke about what Those Ladies meant to her. What a blessing their friendship was. How she'd never be able to put into words the degree to which she appreciated their loyalty, their honesty, their support over the past few difficult years –

'Jesus,' Steph interrupted. 'I can't take any more. Not after the messages for Laks and the last-meal stuff. Can it wait for another time? I mean, you're not dying *tomorrow*, right?'

Gina gasped and Mara blanched. Mara recovered faster than Gina and gave Steph her most casual laugh. 'God, I did sound dark, didn't I?' She waved a hand, dismissing her macabre speech as silliness. 'Thiry has me on this new head-shrinking drug,' she lied. 'Makes me all sappy and dramatic. You think that was bad, you should've heard what I said to Tom last night . . .' She arched an eyebrow.

It worked. Steph leaned across the table, a strong hand gripping Mara's. 'Ooooh, now the conversation's taking a nice turn. Tell me, just what did you say to hunky Tom? I can think of a few things I'd like to tell him myself.'

'Did you go through the twelve-step program?' Mara asked Harry as he drove her home from the restaurant.

'Nah. I'm old-school. Cold turkey on my own.'

'Wow. Impressive.'

'Not hardly. Took me twenty-five years ta get round to it.'

'So you're not familiar with that bit in the program where people go around apologizing to people they've wronged in their lives?'

'Nah. Can't say I am.'

'Well, I've been doing a little twelve-step of my own, this week. Not apologizing, though – thanking. People who've helped me, or who've been particularly important to me in my life.'

'Kinda like countin' yer blessin's, only you're comin' right out and thankin' yers.'

'Kind of. And, Harry? I want to thank you, too.'

'Me?' he asked, feigning surprise. 'I been particularly important in yer life?'

'I think you know you have.'

'Yuh,' he said, smiling. 'Maybe I do.'

'I wasn't happy to have to give up driving this week, to give up that control. Not that I need to tell you. But I've started thinking maybe there's a reason it happened. And the reason was so I could meet you. I'm very happy I was able to spend this week with you. So, thank you.'

His smile widened. 'Welcome.'

They drove the rest of the way in silence. When he pulled up in front of her house, she took an envelope out of her purse and handed it to him with the cash for the fare.

'What's this now?' He turned the envelope over in his hands.

'It's nothing, really. Just something I thought you could use.'

'Should I open it?'

She nodded and he opened it carefully, unfolded the typed letter inside and read the opening line. 'Dear Caroline.' He turned quickly to Mara.

'It's what I think you'd want to say to her,' she said. 'It's everything you told me, the way I think you'd write it if you could . . .'

'Get my head ta make the words come out how they sound in my heart,' he finished.

'Yes.'

She waited while he read the rest of the letter. When he was finished, he folded it carefully and put it back in its envelope, which he set on the passenger seat, under his jacket. 'You're right,' he said. 'It's exactly what I've always wanted ta tell her. In all the words I've felt inside but could never get ta come out right on paper.' He shifted in his seat and leaned toward her. 'Thank ya. For doin' this for me.'

'You don't have to use the whole thing. Only the parts you think are good.'

'I'll use every single word.'

She took his arm after he opened her door and they walked to the house in silence. When she started to turn the door handle, he put his hand on hers and stopped her.

'Why is it, I wonder, that you're doin' yer own little twelve-step program this week? Thankin' people? Givin' me this gift?'

She looked up at him and smiled. And then she leaned toward him and kissed him on the cheek. 'Harry. You know the rules. No questions, no comments, no sympathy, no judgment.'

'Huh,' he said, frowning, and she could tell he was regretting his own rules. But he gave a small smile and nodded. 'Okay, then,' he said, and started down the walk to the cab.

After a few steps he turned to her and said, 'This ain't goodbye, though, right? We'll go ta the school again together on Monday? I'll get ya a little after eleven?'

'Sure,' she lied. 'A little after eleven. That'd be great.'

'See ya Monday, then.' And he turned around and walked to his car, thrusting an arm high in the air as he went.

39

Scott

Curtis had cried from the minute he woke up in the morning until long after they returned home from LaDania's memorial service. Scott couldn't calm him down, and Bray and Laurie didn't do any better. Finally, Pete threw out a Hail Mary involving ice cream and the boy's tears stopped for the time it took them to drive to the ice cream place and watch him inhale a gigantic sundae.

They started up again close to bedtime. Laurie took a shift cuddling with him on his bed until he cried for Scott, who stayed for well over two hours before Bray tagged in. Around eleven, Bray dropped onto the couch, spent. The boy was still whimpering a little, he said, but he was close to sleep. Scott went upstairs and poked his head around the door. Curtis didn't stir, so Scott stole into his own room and slid into bed beside his soundly sleeping wife.

He lay beside her for ages, trying to coax his body into sleeping. He was beyond exhausted, yet the gears in his head would not stop spinning. He glanced at the rise and fall of Laurie's shoulder and wondered if he should wake her. But what good would that do? Lifting himself carefully out of bed, he crept out of the room and down the hall, pausing at Curtis's door. The boy was still splayed on his bed, legs spread wide, arms flung at right angles above his head. His breathing was slow, the emotional toll of the last twenty-four hours having dragged him into a deep slumber.

Downstairs, Scott poked his head into the family room, where Bray lay sprawled along the length of the couch and then some, looking as comatose as his younger brother. The kitchen clock read five after one. He spotted his laptop on the table and wondered what the chances were that any of his friends would be online. 2boys was a night owl, and he'd been uncharacteristically sweet since Scott had given them all the tragic update late yesterday, but his boys always had Sunday morning hockey or lacrosse practice or both. LaksMom and her husband had a date night, and while it had never stopped her before from popping in with a short comment while she powered down from the night and her husband crashed, she had warned that she might not be on.

Muttering a silent prayer that Phoenix or flighty or SNW would be around, Scott carried the computer to the living room couch, opened the forum and clicked to the end of the day's thread. They had been discussing religion last, he saw, either because that was the subject SoNotWicked had introduced in the morning or because that's where the conversation had led over the course of the day. As a group, they weren't the best about staying on topic. To Scott's delight, the time stamps on 2boys's and flightpath's most recent posts showed they had posted only minutes ago.

347

Sunday, April 10 @ 1:08 a.m.
MotorCity wrote:

Hi all. Checking in to say the memorial service was good. LMan produced his body weight in tears and won't be able to cry again for another six years or so, but he's (finally) sleeping now and I think with time, he'll be okay.

He hit 'post field,' walked to the kitchen and poured himself a glass of scotch. He took a long sip, grimacing as the liquid burned down his throat before returning to his laptop and hitting 'refresh.' Bingo – friends awake and to the rescue.

Sunday, April 10 @ 1:12 a.m.
flightpath wrote:

@MotorCity – Thanks for the update. We've been thinking about you. My heart goes out to you and the little man, his brother and your wife.

Sunday, April 10 @ 1:15 a.m.
2boys wrote:

dude, been thinkin of you. i know the little man will be okay. kids are resilient. which doesn't mean it'll be easy – we have our share of motherless-boy tears here every now & then as you know. your guy's got big brother to help him through, and that'll help a lot. so how's brother doing? and how you feeling about it all?

ps – note how i'm refraining from mentioning the drubbing the tigers took last night. see how sensitive i can be?

348

Sunday, April 10 @ 1:19 a.m.
MotorCity wrote:

@flighty – thanks. What're you doing up so late, btw?

@boys – you're a real gem for not mentioning the loss. As for how I'm feeling about it . . .

Scott lifted his hands from the keyboard. He wasn't sure how he was feeling about it. He had been so consumed with the funeral, and with attending to Curtis, he hadn't had a chance to consider it. Which was a good thing, now that he thought about it. It hadn't been a cheerful day by any stretch but he hadn't been aware of the knot in his stomach or the pain at the back of his head that had plagued him last night. Until now.

He walked to the front window, a hand on his neck, massaging. Glancing up and down the street, he eyed with envy the blackened windows of his neighbors' houses and imagined them all sleeping peacefully inside. He wondered if he would ever fall asleep easily again, after this. Or would he be up night after night, looking for someone to talk to online? Pacing. Regretting. Resenting.

He drained his glass and carried it into the kitchen. He couldn't make a habit of this, he told himself. Insomnia was one thing, but drinking alone late into the night wouldn't work long-term. He would let himself have a second glass tonight, given how hard today had been. But from now on, he would limit himself to one. He poured a double.

On the way back to the living room, he stole another glance into the family room, expecting to see a sleeping basketball player still stretched out and snoring on his couch. But Bray's feet were on the floor and he was bent forward, head in his hands. Scott could hear him taking deep breaths as though trying to keep from throwing up. He cleared his throat and Bray's head snapped up.

'Coach! I didn't know you were still up.'

'I was on the computer. Couldn't sleep. Guess I'm not the only one.' He smiled sympathetically. 'Thinking about your mom? It's got to be tough, man. I'm a lot older than you, and I still like having my mom around.'

'It isn't her. I mean, I'm sad about her, for sure. But I've got to move on, take care of the family still around me. Curtis.' He struggled to give a confident smile, but his mouth ended up in a frown. And Scott had caught the strain in his voice.

'Something wrong?' Scott asked.

'No. Yes.' Bray sighed and leaned back against the couch, looking exhausted. 'I don't know. I thought I had it all worked out in my head, you know? But now I'm not sure. I talked to some of the guys at the church today.' Bray's teammates, as well as his coaches, had made the trip from Ann Arbor for LaDania's service.

'And?'

'And I was telling them how I was planning to quit school, come home and raise Curtis. And some of them got it straightaway. My roommates, you know, they've been on board all along. And some of the others, too. They'd do the same thing, they said, no question. But a couple of them were saying it'd be the biggest mistake I could make. And not only for me but for Curtis, too. And then the Johnsons came over, and Pastor John. And Mr Johnson and the pastor, they got it right away, too, how I'd want to step up, keep him out of the foster care system.

'But Mrs Johnson, she was not having it.' He leaned forward again, elbows on his knees, and let his forehead fall to his hands. 'She said my quitting and looking after him is stupid. She said as much as I owe it to myself to keep going in school, I owe it to Curtis to let him be raised by people who know how to be parents. She was all on me about how thinking I can raise him myself isn't putting him first at all. Letting real parents do it is the best for him. I thought quitting, moving home with him, was best. But Mrs Johnson, she's right about me not knowing how to raise him. And now I don't know what I should do.

'Do you think I should do what she says, Coach?' He looked up at Scott. 'Do you think I should let someone else take him—?' His voice cracked and he paused for a few seconds before speaking again. 'I want to do what's right. What's best for him. And sure, I want to get my degree. Get drafted if I can. But sending him to live with strangers . . . ?'

He dropped his head again and covered his face with his enormous palms. 'I don't think I can do that to him, Coach. I don't want to do the wrong thing by taking him myself. And I don't want to quit Michigan. But strangers?'

Lowering himself to the couch, Scott set his glass on the coffee table and slid it sideways. Bray took a sip, made a sour face and pushed the drink back. 'Don't think throwing up is gonna help me, but thanks.'

They sat quietly for a few minutes, and then Bray asked, 'What do you think I should do?'

'I've been biting my lip for the past two days,' Scott said. 'Gnawing on it, really. Because you told me you wanted my support, and I promised I'd give it. And my wife ordered me to keep my mouth shut and keep my promise. You sure you really want to hear what I think?'

'Please.'

'I think Mrs Johnson's absolutely right,' Scott said. 'I think you should stay in school. Not only for your sake but for Curtis's, too. I know you think the right thing to do is for you to stop everything and look after him because you're family. And I think you're amazing for even considering it. But Jesus, Bray. I'm twice your age and most of the time this year I was in way over my head looking after the little man. He's a great kid, but—'

'I know. He's a handful.'

'He is,' Scott said. 'And I would've had a hard time with him at thirty, let alone twenty. Especially if I'd been on my own. There were two of us here and we were so tired some nights we could barely keep our eyes open through dinner. It's exhausting. All the homework and discipline and cooking and laundry and tuck-in time and . . . all of it. And you add work to that, and doing it without help? At twenty?'

Bray nodded slowly. 'I could screw it up for both of us.'

'Anyone could,' Scott said. 'But maybe someone who's done it before, who has someone else to help, has a better chance of making it work.'

'I can see it,' Bray whispered. 'I can see the sense in it. But if I send him to be with someone he doesn't even know? I don't know if I could live with myself.'

'I know.'

They were both quiet for a while, until Scott said, 'Look, I don't want him to be with strangers, either.' He took a deep breath, and another, trying to collect his nerves. He rubbed his hands over his jeans, from hip to knee, then the other way. He stood, walked to the fireplace, set his drink on the mantel. He picked it up again. Glass in his hand, he turned to the couch where a confused and anxious-looking twenty-year-old followed his every move.

He tilted the glass to his lips, feeling the scotch burn down his throat and into his stomach. The knot of tension that had been there since the day before loosened a little. Was it the scotch, he wondered, or was it that he was finally going to say precisely what his body had been urging him to say?

He cleared his throat. 'What if you don't leave him with strangers? What if . . . you leave him with me?'

'But I thought . . .' Bray stammered, looking confused. 'I thought Laurie didn't want . . . He's been such a pain, and the new baby and all—'

'Maybe she'll change her mind?' Scott said, shifting his gaze quickly. He took another sip of scotch, hoping to drown the doubt.

'You'd do that?' Bray asked. 'You'd keep him till—'

'Until whenever,' Scott said. 'Until you graduate, if the pros lose their minds and don't take you. Or until you retire from the NBA, if they're smart and snap you up. Or until forever, if you want to live your own life, have your own family. I'd understand it if you did. Anyone would. And you could see him anytime. Come here for Thanksgiving, Christmas, same as you did last year. Have him come see you for a week here and there if you want, or for the summer, or whatever. You could still be his brother. But you wouldn't have to feel responsible. Stuck. Trapped. Whatever it is you're feeling.'

'It's all those things,' Bray whispered, running a massive hand over his head. 'I feel bad. I feel like I'm a bad brother, a bad person, admitting it. But yeah, it's all those things, like you said. Trapped. Stuck. There I was in the car yesterday, talking this big game about how I'd never do that to family, that's not who I am. And it's not. I don't want to leave him stranded. But I don't want to screw things up for him, either. I'm twenty years old, Coach. I've got no idea how to raise a kid. I'd mess it up. For him and for me.'

'I'll talk to Laurie,' Scott said. 'See if we can work something out. Okay?'

'Okay,' Bray said, wiping his cheeks. 'But if she says no, I don't want you worrying about it. I'm crying now like a baby, but it's only because it's been a tough day, seeing Curtis cry so much, saying goodbye to my mom. Thinking about all of this. But this isn't your problem, Coach, it's mine. And I'll deal with it, make whatever decision I need to—' His voice broke and he stared at the floor before dragging his eyes up again to meet Scott's. 'I'll be fine.'

'I know,' Scott said. 'But don't decide anything yet, okay? Give me a little time to see what I can do. Give me until tomorrow night. I've got a little time left, before I take the little man to Monster Trucks in the morning, and after we get back. If I can't figure out a way to make things work here, you can go to the hearing on Monday, tell the judge what you've decided. Just give me till then, okay?'

Bray nodded, his shoulders now shaking with sobs.

'Hey,' Scott said, sitting beside the young man again and reaching an arm around his broad shoulders. 'That was supposed to make you feel better, not worse.'

'I do feel better,' Bray said. 'I feel . . . I can't describe it.' He wiped at the tears but they kept coming. 'It's just that since I heard about my mom, I've been thinking my life was over, you know? And now you're saying maybe I get to keep living it. Curtis, too. Second time, Coach. This is the second time you're stepping in to save us.'

Scott opened his mouth to answer. But no words came.

40

Mara

Since arriving home from lunch with Steph and Gina, Mara had picked up the phone at least a dozen times to call her parents. Just one more goodbye, she told herself. One more chance to tell Laks how much she loved her. One more chance to tell her parents. One more opportunity to hear each of them say it back to her. But she had hung up the phone each time, before the connection was made. If she heard their voices again, she didn't think she'd be able to go through with it.

Now she and Tom were driving east on the highway, headed for her birthday dinner. Mara bit her lip, thinking about how Tom, Laks and her parents were planning to give her presents tomorrow, when Pori and Neerja brought Laks home. Knowing her mother, Mara suspected one of tonight's activities at her parents' place involved cake batter, icing and candles. It made her sick to think of them working away in Neerja's kitchen, making Mara's favorite cake, Laks taking care to decorate it neatly.

'That is one amazing sunset, love,' Tom said, and Mara was grateful to him for interrupting her self-loathing session.

'Can you see it?' He angled the rearview mirror for her, and a red-and-orange ball, shot through with streaks of deep mango yellow, stared back at her. The few thin clouds surrounding the sun were in shades of purple.

'Wow,' she said, though the word didn't come out with enough force for him to hear.

'See it?'

She nodded, her lips pressed firmly together in a tight smile. 'Lovely,' she finally choked out. She had thought, at one point, about making a list of all the small things in nature she'd miss, and making sure she enjoyed them one last time: the sound of August evening crickets, spring's first daffodil, the whir of a hummingbird, the feel of sun on her face. And this, the dramatic, colorful canvas of a Texas sunset.

At some point along the way she'd lost the list, or forsaken it for one describing things she was far more desperate to experience: the sound of Laks's laughter, the feel of Tom's five-o'clock shadow against her cheek, the smell of her mother's shampoo, her father's aftershave. These were the sights and sounds and physical sensations most glorious to her. She had not run out to the garden at the first thaw this year to find the buds of daffodils. She had not paid specific attention to the mournful sound of wind in the chimes, the heavy, electric feeling in the air before a thunderstorm, the rich, thick, earthy smell after. She had not sat listening for hours on end to the calls of birds in the yard. Now she felt a pang of regret that she hadn't taken the time for those things.

Tom turned back to the road while Mara watched the sun sink a little lower behind them. 'Could we pull over and watch it?' she asked. 'It'll be gone in a few minutes and it's so beautiful.'

'We're already running late. Which, as you know, doesn't bother me one bit. But I can't say the same for my always-punctual wife.'

'I really want to watch it.'

'So let's watch it.' He took the next exit ramp, found a parking lot and pointed them west before turning off the engine. 'It really is lovely.'

'Mmmmm.'

He shifted in his seat to be closer to her, put his right arm around her shoulders and held his left hand out to her. She took it, intertwining their fingers as she edged toward him. She rested her head on his shoulder and he laid his cheek on the top of her head. Without speaking, they watched the sun dip lower and lower, the purple clouds changing shades as the light source moved horizontal to them, then below.

'Is it the most amazing sunset we've ever seen,' she asked, 'or is it simply the most time we've ever spent sitting still and really seeing it?'

'Hard to know.' He ran his hand up and down the length of her arm. 'This is nice. We really don't sit still all that often.'

'You mean I don't sit still. You're always trying to get me to do it with you but I'm always making excuses for why I can't. It's never been my strong suit, has it? Relaxing. Slowing down. Savoring the moment.'

'Or the sunset.'

'Right.'

'No matter. We're doing it now.'

Nodding, she studied their intertwined left hands, gently touching the wedding band on his. 'Marrying you was the single best thing I ever did, and the thing I'm most proud of.'

'Nah,' he said. 'I married up. Way, way up.'

She laughed. It was an old joke between them. 'For all your overachieving,' he'd say, 'you certainly didn't marry half as well as I did.'

'Up or down, backwards or forwards or sideways, I'm glad I did it,' she said.

'Me too.'

She adjusted her head a little on his shoulder. 'Settling in for a long spell?' he asked.

'Why not? We've been out to dinner a million times. This is the thing we haven't done enough of.'

'Oh, no,' he said, sitting upright again and moving to start the car. 'You're only saying that because of me. And I'm fine. We've been here a few minutes. I've gotten my quota of sitting still, and you must be long past your limit.' He winked at her. 'No need to torture yourself on my account.'

'I want to,' she said, pulling his arm away from the ignition, his body toward her again.

'You want to torture yourself?' He laughed, letting himself be pulled down. 'On my account?'

'There's no better account to do it on than yours.'

41

Scott

Scott sat on their bed, working up the courage to wake his sleeping wife. A hand on her shoulder, he shook her gently. 'Laur?'

She opened an eye and his heart pounded. Now that he was here, and she was awake, he didn't feel so sure. It was a bad idea, starting out by waking her. How many times had she lamented never getting enough sleep?

She glanced at the clock. 'What's wrong?' Her voice sounded panicked and she started to sit.

He pushed her gently back down. 'No need to get up,' he said.

'Good,' she murmured sleepily. After a second, she seemed to register he was out of bed himself and asked, 'But then, what are you doing up?'

'I was talking to Bray. He's a mess.'

She clucked sympathetically. 'It's a lot for him to deal with.'

'Yeah . . .' He looked down and noticed his right leg was bouncing a mile a minute.

She noticed, too, and pulled on his shirt to get him to face her. 'What?'

Scott took a breath. 'He's been talking to some people, and he's had a little time to . . . think about everything, you know? And . . . he's not certain anymore whether . . . he can handle a kid on his own. He's convinced he'll screw things up. For both of them.'

'But that's a complete change from the way he was talking yesterday.'

'Yeah.'

'So now he's thinking . . . he'll put him in foster care?'

'He's considering it. Only he thinks that would be an equally bad idea.'

'Wow.' She rolled onto on her back and stared at the ceiling. 'What a mess. And knowing Bray, he's—'

'A complete wreck. He's convinced that whatever he does, it's the wrong thing. I'm worried he's never going to forgive himself, either way.'

'So what now?' she asked. 'When's he going to decide? When's he going to tell Curtis?'

'I asked him not to make a decision until tomorrow night.'

'Oh, right, because you and Curtis will be at Monster Trucks all day anyway. And he wouldn't want to say anything in the morning before you leave. It could ruin the entire day.'

It made perfect sense, and if he'd been quicker on his feet, he'd have pretended that was precisely the reason. He wasn't, and his expression showed it.

'Scott. What's Bray waiting for?' She raised herself to sitting and leaned against the headboard, regarding him narrowly. 'Scott.'

His throat went instantly dry and he reached for the glass of water on her bedside table, took a long sip. The second he set the glass down, she grabbed his wrist and held it firmly.

'Answer me. Why did you ask Bray to wait?'

'I told him to wait . . . to see if maybe . . . you and I could . . . uh . . . keep the little man.'

She dropped his wrist. 'You told him *what*?'

He moved closer, taking her hand in his. 'Hear me out,' he said. 'I know the year has been . . . challenging. But maybe a lot of that was the temporary nature of it, you know? The fact that we all knew he'd be moving home with his mom. Miss Keller said as much, and you, too, remember? How the impending transition has been tough on him? And really, the whole year's been a transition, right? Moving here, and by the time he gets settled in, he's moving out again. One big twelve-month transition.

'Plus, the question of whether she'd keep it together once she got out of jail – I mean, that had to be stressful for the kid, right?'

He waited for her to nod in agreement. She didn't.

'Well, anyway,' he continued, 'if he hadn't had that in the back of his mind the whole time, who knows how he might have done. So I was thinking, if he knew he was going to be here permanently, and if he didn't have to worry about whether his parents were going to be home or in jail when he got home from school, maybe he'd be . . . better. Less . . . trouble. Maybe he'd even, over time, you know, get . . . easy.' He eyed her warily, guessing he was pushing his luck predicting Curtis would ever be 'easy.' The look she gave him let him know he had guessed right.

'I know you're anxious for time alone, for yourself and for us.' He squeezed her hand, smiling. 'And I am, too. But again, I think if he knew he would be staying here for good, he'd be better about that, too. A lot more likely to go play alone in his room for a while after school, give you time to yourself. I think it was the idea that his time was going to be so limited here that kept him underfoot all the time. And I know Pete would help out for the next few months, so we could still fit in all the date nights and everything, before the baby.' He lifted her hand to his lips and kissed it, then shrugged, laughing at his own weak attempt to show her the kind of romance she could expect from him.

'And I'm sure Curtis would fit right in with the new baby. He's been so excited about meeting her, talking all about how he wants to come over and see her, sing to her, teach her to shoot hoops. He'd be a fantastic big brother, I know he would. And look how well he's already fit into our lives, right? We've had those family dinners all year, like you've always wanted. And he's gone grocery shopping with you, and helped you bake cookies. Things you've always imagined you would do with kids one day.

'And remember how much fun it was at Christmas, with both of them here? Remember Christmas morning? How you explained the whole thing about lining up shortest to tallest at the top of the stairs and singing "Jingle Bells" on the way down, and they were both all over that?' He gestured to the hallway behind him, and the top of the stairs, trying to get her to remember how much fun they'd had that morning. 'And you said it was a real family Christmas? The four of us, a family?'

Breathless, he reached for her water glass again, staring intently at the book on her bedside table while he took another long sip and built up the nerve to look to his left, meet her gaze. Hear her answer.

She cleared her throat and he turned. Her lips parted slightly, and he realized with relief that she was at a loss for words. He wasn't ready to hear what she might say. He started to speak again, thinking it would be best if he filled the silence with more words of his own, talked his way past her shock, past the questions he knew she was going to ask when she recovered, the reasons he suddenly knew she was going to give for why his idea could never work.

She found her voice before he could think what to say next. 'You want us to adopt Curtis?'

He lifted a shoulder. 'He's so excited about the baby. He'd be a terrific big brother. Even you said so—'

She sputtered, pulled her hand away from his and held it up, facing him, stopping him from going on. 'That was months ago. And mostly I was praising him as a reward for being so sweet about spending all that time looking at baby clothes with me that day. I didn't mean it literally. You know that. I meant it theoretically. If his mom were to have another baby, I meant. I didn't mean he'd be a good big brother to our baby specifically, so he should stay for good. Don't use that against me to—'

'You're right,' he said. 'I'm sorry. But he would be a good big brother. And he has fit in here, right? We've had some great times this past year, haven't we?'

'Sure we have,' she said, now fully awake. 'We've also had hundreds of time-outs and almost as many temper tantrums. Half a dozen meetings in the principal's office—'

'Right,' he said, nodding agreeably. 'And that's what I'm saying. That so much of that was the product of inconsistent parenting for the first seven years of his life and . . . stress. But how much of all that would go away if he knew the rules were going to remain consistent? And if he knew this was his permanent home? That we were going to take care of him for good? And he didn't have to worry about where his next meal was coming from, or whether we'd be sticking around?'

'I don't know, Scott. Maybe all of it. Maybe none of it. And you don't know—'

'Well, yeah, I mean, there's no guarantee. And he won't turn into some dream child overnight, but—'

'It's not only about the behavior anyway,' she said. 'Or about wanting time to myself, or having time alone with you before the baby comes. You know that.'

He cocked his head. He hadn't known it would be about more than those things. The look on her face told him he should have.

She scowled. 'Don't look at me that way,' she said, 'all surprised, as if it's news to you how I feel about this.'

He tried to guess where she was going with this.

She raised a brow skeptically. 'Really? The biggest fight we've ever had, and you've forgotten?'

Ah. The older-child adoption argument that had landed him on the couch for a week before he was promoted to the outer edges of his side of the mattress for another two and then, finally, allowed closer. He blinked. That must be the argument she was talking about now. It was the only really big one they'd ever had. But how did it relate? Those were hypothetical kids. Curtis was real.

He said it out loud.

She shook her head and looked at him like he was completely clueless. Which he felt, suddenly.

'That makes it harder,' she whispered. 'A lot harder. But it doesn't change how I feel. I still want the same thing.

Our own family, our own biological family. You, me and our baby. And maybe others, if we get lucky enough to conceive again.'

He couldn't believe what he was hearing. 'But Curtis—'

'I know. And I'll feel sick about it if Bray decides not to take care of him. But I can't take him in just because I feel bad for him, Scott, I can't. It's not the family I want. I can't suddenly be okay with it because their situation is now different.'

Reflexively, he frowned and he shook his head once, hard, as though trying to clear something unsettling from his thoughts. He had anticipated hearing how difficult Curtis had been, how reluctant she was to sign on for more challenges, how he would owe her big-time, in ways she would look forward to dreaming up. He hadn't anticipated this.

He felt his wife's gaze and he lifted his chin to her. She was crying, and he realized she had seen the face he made, registered his disappointment.

'Don't pretend that's news,' she whispered, and he could hear anger laced into her tone, along with pain. 'And don't you insinuate it's such a terrible thing for me to say. This is something I've been waiting for, dreaming about, for years, and it's finally happening.' She put a hand on her belly. 'Don't you pretend it's an awful thing for me to want to enjoy it completely.'

He swore at himself. 'I didn't mean—' he started, reaching a hand toward her.

She batted his hand away and pushed past him, sliding off the bed. 'Don't tell me you didn't mean it. I saw the face you made.' She swiped angrily at her tears. 'After everything I've done for those boys this past year.' Her voice was barely above a whisper and he had to lean forward to hear. 'All these months I could've been getting the nursery ready or reading all those baby books that are gathering dust in the corner because I haven't had time to get to them. Because I've been helping with homework, reading stories. Arguing about taking a bath and going to bed on time. All the weekends I could've spent doing all the relaxing everyone tells you to do before the baby comes and you never have a quiet moment to yourself again.'

'Laur,' he said softly, 'I know. You've done so much for him. I'm sorry—'

She raised a hand. 'Don't tell me that now. Don't you dare try to tell me that five seconds after you've looked at me as if I'm some evil monster for not wanting to keep the boy forever. I've done my part. I said I would keep him for twelve months, and I have. I've done everything I said I would do. And I've done a damn good job.

'I've made that boy feel loved and cared for and safe. I've opened my home and my family and my heart to him. And they're still open, and they always will be. I've told Curtis and Bray they're welcome here anytime to visit, even to stay over. Come for holidays, even. As visitors. I don't owe them more than that, and I don't owe you more than that. I signed on to be a limited guardian. Not to adopt.'

'I know,' he said. 'I messed up. I shouldn't have reacted that way. I wasn't thinking. I was only—'

'You were only assuming I'd forget everything I want and say yes. Because that's so easy for you to do, you assumed I'd do it, too. And I didn't, and now you're, what? Disgusted? Disappointed? What was that look, exactly?'

Her voice broke and she took a step away from him,

toward the bathroom. Scott moved quickly toward her, standing himself now, reaching for her.

'No, that's not it,' he started. But he couldn't think of what to say next. He dropped the hand that had been reaching for her, dragged it across his chin. He rocked on his heels and stuck his hands in his hip pockets. 'Is there no way you could be happy,' he asked, 'with this . . . change of plan? I know it's work – he's work. But what if I promised to handle all the stuff at school, so you wouldn't have to do any of that? I'd do all the homework . . . all the everything. You could focus on the baby.'

'That's not a family,' she sniffed. 'Me and the baby in one room, you two in another. You wouldn't be happy with things that way. Neither would I. And it wouldn't be fair to him.'

'Right,' he said. 'But then . . .' He cast about for something, anything. 'What about . . . I don't know. Is there something else? Some other way we could make it work? You don't think there's any way for you to get used to . . . ?'

She shook her head slowly and stared at her fingers.

'And the fact that we're talking about Curtis here . . .' His voice faltered and she snapped her head up.

'Doesn't change how I feel,' she said. 'I love Curtis. Don't use that against me. I feel like you're setting me up here, suggesting that because he's been here for the last year, we're the ones who need to take him. That's not fair. Don't make me regret agreeing to take him in the first place.'

'I guess I don't really understand,' he said quietly. 'I mean—'

'I can't have this conversation again,' she interrupted, raising her hands to stop any further questions, any more suggestions about how they could make it work. 'And I don't think you really want to, either. Because my not wanting to dedicate my entire existence to these boys isn't the only issue here. There's also the matter of you being this total family man when we moved into this house, wanting nothing more than to load the place with babies and spend all our spare time together, as a family.

'And then you get this job at Franklin and bam, now you're vapor around here, with time only for your students. And your former students, for that matter. I've always wanted my own family. You knew that when you married me. I haven't changed. You're the one who has.'

He considered that for a moment. 'You're right,' he said. 'I have changed. It was easy to talk about a white picket fence and a house full of perfect children when we were in college, when we were kids who didn't know anything, hadn't seen anything. And even when we first got married and I was coaching at that cushy private school in Bloomfield Hills, where every kid had an overinvolved parent at every game, sometimes two. But then I went to Franklin. And yeah, I changed. Who wouldn't?'

'Right,' she whispered. 'Who wouldn't? Only a heartless beast.'

'I didn't mean—'

'Yes, you did.'

He stared at his shoes.

'Don't do this to me,' she said, her voice a strained plea, her shoulders starting to shake with sobs. 'I'm not a terrible, selfish person, no matter what you might think. This isn't easy for me, saying I won't take him, after everything. But I can't let guilt make me do something I don't want to do. Give up what I want. What I've always wanted. What you always wanted, too, until you decided you wanted something different. You can't ask me to do that.'

'Is there really nothing . . . ?' he started, but the look on her face was his answer. He was stunned. But she was right that they had been through it before. All the yelling and tears and threats hadn't gotten them on the same page then, and wouldn't now. Plus, the topic of their discussion was sleeping only a few feet away, on the other side of the wall. The last thing he needed was to wake up and overhear all the reasons why he wasn't wanted.

'Okay,' he said softly.

They stood a few feet apart, Laurie sobbing quietly, her face blotchy and red, Scott with his hands in his pockets, rocking on his heels. He thought of holding his arms out to her, stepping toward her, but his body wouldn't move. He opened his mouth a few times to speak, but nothing he believed right then would make things better between them.

After a while, her sobs slowed, then stopped, and he felt her watching him. 'Say something,' she said.

His lips parted, then pressed together again. He raised his shoulders and twisted his mouth in apology.

'Scott,' she whispered again. 'Please. Say something. Say you don't hate me.'

'I don't hate you,' he said. 'I could never hate you.'

He bit his lip and hoped she wouldn't ask him to say he loved her.

PART VI

Sunday, April 10

42

Mara

Tom stood at the kitchen counter, pouring coffee. 'Happy birthday!' he said as she walked into the room.

'Thank you.' She slid her hands around his waist and pressed her cheek in the space between his shoulder blades. She breathed in, filling her lungs with the scent of him.

'Mmmm,' he said, turning to face her. 'We need to send Laks to your parents' more often. Last night was amazing. Not that the rest of the week hasn't been the same. But last night was particularly—'

'I love you,' she said, hugging tighter. 'And I'm so grateful for you. You've been such a rock, for me and for Laks. I haven't told you often enough lately.'

He laughed. 'Other than last night, you mean. You told me the same thing at dinner, remember? And on the way home, and once we got into bed.'

She felt her cheeks redden and he put a cool hand on one of them. 'Not that I'm complaining,' he said. 'Of all the things to forget you've told me, and tell me again, that's a fine one.'

She allowed herself one last, long hug before she made herself push away. 'So, you going for a run?'

'Yeah, but I need a quick hit of caffeine first. I was thinking I might do nineteen or twenty today, if you don't mind my being gone awhile. I'm feeling extremely energized, after the solid ten hours I slept last night. Thanks to you.'

'Nineteen or twenty, eh? That takes you, what, two and a half hours? Two forty-five?'

'About that. But I don't have to go that long today. I don't have to go at all—'

She raised a hand to interrupt. 'Tom Nichols. We are not having this conversation again. You're a runner. You run. You're going twenty.'

He raised his own hands in surrender and laughed. 'Okay, okay. I'll go twenty. What are you going to do while I'm gone? Any chance you'd consider a nap?'

She looked at him as if to say, 'What do you think?' and he laughed.

He handed her a cup of coffee and she blew on it, then said, 'So, two forty-five, then, you think?'

He squinted at her over his cup. 'Um, yeah. Two forty-five. Are you feeling okay?'

She looked at him blandly, pretending it was a memory thing.

'Are you going to miss me?' he asked, teasing. 'Is that why you keep asking how long I'll be? Are you trying to decide if we'll have time for more' – and now he smiled – 'adventures in our room after I'm finished and before I go pick up Laks? Because I'm in. Should I just go five or six right now? Conserve my energy?' He winked.

An iron fist of regret clutched her heart and her throat felt parched. *Yes*, she wanted to say. *Yes, let's spend another hour in bed together. One more hour.* She closed her eyes quickly and called up the image of the sullen teens rolling their eyes at each other while their mother knocked her blanket onto the floor and their father stooped a tenth time to pick it up. Opening her eyes again, she shook her head, feigning annoyance. 'Go twenty.' She reached for his hand, lifted it to her mouth and pressed her lips against his knuckles. Turning her face to his, she opened her mouth to speak.

'Let me guess,' he said, still teasing. 'You love me. You're grateful for me.'

She nodded, pressing her mouth more firmly against him, and he laughed quietly. She had told herself earlier she would need to force herself to smile at him this morning. She had even practiced in the mirror a few times. But now her lips curved upward on their own as she realized she didn't need one more hour in bed, one more kiss on the lips, one more hug. This – his skin against her lips, the light, flirtatious tone in his voice, his laughter – was as good a final moment as she could ever want.

He leaned forward and kissed her on the forehead, a hand firm around her jaw. 'I hate to break up this nice moment,' he said, 'but if I'm going to fit in twenty before it gets too hot . . .'

'Go,' she said.

He gave her one last smile and walked out the door.

Tom had only been gone about a minute when the phone lit up. She didn't have to look at the screen to know it would be Laks and her parents, calling to sing 'Happy Birthday.' Mara's mouth fell open in delight: What better birthday gift could she receive than a chance to hear the voices of her daughter, her parents? She lifted the receiver from the base, but before she pressed the button to answer, she thought of what she'd told herself a dozen times the day before – that a few seconds of her daughter's giggling would loosen her resolve significantly. And her father's low chuckle, her mother's soft 'Beti' would undo it completely.

Mara stared at the phone in panic as the lights continued to flash. Another few seconds and it would go to voice mail. Finally, she pressed the button, raised the receiver and let the voices of the other three loves of her life sound in her ear.

43

Scott

'Would you rather get driven over by a monster truck, or . . .' Curtis pressed his lips together and thought about a sufficiently excruciating alternative. They were driving home from Monster Trucks, both exhausted from the long day. Curtis had spent the day vacillating from hysteria to depression, excited about being with Scott and seeing the trucks one minute, subdued about his mother the next. Now he was slouched in the backseat, looking half asleep, but Scott could almost hear the gears turning in the boy's head as he asked question after question. It was as though Curtis didn't want to squander one minute without trading words, now that the two of them were together again. Scott didn't blame him.

'Would you rather get driven over by a monster truck or . . .' Curtis tried again but he couldn't seem to think clearly enough to finish.

'I feel like I already have been,' Scott wanted to say.

A few minutes passed in silence before the child spoke again. He was quieter this time and Scott had to turn the radio down to hear him. 'I heard Bray talking at my mom's funeral. To some of the guys from the team. He said he's thinking about quitting school to stay with me. But then he won't get drafted, I heard them say. So why can't I live with you, and he stays in school, like we did this year? Why can't I do that forever?'

'It's not that simple, Little Man.'

'Why isn't it?'

Scott ground his teeth so hard he could hear the noise above the radio. He couldn't throw his wife under the bus but he couldn't stand not telling the boy how much he wanted him, how he'd fought to keep him. He made a fist with his right hand and brought it down hard on his knee. Self-flagellation for not knowing what to say at such an important moment. For not having won his wife over last night. The most important debate he'd ever been in, and he'd blown it.

'You look mad,' Curtis said, his voice unsteady. 'Are you mad I asked?'

'I'm not mad. I'm sad.'

'Because of me.'

'Well . . . yes.'

Curtis sighed. 'I'm sad because of me, too. I kind of feel like I did get run over by a monster truck and now my guts are all spilled out.'

Scott let out a noise, not quite a laugh, and considered whether he should tell the boy about telepathy. His eyes were stinging now, though, and he didn't trust himself to say more than a few words. 'I know the feeling, Little Man.'

He reached a hand into the back and Curtis snapped forward in his seat with more energy than he'd displayed in the past few hours. He grabbed Scott's hand in both of his and held it so tight it started to tingle a little. Scott told himself he deserved it.

'You're crying,' Curtis said. 'I've never seen you cry.'

'I am. And a lot of people haven't. Most people.'

Curtis let go of his hand then and fell against the seat once more. He leaned his head on the door and closed his eyes. He stayed that way for a few minutes and Scott was about to turn the radio up, having concluded the boy was asleep, when Curtis spoke again. 'Would you rather be so sad you feel you just got run over by a monster truck, and like your guts are all spilled out, or . . . never have even met Bray or me? So that now you wouldn't be so sad? And you could just be out jogging or shooting hoops or something right now and not even thinking sad things?'

'Guts spilled out, Little Man. No-brainer.'

'Me too.'

Laurie was on her knees in the garden when Scott and Curtis pulled into the driveway. Scott eased out of the car slowly.

She looked up from the bush she was trying to dig out. 'You're early!' She rose slowly, dropping her trowel at her feet, and hugged him, laughing when her belly kept them from getting too close. 'We weren't expecting you for another hour, at least!'

'Why are you gardening? What happened to resting?'

'Oh, I've only been doing this a minute. I was anxious for you to get home. Nervous energy. I had to find something to burn it off.'

'Nervous energy?' he asked.

'Hey, Curtis,' she said, 'would you mind staying out here a minute?'

379

The boy, who'd been bounding up the porch steps, did an about-face and jumped down to the front walk.

'Maybe shoot some hoops for a few minutes?' she asked. 'I'd like to talk to Scott. Alone.'

'Sure.' The boy ran to the garage to get a ball and a few seconds later Scott heard the rubber *thwang* of dribbling from the other end of the driveway.

'What's up?'

'I just wanted to . . .' she began. She wiped a dirty wrist across her forehead, leaving a trail of black earth. She held a hand out for inspection and made a face. 'Actually, could you give me a few minutes? I'm a mess. Could I clean up, and then maybe we can sit on the porch for a minute, before Bray gets back? I sent him out on an errand.'

'Sure. But I don't want to argue again, Laur. I don't see the point—'

'Me neither,' she said. 'Look, I'm a mess. Can we save this till I feel a little less grungy?'

'Sure.'

They walked up the steps together and he took a seat on the porch while she went inside. He heard her walk through to the kitchen, heard the faucet turn on. The sound of running water reminded his body that they hadn't stopped for a restroom break since he'd filled with gas last and bought a large coffee. No sense being distracted during whatever it was Laurie wanted to talk about, he thought, opening the front door.

The smell of paint hit him the second he stepped into the house. What the hell? He took another step and sniffed. The smell was coming from upstairs, he realized, and he took the stairs three at a time. He could hear a fan to his left, and he followed the sound into Curtis's room.

What used to be Curtis's room; it was unrecognizable now. There was a crib where the twin bed had been, a pastel-colored rug in place of the city map. The low bookshelf was gone and in its place was a changing table. A new glider and ottoman sat in the corner – no more old rocker.

What. The. Hell?

A fan oscillated in the corner, drying walls that had been stripped of their Michigan basketball posters and Curtis's toy hoop and were now painted a soft green. Sweet Fucking Pea. No jeans or hoodies lay in a heap on the floor of the closet. Instead, a shelving unit had been fitted inside and held stacks of neatly folded receiving blankets and infant clothes.

He looked at the crib again. It wasn't the unique, expensive, claw-footed one she had been so excited about but a plain, cheap-looking one they had seen in a million baby catalogs. She was so eager to get the room done she couldn't even wait for the crib? Couldn't wait till the kid was gone before doing all this?

He held his arms rigidly at his sides and made tight fists with his hands. He felt his cheeks flame and his heart pounded in his chest, into his throat. How could she be so goddamn cold? Taking an angry step toward the doorway, he considered whether he should go back to the porch and wait for her or burst into the kitchen to confront her. He stomped into the hallway, the first step to either decision.

And stopped, tilting his head. More fans, from across the hall, in the empty room they used as an office. What the . . . ? Maybe she used the rest of the Sweet Goddamn Pea in the other rooms, he thought. She had dedicated every fiber of her being to this baby – why not dedicate all the rooms in the house to it, too? He strode to the office, raised a foot and kicked the door hard. It swung open, banging loudly on the wall behind.

Seconds later, Laurie appeared at the top of the stairs, soapy water running down her arms. 'Scott? Everything okay? I heard a noise. Did you fall?'

He turned to look at her, a thousand emotions in his expression.

44

Mara

Mara stepped into the garage, pushing the door behind her closed. For a few seconds, she allowed herself to lean back and let the door support her. The vodka bottle hung by its neck from one hand and she clutched a bag of sleeping pills in the other. Tears ran so fast down her cheeks she saw no point in trying to wipe them away anymore.

'Okay,' she said, straightening. 'No time for this.'

She set the bottle and bag on the hood of her car and got to work. Behind some large bags of fertilizer, she had hidden four rolls of duct tape and a stack of towels she had bought months ago. Carefully, she taped over the outline of the door into the house, sealing it shut. She had read online that newer houses had good enough door seals, so there was no need to bother with this step – the carbon monoxide wouldn't get into the house. But who would take the chance?

All along, she had planned to leave the top of the door – she couldn't reach it without a ladder, and taping the other three sides was already overkill. But looking at it now, she frowned. The untaped length of door was unsettling. It made her feel she was leaving something undone. She pulled the stepladder over and, holding her breath, climbed up, one hand holding four long strips of tape, the other pressed firmly against the door, holding her steady. She hadn't been on a stepladder in over a year and it was more difficult than she would have thought. Her parents and Tom had been right to insist she not do it.

Next, she pressed three towels along the bottom of the door into the house, ten more along the bottom of the garage door. Reaching behind the bags of fertilizer again, she extracted a garbage bag she had hidden there, and from inside she pulled out a length of soft plastic tubing. It had been easier to pull off the role of DIY home repairwoman than she would have thought possible – the guy at the hardware store simply asked her the length, cut it to size and handed it over along with a roll of tape, wishing her good luck.

Now she taped one end carefully around the tailpipe of her car, fed the other end into a small crack in the rear driver's-side window and taped it in place there. She had read about this online, too – modern engines didn't create the same concentration of carbon monoxide as the old ones did. Ultimately, more than the tubing, it was essential to have the right number of pills. But this was not the time to do anything halfway.

She reviewed her handiwork and nodded, satisfied, before moving toward the bottle and pills. With one hand on the bottle, she turned her head to consider Tom's car, behind her. She had been faster at taping than she had accounted for, she told herself. She had a little extra time. She left the vodka, opened the passenger door of Tom's sedan and lowered herself onto the seat.

Running her hands over the beige leather, she inhaled deeply – Tom's aftershave. She reached a tentative hand to the driver's seat and ran her hand over it longingly, as though instead of cool leather, she could feel his warm body. She slid her hand around the sleek circumference of the steering wheel before dropping it to the gearshift, which she held softly, as though it were his hand.

She ran her palm along the dashboard before opening the glove box and touching a fingertip to his car manual, the envelope that held his registration and insurance, and his CDs. She smiled. He refused to put one of those CD holders on his visor, but he couldn't reach them in the glove box as he was driving, and it was never until he was on the highway that he remembered he had meant to take one out of its case, slide it into the player. For almost a year, he had listened to the same CD – Tom Petty, the one she had put into his player for him the day he brought the car home. She eased herself out and closed the door gently.

Inside her own car, Mara set the vodka bottle on the passenger seat and emptied the bag of pills into the cup holder. She leaned against the seat and took a deep breath.

Stale apple juice.

Laks.

She craned her neck toward the backseat. Her daughter's booster was covered in crumbs, and an hourglass-shaped juice box lay beside it, squeezed in the middle so every last drop could come out. There was a pink flip-flop wedged between the booster and the seat belt. Mara clutched a hand to her throat.

As she considered the little sandal, it struck her that in Harry's cab, with its smell of cologne, its shiny vinyl seats and spotless floor, it had been so easy to wrap herself in a shroud of her own pain and fears, her stringent rules about what she could and could not tolerate, what she could and could not allow her daughter, her husband, her parents, her friends to abide. She might not have been able to keep so focused with the faint odor of stale juice around her, the tiny fingerprints on the window. The flip-flop.

She closed her eyes and heard Laks's voice singing 'Happy Birthday,' giggling as she finished the song with the 'Are you one? Are you two?' chant her friends all sang at their parties, going up the numbers until they reached the age of the birthday boy or girl. When Laks reached twenty, Mara heard her parents whispering in the background, helping her get the numbers right. They were eating pancakes, Laks announced, and Mara could picture the sticky syrup on the girl's cheek – and now, likely, on her parents' phone.

She thought about the honey she'd found behind Laks's ear when she'd lain beside her the other night. She thought about the tufts of hair that stuck out on the side of the girl's head, courtesy of Susan and her 'fix' for the glue incident. She thought about the five big pushes Laks begged for on the swing every day, the new 'spider guy' technique she'd mastered for climbing up the plastic slide. She thought about how they'd cuddled on the couch together yesterday, Laks gripping her mother's arm tightly, nestling her bony bottom into Mara's stomach, sighing contentedly like there was nothing she would rather do than watch TV with her mother.

Mara drew in a sharp breath, pressing a thumb and finger against her eyelids.

'Turn around,' she said. And she did, quickly, and just as quickly she reached for the bottle of vodka and took a long swallow. She pressed her head into her headrest, keeping her gaze fixed forward, out the windshield, and told herself this was why the universe had sent her Harry. She couldn't have gotten through these last days in her own car, with this – her daughter, her life – all around her. She needed the safe cocoon of the taxi, away from everything and everyone she was leaving behind.

Quickly, she tilted the bottle again, and as she swallowed, she fished in the pocket of her robe for the keys. A crinkling sound reminded her that she'd folded the haiku and put it there last night. Her fingers grazed the edges of the paper.

Her proud daughter. How proud would she be now? How strong would she think her mother was? There was no strength in escaping.

Mara snapped her hand out of her pocket and trapped it under her thigh, away from the poem. She put a handful of pills in her mouth, tilted the bottle and washed them down.

Then she started the car.

45

Scott

Scott swiveled his head from Laurie to the office. The desk, filing cabinet, ironing board and plastic storage bins that had taken up most of the room were gone. In their place was a twin bed with a maize-and-blue comforter, an area rug that imitated the streets of a town. A low bookshelf ran under the window, *Stuart Little* propped on a book stand on top, alongside a small framed photograph: the one of Scott and Curtis reclining on the boy's bed, reading about the mouse.

There was no Warm Ecru in sight – the walls were blue on the bottom half, maize on the top half, with a 'Michigan! Go Blue!' border dividing top from bottom. Curtis's toy basketball hoop hung on the wall near the window and a half dozen framed Michigan basketball posters leaned against the closet door, waiting to be hung. He looked at Laurie in confusion as she stepped toward him.

'Pete and half the boys tackled this room while Bray and I and the other half worked on the nursery,' she said. 'We started the minute you pulled out and, taskmaster that I am, I didn't let them take one break. They ate pizza while

388

they worked. Thank God the season's over – you have no idea how fast you can get things done with eight varsity athletes on hand.'

He looked at her, part thrilled about what he thought this meant, part terrified he was wrong. 'For . . . ?'

She nodded. 'For Curtis.'

'For when he comes to visit?' he whispered.

She smiled, shaking her head. 'For when he goes to bed at night. Or wants to play with his toys. Or escape his little sister.'

Scott's knees were liquid and he took a quick step into the room, sitting heavily on the bed. Leaning forward, he put his head in his hands and felt dampness from his cheeks cover his palms.

Laurie knelt in front of him, a hand on each of his knees. 'The craft room looks pretty much the same. Minus the town rug and *Stuart Little*. And we didn't get around to painting yet. But I took the money I saved on the cheaper crib and bought a bed – extra-long. Want to see?'

He spread his fingers and peered through them at her, confused.

'For when Bray comes home,' she said. 'You know, for holidays, summer vacation, the NBA off-season. Whenever it is that grown kids go home to see their families.'

Gently, she moved his hands away from his face and kissed him. 'I am not oblivious to the sacrifices you've made for me over the past however many years. Buying this wreck of a house and doing all the work ourselves all those evenings and weekends. Trying for a baby long after you were ready to accept our fate and move on. Spending all our money on IVF.

'After you went downstairs last night, I felt miserable

about our argument. And I tried to make myself feel better by imagining what it would be like to walk into that room' – she pointed across the hall – 'and pick our daughter up out of her crib. I tried to picture it – our house, with just that one room occupied, and the rest of this long hall empty while we wait for more babies. And I kept waiting for this feeling to kick in – this feeling of, I don't know, content-ment, I guess, or peace. This thing I've been waiting so long for would finally be happening. We're going to have our own family, just the three of us. I should be the happiest woman alive.

'And I was imagining it, and I didn't feel content at all, or peaceful. Or happy. All I felt was sad. Brokenhearted. Filled with regret. And it hit me that you would feel that way every day for the rest of your life if we didn't do whatever we could to help these boys.'

She sniffed. 'And I realized that no matter what I thought I wanted my life to be five days ago, all I know now is that whatever my life is, it won't be anything if I know you're not happy. And if I'm the one who kept you from being happy. So I started imagining something else.' She swept an arm around the room. 'I started imagining this. And that's when I felt the contentment and peace I'd been waiting to feel.'

He cleared his throat. 'Are you sure? Do you think maybe you're just feeling . . . sentimental, or something, because of what they've gone through? Do you think you'll regret it the next time Curtis gets sent to the principal's office or comes home with a bloody nose?'

'Of course I'm feeling sentimental because of what they've gone through. So are you. And I've thought about how I'll feel when he messes up next, as kids do, and whether I'll feel resentful when it happens. And I hope I'm right about this, but what I decided was that you were right about how it's easy to focus on white picket fences and perfect children, like I've been doing all this time. But maybe that's not what our life is supposed to be, after all. Maybe it's supposed to be about broken chain-link fences – the ones at Franklin. And the imperfect kids who come with it.'

'Are you absolutely sure?'

'Sure we can handle him without wanting to tear our hair out sometimes? No. Not even close. I promise I'm going to look at you a hundred times a year and ask what the hell I was thinking. And you'll have to remind me of this conversation. And then hand me a drink.'

She smiled, raised herself a little higher and kissed him again. 'But I am sure I love him, and Bray. And I have never been more sure that I love you. And that's all I need to be sure of.'

46

The Forum

Sunday, April 10 @ 10:30 p.m.
MotorCity wrote:

I'm happy to announce I feel tired and am about to go to bed . . . and to sleep! You know you're getting old when that's news. . . .

@Moms – I sent you some PMs about this already. Will jump over to PM again after this for a bedtime chat. I'm worried now about you resorting to juicer ads while I'm snoring away. ;)

Sunday, April 10 @ 10:32 p.m.
2boys wrote:

dude, you catch the highlights? pettitte's healthy and strong and lookin' to log a couple no hitters, starting in detroit . . . seriously though, glad you kicked the insomnia – that mean brother's made a choice you're happy with? do tell – inquiring minds wanna know

Sunday, April 10 @ 10:34 p.m.
flightpath wrote:

Yes, MotorC, do tell. I've been logging in all w/e – something I ordinarily don't do, as you know – to see if you've had news to share. Has brother made a decision?

Sunday, April 10 @ 10:35 p.m.
MotorCity wrote:
If I didn't love you all so much, I'd make you guess, take wagers, the whole bit. But I do, so . . . I'm adopting LMan. And brother. Well, you can't adopt a 20-year-old, exactly, but I'm claiming him as my own. Have a room for him for when he comes home from mopping up the college courts with the fools who try to face him, then when he starts doing the same in the pros. Or in the boardroom . . . however it turns out for him.

And b/f 2boys can ask, my wife is all for it. You heard me: All. For. It. LMan and I came home from Monster Trucks today and damn if she hadn't put brother and some of his teammates to work, along with Pete (who likely ate pizza, drank beer and delegated most of the day away). By the time we sauntered in, they'd fixed up permanent rooms for both boys, alerted the social worker, all of that.

I feel as if my life started again tonight. (Cue flightpath to tell me I'm way too sappy to be a coach.)

@Moms – I've got details for you that the rest won't be as interested in. Can't wait to hear your reaction.

Sunday, April 10 @ 10:37 p.m.
2boys wrote:
wow – great news on getting the kid AND the girl in the end, not to mention the tall guy who can clean the eaves every fall ;)

393

Sunday, April 10 @ 10:40 p.m.
SoNotWicked wrote:

WAHOO, MotorC! SO HAPPY! So glad I stayed up late enough to check and now, night all! See you in the morning. I'm gonna fall asleep thinking about NEW TOPICS to discuss. Something *LIGHT* is in order after the week we've had, don't you think? SUGGESTIONS?

Sunday, April 10 @ 10:45 p.m.
2boys wrote:

sonotwicked – yankees. let's have a whole week of chatter about the yankees. motorc's in too good a mood to say no.

Sunday, April 10 @ 10:48 p.m.
MotorCity wrote:

@2boys – I'll never be in that good a mood. Tigers alllll the way.

@Moms – You must be busy – still no answers to my PMs from earlier. I'll check again in a little while, after I look in on the boys in their beds for the hundredth time.

Sunday, April 10 @ 11:32 p.m.
MotorCity sent this private message:

LaksMom, not to sound too dramatic, but is everything okay? I've kind of been waiting for you. I feel like this whole thing won't really feel official until you know about it.

I'm starting to wish we'd traded real names and numbers at some point, so I could look you up and call. I feel certain you wouldn't mind if I invaded your privacy for this. :)

Sunday, April 10 @ 11:55 p.m.
MotorCity sent this private message:

Hey LaksMama. Thought I'd check one last time, but looks like you're still offline. I'm sure there must be some simple explanation on your end, like no Internet service or something, but man, I'm going crazy here, waiting to talk to you! I'm so psyched to tell you all the details about how today went down, and to hear what's up on your end.

Are you there?

Epilogue: The Letters

My sweetest Laks,

I left this letter with Daddy, and asked him to give it to you when he thinks you are old enough to read it. The fact that he has given it to you now means he thinks you're old enough, mature enough. Good for you for being so mature. I am so proud of you. I was always so proud of you. I always will be.

I honestly don't know if there is a God, or a Heaven. We didn't talk a lot about it, you and I. By now, Auntie Gina may have taken you with her to church a few times, and you may know more about all of it than I ever did. If you believe, then I do, too. Children are often able to understand things like this better than their parents are. And I hope it makes you feel better to know I am in Heaven, watching you, loving you. With you. But even if you don't ever believe, I will always be with you. Just close your eyes and think of me. It doesn't matter if you can't remember what I look like – you just have to think, 'Mama,' and I will be there.

And that leads me to a few important things I want you to know. The first is that I love you. More than anything in the world. And I don't want you to ever think that if I'd loved you more, I'd have stayed. I couldn't love you more.

The second thing is that it's okay if you stop remembering what I look like. Or what my voice sounds like. That is totally normal. I don't remember how my mother looked or sounded when I was five. You can look at my pictures if you want to see me. And if you don't want to see me, that's okay, too.

The third is that if Daddy remarries, it's okay if you love your new mom as much as you loved me. Or more than you loved me. That's normal, too, I promise. And I also promise that it's what I want for you.

The fourth is that my dying is not your fault. It was Huntington's fault. You know this. We talked about it many times, how Huntington's made Mama sick, and how it couldn't be stopped. I know Daddy will have already told you this. Your grandparents will tell you, too, and I know Those Ladies also will. Please believe them. Huntington's is a very powerful disease that I couldn't fight any longer. There was nothing you, or Daddy, or even the doctors could have done to save me.

The fifth is that if you ever need anything, Those Ladies are there for you. Daddy knows this, too. He also knows I believe he is the most amazing father in the world, and that he can help you with anything that comes up. But if there is ever a time when you think it would be helpful to talk to another woman,

Daddy will not be upset if you tell him you'd like to speak with them. Or shop with them, or get your nails painted with them . . . or any of that girl stuff.

The sixth, and last, is that well-meaning people will probably tell you that now that your mother is gone, you must 'be good' or 'be brave' or 'be strong' or 'be a big girl' and that you need to do that for your father, or for your grandparents, or even for me. And I want you to know those well-meaning people are wrong. You don't need to be good or brave or strong or big or anything you don't feel like being. You need to be who you are, and act how you want to act, and feel what you want to feel.

And you need to do that for you, and not anyone else. And anyone who tells you different is wrong. Don't tell them that – but you can think it. And when you do, think of me, and know that I will be nodding my head and saying, 'You're right.'

I love you, my sweetie, my Lakshmi. And I have loved every second of every minute of every day of being your mother.

Thank you. Thank you for making me the luckiest mama in the world. That's what I was, because I had you for a daughter.

Love, Mama XOX

Dear Tom,

My one true love, my darling, my heart, my every-thing.

Do you remember the first day you asked me out? We were standing in the foyer of Morrice Hall. I had run in there to escape the rain and you walked into the wrong building for an interview. We talked for a while, waiting for the rain to stop. And then you asked me out. I didn't answer you for a long time and you thought it meant I wasn't interested, and you apologized and turned to leave. I stopped you and explained that I'd thought I was about to sneeze and that's why I delayed responding.

That was a lie. Do you know why it took me so long to answer?

Because I couldn't breathe.

You were the most beautiful person I'd ever seen. And when you looked up and saw me there and struck up a conversation, I told myself you were only being polite. We were the only two people in the foyer – you had to talk to me. I told myself you likely had a line of gorgeous women standing outside your door every night, vying for your attention. If any of them had been around then, or if it hadn't been raining, if you hadn't been forced into that enclosed space with me, you'd never have given me a second look. So when you kept talking to me for ages, even after the rain stopped, I couldn't believe my luck. And when you asked me if I'd go out with you, well, like I said, I couldn't breathe.

I could have died happy that day. And yet, lucky

me, I was given so many more days after that – so many more happy days with you. Some sad ones, too, as everyone has. But more happy than sad, without question. And more happy than I ever, in all my dreams, thought I would have.

I thought I was the luckiest girl in the world that day and I have thought that every day since – until Dr Thiry came along. But no one can be so lucky for so long, I suppose. And I have come to think of it as a universal fairness that my glorious life with you has come to an end – it's not fair for one person to corner all the happiness, or even as much of it as I have. It's time to redistribute it again.

You are my dream come true. You are everything I ever wanted. Strike that – you are more than I ever wanted. More than I ever thought of wanting, more than I imagined I could want. And my life, since that first day I met you, has been so much more than I ever thought to plan for, or dream of.

Because of you.

I know you will be angry with me, my love, and I don't blame you. And if one day you tell Laks how I really died, and she asks if you were angry, or if you still are, I hope you will answer her honestly, so that if she is angry, too, she won't feel alone.

But please don't only be angry. Please be fond some-times. And please remind Laks to be also.

Also, Tom, please allow yourself to be relieved, and let Laks know it's okay if she is. You don't have to admit it to her – I know you won't ever let yourself say it out loud. But please admit it to yourself. And know that when you finally do, my soul will finally be freed (no, I don't suddenly believe, but I'm allowing for the chance that you may, one day).

I want you to be relieved, my darling. I want that more than anything – to relieve you of me, and this horrible disease that's turned me into someone so different from the girl whose breath you took away that day.

That's why I've done this – to spare you and Laks. And the others, too, but mostly the two of you. You deserve all the happiness and adventure the world has to offer, and you would never get it with me around. I don't want you saddled with a wife who can't be taken out in public without humiliating herself; I don't want Laks stuck with that kind of mother. Or tied to the house, feeding, bathing and changing a grown woman when you should be out, living. I can't bear the thought of you wasting hours of your lives visiting some empty shell of your former lover, Laks's former mother, in a nursing home.

I did this for me, too, yes – I could never fool you into thinking it wouldn't have driven me insane to lose control of my life. But I did it, above all, for you, my dear, kind, altruistic husband, who would have spent the next however many years chained inside, to me, while the best years of your life drifted by outside the window without your noticing.

And no, you didn't drive me to this by acting like I was holding you back. I never felt any kind of resentment from you, any hint that you felt ripped off, choosing the one woman in all of McGill, maybe, with a time bomb inside her DNA strand. Quite the opposite – I have felt, for the past four years, that you were *willing and able and even cheerful about the thought of caring for me as this progressed. That you would have been more honored than bothered to brush my hair for me, to blend my food and feed it to me from a spoon, to wipe my chin after every bite.*

On the subject of getting my own way (you knew this was coming when you found my letter, didn't you?): I want you to date. I know you're shaking your head right now. Stop. Listen to me: I mean it. I want you to meet someone wonderful and I want you to fall in love.

If it helps, don't think you're doing it for yourself. Do it for me. I am torn apart by guilt at leaving you this way, for you being the one who has to face it, to break it to the others. Knowing you will one day be in love again, with someone strong and healthy and vibrant who can travel with you, run with you, be a real partner to you for the rest of your life, absolves me of some small fraction of my immeasurable guilt. Please, please let me have that absolution.

But most of all, do it for our daughter. She's too young now to realize how wonderful a husband and partner her father was. She needs to see you in that role again, when she's old enough to observe and absorb it. She needs to witness how romantic and loving and thoughtful you are. How you remember anniversaries and Valentine's Day and birthdays. How you bring home flowers for no reason. How generous you are with kisses and compliments.

How else will she know what to hold out for?

What else can I say to you, my love, my heart, my best friend, my lover, my husband, my everything?

403

Only that I am so profoundly sorry to have left you without warning or the kind of goodbye I longed to give. Please understand I had to. I could never have risked letting you suspect my plan, and having you prevent it, which we both know with certainty you'd have done.

And thank you.

Thank you for your patience and forgiveness over the last several trying years.

Thank you for being my rock.

Thank you for holding me on the nights I howled in rage at being sentenced to such a terrible and premature ending.

Thank you for telling me every day that you loved me more than ever, that this thing hadn't gotten between us, that you weren't sorry you had chosen me. That you would stay with me forever, and that it was because you wanted to, not because you felt you should. I believe you, Tom. I know you would have stayed with me. I always knew you would have.

I never thought you should have to.

And thank you for taking my breath away in the foyer of Morrice Hall, all those years ago.

And every day since.

Your Mara

Acknowledgments

My profound gratitude to Amy Einhorn for her brilliant editorial insights, for helping to create a new literary drinking game and for letting me sneak in a reference to a certain UK boy band in honor of my three favorite teenage girls. Thanks also to Elizabeth Stein, Anna Jardine and the rest of the team at Amy Einhorn Books, and to Thomas Dussel of Penguin Group USA.

Thank you to my agent, Victoria Sanders, who took a chance on a new writer and whose magical agenting powers resulted in the most exciting vacation my husband and I have ever had. Thanks also to Bernadette Baker-Baughman for answering my many newbie questions, to Chris Kepner and to everyone else at Victoria Sanders Associates. Also, thank you to Eric Rayman.

It was vitally important to me to portray Huntington's disease (HD) accurately. I am more thankful than I can adequately express to the experts who so generously took the time to educate me about the condition, especially Bonnie Hennig, Ph.D., who spent hours explaining the medical, emotional and social aspects of HD, and Kelvin

Chou, M.D., who listened to me run through every plot point in Mara's story and advised whether each was medically accurate and, if not, how to make it so. In addition, Barb Heiman, LISW, and Elynore Cucinell, M.D., provided their significant expertise and experience. Any inaccuracies are mine alone.

I am lucky to have smart and helpful friends. Kate Baker, Jeanne Estridge, Jana Timmer Bastian, Terri Eagan-Torkko, Meghan Eagen-Torkko, Mary Beth Bishop, Jennifer Bondurant, Julia Kailing Cooper, Sarah Roach Plum, Ruth Slavin, Anna Cox and Sonja Yoerg read and commented on early drafts, as did Kate Kennedy. The amazing Benee Knauer helped massage a manuscript with potential into something much better. Rina Sahay, Elisha Fink, Lori Nelson Spielman, Linda VanAcker, Pamela Landau and Meghan Eagen-Torkko provided expertise in a variety of areas, from Indian culture, Michigan criminal law and school district policy to the social environment in Detroit and the emotional challenges related to adoption and infertility. Nicole Ross, The Cool Kids, Glenn Katon, The Monday Night Ladies, Nick Kocz, Mike Coffman, Patrick Cauley, Charley Hegarty, Mary Bisbee-Beek and Adam Pelzman offered moral and other support at various times along the way. Thank you, all of you.

My children, Samantha, Jack, Libby and Maddie, have been loud and enthusiastic cheerleaders, and never once complained about hearing, 'Just let me finish this chapter,' as an answer to almost every question they asked me for twenty-four straight months. Thank you, thank you, thank you, thank you.

Finally, I am so grateful to my husband, Dan, who took on all the work of running our hectic household for two years while I hid in a corner, hunched over my laptop. He served as my first-line editorial adviser, too, and has been labeled The Plot Doctor by my writing friends because of his uncanny ability to solve the thorniest plot and character issues. His 'reward' for this talent was constant interruption – from reading, working, watching Michigan sports and even sleeping – by my repeated refrain, 'Can I ask you one more question about the book?' Always, his answer was, 'Sure.'